Also by Dave Hopwood

Novels

The Shed

- A disgruntled guy takes time out in a moorland monastery, crossing paths with rock stars, wanderers, world-changers and of course… monks

Dead Prophets Society

- A town turned upside-down by a gang of revolutionary punks

Sons of Thunder

- A contemporary gospel, the Messiah in Cornwall with surfers and mechanics for disciples

No More Heroes

- Cain, Solomon & Jacob in a modern tale of men, women, dads and crime

Other

Top Stories

- 31 parables retold with serious and humorous contemporary comments

Pulp Gospel

- 31 bits of the Bible retold with gritty reflections and comments

Rebel Yell: 31 Psalms

- Psalms, God & Rock'n'Roll

Faith & Film

- Movie clips that bring the Bible to life

The Bloke's Bible

- Bits of the Bible retold for guys

The Bloke's Bible 2: The Road Trip

- More Bible bits retold

For more information visit Dave's website – davehopwood.com

The Twelfth Seer

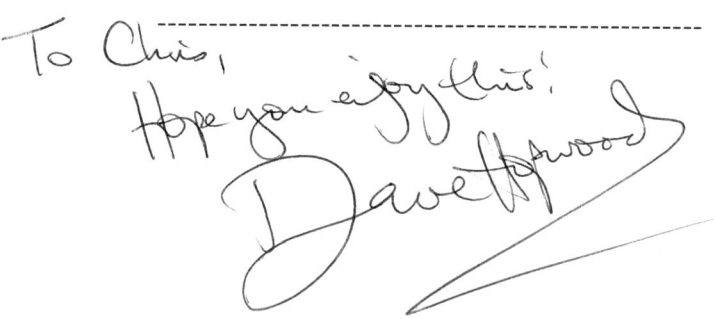

Please don't copy this stuff, it's all copyright D. Hopwood 2012

About Max

Full name Max Maguire. Born in Ireland. December 1979. Son of John and Emily. Great grandfather died at Pacshendale in WW1. Posthumously awarded the DSO, for bravery in the field of battle. Maternal grandfather was a hero in the Battle of Britain, flew sorties all summer of 1940. Lived to tell Max the tales of courage, fear and dog fights in the sky over 'Hell's Corner' – a.k.a. the South-east of England. One sister – Amber, two years older. Emigrated to Canada in 2001. The family moved to Cambridge in 1983 where his father took up a professorship teaching theology at Ridley Hall. Max's mother was an avid skier and climber. She enjoyed an active sports and social life until 1996 when she disappeared in a freak climbing accident. Max's father, fifteen years her senior, never recovered and died of a broken heart four years later. Max dropped out of University one term into his second year. Took a string of jobs but couldn't keep any of them. Left the UK and went travelling, working from to time to time to pay his way. Disappeared for a while and resurfaced in Bosnia during the conflict there. Ended up fighting in a number of skirmishes. Returned to the UK to recover from gunshot wounds and took a degree course in Biblical Theology. Got a first. Drifted for a while. Took an assignment from an old university friend of his father's who took pity on him and sent him to track down the lost treasures of Solomon. Max was surprisingly successful and this led to further quests for his father's circle of university friends. Continued this kind of life until 2009 when he hit an emotional wall, had a breakdown and gave up adventuring. For good.

One

It takes thirteen hours to fly to Singapore and a further two to Phnom Penh. By the time you touch down in Cambodia your ears ache from the descent, your stomach is nauseous from the lack of sleep and your mouth is steeped in the aftertaste of plastic-wrapped food. And if yours isn't, Max Maguire's is. Plus the adrenalin is playing havoc with his system, the flight or fight mechanism kicking in in preparation for the showdown at Angkor Wat. Max has a rough idea about what's waiting for him up North amongst the lost temples of the Khmer Empire. As he steps down from the plane the claustrophobic heat wraps around his being like a clammy hand. Thirty seven degrees and counting. Cambodia's only international air terminal is about the size of a bus station. A sign above the entrance informs him he is standing in Pochentong Airport. He strides towards the doors. He'll recover from the jetlag pretty soon, he's travelled a lot and he's in good shape, though not as good as a few years ago. He's been in his thirties for a while, five eleven, 180 pounds. Broad shouldered, but slouches a little. Never really sorted that out. Never been particularly striking or goodlooking either. Rugged maybe. Handsome, no. Somehow things just aren't quite placed right for that. All the components are there, just not quite in the right order.

The arrivals lounge at Pochentong is little more than a large hall, and as Max queues at the white desk he studies the smartly dressed young men and women sat in a long bureaucratic line behind the counter. It's said that a whole generation was lost in the 70's here under the Khmer Rouge genocide. The old and the wise just disappeared. Along with the educated. Back then the airport was shut down, no one could go anywhere, and the place was swimming in vicious Khmer Rouge troops. Thankfully there are just one or two soldiers loitering nearby. Airport security. They look casual enough. Max has read plenty about the days when Cambodia bore the brunt of American carpet bombing. Collateral damage from the Vietnam war. He also knows those days have long since passed. He reaches the front of the queue and hands over his passport. The girl behind the counter passes it to the man sitting next to her who in turn passes it to someone standing behind him. In the end the little book slips through five sets of fingers and they all have a good look before ushering Max along to collect it again from the far end of the counter. He pays his entry tax and is channelled through passport control and out to wait beneath a ceiling fan someone rescued from the fifties. Max picks up a cheap paperback, a few riels gets it for him. It's hardly light reading. *S21: Four Years in Toul Sleng* brings him the horrors of forty eight months in the notorious torture centre of the Khmers Rouge. The Security Regulations alone are enough to chill the bones, including instructions like,

6. While getting lashes or electrification you must not cry at all.
9. If you don't follow all the above rules, you shall get many many lashes of electric wire.
10. If you disobey any point of my regulations you must get either ten
  lashes or five
shocks of electric charge.

Max is getting sick of having to swallow the twisted logic of the depraved and power-corrupted. He shuts the book and shoves it into his rucksack. He shuts his eyes. Images of barbarity flash across his mind like speeding cars. Eventually they fade and he dozes. The fan above him whirrs laboriously and squeaks every third time round, the rhythm plays on in the background. Hours pass, his flight arrives. He boards and braces himself for the skirmish up north.

He and a few others fly over the great lake, Tonle Sap, aboard an old propeller-driven plane. Max feels every air pocket, every breath of turbulence that grips the little craft. The day is beginning to die as he boards a cyclo taxi through Siem Reap to Angkor. By the time he gets his first glimpse of the mighty Angkor Wat, the sun is dropping like a mythical oracle, mortally wounded and shedding its deathly orange blood across the ancient stone. Three towers rise like mighty fir cones from the monolithic walls, basking in the auburn glow, and below them the symmetrical complex sprawls in splendour, all colonnades, corbel roofs and decorated stonework. Lotus plants, dancers, wild buffalo and snakes are etched in the sandstone.
For a thousand years this place has stood and absorbed the life of the Khmer people. Every pulse, every heartbeat for a millennium. He wonders what that does to a place, must steep it in a time zone all of its own. And he

wonders how much killing it's seen. And if it's about to see more. He pays the cyclo driver and asks him to wait. Gives him a hefty tip for doing so. The driver is reluctant, the darkness is closing in, he wants to be back home in Siem Reap, eating fish and rice by the road with his family. But the money is too good. He stays.

Max checks the slim side pocket of his khaki trousers for his knife. It's there. The pouch is barely visible, an extra seem running down the side of his thigh. He walks and doesn't look back. He doesn't know too much about what's coming, he knows that a one-eyed, saffron-robed monk is waiting for him with a map. Right at the top of the temple, up the stretch of irregular steps, like hundreds of pitta breads piled one on top of each other. This is the end of the trail, the last fragment of map on a journey for a long lost piece of history.
As he crosses the sandstone causeway, over a vast bone-dry moat, he passes a trio of musicians, all of them amputees, playing a repetitive, circular medley on pan pipes and drums. Max tosses a note into a coloured hat beside the single foot of the drummer. A dozen children spot the gesture and herd around him. He shoos them away, it takes some doing. There are amputees everywhere, the legacy from years of Khmer Rouge landmines.

He reaches the steps. Tourists and pilgrims clamber up and down, some of them on knees or backsides to avoid the fall. Max wedges his boot on the first step and starts up. Fifty metres later and he's up there. A little out of breath but nothing to suggest he's not on form. There are dozens of pilgrims up there, all come to see the vista at dusk. They only just made it. He looks out over the other temples buried in the forests that hedge them in. A thousand years of ancient history. Amongst them Angkor Thom, The Great City, with its huge carved heads, sporting the faces of the king who built them, complete with the smile of Angkor on their lips. French writer Pierre Loti encountered them whilst exploring the jungle in 1912 and it very nearly curdled his blood as he bumped into one, then two, then three, five, ten enormous smiles looking down on him from every direction. And Ta Prohm, the Bayon temple with the spung trees sprouting from the tops of buildings, their huge roots gripping the cobalt roofs, clasping the stonework like tight-fisted children clutching at Lego models. There are hundreds of the ruined temples below him, craggy sandstone shells with their crumbling towers and bas-reliefs, but no one-eyed monk here fifty metres up. Then a tap on the leg. He glances down. A child. A boy with a grin and dirt on his cheeks. He beckons and points back down towards a square court far below, the Preah Pean. The Gallery of a Thousand Buddhas.

'You go, you go, you go,' he says, reciting words he has been fed, and he holds out his hand for a few riels.

Max hands some money over and stumbles back down the fifty metres of bunched steps. In the Gallery, near one of the long-dry corner pools, he spots a figure in a saffron robe, small, bent, an orange patch skewed across the left eye. The man is sweeping the cloister floor, he glances up, beckons with a toothless grin. Max crosses the gallery. The monk looks beyond him, checks that no one else is in the gallery. The place is full of shadows as the light dies, any number of pillars could provide cover for assailants. The monk waves a finger and calls Max close. When his body is shielded by Max he leans his brush against the wall, reaches inside his robe and produces a scrap of cloth. He hands the rag to Max. He doesn't wait for Max to study it, just places his hands together in front of his chest, bows and leaves. When the place is quiet Max opens the piece of cloth. Four sketches on it. A lion, an apsara dancer, a pole and a snake. Max scans the walls, the gallery is full of carvings like this. He strolls around till he finds three of them together, the lion, the dancer and the snake. He presses the stone, attempts to twist the protruding pieces. Nothing. And there is no carving of a pole or a stick of any kind. He crosses the gallery and checks other walls. No clues, no sign of all four images together. He returns to the spot. Each image has a hole for an eye, sinking deep into the ancient stonework. He remembers the monk. He placed his hands together and bowed as he left. Which means he took nothing with him. Max looks back to the spot where they met. The brush, he left it. Purposely. He races to it, grabs it and returns to the three carvings. He works the handle free from the base and eases it into the eye of the snake. Perfect fit. And it goes deep, deeper than he expected. It locks home against something, then there's a distant grating sound, stone on stone, as something stirs inside the rock. He glances around. Still no one else about, just voices of the tourists and travellers wandering around outside and above him. He removes the handle and locks it into the eye of the lion. Pushes deep, another connection, more

grating stone. He removes it and eases it into the right eye of the dancer. The handle goes right in, stops, twists from his fingers and is sucked right into the hole. More grating. He steps back, cautious now. Then he hears the click. The hammer of a revolver drawn back and locked in place ready for the release of a trigger. He raises his hands a little, turns. A sleek figure in black fatigues, gun in hand, she waves him away from the wall. He's never seen her before but she's about to steal the greatest treasure he's found. He steps back. As he does the wall behind him cracks. Pieces of stone fly from the faces of the lion and the dancer. He dives for cover. The woman with the gun ducks too. More rocks fly, the ground trembles a little. An explosion. Dust bursts over them like a mushroom cloud. Jagged splinters rain down on them like hail. Then silence. When Max stands up, dusting grit from his clothes, she is kneeling at the wall, reaching inside a newly-formed crevice. She grins to herself, then spits dust and reaches further in. When her hand comes out she is holding a dented silver box. The lid, contorted by the blast, is twisted and bursting open. She peels it back and reveals a huge sapphire. Shimmering blue and 22 carats. Brought here by missionaries in 1168, who claimed it had come from the throne of God himself. A precious off-cut from the divine pavement of sapphire when God appeared to Moses on Mount Sinai. Thought lost forever in the ruins of history and the carnage of time. Once owned by King Jayavarman VII, architect of Angkor Thom, who named it The Eye of Angkor. Now sitting here within reach of Max, in the fist of a gun-woman who'll no doubt sell it for everything she can get. Max stares at her, all the time feeling the dust and grit seeping down the arm of his combat jacket into his cupped left hand. She won't be watching that side, or at least, not as much as his right hand. She stands and laughs, her eye teeth are oddly black, some kind of marking on them. She raises the gun and moves towards Max.
'Give me your rucksack,' she hisses at him.
He glances down, plays for time, allows her a moment to stretch her hand towards him. Then he does it, flicks his left hand up, fist clutching the dust, half a handful straight in her face. She was about to speak again so her mouth is open and plenty goes inside. She gags and splutters, scrapes at her eyes with the black painted finger nails of her left hand. He swings his boot up and kicks the Eye of Angkor from her other fist, high up into the night sky. He lunges forward and shoulders her back so she crashes into the wall, and is left gasping for air. As she crumples to the floor he catches the

diamond, pockets it and turns to leave. A shot rings out, a bullet flies past his shoulder, ricochets off the stonework and flies back across the gallery. Thankfully the dust in her eyes has done nothing for her accuracy but any more shots like that and she'll do irreparable damage round here. An archaeologist's nightmare. Still, he has no time to be squeamish about the history. He scoops up a rock, it's about the size of the sapphire, and turns and yells.
'Here then, have it, just don't destroy this place.' And he tosses her the piece of stone as if he's giving in. Even with her blurred vision it'll only take her a couple of seconds to realise she's been duped, but by then he'll be outside, weaving his way through the crowds and running back across the causeway to the cyclo taxi and freedom.

That was three years ago. Seems like a lifetime now.

Two

Three years later.

Every boy grows up wanting to be a hero. You see enough movies about superman or James Bond and you get ideas about saving the planet yourself. You start to picture yourself fighting criminals and rescuing kidnap victims. Getting accolades and newspaper headlines about how you took out the bad guys and freed a small country.
Yet again.
What you don't dream about is becoming a hero, then falling apart and losing the ability. Having grabbed the headlines and saved the planet a little, you don't expect to find yourself back in the slow lane, shunning the limelight and ignoring the cries for help. But it happens. Good guys fall apart. And then they take some rebuilding.

There are days when he hates his life now. Days when he comes close to punching a wall. Days when he can't believe it's come to this. How did it happen? How did he become this small-minded, fearful guy? Where did he lose his courage, where did he misplace his sense of adventure? This isn't like him. It really isn't. This is not the Max Maguire he grew up with. Not the guy he saw every day when he looked in the mirror before hiking out on some new adventure. Some fresh world-changing, life-enhancing mission. He knows the answer of course. He knows it every night when the haunting dreams play out like warped film footage in his head. Every day when he stands in that classroom teaching and not doing. But he has no choice. Life has ambushed him, cornered him in a way he never expected. So now he makes the best of it. It's hard. Soul decaying. Ludicrous. But not as hard as if he were still riding that adventure trail. Still dodging bullets and wrong-footing criminals. Some things are hard and you live with them. That's all he has the energy for right now. That and teaching the toughest book in the world to a class full of pious renegades.

He clocks in as usual at 7.00am. The first thing he sees is Ginny, night security guard. She is, as ever, going the extra mile. Doing way more than is expected of her. Usually it's mopping one of the floors or tidying a classroom or making a cup of tea for some early rising student. Or a cup-a-soup for one of the homeless guys who knows she's a soft touch. She's well into her fifties, been around the block a few times and can handle herself. But she's all heart really. She always cracks a smile for Max and has a wicked laugh and a terrible sense of humour.
'Morning Mr Maguire, out on the town last night again?'
He gives his usual world-weary shrug.
'Got a spare cuppa for a lost boy?' he asks.
'Maybe. One good turn and all that… you scratch my back, if you know what I mean,' and she gives him a broad wink and one of her earth-shuddering laughs.
He grins back, waits for the steaming mug to appear and wanders outside. The truth is he hasn't been out on the town for years.
The mornings are getting lighter all the time now so these days he plans his lessons outside. Sits on the scraggy lawn near room 33 in the shade of an ancient oak. Guildford School of Theology runs what it calls The Offsite Degree Strand. Students training to be youth workers and priests in parishes around London. They're learning on the job but commute to the GST for the cerebral stuff. That's him. The cerebral stuff. It's in the blood of course, seeped in from days spent fishing with his father, when his old man would pump him full of the weird and extraordinary tales from the Old Testament. His father loved the characters and misadventures and

could tell them in a way no preacher could. As a result the Bible was never really a book to Max. It was a movie, a comic strip, a piece of television, a good joke. His father never read to him from it, he knew the stories too well. He reeled them off like a taxi driver spilling his knowledge. It was characters with glorious names like Nimrod, Blastus, Samson and Ehud that elbowed Max into the life of an adventurer. From an early age they filled his head with dreams of saving the world from the bad guys. Not now though. Now he is doing what he can to pass on the baton. Talking himself out of a job. Let the bright-eyed warriors in room 33 take it on now. Let them change the world.

Three

Iran. Masouleh. A small village in the Alborz mountains 1,000 metres above the Caspian sea. The kind of place where families have lived simple lives for centuries. Children and animals wander the streets, no fear of oncoming traffic. Because there isn't any. All vehicles are banned due to the size and inclining nature of the roads. There are steps and stairs everywhere and roofs serve as walkways to access the homes, shops and café's as they perch on the mountainside like so many tan-coloured shoe boxes. An undulating matrix of carefully-crafted, mud-brick dwellings, hugging the hills, wedged tightly together, one on top of the other. So intricate that it's spawned a saying in Masouleh, 'The yard of the family above is the roof of the family below'.

In a rooftop café a woman in black holds a sheet of fax paper in her leather gloves. It contains a name, and six words scrawled beneath a black and white picture.

Carlos Gomez. Retrieve his Nehushtan piece. Kill him.

It's a cheap contract for murder. And this woman does well with this kind of thing. She fingers the edge of the smudged flimsy sheet and rips it down the middle. A perfect separation. As the two halves of the page fall away, a near-distant face appears through the gap, sitting at a table outside another café. The woman smiles and flings the two halves of the contract away.

She squints at the figure. That's the man, she's tracked him for a week and he thinks he safe now. She's good at that, lulling her prey into a false sense of security before she strikes. She beckons to a waiter. He recognises her

and nods, comes over to her and she orders something. The waiter leaves
and returns with two plates which he places on the table. One has food on
it, hard bread, cold meat, a clutch of figs and dates, the other is covered
with a white cloth. In the near distance Carlos Gomez throws some money
onto his table and begins to walk towards her seat. As he comes near the
woman removes the cover and reveals a pistol on the second plate. As
Carlos passes the table she reaches for the gun, but without looking at her
Carlos grabs the edge of the table and pushes it over so that she and the
gun hit the floor. Carlos begins to run. The woman is up and following. A
chase ensues through the narrow streets, across the roofs and courtyards
and up the winding mountain steps. She calls out, appealing to some of the
locals. The bad man just stole her bag. He's a corrupt westerner, she's a
single woman alone. She needs help, without her money she will starve.
Some of them join in, grabbing sticks and rocks. The occasional cooking
implement. Children abandon their rooftop classes and goats bleat as they
follow the growing crowd. The best entertainment in a long while. With
every new rooftop more people join the chase. Even a few tourists,
abandoning their teas and coffees in the terraced restaurants. And the fog
comes down. Masouleh is famous for its fog. Drifts of mountainous white
that wrap themselves around the yellow clay homes and the villagers inside
them. There are some places in the world where the mist rises in the
morning and is regularly burnt off by the sun. Not Masouleh. You're lucky
some days to get two hours of clear light. Carlos is not out of shape but he
can't run forever, his tanned, handsome features break sweat. He needs to
find a safe place. Eventually he ducks down an ally into a derelict two
story home. It's being refurbished. Piles of mud, ash and straw dot the
floor, waiting to be mixed into bricks. He clambers up the few steps to the
level above. Runs to a dark corner and presses himself against the wall.
The fog has taken most of the light outside, it won't make him invisible but
the gloom inside is certainly greater. He slips down onto his knees. Waits,
listens and prays. The crowd are passing by, he can hear the running steps
and garbled cries, the goats bleating and the kids laughing. They are
moving on. Leaving him alone. He bows his head, stays there for a long
time, kneeling with his forehead pressing against his hands. His gasping
subsides and he wipes his brow with his muscled forearm. Gomez came to
Masouleh to hide, a European amongst Asians, a city dweller in the
mountains, a Christian amongst Muslims. For a while there it looked as if

his plan had failed. But maybe not. There is a cemetery on the southern side, away from what little sunlight there is, away too from the houses and trinket shops and the rest of the village. He prays quietly for a while, words of gratitude and some moments of calm, then stands and makes his way quietly out. The crowds have gone, and the woman with the gun is no more. He slips through the fog and finds the graveyard. Tucks himself behind a huge rock and curls up to wait for the dark.

Time passes.

Then something bounces over the rock and off his shoulder. It's a ball of paper. He picks it up tentatively, unfolds it. It falls into two parts in his hands, perfectly torn down the middle. It is the fax with the scribbled writing and the photograph. The cheap death sentence. Carlos looks up. A black boot appears around the side of the rock. He peers round. The woman from the café is standing there. She's like a homing device. She proffers a gun and jolts the barrel to indicate that he get up. He has no choice, behind him the trees and grave stones make an impassable barrier. In front she has the way covered. The woman from the café places the barrel of her gun squarely against his forehead. A Hechler and Koch P7M13. Plenty of bullets tucked in that fat handle. Carlos crosses his eyes as he focuses on it, the women leers revealing two viper tattoos on her eye teeth. Things don't look good after all.
'You have it?' she asks quietly.
He nods, doubting it will do him much good.
'Who are you?' he asks.
She shakes her head, doesn't smile.
'You don't remember? I'm disappointed. You should do. But it's too late now. And you certainly won't remember this meeting.'
She holds out her hand.
'Give it,' she says.
'Why? What good is it to you? It's powerless on its own.'
'I'm not here for a discussion. I'm here for the snake and I'm here to kill you.'
Her face is hard, cold, she might as well be explaining how to change a tyre. He reaches inside his jacket, feels the weight of the package in his fingers.

'Slowly,' she says.
He does move slowly. Until his closed fist emerges from his jacket. Then he jabs her across the jaw, a short, economical movement, efficient. He knows how to punch his way out of trouble. Her head snaps to the right under the impact. The gun slews from his forehead. He moves to hit her again. But she catches him a hard, backhanded slap which wrong-foots him, then a sudden jab which pushes his head way back. The gun is in his forehead again. The girl has blood leaking from her mouth and a bruise forming, but she is oblivious to it.
'Enough,' she says quietly. 'It's over. This is for Table Mountain. Goodbye Mr Gomez.' And there is a click as she squeezes the trigger.
A click. Just a click. No more, no less. No thundering explosion or searing pain in the head. Just a cold, quiet click. Carlos opens his eyes. His God is with him. He is alright. He smiles. The woman with the tattooed teeth does not. She just squeezes the trigger again and blows his head off. Nonplussed by the gore and the mess she reaches down and opens his fist. Nothing in it. She pulls open his jacket. Checks three pockets and pulls out a canvas pouch. Feels the weight of it. She smiles, hunts some more and finds his mobile. An iPhone stuffed with addresses and numbers. She scrolls through, the vipers glinting as she grins. Nothing will stop them now. Carlos thought he was lucky for a moment there. He was wrong. He was just the first. The hunt has begun for real now.

Four

They move her out of darkness and to a tastefully furnished bedroom, all light colours, mostly blues and yellows. It's a huge relief of course. The cellar was damp and cold and oppressive. Like waking up to death each morning. This new place is a blindfolded car drive away from that cellar. She is shoved into a vehicle and then out again and then a man with a gun steers her into this building, and to the new room. He says nothing, won't answer any questions. He removes her blindfold and the tape from her mouth, then walks out of the room, coughs up phlegm and spits in the cool, stone corridor outside. Closes the door and goes. She sits on the bed to test it. As she presses the duvet she sees that her hand is black from the cellar and the nails are broken. This place is classy. She could be in a hotel room, on a summer break. Except that there are locks on the window and the door is triple-bolted.

*

It's been a long day, eight hours of bending minds and haggling with stubborn students. Larry Hook is a particularly loose cannon. Half his mind on movies and the other on a career as a writer. Doesn't leave much space for the Good Book. Why he's training as a priest Max does not know. Research for his multi-million selling novel maybe. He's intelligent but not inclined to apply his grey matter to those things that count. And the frustrating thing for Max is that Larry reminds him so much of himself. Some days it's like looking in a dusty mirror. Max hates hypocrisy, and trying to force someone like Larry to knuckle down some days feels like the height of it. If he'd ever wanted work experience as a Pharisee tutoring the likes of Larry was tailor made for it.
He spends a couple of hours shuffling papers, doodling supposedly helpful comments on them, and drinking strong but bad coffee. The old clock in room 33 ticks on and the hand scrapes past the nine. Enough. Time to go. Ginny's already in the corridor, checking for stragglers and any left-open, unlocked windows.
'You should be out of here Mr Maguire,' she barks, 'you're wasting precious nightclub time.'
'I wish,' he says.
They banter for a bit about Ginny's days as a minder to the stars. She has more stories than a branch of Waterstones. Every one of them with a suitable punch line.
'You should write a book,' he says.
'I'd be sued. That Simon Cowell autobiography is like an Enid Blyton by comparison.' She holds up a black sack. 'It'd be me in this bin bag if the truth ever came out. Did I tell you about Sean Connery's underpants?'
'No but now's not the time, Ginny. I need my beauty sleep.'
She laughs. 'You'll be lucky. Sleep's regenerative, but it's not that good.' And she laughs again. 'Hey, do me a favour will you, sling this in the bins on your way past.'
He takes the bulging black sack from her. It's heavy.
'Found it in the staffroom. Probably full of empty whisky bottles, spew and used needles.'

She laughs a lot at her own joke, a bronchial, too many-fags-in-the-past kind of laugh, and he does his best to join in.
'See you tomorrow,' he says and he goes quickly.
He checks around as he makes his way around the back and down to the lower car park. On a Friday night at turning out time this place transforms into the fifth circle of hell. The drunks and pub turn-outs using the skips and bins as a toilet area. Fantastic. It's early though, and it's not Friday. He leaps the steps three at a time and does his best to brush no part of him against the bulging and dangerously-thin plastic sack. The level is quiet. His luck's in. The bag is still intact and there are no bladdered drunks spoiling for a fight. He makes it to the green wheelie bins, hoists the bag to head height and stops. What's that noise? Was that fist on flesh? Raised voices, some of them slurred. He turns, squints and strains to see across the car park. He is a little short-sighted, not much, just enough to make those guys across the tarmac a little fuzzy round the edges. Too lazy for contact lenses and too vain for glasses. He can see three, maybe four blurred figures. He sighs, is about to throw the bag, then reconsiders. He turns and walks across the car park, swinging the sack as he goes. This could be interesting.

Some guy is cursing, he's coming into focus as he gets closer. He's one of a gang. Three men in their twenties by the looks of it, staggering, swearing, pinning a fourth smaller guy against the wall. He walks steadily, quietly, knows not to make a fuss or announce his arrival. They are all in focus now, the guy pinned against the wall is easily the shortest, about five four. His eyes are wide but he can see what the others can't. He can see help is on the way. The others keep laughing and swearing, jabbing and slapping the little guy. One of them has a wallet in his fat fingers and is laughing about it. Keep doing that and you'll get a just reward, mate. He lifts the bag, he's glad it feels so heavy now. Glad the sack isn't substantial. Let's see how easily it splits.
'Oi!' he yells for the first time, and does it right behind the guy with the wallet. Two of the gang turn. Perfect. He smacks the bag right across their heads. The plastic splits and waste food splatters everywhere. The little guy ducks. A spray of tea bags spatters the wall above his head like gunfire. The one with the wallet hurls it into the air. Max follows the initial assault with three power-driving deliveries from his right fist. One for each

of them. Smack. Smack. Smack. The three guys go down, one on top of the other, all of them on top of the spewed rubbish. They groan and one of them gags. But they don't get up.
The little guy can't believe his luck.
'Thank you,' he says, 'thank you so much.'
He shrugs. It doesn't smells great down there now. 'By rights I should clean this up,' he says. 'It's a public thoroughfare.' Shakes his head. 'No I'll come back in the morning when these Muppets are long gone.'
He looks at the back of his hand, it has a brown smear across it, he leans down and wipes it on one of the gang. Then he retrieves the wallet from the floor and hands it over.
'Keep an eye on that,' he says and he walks away.
And that's that. Time for home. The little guy watches him leave, a plan forming in his mind.

Five

Larry Hook speed-eats coke bottles. Not plastic or glass. The confectionary kind. He gets them from the corner store by the college and chews them in class when Max's back is turned. He also speed-reads *Total Film* Magazine inside his Old Testament commentary. The smaller compact edition fits snuggly inside Tom McLachlan's legendary tome. Larry lives for movies, eats, sleeps and breathes the things. He is in the process of writing three of his own, and can talk films to anyone who is prepared to lose an hour debating the works of Hitchcock, Spielberg, Sturges and Tarantino. Larry will watch anything. He's no movie snob. He loves every kind of film. Any question about any movie he can answer them all. If he ever goes on Mastermind he'll assassinate the competition, just a shame that you have to do the general knowledge round too. Cause there is so much movie news in Larry's head there just isn't room for anything else. Filmic knowledge is all that lives there. It has often been said that his mind is not unlike a cutting room floor. Bits of film all over the place.
Max just wishes he'd apply that vivid imagination to the works of Moses, Elijah, Jeremiah and Luke. With his refurbished jeans, long black hair and an Iron maiden t-shirt underneath his Oxfam tweed jacket he's no obvious choice to win the badge of Theologian of the Year. But Max is convinced

that he'll find a way to win him over. He just needs to get the guy to see
the Good Book like it's a good film. If his dad were still around Max
would be picking his brains. But no chance of that.
'Larry, you daydreaming again?' Max asks, partway into the afternoon
lesson.
Larry shakes his head, but he looks bewildered and doesn't attempt a reply.
'Did you finish that essay on Solomon and slavery?'
He shakes his head again. Chews. Swallows. 'Nearly,' he says.
'Let's have a chat afterwards.'
Larry grins and nods. He never minds having a chat afterwards. It'll be
another round of verbal sparring, Max attempting to talk theology, Larry
trying his best to abduct the conversation and bring it over to movieland.

*

'Larry how can I help you?'
Larry looks lost.
'Err… You asked to see me. How can I help *you*?'
'You know what I mean. I want to harness that imagination. All that
creativity in there. The church needs it Larry. It's dull in some of those
creaky old buildings. I want you to harness all the colour in that skull of
yours and bring it into the faith.'
Larry scratches his head. He can't quite connect the two worlds.
'Larry – it's no good keeping the two domains separate. You can't keep
your faith in a little priest-shaped bag, while you've got all this energy
going on in the rest of your life.'
Max waves a couple of sheets of paper.
'I won't lie to you, this essay about David and Bathsheba is dull. Dull,
Larry. And yet I hear you cracking on about *Indecent Proposal* and *Dr
Zhivago* and the like and you're a different person. You always hook an
audience. Can't you see? They're the same stories. David and Bathsheba,
Indecent Proposal. Just because it's in the Bible it doesn't divorce it from
reality. Find the human story in there, that's what people connect with,
that's what they want. This book is full of humans tripping over
themselves in their journey with God. Don't give me nice ideas about
glossy faith. Give me something real. Do a Baz Luhrmann. He took *Romeo
and Juliet* and made it something that gripped the kids in the bus shelters.
Teenagers were flocking to see it, dressing up in the outfits. He set their

heads on fire with this old, old story. How much more can we do with the likes of Samson and David and Ruth and Esther? Imagine Quentin Tarantino writing a love story. And then tell it that way. Even better, imagine Tarantino making David and Bathsheba as his next movie. Explore it like that. Grab me, shock me, disturb me. Live up to your name – *Hook* me. But don't bore me.'
Max holds Larry's perplexed frown for a few seconds longer, then he hands him the couple of papers.
'Try it,' says Max. 'Just try it.'

Larry nods and goes, pops another coke bottle as he slips out of the door. He wanders outside and drops onto a bench in the shade of the old oak tree.
'Excuse me, I'm looking for a guy who might work here.'
Larry looks up into the face of a stranger. The guy keeps talking.
'He's in his thirties, late thirties maybe, tall, sort of rugged, bashed about a bit. Broad shoulders, but he slouches. Looks a little bit haunted. Shades of Brad Pitt about him. Can handle himself. Can handle himself very well. Steely grey eyes too. And a scar here, running up his chin where you might have a dimple. Know him?'
Larry blinks and sits back. 'Are you studying him for a degree or something? I mean, hey - you're pretty accurate.'
The guy, short, designer glasses, confident, shakes his head. He taps his temple.
'I have a good visual memory,' he says. 'See something once, I got it. My girlfriend says I'm a walking SatNav.'
He frowns suddenly. His face hardens and he looks down. Then he looks up and forces a smile again.
'Anyway, have you seen him?'
'D'you like Brad Pitt?'
'What?'
'You mentioned Brad Pitt, in your description,' says Larry, 'd'you like him? I admire the way he doesn't always have to play the goodlooking hero. Like *Kalifornia*, seen that? He's a beardy weirdy nutter in that. Brilliant. And *Twelve Monkeys* too. And that episode of *Friends* when he plays a geek from Ross's school.'
The short guy holds up his hands.
'I don't mean to be rude but I'm in a hurry,' he says. 'What's your name?'

'Larry.'
'Larry, I'm Ben. I need to find this guy. I'd love to talk movies but I don't see many.'
Larry shakes his head sadly. 'I'm sorry,' he says.
'You're sorry you can't help me? Or you're sorry I don't see many movies?'
'Absolutely. The second one, the movies one. Max is inside. In room 33. Be careful though, he'll start trying to tell you about how Adam and Eve is really just *The Sound of Music* without the songs.'
Larry points behind him, thumbing towards the window. Ben turns and looks through the glass. Beyond the reflections and smudges he can see a tidier version of the man who rescued him last night. He looks smaller. Doesn't look like the kind of guy who could punch out three muggers. Ben thanks Larry and finds his way in to the building.
'Max Maguire?'
The guy standing at the desk, thumbing through papers, looks up. He has that same haunted look in his steely grey eyes.
'I know you,' he says, and Ben nods.
'You saved my life in the car park last night. I'm Ben Brookes. I wanted to thank you. You saved my wallet too, saved me a whole lot of trouble getting new credit cards. Also saved me losing the best picture of my girlfriend. Want to see it?'
The big guy shakes his head, goes back to his papers. Ben presses on.
'Can I do anything to thank you?'
He shakes his head. Ben glances down at his shoes. They are shined perfectly. Ben considers something for a while. The other guy doesn't say anything, just moves stuff around on the desk.
'Then – can I ask you a favour?'
'You can ask.'
'I can't here. When do you get a break?'
'Forty minutes or so.'
Ben nods. He'll be back. Max doesn't say anything.

*

Forty minutes pass, Ben returns and the two of them stroll down to the café next to Larry Hook's coke bottle shop. They order coffee and sit outside. Ben drinks Mocha, Max stares into a double espresso.

'I need to ask you a favour, a big favour.'
Max nods.
'My girlfriend's disappeared.'
'I'm sorry to hear that.'
'I saw how you handled yourself the other night. You're used to trouble right?'
Max grimaces.
'I'll take that as a yes,' says Ben. 'But you obviously watch out for people too. I mean you didn't have to cross that car park for me. Could have done a Good Samaritan and just walked on by.'
Max smiles. 'Actually the Good Samaritan doesn't walk on by. That's the point. He's the one that stops. So, technically I guess I did… do a Good Samaritan.'
Ben sighs. 'Whatever. Listen. I can pay.'
'You can pay?'
'Sure. Money's not a problem. I want to hire you. I want you to find her.'
Max leans back in his seat, holds up his hands, gives a crooked grin, looks kind of shy.
'I'm sorry I don't do that,' he says, 'I have a job, I teach at the college. Can't just go swanning off into the unknown.'
'You have a family?'
Max shakes his head.
'So… other commitments?'
'Like I say. Just my job…'
'Don't you have the Easter break coming?'
'In a week or so.'
'That's what I thought. Look. She's probably somewhere round here. I'm not asking you to drop everything. But I'm worried she's in trouble. She wouldn't just up and leave me. We have a good relationship. I love her.'
'Great. Call the police.'
Ben Brookes sighs, places his elbow on the table, rests his cheek on his left fist.
'I have done. She's on their list. But… I don't have time to wait for Crimewatch to film a little reconstruction and put it out in a month's time. I'm really worried. Look, I found this picture in her room.'
He holds out a photo. Max hesitates. He doesn't want to see it. He knows this will draw him in a little closer. Too close.

'If this woman is involved it could be mean.'
Max leans in a little, he won't take hold of the photo but he'll look. He winces.
'Oh yea, she looks mean, all right,' he says.
'If you look closely you can see she has tattoos on her teeth. Tattoos! Two snakes or something like it. Normal people don't have that.'
Max nods, stands up.
'I'm sorry... Ben wasn't it? Yea, Ben, I'm sorry. There was a time I could have helped you, and if your girlfriend was being mugged in the street I'd be right in there. But I don't go looking for trouble anymore. I'm sorry.'
Max pushes his chair away, turns, hesitates, then glances back and says again, 'I'm sorry.'
And he walks away, the image of the woman with the tattooed teeth still playing in his mind. It's true, normal people don't have that. Oh yes, he remembers her all right.

Six

It's bright outside. Beyond the white-boarded windows, somewhere through the cracks and the splintered notches in the wood, the sun is trying to get at her. She spends time standing beside the glass, feeling the remnants of heat. Shutting her eyes and remembering the days as a little girl, running and playing and swimming on days like this. Days before she adopted the mad idea of travelling the world researching, interviewing, writing, seeking out other people and their dirt and glamour. Will she ever do that again? Will she find a way back? Perhaps there are people out there looking, knocking on doors, pressing bad guys up against walls. Twisting the arms of criminals behind their backs, pressing cruel faces against crumbling stone in an attempt to extricate truth and track her down. Is that too much to hope for? Perhaps. Perhaps. She always did have a vivid imagination.

*

'So you see Jesus does impressions. It's his best qualification.'
The boy in the back has his hand up. It's always the boy in the back, his blond fringe hanging over his eyes, his arm held lazily aloft like he's tried

to hail a taxi and it passed him by. A wad of gum flicks around his mouth behind his perfect white teeth.

'Yes Al?' Max says with a sigh.

'They're not like real impressions though are they, I mean he doesn't do voices does he?'

Max warms to this. 'No, but voices aren't the point. No one knows Moses' voice anyway. They have no idea what Elijah and Elisha sounded like. How would they? They don't have DVD's or YouTube. It's not what they look like that matters, Jesus doesn't nip down to the costume shop and ask for a Noah lookalike beard and glasses. It's what the old prophets did that matters. And that's where Jesus is very specific. He's done his homework, probably during his forty days of boot camp in the wilderness. He knows his audience and his audience know their Old Testament heroes. So Jesus impersonates those respected guys so that people will start to see the resemblance, they will start to put it together that Jesus is the next in a long line of prophets.'

'But Jesus wasn't just a prophet, sir. He was way more than that.'

It's Stacey. With the startling eye-liner and brain like a planet. She's earnest, always earnest, and has this intense, unflinching stare. The eye-liner makes her look perpetually stunned. She always beams her Stacey-stare at Max when asking him questions, it's disarming.

'Sure,' says Max, 'but he has to start somewhere. And he's in no rush. People misunderstand that. You won't find him cruising around with a loudhailer and a t-shirt with *Messiah* screen-printed on it. He builds his case carefully, slowly, hides it from the people who have power. Look, let me show you this.' He scoops up a PC remote and presses it. The screen behind him flickers then goes blank. Max looks around for a technician.

'He's on a tea break,' says Al, helpfully.

'Great. Ah. Never mind. Let me just tell you, let me do it the old way. The way the Biblical storytellers did it. Skip back to the exodus okay? The account of Moses leading the Israelite people out of slavery in Egypt. It's a dangerous situation. The Egyptians are a superpower. They rule. A man walks out of the desert smelling bad and claiming that God has told him to rescue the Israelites. How can he prove that? They don't have a Bible to check him out, they have no reference books. They live in a land where Egyptian religion rules and no one's expecting a murderous shepherd with

body odour to coming out of the desert and set free the slave workforce. Moses needs qualifications. So Moses does miracles.'
'You can't prove that.'
Max holds up his hands. 'No, Al, but that's another point entirely. Stay with the plot for a minute here. You asked me about the impressions question. So – how does Moses 'prove' he's been sent by God? He does miracles. He does things which demonstrate some kind of supernatural, divine power. The kind of things a man cannot do under his own steam. And everyone starts to take notice. Including the Egyptians. Especially when he turns the Nile into a river of blood. That gets their attention. The Nile was fundamental to their worldview, they had gods associated with it. Suddenly the thing stinks. Okay. Jump forward a few years and Moses dies while the people are still stuck in the desert. They've left Egypt but not yet arrived in Canaan.'
'Wasn't that just land-grabbing?'
'Al, please. Let me wrestle with one difficult concept at a time. Joshua is appointed to follow Moses, but how will he get the people to believe he's the next big guy? Simple… and difficult. Do what Moses did. Do miracles, and not just any miracle, the kind of miracles Moses did. And what's the big one, the one they write songs about? The parting of the Sea of Reeds. Moses can hold back water, so that's what Joshua has to do. He makes a way through the Jordan river and the people follow. Joshua shows he can do what Moses did. And that's what Jesus is doing. Like Joshua he impersonates Moses, and others, so that people will make the connections. The people don't have a script for this kind of thing, they say Jesus is a rabbi, but he didn't train as one. They don't know what else to call him, he's this strange prophet who argues confidently with the authorities, displays incredible wisdom, does miracles and spends a lot of time helping the marginalised. And looks like their hero Moses. He brings his own commandments, he takes control of water, he makes bread appear. All things that the great Moses did. Got it?' Silence. The class look uninspired. Sixteen pairs of eyes look back at him, giving away very little. Apart from Stacey whose penetrating gaze fixes him as she nods once. A hand goes up, lazily chasing that cab again. 'Yes Al?'
'The bread he made. Was it brown or white?'

Seven

A man in a white suit comes to see her. He makes no attempt to disguise himself, he leans on a cane, walks with a limp and is clearly not well. He talks a while but explains only a little. He appears to be a strange mixture of reasonable benevolence and calculated savagery. He asks if she needs anything. Freedom, she says. He smiles and the smiling makes him cough. That will depend, he says.

*

Suzie wakes. She washes off the sleep in the dysfunctional shower, pulls on her clothes and slips out of her room. She exits the small Texan hotel through a side door. She walks for a while, leaves the city behind. Del Rio becomes a distant shadow on the horizon. Mere shapes in the background. Night falls and she finds herself in the San Lui valley. There is a single shack in a cleft in the rocks there and she slips inside. It is deserted so she climbs into the single bunk and takes refuge in it. She is woken in the night by a hand shaking her shoulder. It is an old seer, a Mexican going by the name of Sanchez. No other name. Just Sanchez. He's a recluse. And he took some finding. Sanchez informs her that she is sleeping in his bed. He is an old man and needs his rest. She smiles. She has a good smile, a good face. Hard but kind he thinks. Her black hair frames her expression, she appears pleased to see him. She shakes herself and gets up, the seer points to an old armchair and tells her she can take that. The seer settles himself down and she spends a restless night in the chair.
In the morning Sanchez wakes her again and is frying up a breakfast of strange, unrecognisable food. He slaps an old metal dish down in front of Suzie and tells her to eat it. While she is doing so the seer looks her straight in the eyes.
'I wonder,' he says, 'are you a seeker of truth?'
'Maybe. You could say that,' she says.
'Then it's no accident that you've come this way,' says the seer.
He takes a picture frame from the wall, opens up the back and shoves a black and white shot towards her across the splintered table.
'You know this man?'
She nods. Oh she knows him all right.
'Who is it?'

'Max Maguire.'

The old seer laughs, a wheezy, gravel of a laugh. He rubs his hands together.

'I knew you would come,' he says. 'I saw it. I saw you. In the corridors of my mind. A short woman in black, those three studs you wear in your left ear, that band around your wrist, and most of all your piercing eyes. I had a dream. I saw you. I'm not as sharp as I once was, but I got it right this time. Let me show you something.'

He goes to the wall, removes a stone and pulls out a slim wooden box. It is thick with dust and he brings it to the table and lifts the lid. A layer of dust drops straight into Suzie's plate.

'What you will see now no one has seen for two hundred years.'

He lifts a piece of animal skin from the box, lays it on the table and opens it out.

'This, my friend, is a fragment of Nehushtan. The snake of Moses.'

The woman smiles. Her journey has not been in vain. The seer pulls a huge black book from a shelf and slaps it down in front of her, the dust rising in clouds from it. He flips it open and jabs his finger at a marked page, moving it repeatedly like a speeding woodpecker.

'Read it,' he says.

She blinks, rubs the dust from her eyes and looks more closely. Reads it aloud.

'Then the Lord told Moses, "Make a replica of a poisonous snake and attach it to the top of a pole. Those who are bitten will live if they simply look at it." So Moses made a snake out of bronze and attached it to the top of a pole. Whenever those who were bitten looked at the bronze snake, they recovered.'

He takes the book and flicks pages again. Jabs his finger at the paper again like the same demented woodpecker.

She reads, 'Hezekiah broke up the bronze serpent that Moses had made, because the people of Israel had begun to worship it by burning incense to it. The bronze serpent was called Nehushtan.'

The seer smiles and holds up the two inch fragment.

'The snake was smashed seven hundred years ago by the Judean King Hezekiah,' he says. 'It has been guarded carefully ever since. All you have to do is find the other pieces. Who knows what you might accomplish.' He grips her arm. 'But be careful, beware the vipers.'

She thanks him, stands, takes up the piece of snake and wraps it back up in the animal skin.
'I've waited a long time for this,' he says.
'Really? In your vision did you see any teeth?'
'What do you mean?' the old seer looks uncertain for the first time.
She smiles a broad, hungry smile and bares her eye teeth in a wolfish grin. He looks closely to study the tattooed vipers. He recoils, suddenly short of breath. Her face seems to have changed, she doesn't look so kind anymore. He blinks repeatedly, tries to speak but can't. She figures she may not have to do much here.
'You see I am not so much a seeker of truth…' she says, 'as an assassin.'
She thinks for a moment, takes out her gun and shoots him in the heart. It's all over so quickly.

Eight

The man with the cane starts turning up regularly. Three times a day. He chats with her, asks her about her work and her writing. It sounds innocuous enough, and she entertains him calmly and politely, but all the time she is angling for information. Where is she? Why is she here? When can she go home? Nothing. He gives her nothing. He seems lonely. Why else would he come so frequently? When she asks about his health he ignores the question.

*

'Why did the prodigal's father run?'
Silence. Max stares. The class stares back. Larry pauses chewing.
'Al?' Max says. 'Nothing to say?'
Al shrugs. 'It's obvious.'
'Well humour me.'
'How about because he hated his son and didn't want him home…'
Lena, sitting in front of Al, laughs then blushes when no one else does.
'Sorry,' she mutters.
'Close, but no cigar,' says Max.
'Look we all know, it's a loaded question,' groans Al, 'He runs 'cause he's pleased to have the boy back.'

'Yet again, close but no cigar. Larry? Stacey?'
'There's this scene in *French Kiss*,' says Larry, 'where Kevin Kline goes home expecting his family to hate him. But they throw a party.'
'Okay. Why?'
Larry shrugs. 'Cause they like him.'
Max sighs. 'Stacey?'
'Is it something to do with the Old Testament, sir?'
Max snaps his fingers. 'Now we're getting somewhere.'
'It's about Jacob and Esau isn't it?' she says. 'The prodigal is Jacob isn't he? The boy who ran off and abandoned his family.'
'Absolutely. And you know what Deuteronomy says about that?'
She doesn't.
'Okay. Deuteronomy chapter 21 verse 18 – bad news for teenagers. If a couple have a wayward son who refuses to obey his parents then the family must take him to the elders of the village who will then stone him as an example to all the other teenagers. So, here, in Jesus's retelling of Israel's history, we have a young son who acts as if his father is dead, takes the money from the estate and then wastes it all. The village declare him dead in his absence and should he return they are likely to stone him. And this is where the father is counter-cultural. He looks for his son, refuses to think of him as a dead, and so, when he sees the boy returning...'
'He runs to protect him,' says Larry, the sound of a penny dropping as he speaks.
'Bingo,' says Max. 'And what does the father say at the end of the story? Stacey?'
'My son was dead but now he is alive again.'
'Exactly. The villagers had written him off to the grave. But not the father. The father believes in resurrection. That's why he runs.'
Bang on cue, as he delivers the punch line, the bell rings. Like the drum beats at the end of *Eastenders*. He sits back and watches them leave, wonders how many will give it a second thought as they return to their lives in the London rush.
As the crowd funnel through the door, disperse and leave the empty doorframe, Ben Brookes appears in the space. His body propped against the wood. Sharp and tidy as ever. Apart from that wiry hair. Ben smiles. Max does not.
'I was wondering what it would take,' Ben says.

28

'No news, then?' says Max.
Ben shakes his head.
'I was wondering what it would take,' he says again.
'You got me wrong,' says Max. 'I'm not a hero. I just scared off a few punks in a car park. Anyone would do it.'
'I couldn't,' says Ben. 'I'd be on the floor in a pool of blood. I don't know much about this kind of thing but you look to me like you have experience. Like you can handle yourself.'
'Maybe, but it doesn't mean I want to be the next James Bond.'
Ben frowns. 'Please, just think about it,' he says. He turns to go then throws Max one final hopeful glance.
Max waits until the steps in the corridor have faded to nothing then he sits back and throws his feet onto the desk. Why won't the past let him go? He glances up at the ceiling, says a silent prayer and shakes his head.

*

It takes eight minutes to ride the train from Guildford to Woking, another five to walk to his flat opposite the station on the town side. He lives in a two roomed affair. Bedroom and kitchen-diner with a sofa. These days he crashes out on the sofa as often as sleeping in bed. He collapses on it now, his head full of Ben and that final glance he threw at Max as he walked away today. The look in his eyes. The longing and the hope. There were times recently where he'd rely on a bottle of whisky to escape from a day like today. But not now. Now he stares at the curtains, still hanging there from the 1970s, and he waits for sleep to take him out. It does, and it takes him to that deserted railway station. Not a soul about. The wind gusting around, kicking up litter. The eerie silence. Maybe only a few minutes of it but it seems to go on all night. He wakes, lies staring at the ceiling, the images flashing through his mind. An old picture show. Black and white footage infused with the colour of blood. So many he couldn't save. So many innocent victims. Why was saving the world so hard? It hadn't felt that way when he started out. Those early days when he felt nothing but bulletproof. No mountain too high, no villain too hard. He dozes off again. He's back on that station. The wind. The silence. The steps approaching. He wakes. He's sweating. He can't go back to all that. Can't relive those things. He gets up. Walks to the window, pulls back the '70's curtains. She's there, on the street, the collar of her black leather coat pulled up around her face. Ear studs glistening under the street lamp. She's on the phone and laughing. She thinks he can't see her. He stares at her for a long time. So long that she fades away. Where is she? Where did she go? Not here anymore. Not down there in that street below his flat. He imagined that. Just an illusion. An apparition that still stalks the corridors of his mind. But somewhere, somewhere out there, she's very real. Spitting poison from those viper teeth. He pours a glass of water. It comes out cloudy at first, so he lets it run, swills the glass and fills it. He drinks it down and goes into the bedroom. He lies down, sleeps, and dreams again of that station. The young, vulnerable seventeen year old pacing the platform. The sudden violence. The life ebbing away in Max's arms. He wakes again. Listens to the couple next door arguing through the wall while Bob Marley plays in the background. 'Don't worry about a thing, cause every little thing is gonna be all right...' The man from Nazareth said something to that end. He pulls out his battered brown Bible and thumbs it. Falls asleep reading and this time makes it through without too much dreaming.

Nine

Eight o'clock the next morning. Max is at his desk. The sun is out, the promise of a bright spring day. Larry sticks his head in, sees his tutor and strolls in, magazine in hand.
'Seen this this Mr Maguire? They're gonna make a movie about Don Cortez. Better do it soon – he's not looking well. Not at all. Hopkins is gonna play him.'
Larry holds up his copy of *Total Film*. 'Should be good,' he says, 'Haggis is writing and Gerard Butler's gonna play the bad guy.'
'I thought Cortez was the bad guy.'
'Not in his own movie.'
Max didn't care about Cortez right now. Rich businessman and their ensemble cast of dark eyed beauties and thick set heavies was of no interest at all.
'More to the point, Mr Hook - how's the paper on Solomon and slavery?' he asks.

'Ah, well, see - I don't get it. If Solomon is supposed to be this great, good-guy king, how come he uses slaves to build his palace?'
'Not only his palace, Larry, his temple too. Which is the point of your essay. Why do good people lose the plot? How can a man like Solomon build a temple for God and yet use slave labour, what's going on there?'
Larry shrugs. 'Seems stupid,' he says.
'Yes. But that's what so fascinating about the Bible – it doesn't hide the crimes and misdemeanours. What does the guy writing psalm 139 say – "you have made me wonderfully complex." People are complex Larry. The older you get, the more you'll see that.'
'I dunno, it's religion isn't it? Just seems to screw people up. I was reading about Stephen last night, you know, the guy who got stoned in the book of Acts. Not on pot you understand.'
'Yes Larry, I know where you're going here.'
'Well, it's the religious leaders who stone him, the vicars and bishops and priests. And they have the cheek to take off their coats so they won't get them dirty while they're doing the job.'
'More than that Larry, they remove them so they won't get blood on them, so it won't make them "unclean" in the eyes of God.'
Larry snorts. 'Like – killing a guy who's feeding the hungry and helping the poor doesn't make them "unclean" then?'
'It's the same thing as Solomon. People lose the plot. They become so focussed on the rules they lose sight of what really matters. Put that in the essay. Write about Stephen and the guys who stoned him. Don't be afraid to wrestle with the Bible. Before it was ever a book it was a collection of stories and people were always haggling over the meanings. It was the way. Why do you think Jesus says to his audience, "Here's a story, what do you think about it?" Go explore Mr Hook, find me a movie that wrestles intelligently with faith and hypocrisy.'
Larry's face crease like paper jammed in a photocopier. 'Hmm, I might,' he says. 'Plenty of movies like that.'
He wanders out.
'Be intelligent though, Larry,' Max calls after him, 'plenty of films use religion as a soft target. Be intelligent.'
There is a mumble from the corridor. Max takes that as a 'yes'.
He stands and stretches and takes a stroll himself. Ginny's packing up for the day, getting ready for home.

'Got me a nice roast waiting for heating up,' she says, 'then it's "hit that sack".'
'How d'you cope with doing nothing all night?' he asks.
She looks affronted. 'I don't do nothing. I patrol, I watch out for waifs and strays. And trespassers. Plus I stick my nose into other people's affairs. So be careful what you leave lying around.' She laughs. 'And anyway, I like the quiet, I've had plenty of clatter in my life. Plus I've always got Mr Loaf for company. I can always snuggle up to Meat, as I call him.'
She taps her iPod.
'Meat?'
'Yes. You know - *Bat out of Hell*. You'd like him. He's religious too, you know. He's a lovely guy. Met him once. Wouldn't mind a slice of that.'
She roars with laughter, pats Max on the shoulder and squeezes past him. 'Enjoy your Bible study,' she says and she's gone. The silence is suddenly very obvious. He picks up yesterday's paper from the table. Walks out to the oak tree and drops onto the bench out there. He strums through it, the pages rustling in the light breeze. He stops. Stares at the lines of print. Just a little story. Bottom of page fifteen. But not a little story at all. Not to him. Carlos Gomez. Murdered in Iran. Possibly an underworld killing. Possibly not though. Max stares into nothing, students pass him by and acknowledge him but he doesn't see them. Carlos Gomez. Dead. The man who had once saved Max's life. Gone. He'd never save it again and Max can't return the favour now. Just ten lines in a broadsheet paper. Carlos Gomez, a strange reclusive guy travelling in Iran. An unknown hero. Max folds the paper and walks around for a while. He is so distracted he is nearly late for his first class of the day. It's a good job he's planned it well, because his mind is absent for a lot of it. And when the class is done and he is alone again with his thoughts he sits staring into space for the longest time. And in his mind's eye he can make out a figure leaning in a far, dark corner of his head. A figure that looks for all the world like Suzie Kruger.
'Stay out of this Max.'
Sounds like her too.
'You know what happened before. You know you lost the game. Stay out. You wouldn't want to end up like Carlos. Would you? You made the right choices. Quitting while you were ahead. Quitting while you were *alive*. Don't foul up now.'

He shivers, looks away, stares at the Bible open on his desk. *Wake up! Strengthen what remains, and is about to die.* They have been studying Revelation. Death, thunder and pestilence. *Strengthen what is about to die.* Beside the Bible there is a cartoon tract given him by Lena. One of those booklets about the end of the world, where giant locusts attack mankind like swooping helicopters, and all the non-believers run screaming to the hills. The four horseman of the apocalypse resemble ninja turtles and death itself is not unlike Chuck Norris in a trench coat. It depresses him. Not only the depiction but also the way people predict the future like this. So much for the good news. *Wake up!* He shuts his eyes, searches the corners of his mind but all is well. The dark figure is gone. Suzie Kruger or not, she has taken off. He laughs at himself, forces himself to see the funny side. Just a mirage. That's all. Just a trick of the light, a glitch in his imagination. There was a time he would have barely batted an eyelid at the sight of someone like Kruger, but now… he gathers up the papers and books from his desk and goes in search of some lunch in a quiet corner of Wetherspoons. Carlos Gomez, Suzie Kruger, Chuck Norris in a trench coat. It's been a busy morning.

Ten

'Sir. Can I ask you something?'
It's Larry Hook again. He can't keep away. It's been a full afternoon and Max has his mind set on an early finish. There's a six o'clock showing of *Spondulix* at the Guildford Odeon. He needs a little pulp fiction to help him forget today. A fix of Ellen Page and Joseph Gordon-Levitt would do the job.
'Let me ask you something first,' Max says, leaning back in his seat.
'I haven't done it, sir, but I am working on it.'
'Really? I'm sure you are. But that wasn't exactly what I had in mind. I was thinking more of *Spondulix*.'
Larry's face lights up. He may even have forgotten his original question.
'It's just opened,' he says.
'So I heard. Any good?'
'Haven't seen it. But Ellen Page is always a hundred per cent watchable.'

Max glances at his watch. 'How about I give you permission to have a night off from you're assignments, I know how much you love doing them.'
'Cool. When's the showing?'
'Six at the Odeon.'
'Meet you there at five thirty. Don't be late sir, I'm never late for movies.'

*

The Guildford Odeon is a six minute walk, a ten minute stroll, from the School of Theology. Max takes his time, he has plenty of spare minutes. The weather is cooler now, the sun's melted into a drab sky, a remnant of winter replacing the early hint of summer. He waits on the bench outside the cinema, staring at a life-size cardboard image of Ellen Page lurking beside the door.
Larry rolls up bang on time, force-feeding himself coke bottles. He has his notebook in his hand, an old exercise book plastered in a hundred movie stills. They join the meagre queue and plump for the 2D showing rather than the 3D.
'A good movie doesn't need an elbow jutting out of the screen in your face,' Larry tells the girl on the ticket desk. 'I mean - have you never seen *Notorious*?'
It's hardly the best chat up line in the book.
'Notorious what?' she asks.
'Alfred Hitchcock.'
'Who?'
Larry shakes his head and sighs, looking suddenly as if he's forty years her senior.
'Sorry,' she says, attempting a grimace.
'I'll show you it one day,' says Larry.
'Is that Robert Pattinson's new movie?' she asks, suddenly perking up.
Larry just shakes his head. It's all he can manage. Max buys his ticket and they head for screen two. He half-expects Larry to make some comment about 'the younger generation' but he is spared that.

*

'What did you do before working at the college?' Larry asks as they watch local adverts glide across the screen.
Max allows himself a sly smile.

'What are you angling for Larry?'
'Well, you just don't seem like the professor type.'
'I'm not giving you ideas for your next blockbuster.'
Larry laughs. 'Oh come on. A guy like you, you must have done stuff.'
'What do you mean? A guy like me? Is this the question? The one you came to see me about earlier?'
'Well, you know, I just wondered. After that mugging an' all.'
Max turns slowly and deliberately to look at Larry. The young guy shrugs, shakes hair out of his eyes.
'What?' he says.
'Who told you about that?' Max asks him.
'That guy, your number one fan. He came round looking for you again.'
'Again?'
'Sure. He's been in every day this week. You're not always around when he comes. Normally I just fob him off with stuff about your drug problem… shooting up in the toilets and everything…'
Larry throws a coke bottle in the air, catches it in his mouth. He chews and grins big.
'Just kidding. But he is here every day. He's dedicated.'
Max turns and stares at the screen again. A local car dealer with slick hair and a bright green suit tells him how wonderful his life would be if he bought a Guildford Ford.
'What did he tell you?'
'That you took out three bad guys with your bare hands and a bin bag.'
Larry taps his book. 'I already put it in. Opening scene. But the thing is… you must have done that kind of thing before. Army? SAS?'
Max shakes his head. Larry's harmless enough.
'The thing is Larry,' he says, 'it's like they say. I could tell you, but I'd have to kill you.'
'With a bin bag?'
'With a bin bag.'
Larry nods and chews for a while. A family of five roll up and sit in front of them. The father is about eight feet tall and places his skull right in front of Larry's eyeline. The kids chew noisily on Doritos and popcorn. Larry throws his hands up and shrugs with every fibre of his being. He raises his thumb and jabs it in the direction of two seats along. He and Max shift sideways.

'Ever hear of a thing called *The Cordoban Cross*?'
Larry drops this in as they settle in their new seats, he speaks out of the side of his mouth as if they're under surveillance. Max turns in slow motion and stares at him.
'How d'you hear about that?'
Larry pulls a newspaper cutting from his notebook.
Max shakes his head. 'You're good, Mr Hook,' he says. 'Too good for your own good.'
'Will you have to kill me?'
'Maybe.'
'The thing is,' says Larry, still out of the side of his mouth, 'it doesn't mention you here in the paper, but your number one fan is pretty convinced. He checked you out, said he found something on line. You did this didn't you?'
Max wasn't listening. Ben Brookes was starting to get him down. He took the cutting, stared at the black and white photo of the tiny cross.
'It was just a favour for someone. An old lady I met in a park one day. She was looking all sad and lonely. Told me about this ancient golden amulet she once had. When she lived in Spain. A family heirloom that got stolen, that's all. I went looking for it for her. Got more than I bargained for.'
'And how does this fit in? The Cordoban Cross?'
'Goes all the way back to the days when the Moors ruled Spain. These guys called the Berbers invaded from North Africa and ended up creating the Mezquita, or Great Mosque, in a place called Cordoba, in Andalucia. They converted an old church and then added bits and redesigned it and it became this incredible Cathedral Mosque. Still one of the biggest temples in the world. Was a centre for art and education and study of all kinds of things.'
'And the cross?'
Max leans on his elbow and narrows his eyes at Larry. 'You don't give up do you?'
Larry grins. 'I'm a simple guy. I just want to make a million dollar movie.'
'Well, here's the science bit. The Cordoban Cross had been crafted from Moor gold in the 13th Century for the church tucked inside the Great Mosque in Cordoba. Place is full of that kind of thing. The crucifix was known for the three tiny blue jaspers that held the silver Christ to the

golden cross. Work of real craftsmanship. It had been thought lost for centuries.'

'Till you met an old lady in a park.'

'Yea. Kind of. Elli, that's her name. She's this beautiful, olive-skinned, bright-eyed widow. Once owned a house in the street opposite the Great Mosque, and just before she left Spain her golden amulet got stolen. It was worth a bit but it was really all about the sentimental value. Been in her family for centuries. So I went looking.'

'Because?'

'Because… I… I had nothing else to do that afternoon. Okay? Wasn't hard. I had contacts then. After a series of dark encounters and close shaves, no I'm not going into detail, I found myself at three in the morning, digging as quietly as possible into the floor of that old church inside the Mezquitta.'

'And what d'you find?'

'The amulet. All wrapped up in a little leather pouch. Along with this.'

He points at the picture of the cross.

Max stared at the cutting, fingering the scar on his chin. According to the article the cross had been mysteriously returned to the Cathedral Mosque. Was now under lock and key and an impregnable security system. But there was plenty the newspaper didn't tell.

'You get injured finding it?' Larry asks suddenly.

Max looks up, stops rubbing his chin.

'Just a nick,' he says. 'So you see, not really much to tell.' He points at Larry's wristwatch. 'There'll be ten minutes of trailers. I'm going for a Sprite. Want one?'

'You're not going out? You have to stay in character, stay in the movie-zone.'

'You stay in it for me. I'll be back for the film.'

*

Not really much to tell, no, not if you disregard some of the murkier details. Like the way he was forced to dig up the floor of the church at gunpoint. Or the teaming up with local gangster, Ismail Cruz. Cruz had also been on the hunt for the amulet and so he and Max joined forces over two bottles of Alhambra beer and a squid bap. And they worked well

together - until they located the treasure buried inside the Mezquita, then Ismail turned nasty, pulled a gun and nominated Max to do the digging.
'You don' know wha' you 'ave here, do you, Maguire?' Cruz said as Max laboured under flickering torchlight.
Cruz chuckled and casually tossed his gun from one hand to the other.
'You ever 'ear of the liddle famouth Cordoban cruthifixth?' Cruz said.
Max hadn't, right then he didn't care, he wanted a cold beer and a warm bed. He stopped digging.
'Hey! Ismail,' he said, leaning into the hole. 'Take a look down here!'
Ismail leant over Max's shoulder and Max swung the spade up and cracked the Spaniard on the forehead.
Cruz ejected a whole string of Spanish curses before leaping back, raising his gun and firing off two shots. Fortunately there was blood in his eyes and it stopped him from shooting straight, but one bullet still tore through the edge of Max's hand, while the other ricocheted off a pillar and sheared off a sliver of stone, which bounced off two walls and the floor before slicing upwards through Max's chin. This only heightened Max's sense of injustice, and made him pummel Cruz twice with his injured hand. Then, alarms wailing in the background, Max snuck into the shadows of the massive Mosque and waited for the police and their dogs to raid the building and drag Cruz away. In the darkness he turned his jacket inside out, and slipped out looking for all the world like one of the cops. It was a useful trick. The lining had a dark uniform look that enabled him to blend in.

Outside, in a back ally behind the Mezquita, Max pulled a tattered leather bundle from inside his shirt. There inside was the gold amulet. But it wasn't alone. Something else had been hidden with Elli's precious heirloom. Max unravelled the rest of the leather to find himself staring at the little golden crucifix. The three jasper nails were glinting softly in the low light and he guessed there was something more going on here. When he returned to Elli's little Cornish cottage, jammed in the cliffs off The Lizard, Elli Ramirez could not believe her eyes.
'So, it's true. My boy told the truth.'
'What boy?'
She looked more than a little sheepish.

'Don't be angry with me Mr Maguire. But I did mix my truth with some lies. My nephew Ismail, he's my brother's famous son. He's what you call a big shot in Cordoba. People everywhere know my brother's son.'
'Including the police.'
'What do you mean?'
'He's not Ismail Cruz is he?'
Her chestnut eyes lit up. 'You know him?'
'You could say we met, yes.'
'Ah my sweet boy. The apple of all our eyes. Wouldn't hurt a fly…'
Max jabbed a bandaged hand in the direction of the dressing on his chin. 'Mrs Ramirez, he nearly took my head off.'
'No! Why?'
'Long story. What does he have to do with your pendant?'
'I owed money… taxes to the government… they would have made me sell my precious amulet. You see – it is worth quite a lot. So I gave it to Ismail to hide for me. Only… he lost it. In a game of cards. And I thought it was gone forever. That was a year ago. But now look, you found it! Everybody's happy.'
'I didn't just find that, Mrs Ramirez,' Max laid the leather pouch on her coffee table and unwrapped the crucifix. 'I found this too. It wasn't alone.'
Elli Ramirez put on her winged reading glasses and came close to the table.
'Oh my… so Ismail was telling the truth!'
Max sighed. 'About what?' he said through gritted teeth.
'He always claimed that the night he bet my amulet on his three jacks and two nines, that an Australian girl he was playing, what was her name? Funny name… oh yes… Beluga something. Odyssey I think. Yes. Well she produced a strange gold cross with three blue stones and she bet that against him. I never believed him, but I didn't tell him 'cause he can get a little tetchy…'
'You're telling me,' said Max.
Elli Ramirez picked up the crucifix and gently dabbed her fingers on the blue jasper nails.
'So much life,' she said softly, 'so much life.'
She closed her eyes and reverently laid the cross back down, nodding as she did so.
'Anyway,' she said suddenly, 'they say that little cross is seven hundred years old. Seven hundred! Might be worth a few pounds, eh?'

'No doubt, Mrs Ramirez. No doubt. Look I'm gonna leave you know, I have to get my chin stitched properly. In the meantime, look after that little amulet. Please. I don't fancy going head to head with your nephew again.'
As he limped into the darkness Max looked back to see Elli Ramirez happily waving him off from the door of her cottage. The crucifix went back to Cordoba. Max did not.

*

When he returns with a couple of drinks Larry is chewing on his pen and still studying the news cutting.
'I think you should help this guy,' he says. 'You know, this whatshisname...Bill Brookes.'
Max sighed.
'Larry, I teach theology. To people like you. That's what I do. I can't go swanning off to help every Tom, Dick or Ben - actually that's his name - whenever I feel like it. I'm here. At the college. Most days. This is what I do.'
Larry shook his head. 'I dunno,' he tapped his notebook. 'I think you do other stuff too.
Lots of guys can teach theology. Not everyone can take out three muggers with a bin bag.'
Why was it like this? Why was the past like a dog chasing cars that just wouldn't let up?

Eleven

The guy with the rifle brings the food again. He always brings it and always brings the same thing. Bread, fruit and fish. Always fresh and well prepared. She asks him how long it has been, she asks him what they want, she asks him his name. Nothing. She wonders about making attempts to seduce him. He doesn't smell good, but she guesses that she doesn't either right now. All she has is a bowl of cold water, a tiny bar of soap and no deodorant.

*

Another night of bad dreams for Max. These are full of bullets. The ricochets in the Mezquitta rattling round his brain. Again and again and again. Then Ak47's spitting blood at him. Suzie Kruger's sinister sneer and some woman he's never met playing cards. Could be Beluga Odyssey. Or just some woman he passed in a street once. You know how dreams are. Then he's back at the railway station and there's that eerie silence. He wakes to sunlight, exhausted from his sleeping.

*

Casper Mack hands his passport to the girl behind the desk. She glances up. He smiles, she doesn't. It's been a hard day for her. She's still learning her job, still being supervised. She's sure it'll be less stressful when she can work on her own. Being watched all the time is a nightmare. Casper smiles again as she hands the passport back. It's not a bad likeness. Makes him look like a criminal, but then, what are passport photos for? He's really not a bad man. He's done some bad things, but hasn't every one? And he likes to think his heart was always in the right place. She attaches a label to the handle of his blue Tumi suitcase. This guy is rich. Rolex watch. Armani suit. Goodlooking too. Especially when he smiles. Any other day and she'd be up for that. Sneaking her number in the back of his passport before she handed it back. But not today. And it won't happen with this guy. More's the pity. Casper pockets the passport and thanks her, she thanks him and urges him to have a good flight. He walks away. She glances at her watch. Coffee break. One customer to go and she's on her own time. She smiles at the old couple tugging their cases towards her.

Casper gets himself a coffee. A macchiato with extra shots of Bourbon. Drinks it slowly while he pores over the lengthy story about Sanchez. He can't believe it. They go way back. Never thought it would end like this. A harmless old guy, living out his last days quietly, gunned down. Crazy. Another broken link in the chain. The papers have some details right, but they are guessing when it comes to the snake. They can't even spell Nehushtan correctly. They have the vowels in the wrong order. Are they just spitting in the dark with this? Journalists sniffing out a story from the last century to fill a few column inches. Why now? Why the sudden killing? Hopefully Marty will know. Marty's a wise guy. Sensible, logical, won't let his imagination run away from him. That's Casper's problem.

When you're a screenwriter you live with the preposterous. Anything is possible. His job is to imagine the worst. He glances at his Rolex. Just time for a bathroom break. Casper drains his coffee. Slips his phone from the table into his suit pocket. Strolls to the men's room.

The old couple safely checked in she stretches and slips off her stool. Closes up her desk and walks out the back. Just one more job then coffee. She walks, she goes through the door, she waits. It's not long and in the end the first part is easier than she expects. She hears the sound of the flush, and then the running of the taps and the gush of the dryer. She's there when he turns around. She does smile now. Casper doesn't. She pulls the razor from her waistband and presses it under his chin. She must get this right.
'Where do you keep it?' she asks quietly.
He glances towards the door. She punches the blade higher, further into his smooth skin.
'Where?' she repeats, her voice smooth as cream.
'What? What do you mean?'
'You know what I'm talking about. A safe deposit box is my guess. You have a key? A combination?'
He can feel the blade beginning to slice skin. The back of his head presses hard against wall tiles. His eyes widen, this woman is not fooling.
'Is this about Sanchez?' he says, 'did you do that?'
She frowns for a moment, looks confused. He glances over to the door again, it's beginning to open. He feels hope start to seep back into his being.
'Sanchez?' she asks, frowning.
'Yea, Sanchez? Was that you? Why? Why do that?'
The door opens a little wider, if he can just keep the conversation going a little longer help will be at hand. He may live to tell this tale.
'I don't know what you're talking about,' she says.
Blood, he can feel a single line running down his neck, she has pushed the blade further in. The door cracks wider. A foot appears.
'Where is it?' She speaks slowly and hoists her knee towards his groin, begins to apply pressure. He's starting to sweat, doesn't look so handsome anymore.

The door is wide now. The figure walks in. Another woman. Must have made a mistake coming in here. He stares across at her, pleads with his eyes, begs her not to leave. Shouting would be good though. Screaming, yelling, anything loud. If she could do that it might save him. The woman comes in, closes the door and leans against it. She stares at him and says nothing.
'Where are you going today?' the girl with the blade asks, her voice still calm and gentle.
'You know where I'm going,' he says, his voice rasping, 'you checked me in - London.'
'Who were you meeting? Is that where it is? Is that where you hide it?'
Did he nod then? Or was that just a nervous movement, an attempt to ease away from the blade at his neck. She glances for the first time towards the door. The other woman is still standing watching. She blinks once. The other girl pushes the blade up and across. He cries out and she has to slap a hand across his mouth to suppress the sound. In doing this she can't move away in time to avoid getting spattered with blood. It's suddenly not as smooth as she had hoped. He crumbles in her arms. The other woman is immediately next to her. Pushes her back. Grabs towels and starts mopping the tiles. They grab him and haul his body into a cubicle. Lock the door and squeeze out underneath it. It's harder for the check-in girl, being taller and less experienced. They splash water on the tiles and wash them down hastily. She rinses the razor and conceals it again, buttons her jacket to cover the red splashes on her shirt. They head for the door. The other woman is carrying something. They are just in time, the door opens as they reach for it. Two teenagers bump them, yakking about music as they come. The women step back, the guys look them up and down, then at each other. They laugh and let them out. Outside in the departure lounge the girl from the check-in desk shakes her head. She hates being monitored like this. Would have done the job properly if she hadn't been worried about being watched. Suzie Kruger looks at the phone in her hand. Casper's phone.
'You're lucky,' she says, 'we'll find out what we need from here.'
'I need to change. Now,' says the check-in girl.
Suzie Kruger shakes her head. 'That was a mess. Could have gone badly wrong. Very badly wrong. You got to do better, girl.'

She nods. She will. They walk away, parting company as they go. Inside the men's room Casper Mack is breathing his last. And two teenage boys still laugh about two women hanging out in the gent's toilets.

Twelve

Don Cortez has his own doctor. The best that money can buy. He is a short barrel of a man, all braces, pinstripes and sweat on his brow. More like a lawyer than a quack. But all quack he is, and though he fears Cortez he knows better than to soft pedal the truth. The prognosis he made six months ago has proved alarmingly accurate, the short barrel of a man has excelled himself. He leaves Cortez nodding quietly and softly fingering the right side of his thin moustache. Cortez is a pragmatic man. Even in the face of terminal disaster.

*

'What did you make of *Spondulix*, sir?
It's Stacey. The rest of the class are filing out but she stops to chat. He thinks.
'I enjoyed it. Made me forget my troubles for a while.'
She adopts her concerned face.
'You have troubles sir?'
'We all have troubles, Stacey.'
'D'you think it made a serious comment about money?'
'It was clever. Full of parables.'
'Really?'
'Yes. You didn't spot them? Think about it. Felix found treasure hidden in the field. That old lady Millie, the one who blew the bank manager's head off, she was pretty much a persistent widow. Fenella Fury had to raise cash quickly so she slashed everyone's debts in half. Mugs Medina was a rich fool. All Biblical.'
She narrows those earnest eyes. Nods slowly, but doesn't really appear to agree.
'But... they weren't exactly the parables.'
Max sits back in his chair, throws his hands behind his head.

'Stacey, parables work on lots of levels. Take the lost sheep for example. Fundamentally it's about lost things. It comes out of the Old Testament stories but it also has resonance with everyday life. People lost sheep back then. They knew that story. Nowadays the lost TV remote, or the lost reading glasses, would be more appropriate for us. *Spondulix* seemed to me be doing that. Updating the stories.'
'So you think it was a Christian film?'
'I doubt it. I don't know. What's a *Christian* film anyway? Did it have truth in it?'
'I guess so.'
'Was it entertaining?'
'Well, I found Ellen Page annoying, but… yes, okay.'
'So it was in keeping with a lot of Jesus's parables. Entertaining and truthful. My guess is the writer may have grown up with those Bible stories. But I'm not bothered one way or another really. It made me think about money and how it controls me. Plus – it was action-packed with a clever story. Can't ask for much more in two hours.'
She thinks. 'Have you ever read *Millions*, sir?'
He shakes his head.
'That's a sort of parable I suppose. Makes you think about money. It's really good. I could lend you my copy.'
'Great.'
She smiles. It changes her face. Lifts the intensity. He smiles back. She goes.

*

10.30pm. He's in no rush to go home. Too many dreams these days. He leaves the college and strolls for a while, out of town towards the river. There's a good moon tonight. And the sky is clear. He recalls the sun going down over Angkor Wat. That was a sight. Late night Guildford can't match it, can't come anywhere near it, but it's enough to bring the memory back. The night he first met Suzie Kruger. He thinks on that for a while. Finds himself climbing the incline of St Catherine's hill. Wanders up the sandstone paths to the chapel at the top. Legend has it that St Cath was a giant who wielded a colossal hammer to build the chapel up there. She and her sister Martha shared the massive work tool, tossing it between them as they built their chapels on their respective hills. St Martha's place has fared

better, looking nothing like its 800 years of age. Cath's is every bit the ancient ruin. Roofless and craggy. And as Max drops to the ground and leans against its scarred walls, head back and looking up at the night sky, he thinks again of those Khmer temples. The spung trees, the cobalt roofs and honeycomb towers, the endless, carelessly piled steps, and the burning sky behind it all. History and faith collide in his mind and he mutters silent pleas, longings and complaints to the night sky. Some words of thanks too. And some apologies. His mind drifts away and his eyelids feel suddenly heavy. He lets them drop for a while.
'You never saw her did you?'
Max is dreaming again. The damn dreams just won't give up. Whose voice is that? He knows it. He's heard it recently, it's not a distant memory.
'Max.'
There it is again. He looks around. It's dark. Where is he? There's a cold breeze. And an elbow jabbing his ribs. He straightens up. Eyes wide. He's awake. He's not asleep.
'Max.'
There's the voice again.
'You never saw her did you?'
He turns and looks up, his heart sinks. He's awake all right.
'You're kidding me,' he says, 'you followed me up here?'
Ben Brookes looks embarrassed.
'I spotted you by the river, but you started up here before I could catch you. You're way fitter than me. I couldn't keep up.'
Max notices the other man is panting a little.
'You never saw her did you?' Ben says.
'Never saw who?'
'I realised. I thought it might make a difference. I have her picture.'
'No news then?' Max always asks this in the vain hope that one day this haunting by Ben Brookes will end.
Ben shakes his head. 'Nothing. Look.'
He pulls out his wallet, reaches in for the picture. Max pushes the wallet away.
'Please don't. I told you, I can't.'
He scrambles to his feet. His clothes feel wet from the ground. Ben is still searching for the picture. Max dusts himself down, walks past him and out through the grizzled doorway. He stands and stares at the moon, his face lit

up by the silver light. He looks older like that, his face full of clefts and shadows.
'What can I do to stop this?' Max pleads. 'You don't know what this is doing to me.'
Ben comes towards him, a photo in his fist.
 'Say yes, help me.'
'Listen, you don't know me. Nobody knows another person, nobody sees what's behind the plastic front do they? The woman on the tube who looks as miserable as sin. The homeless guy with his dog and his sleeping bag. We've all got our stories. I may seem like a selfish person to you. Just another coward. But I have my reasons. I don't talk about this to people but I've been to places where the police torture homeless children for sport. I've sat in streets where teenagers are mutilated for money. Met kids who were forced to kill their own parents. These things build up in you, you know? Ah… of course you don't know, 'cause you're not me. And I'm not you.' Max sighs. 'You can take these things for a time, but then they start to accrue in your soul like a bad bank account, a toxic asset. I've seen enough barbarity. I've had it. I've OD'd on it, I have to give it up. You do your best to change the world but along the way you can't help absorbing the darkness.'
Ben nods. He's finally starting to get the picture.
'I'm sorry,' he says, 'I didn't realise.' He starts to go. 'I won't bother you again.'
He shoves his wallet in his back pocket and a photo falls from it as he does so. Max doesn't want to pick it up, but Ben's walking away. Hasn't noticed. He moves forward and reaches down. Can't help but stare at it as he lifts it. The girl is beautiful. Short brown hair, hazel eyes. She is crinkling her nose in the shot, laughing and saying something. Max looks at her for a long time. This is too much. The clincher. He knows now he can't pull out. When he glances up Ben is standing looking back at him. Max steps up and hands it back to him.
'This is your girlfriend?' he asks.
Ben nods. 'Yep. That's her. Her name's Aretha. Aretha Kiss.'
Max stares at the picture for a while.
'I'll do it,' he says eventually.
Ben bows his head, sniffs and brushes something from his eye.

*

At 3.27am Max wakes up and realises. He said *yes*. He said *yes*. He can't believe it. What was he thinking? He broke his own promise. He swore to himself that he wouldn't put himself in the firing line again. Will he never learn?

Thirteen

'I don't think Casper's coming.'
The three men have been waiting almost an hour. Casper is a man of detail. He is never late, and if he were going to be he would call ahead. They would know about it. As it is, they know nothing. Just that Casper Mack is not there with them at the planned meeting.
Stan Deal drums his fingers. He has things to do, people to see, he doesn't need to waste time waiting around for something that will never happen.
'We shouldn't have brought them with us,' Marty Zeus jabs a fat finger at the black attaché case on the table. 'That was stoopid.'
'What else are we gonna do?' asks Dean Amble. 'Seems like wherever we keep them they ain't safe. Sanchez was half way up a mountain. Carlos was hanging out in some two bit town in Greece. They're both history and their pieces are gone. They might as well be here with us than in Fort Knox. These guys are smart. Whoever they are.'
Stan walks to the window, looks out over the city.
'Who are they?' he asks, mostly to himself.
Marty snorts. 'Does it matter? It's what we always feared. It's what our forefathers feared.'
'Forefathers? You make it sound like the Magna Carta,' Stan mutters.
'Look, whatever. The point is obvious here. These guys want the power of the snake, or the power they believe it has, and they'll stop at nothing to get it.'
'Why murder Sanchez? He was practically on death's doorstep anyway.'
'To cover their tracks?'
'Hardly,' says Dean, 'more likely they were trying to disguise their intentions. Make it look like a series of unconnected killings. Just a few guys getting mugged around the globe. Welcome to planet crime.'
He grabs a handful of pistachios and hurls them at his mouth. His face glistens with sweat as if he's been working out. But he hasn't. Not Dean.

The only working out he does these days is the size of his clients fees. Even the time spent here, hiding in this hotel room, is being billed to someone or other. He has a case full of briefs on the sofa there. He's still working even if this meeting seems about something else entirely. Stan isn't working though. He hasn't worked in years. Peacefully retired and happily married. He got the golden handshake seven years ago and fell in love with his wife in the years that followed. They've been together for 35 years, but only recently fallen for each other. He looks thinner than ever as he stands by the window in the glow from the city there. His shoulders are sagging and his head seems too heavy for his neck. He's a man undone. Afraid and alone in a big city.
'Why do people do this?' he asks. 'Take what is sacred and make it profane?'
'Greed,' says Marty. 'Money makes the world go around and money makes the wheels fall off.'
Dean snorts and a few shavings of pistachio fly from his mouth.
'What the hell's that mean?'
'You know the old saying,' says Marty. "Money's the root of all evil."'
'Wow, back up a minute,' Stan holds up a silhouetted hand. 'It's "The love of money is the root of all evil." There's a difference. Believe me there's a difference.'
Dean snorts again. 'Sure is, tell that to some of my clients. They might pay their bills on time.'
'That's rich coming from a big shot lawyer,' says Marty. 'What's that other old saying? Oh yea, "99 per cent of lawyers give the rest a bad name."'
Dean drops onto the sofa, the cushions reverberate around him.
'That ain't in the Good ol' Book, is it?' he says.
'No but it should be. You bill people for just breathing.'
'Well, some of them use up a lot of air.'
Marty walks to a crowd of bottles, pours himself a Jack Daniels.
'They won't find us here will they?' asks Stan.
'I wish I could say yes,' says Marty. 'But these people seem clever.'
'Do we know anything about these losers? How many? Where they come from? If we can haggle with them?'
'The only thing we know is they are not losers. They are clearly organised, knowledgeable and dangerous.'

'Is it something we said? Did one of us upset them one time?'
'It's nothing like that,' says Stan, still at the window, his back to them, 'it has to be the snake.' He shivers. 'Sometimes I wish I'd never heard of Nehushtan.'
Dean throws his hands in the air. 'But you're not telling me they're going to work their way through the whole bunch of us, picking us off one by one. We'll get back up. We'll get protection.'
'That's not a bad idea,' says Marty, peering at Dean over the top of his glasses. 'You must know people.'
'Oh I know people. And I know people who know people. And Casper does too. He moves in all the right circles. I say the moment he gets here we get a strategy. We get protection and we get a plan. With Casper and my contacts we got nothing to worry about. They got to Carlos cause he was unprepared, they got to Sanchez cause he was, let's face it, old. He probably handed it to them on a plate. Sanchez was a great man, but always way too naïve. We are none of those things. We will be more prepared than Noah and that ark of his.'
'Wish I had an ark I could hide in right now.'
'You will have. I'm telling you. These babies won't know what's hit them when they come looking for us.'

*

A knock at the door. An efficient rap, the sound of someone who does this all day. Someone who does it for a living. Dean makes for the door but Marty raises a hand. Stan turns from the window, gives a nervous lick of the lips as he glances from one man to the other. He looks like a scared rabbit. Frozen to the spot, eyes wide, body stiff. Marty indicates to Dean to stand behind the door. Dean shrugs but does so. Marty steps to the eyehole.
'Room service,' he mouths at the others.
Another knock. He reaches for the handle. Stan starts to gesticulate. Dean rolls his eyes.
'One second,' Marty calls, and he waves to the others. They make a conference in the middle of the room. Whisper urgently.
'Look,' says Dean, 'we ordered food, I'm starving. Food is here. What are they gonna do, poison the salmon?'
'Probably,' says Stan. 'That's exactly what they'll do.'
'Well I'll risk it, I'd eat a toxic horse right now.'

Another knock. Louder now. Three heads turn, their breathing on hold, as if they expect the lock to burst and the door to swing wide. Nothing happens.
Dean makes for the door again. But Marty places a hand on his shoulder. He's taller than the others, has a natural command about him.
'Wait,' he mouths, a faint whisper to it. 'Let's not be stupid. It's probably fine. But you two go in the bathroom, I'll open the door on the chain.'
Dean rolls his eyes again. 'Let's get the cavalry here, soon as possible,' he mutters. 'before I die of hunger.'
Marty goes to a drawer. He takes something out, walks to Stan.
'And take this,' he whispers.
Stan's eyes bulge wider.
'It's a gun!' he gasps.
Marty nods. 'Well done. Got it in one. Ten points to Gryffindor. Now take it and hide it in there with you. Anything goes wrong, you've gotta use it. And I mean got to.'
Stan holds the pistol as if it's about to explode.
Dean looks impressed and pulls it easily from his grasp. He feels its weight, passes it from hand to hand, holds it up and swings it about. Marty pushes the weapon down and points to the bathroom. There is another knock at the door. Sharper, more insistent than ever.
'Room service!'
There is a gentle click as the other two disappear into a room not made for two grown men to hide in.
Marty fixes the chain, cracks the door a little, a young woman in a uniform, all neat and blue, stands there with a trolley loaded with food. There are numerous dishes cornered with white cloths, could be a whole armoury under there. Hand grenades, explosives, assault rifles…
Marty smiles and opens the door.
'I'm sorry about the hold up,' he says, as if he hasn't a care in the world. The girl wheels the trolley in and Marty checks the corridor behind her. Empty. No gang of professional killers waiting to do their work. The food smells great. And it isn't accompanied by the aroma of gun oil.
'Where shall I leave it, sir?'
Marty points towards the table near the window. She wheels it over. Marty watches her intently. The girl glances back and Marty forces a grin. He remembers himself and reaches in his pocket for a tip.

'That'll be great,' he says and he proffers his hand.
The girl nods gratefully and takes the money.
'You alone tonight, sir?' she asks.
Marty nods. Resists the temptation to make any apology for the absence of the others. He does ask 'Why?' though.
The woman doesn't bat an eyelid.
'We do offer an escort service, sir, if you wished to take that up. If you had plans to go out or...'
She doesn't finish what the 'or' might be but Marty shakes his head with a benign smile.
'No thanks,' he says.
The young woman nods and leaves. It's all over. The moment she is gone Dean bursts from the bathroom.
'Man that smells great,' he says, undressing the dishes with a certain panache.
Stan emerges more cautiously. 'Escort service?' he asks.
Marty laughs. 'Oh yea – sorry I didn't check with you guys before turning it down.'
Dean rips meat from a spare rib with his teeth.
'You're kidding me,' he says. 'I'm eating and sleeping and then I'm done. Now, where's that toxic horse?'

Fourteen

Dean is dead. The bullet just ripped through the window, took out one side of his head, and left a collage of his brain across the meal trolley. One minute he was sitting on the sofa eating a cold turkey leg in the dark, watching a movie with the sound down, the next he was nowhere. History just made. His body is still upright, the kill was clean and quick and efficient. It barely disturbed his sitting position. But he is gone. All over. And all over the leftover food. Marty hurls himself from his bedroom, stops dead when he sees what has happened, then turns and throws up into his hands. He staggers to the bathroom and runs the taps. Washes, spits, throws up again, then repeats the process and eventually re appears, his hand held up to block out the sight of Dean. Stan is still in the shared bedroom, crouching against the wall, his hands pressed to his eyes.

'Are we… are we all dead men?' he mumbles through the open door as he hears Marty approach.
'Depends,' says Marty, 'depends when Dean's cavalry gets here. One thing's sure though. They'll be too late for Dean.'

*

They sit hunched against the bedroom wall for an hour. Waiting, listening. Not daring to move or speak. The darkness and the stillness are their best friends right now.
'I've been thinking,' Marty says, pushing his mouth close to Stan's ear, 'they won't kill us all. It's illogical.'
Stan can still barely speak. He looks at Marty with his frozen stare. Just turns his head, that's all. No real reaction, no emotion.
'Think about it, if this is about the snake…'
'Damn snake!' Stan bursts out, and Marty pulls back. 'damn, damn, damn snake!'
If Stan had not been the restrained, religious guy he was, the air would have been blue now. Marty is sure of that. He lets a smile slip across his lips. Pats his old friend on the arm.
'I wish I'd never heard of it,' Stan continues to fume, 'shouldn't mess with what you don't understand. Shouldn't! Shouldn't play at being God. Damn damn damn! DAMN!'
Marty relaxes a little, lets his hunched knees drop straight, and his shoulders sag. He even laughs gently.
'If Moses could see us now, eh?' he says. 'D'you think he'd believe it? Two grown men cowering in the dark because of something he made in a desert thousands of years back.'
Stan frowns. 'Moses did plenty of cowering,' he says.
'Really?'
'Of course. He was like all of the great Biblical heroes. Courageous one moment, irresponsible the next. He made his gaffs, plenty of them. But he was humble too. Humble. Something men with a gun will never understand.'
More silence. After a while Marty returns to his plan.
'They won't kill us,' he says, 'not if they want the snake. We are their means of getting it.'
Stan grips his arm. 'Where is the case? Is it still here?'

'Of course. It's where we left it. On the table in there.'
'Then we have to get it.' Stan grips Marty's arm again. 'That's our ticket out of here,' he says, the penny dropping, 'if we give them the pieces they'll leave us alone. It's true isn't it?'
Marty wants to say so, he desperately wants it to be true. But he can't be sure.
'Let's just go,' says Stan, 'let's leave the case and get out. Now. Go anywhere, get the first plane. Take a vacation. Our families could join us. We could just disappear.'
Marty considers this. Stan can't stand the silence while he does so.
'Well? Well?' he says.
'It's possible,' Marty says. 'It's certainly possible for you and Jean to disappear. It's more complicated for me. Work commitments. The kids, you know. Schools.'
He chews on his thumb nail.
'Plus what about the cavalry? Dean called his friends hours ago. They'll be on their way. We can trust them. They're professionals.'
'Yes, but they won't be much good if they get shot through the window with a high velocity rifle.'
'Maybe we should call room service.'
'What?' Stan's turn to finally crack a smile. 'You want caviar and champagne now?'
'No. But it will make everything public. If the hotel staff see what's happened the police will be called in. We'll be surrounded by other people. Safety in numbers.'
Stan nods. 'Like Jesus,' he says quietly.
'What?'
'It's why they needed a Judas,' he says, 'Jesus was safe as long as he was with the crowds. Let's get the crowds.'
Stan begins to stand.
'Wait.' Marty's turn to grab his friend's arm. What happens if we call the police and Dean's cavalry turn up? I'm not sure that his friends are all above the law.'
'Surely they can handle that themselves. They must be well used to keeping a low profile if the situation requires.'
Marty isn't convinced. 'Could be... incriminating,' he says.

'What? What do you mean? We've done nothing wrong! We're just guarding pieces of a powerful Biblical artefact. We're trying to keep it out of the wrong hands.'
'Yea, but it should have been declared years ago. Technically it belongs to the Israeli government surely. I mean, you didn't buy your piece did you?'
'It came to me. Like an heirloom. My grandfather was a Nehushtan Seer.'
'Exactly. But I bet there's no paperwork or proof of ownership. We could end up losing our pieces to a museum.'
'Better than losing our heads to a marksman.'
Marty shakes his head. 'I don't know. This feels suddenly complicated. I swore to guard this. I promised I'd respect what it stood for, be upright about it.'
'Even to death?'
Stan glances at Marty, he can't be sure in the dark but he looks as if he nodded just then.

Fifteen

Time passes.
'One of us has to go and get it.'
'The case?'
'The case.'
'We need to conceal it somewhere,' Marty says checking his watch.
'Dean's friends are late and it's time we called in the authorities. We get the case, we call the cops, and we play dumb.'
'Go on then.'
Marty looks at Stan. They are both still on the carpet, backs against the wall. Marty can still taste the bile in his mouth from earlier.
'I'm not sure I can face Dean again,' he says.
'Well you know I can't.'
Marty pulls a coin from his pocket.
'We're flipping for it?' asks Stan. 'You're kidding me?'
Presumably Marty is not because there's the sound of thumbnail on metal and silver flashes in the darkness. That's when the second shot rings out. Marty flips the coin too high. The bullet rips through it and they are showered in metal slivers and wall plaster. They both drop sideways,

falling in opposite directions away from each other. Faces pressing into the carpet. Pushing down hard, trying to disappear, trying to find a way out through the floor. It doesn't smell great down there. Marty can hear whimpering. It's Stan.
'You okay?' he calls out, his voice muffled by the floor.
No reply, just more whimpering.
'I said are you okay?'
Nothing. So they lie still. And Marty tries to think straight. That shot came from a completely different place, through a completely different window. Either the marksman is agile, or they are surrounded. They need to get hold of the case. They need to do that now. And quickly so they can get out. Stan is still whimpering, so it's down to Marty. It will have to be him then.

*

He opens the door a crack, sees and hears nothing. He drops flat in the doorway, crawls through inch by inch, his body never losing contact with the floor. He can smell Dean. It's not good. He gags, pauses, swallows it down and focusses his mind on the case. He crawls on. He does not need to stand. To stand would be death. He can just reach up from the floor and pull the case down. Another inch, then another. He keeps pausing, expecting another shot, imagining what it will feel like to have one of those bullets tear through him. He crawls again. Inch by inch by inch. The table is not far now. A few more seconds and he'll be there. Just a little more effort. Inch by inch. He's there, his head nudges the table leg. Now for the moment. He has to reach up, that'll mean lifting his chest from the floor. How visible will he be? How vulnerable? He pushes his head down to keep it as low as possible and starts to turn his shoulder upwards. His hand is rising. His brain is telling him not to do it, but his hand has a life of its own. It's going to make it. Must be visible by now and there's been no gunshot. He reaches higher again, his fingers touch the edge of the table. He throws his hand up over the table top and reaches for the case. It's not there. It's not there! What the... He feels around, slaps his hand against the surface. Nothing. Who took it? When did that happen? Then he hears it. A loud bang. He freezes, hand pressed on the table top. Another gunshot. Or was it? No. Not this time. Something else. A knock at the door. His heart thumps against his chest, his hand retracts, he rolls onto his back and lies still. Two more sharp raps. Then a voice.

'Is everything all right, sir? We've had reports of noises up here. Is there a problem?'

It sounds like the young woman again. The trolley girl. This may be their salvation. Just one problem. To open the door he will have to stand up. If he crawls it will take forever. But if he stands…

A cardkey scrapes in the lock. The handle on the door drops down. The door swings. Marty gets ready to leap up. It is the young room attendant. She looks in, can't see Marty from where she is standing. So she knocks on the outside of the door again and calls out.

'Hello, is anyone awake?'

That's when Stan opens the bedroom door. And that's when the third shot sounds. For a brief moment Marty can't work it out. He looks from the hotel girl to his best friend. Neither has moved. Then it happens. Stan crumbles to his knees and as he drops Marty sees the seeping mess that is now his chest. Stan falls forward, face down on the carpet. The hotel girl puts her hand to her face. Marty leaps up and throws himself at the young woman, forcing them both out into the corridor. Thank God is all he can think. There are no windows there. No more gunfire. Thank God. The girl pulls herself out from under Marty. Marty rolls to let her free and lies on his back mumbling.

'Stan's dead. Stan's dead. Stan's dead…'

The young woman clambers up. Marty can't move. He feels a hand on his arm, tugging at him.

'Come on, you can't stay here.'

The young woman seems calm beyond her years. She's taking hold of Marty, making him stand, urging him to move. Marty has no strength but somehow he gets up, the girl leans him against the wall.

'Thank you,' Marty says, 'you saved my life.'

Then he notices the case in the hotel girl's hand and he feels something jam into his ribs. He looks down. He can't speak. This is surely not happening.

Sixteen

Cortez eyes the man with the rifle. He dismisses him then reaches inside the top left hand drawer of his massive oak desk. He removes a bottle of

Jack Daniels, a small crystal tumbler, and a snub nosed Smith and Wesson revolver. He sits and stares at all three for a long time. He wonders about ending it all. His plan seems suddenly reckless, desperate black magic to ward off the inevitable. Enough. It's over now.

He glances back at the drawer. There is a fourth item in there. A gold leaf leather Bible.

Decades ago, when Sundays still had schools, a kindly, wiry-haired Catholic priest had loved to regale him and the rest of the class with a story about money and death. The rich fool he called it, and he flapped the weathered pages of his Good Book at the boys as he told it again and again. Cortez flips to it now. Ironically, the tale intended to chill the bones had become his favourite, he loved the story of the filthy-rich, self-made man. Okay so death got the old scheme-ster in the end, but not before he'd made his fortune, built his barns and stored his riches in them. Death was gonna drop by on all of us, the young Cortez had reasoned, may as well shake hands with the reaper a rich man. Back then he had felt indestructible, and death had been a long way off. A mere speck on the clear blue horizon. Now there is a storm in the sky and the cloaked, hooded one is on his doorstep and ringing the bell.

He had considered becoming a priest for a while, applied to seminary and had a few of the right interviews. But two things got in the way. Firstly his gangster father would never have consented. Tony Cortez was as hard as the concrete he used to encase his enemies No son of his would take vows anywhere in the neighbourhood of poverty, chastity and obedience. Then there were the gambling debts he had acquired in a string of enthusiastic nights over a dimly lit card table.

Which led eventually to the small matter of the killing of Toby Jones. Don and Toby grew up together. Played happily as boys and schemed enthusiastically as teenagers. They were going to be rich and powerful, take the world and lay it at their feet. The problem was Toby was a dreamer, Don was not. Don was serious, Toby was just a waster. A waster with too much luck at cards. Way too much luck. So much luck he had to be making it himself.

Don took Toby outside to a back alley behind the small gambling den where they had been meeting to play poker. There he shoved him against a wall and told him their friendship was over. Too many unlikely wins. Too much money stolen from Don. That was the night Don discovered he had a punch like a jackhammer. One sudden, ferocious strike and Toby was writhing in the dirt. Then, while his old mate was pleading in the dust and the darkness, spinning yet more imaginative lies, Don Cortez beat him to death. It didn't take long. Afterwards he took the body to a nearby building site and buried him in a place that would soon be covered in concrete. The body was never found and Don's father put out the story that Toby Jones had quit town.

'Store up your treasure in heaven', Father Tom had said, 'where rust can't get at it and no one else can steal it from you.' The young Don had placed a hand in the air and asked how you could possibly do your banking like that. 'Heaven deals in compassion and justice,' Father Tom said, 'humility and truth. Invest in those and you'll be doing business with God's bankers.' Cortez discovered his own kind of truth and humility, the kind you could buy with gold and a gun; and he'd taken it on himself to dish out the justice. Toby Jones had been mouthing off to too many people about the debt Cortez owed him. He might have paid Toby Jones properly if the man had just kept his mouth shut a little more. And stopped cheating at cards.

A lifetime of savagery and moneymaking followed in the wake of Toby Jones. Now it's pretty much done. The barns are all built and there is little else to do. Cortez shuts the gold leaf Bible, raises the revolver and presses the barrel to his temple. He feels the two twinges of arthritis, firstly in his thumb as he cocks the hammer, then in his finger as he curls it around the trigger and starts to squeeze.

*

The class finishes at 3.30pm The last class of term. And you can tell. Today they all seem lethargic, no one wants to debate or argue that much. Max sits on the edge of his desk and talks to them about the coming break. 'I'm away next week,' he says, 'and maybe for the week after too. So you get a reprieve on your assignments. However Larry, in the words of Mr

Schwarzenegger, 'I'll be back'. And when I am, I expect all outstanding essays to be complete and ready for handing in.'
There isn't much dissent. With Easter looming the next term seems a lifetime away. They wish him a good holiday as they file out. He reciprocates, hoping like hell he'll make it back alive. Al gives him five as he slopes past.
'I'll stockpile you some tough questions,' he mutters as he goes.
Only Stacey hangs around.
'Here's the book, sir,' she says, slipping it onto his desk.
'The book? Oh. *Millions*. Yes. Thanks Stacey.'
'Would you like to come for a drink?' she asks. 'A few of us are going down the road.'
He looks at her, doesn't mean to seem like he is sizing her up, but it has been a hard week. He is tired and his resistance is low. She has long hair, very long, beautiful hair. Must've ended up sitting on it sometimes. He takes a protracted look at those eyes and the startling eye-liner.
'I'd better get home,' he says.
She shrugs. No smile now.
'Maybe when you get back,' she says and he nods.
She's fifteen years younger. Another generation. It could only be complicated.

*

Ben Brookes can't find it. It was here but it's gone. He refuses to believe it. Turns out her cupboards and drawers again. Underwear, socks, t-shirts, jeans, jackets. Plenty of all that. He stands and looks around her bedroom. Retraces his steps in his mind. He saw it the day before she disappeared, and she may have taken it with her, but not if she left in a hurry. If she went because she had to she may not have had time. It was definitely here. A snapshot in his photographic memory places it on the beside cabinet. But it's not there now. He rifles through the piles of stuff on the floor. Magazines, coffee cups, clothes. And notebooks, plenty of them, but not that one. Not the one with the snake etched on the cover. Her room's a mess, but not from him. Not from his searching. It was always thus. He sighs and sweats and leans against her wall. Stares into the mirror opposite. He needs a haircut. His wire hair is starting to look like Dennis the Menace. She'd be on at him to crop it back. There are photos around the mirror. Places she has visited with her work. Writing for top women's magazines gets you places. Aretha in Paris. Aretha in Cologne. Aretha in Dubai. Aretha in Phnom Penh. Aretha. Aretha. Aretha. Where are you? He looks deep into his own eyes, light glinting off his glasses. Then he stops, leans forward, sticks his neck out like a turkey. He swings round. The picture. He's been leaning on that appalling snake picture she keeps up there. The winged serpent from the desert. He steps back, reaches up and feels for the hooks that support it. They're just tacks, tiny nails so loose that one of them comes free as he eases the glass frame off the wall. Aretha was never much good at DIY. She'd have put her mirrors up with blue tack if it held well enough. There it is. Embedded in another appalling display of Aretha's handiwork. A small blue journal jammed into a hastily chiselled square crevice in the wall. Goodness knows what the landlord will make of it. He pushes his fingers around the book, it's not easy, it's jammed in tight and Aretha's fingers are way smaller than his. But he gets hold, pulls hard and prizes the journal free. Amongst a shower of dust and plaster. He runs for the door, thinks again, replaces the snake picture and leaves.

*

Max stares at his coffee. Double espresso. He's in no hurry to sleep. No hurry at all. Since he crossed the line a couple of days ago things have moved swiftly. His job at the college is effectively on hold, at least in his own mind. He told the principal he was off travelling. Tried to give him some guarded hints in case he didn't show up next term. Principal Kirkwood's a wise old bird. He knew something was up. Didn't say much but then that's his way. Gives those quick little nods of his while he strokes his goatee beard. There are times when he's not unlike Abe Lincoln. He shook Max's hand firmly as they parted, wished him 'the best of things', a send-off which seemed somehow loaded with meaning, a multitude of cloaked encouragements. Having pushed him into doing this Larry was all 'Hey! Come back soon!' when he spotted Max clearing his desk at the end of that last day. Stacey wasn't so sure. When he strolled to the station and passed her sitting outside the pub with her mates she could only muster the ghost of an enigmatic smile. The acceptance of her book and the rejection of the pub invite had seriously confused her, disorientated her well-ordered, earnest world.

*

He downs his coffee and goes to get another. The girl behind the bar makes animated small talk. Asks him if he's passing through, heading anywhere nice. She has ginger-red hair and a broad Australian accent. When she talks, and she does that readily, her face is never still, she's as expressive as a mime artist. She hands him his coffee with a wink. And that's when Max notices her name. He frowns, she frowns back then laughs. There can't be that many Beluga Odyssey's in the world surely?
'Ever been to Spain?' he asks.
Her eyes light up. 'Too right! You?'
'Yea. D'you play cards?'
'Too right! You?'
Max shakes his head. 'Not against you,' he says and he walks away, leaving her for once lost for words. Max can barely believe it. The past really won't let him go.
'Got it!' Ben steps out of nowhere and slaps the journal onto the table top. Max's coffee rocks like the titanic. He steadies it.
Max lifts the book and studies the cover. There is a detailed sketch of a winged snake on the cover. Underneath, written with a flourish, is the word Nehushtan.
'If there's anything that can give you clues about Aretha. It's this. I never liked her being so obsessed with it. Her disappearance has to have something to do with it.'
Max flicks through the pages. It's full of newspaper cuttings and scribblings about the bronze snake.
'D'you know all about this?' he asks.
'Kind of. Bits of it. Some sort of a powerful snake that got worshipped and smashed up and the pieces got lost.'
Max nods. 'Nehushtan,' he says quietly. 'The snake with healing powers. According to the book of Exodus when the Israelites were crossing the desert they got attacked by poisonous snakes. They'd set out from a place called Mount Hor when these winged, fiery serpents appeared and ambushed them. Many of them got bitten - the kind of bites that burn flesh and bring on slow death. It was a desperate time. No medicine or health service of course for those guys. So the people go to their leaders, Moses and Aaron, and send up a cry for help. And that's when it gets supernatural. Moses makes an image of the thing that's killing them. A

bronze effigy of the winged serpent. It's up to the people then to exercise some faith. Moses puts the snake on a pole and invites them to look to it as a kind of prayer to God. Those that do get better. Those that don't…' he runs a finger over Aretha's detailed drawing, 'die.'
'So…' Ben shrugs. 'D'you think she's off somewhere looking for it.'
'Who knows, if she is she won't find it. Got destroyed. Two and a half thousand years ago. By a king going by the name of Hezekiah. Usual kind of story really. People forget the purpose behind the snake. They think the snake itself has the power, which was never the intention. Happens a lot. So this king decrees they'll have a little vandalism. Smash up the snake. Get the people back on track.'
'And then?'
'Who knows. Some think the pieces are dispersed around the globe.'
'And what's Nehushtan?'
'That's the name of the snake – means bronze serpent or, as Hezekiah called it, "Unclean thing." Your girlfriend, how serious was she about this stuff?'
'Oh she was serious, I mean look at the journal. That's years of research. Every time she went somewhere with a magazine she'd be checking out the snake, seeing if there was any chance she might come across it where she was going.'
Max had stopped listening. He had come to a page with a name and address on it.
'Who's this?' He held up the book.
'Blyton Gann? Never heard of him. Probably some old university professor with some weird conspiracy theory about snakes taking over the world.'
'And the Nehushtan Seers?'
Max pointed at the page opposite, Ben shrugged.
'Maybe a group of university professors with a weird conspiracy theory about snakes taking over the world.'
'Well, we'll find out. I think we got our first lead. Our only lead. Can I keep this?'
'I can carry it for you.'
'No you can't.'
'I can.'
'No.'

Max and Ben eyed each other. Max's face was like granite. Ben was the first to blink.
'Oh come on...'
'Ben, I do this alone or I don't do it at all. I don't carry passengers.'
'Why not? I could be useful.'
'I have my reasons. Good reasons.'
'But she's my girlfriend.'
'I know and I'll do everything I can to get her back for you. But I have to do it alone.'

Seventeen

There is something odd here. Max turns the journal in his hand and thinks about it as he sits on the train and waits for it to pull out. Doors slam in the background and last minute passengers hustle their way down between the seats.
'This free, mate?'
He nods. Takes his leather rucksack off the seat and shoves it between his feet. He turns the journal again.
'Hey! We just met. Remember?'
Max turns to look. Oh great. It's the animated red head.
'Beluga,' she holds out a hand.
Max doesn't take it so she just pats him on the shoulder. He forces a smile.
'The card player,' he says.
'Sure but how the dickens d'you know?'
Max considers for a while. How incriminating is it to tell her about Ismail and the Cordoban Cross? How much conversation will he have to pursue if he mentions it? She grins at him and chews gum, waves her hand to encourage his reply. He figures whatever he tells her he's gonna get questions. He can see that his quiet night-train ride to Devon just got shot to pieces.
'Ever met a guy called Ismail Cruz?'
She stares ahead, thinks and chews. Then she stops and turns her head slowly, eyes like beacons.
'You bet I have! Man, I took that guy to the cleaners. He thought he could play poker. He was wrong. I didn't even have to cheat or anything.'

This'll be interesting, thinks Max.
'So what did you win?' he asks.
'A whole load of stuff. All his money for one thing. A watch. And a ring. Oh yea and this weird bracelet thing. Gold. Yea.'
'D'you still have it?'
'Sheez, I wish. I lost it again. In another game. Not to Loser Cruz I hasten to add. To this weird girl with tattoos on her teeth. Suzie something or other. Man she was a bitter opponent. It hurt to lose to her. She scared me too.'
'I know what you mean,' says Max quietly.
She slaps the back of her hand against his shoulder. 'You lose to her too, eh. What game? Poker?'
'No. Not poker. The game of life.'
'Deep' says Beluga and she chews on her gum for a while, twists her index finger round it and stretches it out between her teeth. Then she hooks it back in and says, 'Wonder what happened to that old bracelet?'
'It's in Cornwall,' says Max. 'I gave it back to the woman who owns it.'
'Sheez! No! Really? Man that's crazy. Where d'you find it?'
'In the Mezquita.'
'The Mez... What? You mean that old Mosque? Where? In the collection plate?'
'No, under the floor. Along with another bit of treasure. The Cordoban Cross.'
'Wow, you been busy mate. How d'you find the time? What do you do for living?'
'Well I used to do that, track stuff down. Now I'm a teacher.'
She laughs, a real gut-wrenching belly laugh. People turn and look, including some who have earphones in. She slaps his shoulder again.
'You're great you know. You're funny. But I gotta get some kip. Been up for two days solid. Mind if I borrow your shoulder?'
Seeing as she's been handling it so much in the last few minutes Max figures it isn't worth the arguing. She presses her face against his jacket, turns herself sideways in her seat and pulls her feet up.
'Nice jacket,' she says, 'military?'
'US Army. Got it from a friend who claimed Stallone wore it in *First Blood*. But I've seen that movie, I'm not convinced.'
'Cool. I like it.'

'Works for me,' he says, 'plenty of nooks and crannies.'
'For what?'
'Stuff. Just stuff.'
She grins at him one last time, closes her eyes and drifts off. Max checks the lining in his jacket, pats a couple of hidden pockets. Leon had stitched them in there. Custom designed the thing for action. Shame about Leon. The end came just when he was on the up. Max hasn't worn the jacket for a good while. Hung it up when he started to fall apart and gave up the wild life. The thing is pock-marked from too many adventures. Carries too many stains and scars. He never thought he'd need it again, jammed it into a tea chest with his boots and his belt. Leon's face flashes before his eyes. He shakes the memory off and drags himself back to the present. Turns the Nehushtan journal in his hands again. He traces her name with his finger. She has inked it so many times it is embossed into the first page. Graffitied again and again. Like a schoolgirl bored in her history lesson.
What is odd, he thinks, as his finger travels, what is very strange, is that if this has something to do with the Nehushtan, if this is all about the bronze snake, what is he doing with Aretha Kiss's journal in his hands? If she went on a quest to get the serpent, why did she leave the diary behind? And if it isn't about the Nehushtan, what's he doing sitting on a train heading for deepest Devon? What good will that do?

*

'You took it, didn't you? When you bought the food. There I was creeping across to get it, when all the time… Talk about sleight of hand.'
Marty and the hotel girl are in the lift, travelling down too many floors.
'Shut up,' she says.
His eyes fall on the attaché case in her hand.
'Why d'you bring it back? And what's going on? Who are you?'
'I said shut up.'
Now that Marty had a mission, now that there was some action, it had centred him again. As dangerous as the situation was, at least he wasn't sitting hunched in a dark hotel room waiting to die.
'It's the combination, isn't it? You can't open the case.'
The girl moves in on him and jams her gun hard into Marty's ribs.
'I killed one of you already. I'll do it again.'

He'd suspected as much. Worked it out as she walked him to the lift. Stan's wound had been shocking, but nothing like the damage wreaked on Dean's head. The bullet that killed his best friend had not come through the window from some high velocity rifle. It had been fired in that room, from the woman he thought was their saviour.

'How old are you?' Marty asks.

'Twenty.' It is the first straight answer she's given.

'Twenty? And you're… I can't believe it… I cannot believe it. You're killing people. You're some kind of assassin.'

'Trainee assassin. It's a job, now shut up.'

'It's not a job, it's a crime. Ultimately it'll destroy you. It'll eat you up. Or some bigger assassin will take your life. Those who live by the sword, die by it.'

'What? What are you talking about? Swords, what swords? Who's got swords?'

'It's a quote, from the Bible.'

'I never read the Bible. I never had one.'

'Maybe if you had you wouldn't be in a lift pointing a gun at me now. Having killed one person already.'

'Two,' she says. 'I killed two.' She is matter of fact about it.

'What? When?'

'I killed one in an airport. Anyway shut up. I don't want to talk to you. It's not my job. My job is to get you to Miss Kruger. That's it. And I'll do it. So don't mess with me.'

He opens his mouth.

'Shut up,' she says, and he does.

Two floors to go. Marty suddenly realises time is running out. Something will happen when they reach the basement. There will be others there. This Miss Kruger perhaps. Escape will be so much more difficult. He grabs her arm.

'Please, please, let me go… I'll tell you the combination… I'll tell you now. You can have it.'

He's a trembling wreck, shaking her arm, setting her off balance, so much so that her gun hand smashes against the wall and she momentarily loses her grip. And that is the moment he pulls his own gun from his jacket pocket. Stan may not have known how to use it, but he sure does. He thumps his fist against the lift control panel, smashes it on the stop button.

The lift lurches to a halt. The gun falls from her grasp entirely. She reacts, smacks him across the face with the back of her hand. His head swims, his vision goes for a moment. She disappears from his line of sight then reappears with the point of her pistol indented in his forehead. She is good. Very good. But only up to a point. He too has brought his gun up and jammed it into her chest, just off-centre and towards the left. It's an outright invasion of her physical privacy, she could sue him for it, but that won't be on her mind right now. They stare at each other. She knows she can blow his brains out, the question is, can he put a bullet through her heart?

Eighteen

He is not an assassin. He is a businessman. He is a do-gooder, a churchgoing freak who hides bits of bronze snake in his house. He has a wife and two kids. He is Mr Average. He pays his mortgage on time and goes abroad for his holidays. He's good at his job and drinks Dutch lager and Fairtrade coffee. He's never been in trouble with the police and runs errands for his elderly neighbours. She knows all about him. She's read the file. A guy like this will not pull the trigger in a lift and take the life of a twenty year old woman. On the other hand, he does own a gun, seems confident with the use of it and has it pointing right at the vital organ that keeps her alive. They stare at each other.
'What's your name?'
'Anya. No. Shutup. Stop talking.'
'Well, we have to solve this Anya. Two of my friends are dead and this place is crawling with cops.'
'No it's not. Not yet.'
'How do you know, Anya?'
'Stop using my name. Okay? Stop it. I know what you're trying to do. Just shut up.'
She tightens her grip on the gun. Pushes it hard against his skin. It must hurt him but he doesn't show it. There is no flinching. He just smiles. Smiles? What? Really? He's smiling? How can he be smiling now? She realises she's tensed up, so she forces herself to relax. Stay calm. It's the bottom line. She already fouled up one killing with that Casper guy. What

was his name? Casper Black? Slack? Flack? Who cares? Just don't mess up this one. This one is the opposite problem. She cannot kill this guy. She must not. She has to get him to Kruger so they can find out what they need and then dispose of him. His brains on the back wall of this lift is the last thing anyone needs right now.

'I have a daughter,' he is saying. 'Bit younger than you. She's called Anya.'

'Don't be stupid. You do not have a kid named after someone who is gonna blow your head off.'

'True. We named her that because we loved the name. It's a beautiful name. Do you like it?'

'I'm stuck with it. What do you think?'

He is trying to soften her up. And he's confusing her. Does he really have a daughter called Anya? What kind of coincidence is that? She wants to know how old the girl is, but she daren't ask, that would be totally unprofessional.

'Why aren't you in shock?' she says suddenly.

His eyes widen. He grimaces. 'Should I be?'

'Yes. You just said yourself - two of your best mates are dead. Dead! Horrifically. Professional killings. You should be very worried.'

He should be. But right now there is so much adrenalin in his system he can only think about the gun and this girl and whether he'll squeeze the trigger before she does.

'I've seen action,' he says. 'You may know that if you've been doing your homework. I was an army chaplain for a while. Before I gave up being a priest. Before I changed vocation. Look, how about we both put our guns down?'

'What – and play rock, paper, scissors instead? You know I'll never do that.'

'Come on Anya. This can only end badly unless we think it through. You planned to abduct me and take me down to your Miss Kruger without a struggle. Well, the struggle has arrived. It is not going to be as planned. Either you kill me, or I kill you, or there's the mother of all shootouts in that basement and everyone bleeds to death.'

She laughs. More of a sneer really. 'This isn't the movies,' she says.

'Well, it ain't *The Sound of Music*, that's for sure.'

'It ain't *Die Hard* either. You won't be a hero. You'll be dead. If it's not me doing it, Suzie will get you. She's unkillable.'
'Is that a real word?'
'Shut up. You can't kill her. She's one of the best assassins in the world. She's killed on five continents. Seriously. She has no conscience. And she's totally professional. She does what's needed, then goes home, has a goodnight drink and sleeps like a baby.'
'How many are there?'
'How many what?'
'World class assassins, if she's only one of the best?'
Her eyes burn fire at him. He just won't take this seriously.
'Plenty,' she says. 'There are plenty.'
'You know what world class killers do? Get dropped into war zones, and lie motionless for a week, in their own excrement and urine. Just waiting to do their job. Waiting to take out the bad guy. Suzie ever do that?'
'That's disgusting.'
'It's professional. Apparently there are way more volunteers to fly them out than fly them back home afterwards. It's a true story.'
'She ain't that kind of killer.'
'What? Not up for that then?'
'Shut up. She'll do anything if she needs to. Now push the button and start the lift. I've had enough of this.'
He shakes his head and smiles. He's calmer than he's been all day. He won't move the lift. She glances across at the control panel, her finger twitches a little. She contemplates knocking his hand from her chest with a side swipe, dropping low and kicking the button as she goes. It might work, or she may end up dead.
'I wouldn't if I were you,' he says. 'Got a boyfriend?'
She laughs for a second time. His question is so unexpected.
'Why? You offering? Marriage not going well?'
'Marriage is great. You should try it.'
'Assassins don't settle down with two kids and a mortgage. Get real.'
'Anya, you know if you do this you'll be running all your life. You'll need drugs to sleep and alcohol to kill the nightmares. You'll know the view from your own shoulder better than anything, because you'll always be looking over it. Do you want that?'

She licks her lips. He's right. Of course he's right. He's hit the nail on the head. The only problem is, she thought that through a long time ago. The day she met Suzie Kruger and together they plotted the 'accidental' death of the boys who had assaulted her. The day those punks got theirs for the years of hell at that school for scumbags. She thought it through then and the question was laid to rest a while ago. It's lying in an unmarked grave with no one shedding a tear.
'You make your choices and live with them,' she says, tight-lipped.
'Never too late to make other choices.'
She swallows.
'Anya, I'm serious, it really isn't.'
'Oh yea? You trying to convert me now? Make me into a saint?'
He shakes his head. 'Don't forget. I've seen plenty of people traumatised by what they had to go through. I know that some of them come back from the brink. I know that life can get better.'
Enough of this now. It's getting to her. She wants out.
'Press the button or I blow your head off. I'm serious. Enough of the 'sweet Anya' crap. Push the button or you die.'
'Anya, you know you can't kill me, you know you need me.'
The gunshot storms around the confined space with all the thunder of a wall of sound at a heavy metal gig. She staggers back. Drops to her knees. Looks down at her chest. Expects to feel warm blood there. She does. His blood. It's everywhere. He was a nice guy. A good guy. And in the end that's why she had to kill him. He was waking her up again, softening her conscience. She couldn't have that. If she's gonna be Suzie's sidekick, Kruger's right hand woman, she has to stay strong. She can't become some stupid average citizen with houseplants and a heart. She can't be like Marty Zeus. She can't believe in things like compassion and hope. Those things always lead to despair. She has chosen the better way. She has killed Marty Zeus. She had to do it. She had to.

Nineteen

He continues to visit. Regularly and frequently.
He asks her about the snake. She has been waiting for this. The conversation has turned from enquiries about her life and work, to

questions about her Nehushtan research. How much has she discovered? What does she know? How powerful would the snake be now? She does her best to answer without giving too much away.

*

The train pulls to a halt. Exeter, St David's. Max stretches, flexes his shoulder gently to nudge Beluga awake. The girl next to him yawns. She still has the gum in her mouth. She grimaces and takes it out, looks around for somewhere to stick it. Glances down towards the underside of the seat.
'Don't,' says Max. 'Just don't.'
She raises an eyebrow and shoves it in the instep of her crimson ankle boot.
'You getting off here?' she asks.
He nods, pulls the bag from between his feet.
'Mmm,' she thinks, messes with her hair. 'Maybe I will too.'
Oh he doesn't like the sound of that. Not at all.
'Where are you going?' he asks.
'Somewhere,' she says and she grins. 'Come on.'
She hauls a blue and yellow carpetbag from the overhead rack. It crashes as if it's full of cement. Reluctantly he follows her out. It's dark outside on the station platform. Cold too. She pulls her fleece-lined denim jacket round her.
'What time is it?' she asks.
He squints down the station towards the clock. It's a blur. If he creases up his eyes he can just make it out.
'12.30.'
'Wow! I need to be in bed.'
Max drops his leather rucksack between them and turns to face her.
'Yea. Can I ask you something? What are you doing here?'
'What?' She's still sleepy and her face is pale and less animated now.
'I mean, one minute you're working in a bar serving me drinks. The next you're nuzzling up and getting off at the same station. Seemingly on a whim.'
She sighs. Rolls her eyes a little. Blows in her hands and then hugs her jacket close.
'Okay. Okay. Here's the deal. I got fired. Sort of. Happens all the time. I get bored, they get fed up of me. It's kind of mutual. Can't hold down a

job. Talk too much. Mess about too much. Apparently I'm a "space cadet".' She makes speech marks with her fingers as she says this. 'If I could make a living playing cards I'd do it. But there's no job security in that. So I drift. And I'm drifting tonight. With you.' She gives him her best grin.

'No you ain't.'

'Oh, but…'

'No. No way. Look Beluga…' He stops. 'Is that a made up name?'

'You betcha. Made up by my dear old mum and dad. They always called me Blue though, so feel free. Seems less like a bowl of sturgeon's eggs, don't it?'

'Listen. I have something I have to do and it'll be a lot less complicated without passengers.'

'I won't be a passenger, I can handle myself. Remember I beat Ismail Cruz in a high stakes game of poker. Texas Holdem.'

'I don't care Beluga, Blue, whatever. I want you to be okay, and if you're with me, you may not be.'

She moves a little closer. 'I come with perks,' she says with a wink, and then she pulls two sticks of gum from her pocket and offers them.

He shakes his head.

'You got cash?' she says.

'I am not paying you off.'

'I'm not asking,' she says.

She bends down and pulls a wad of twenties from her ankle boot.

'And there's more in the other one too.'

'You steal that?'

She looks horrified. 'No way. I told you, I'm good at cards. Best thing about working in a bar is it's full of guys who have no idea how good I am. That's where drifting really pays off. Every town has a bar full of ignorant guys. Suckers incorporated. You sure you don't want gum?'

Max considers. 'How much you got?'

'Er… four sticks.'

'Not the gum.'

'Oh! A grand. What about you?'

'Not much. Not that much.'

Tutoring theology pays. But not that well.

'Thing is,' she says, 'making money at cards is like making yoghurt. As long as you got a little left over – you can always make some more.'
He laughs. Not much, just a little. But he's starting to be persuaded too. Easy cash might come in handy. He hasn't needed to grease palms in a while. She might just be an asset.
'We play this my way okay?' he says. 'My way or nothing.'
'Sure, sure. Now can we go somewhere, it's freezing.'
'Well I was gonna see someone but it's late now.'
He points to the station exit.
'Let's get a taxi to take us to a hotel.'
'A luxury one?'
'It's your money.'
'Excellent! By the way, you know the difference between yoghurt and Australia?'
He shakes his head. They walk on, he waves a taxi. The driver needs a shave and his car needs a wash but they take it. She presses up against his jacket again for warmth as they collapse in the back.
'Yoghurt's got a culture,' she says.

Twenty

She stares at the attaché case now lying on the table. Then at Anya Barlowe. Then at the open lift.
'Twice now,' she says, her voice emotionless. She has an eerie way of speaking sometimes. Unnerving. Automated. 'Twice now. I swear you got one more chance then I kill you myself.' She nods towards the open lift doors. 'What are we gonna do about that?'
The steel space is awash with red and grey gore.
'He was trying to turn me against you, Suzie, I swear I had no choice. I had to do it.'
'I'm not interested. All that matters is getting clean away now.'
Anya catches sight of the Vanquish multi-calibre rifle leaning in the corner.
'He said soldiers lie down in their own crap for a week,' she mumbles.
'What?'
'You ever do that?'

The other woman's hand slams the table. The case shudders and bounces an inch.

'I don't give a damn what he said. He's dead along with his snake buddies. Along with you if you look like an amateur one more time. I want you to get in that lift and jam it up so badly it goes nowhere for the next six months. When you've done that, get everything out of the dead guy's pockets and pray that he has information about the rest of the Nehushtan freaks.'

Her voice is cold. Her eyes are cold. Everything about her is cold.

'Got it?'

Anya nods. She has got it. Kruger stands, picks up the M24 and the case and leaves the basement through a narrow slit of a back window. Anya grabs tools from a bag, goes to work on the lift panel and tears out its guts. But it's not the lift she's killing. It's the scumbags from school. It's the boys who did things that made her into this. The screwdriver rips into their bodies and tears out their entrails. The hammer smashes their skulls and renders them useless.

*

Max can't sleep. He's made a grave mistake already. He learnt a long time ago to work alone. Spectators and civilians always get in the way. Always. It was the money. It conned him. He's out of practice and he saw an easy way forward. Free money. And from a bright-eyed, sparky girl with too much wit for her own good. Now he's trapped. Needs her money for a while and the longer she hangs around the more she'll think they're some kind of team. She has too much optimism. She thinks they'll be good together, she doesn't understand. She may have won the gold amulet from Ismail Cruz but she soon lost it again to Suzie Kruger. Suzie Kruger? How did she end up in a game of cards with that predator? He walks from the window to the adjoining door. Cracks it a little. Beluga's asleep on the bed, collapsed in her clothes, her carpetbag lying next to her, the crimson boots strewn skewed at the foot of the bed. Max pushes the door a little more. It creaks. He stops. She stirs, mutters something, then lies still. He waits. He's done a lot of waiting in his life. He can do some more. He stands there for a full ten minutes. Her breathing is steady and regular. He slips into the room. A couple of steps. A couple more. He crouches, takes hold of her boots. Feels inside. He won't take much. Enough for the next day. A couple of hundred. And he'll get it back to her. Somehow. He stands, turns and slips back to his room. He picks up his rucksack as he passes it, pulls on the door and is out in the corridor just as she starts to wake.

*

Leon's jacket has a double lining, which means it's warmer than it looks, and you have a world of space to conceal things. Max shoves the money into one of those nooks and crannies as he slips out the main door of the hotel. A sleepy receptionist doesn't say anything. By rights he should leave his key, but he might need that again. He slings his rucksack over his shoulder and pulls the journal from the left pocket of his jacket.

Blyton Gann
The Old Bookcase
237 Shrimpton Street

He goes back inside. The receptionist rubs his eyes as he talks. Points to a rotating rack. Max finds the pocket map of the city. Still doesn't leave his keys. He goes. Shrimpton Street is not close but he has hours to walk it. The hotel is on the rural edge of civilisation, space for a golf course and acres of woodland. The Old Bookcase is buried in the hub of the city, some side ally in a minor artery deep in Exeter's heart. He makes a start. At six he passes a coffee shop just opening for the breakfast crew. He buys a paper from a vendor across the street, then goes in, orders two double espressos and sits in the window ingesting caffeine. The place is waking up. Traffic moves, kids shout, commuters walk like the living dead homing in on trains and buses. There has been some kind of shoot-out in the capital. At The Republic in South Kensington. It's all over the front page. Night time attack. Rumours of dead civilians. Blurred and pixelated pictures of broken windows and bullet holes in concrete. There's enough rumour and speculation to suggest some kind of cover up. But it doesn't have the stench of terrorist action. Could be drug-related. Though The Republic is a surprise if that's the case. He flicks pages. It takes a while to find any other stories. Then one word in the comment column catches his eye. Nehushtan. He flicks back to the top story. There's no mention of it there. But here, on page seven, the resident celebrity hack has caught a sniff of something. Word on the street. Hearsay and whispers of a secret serpentine society. Something to do with an ancient Biblical artefact. Bronze snake remnants that could be worth millions.

*

Max checks his watch. Closer to seven now. Blyton Gann may be awake. He drains his coffee. Leaves the paper and goes.
The Old Bookcase is snuck down a narrow side street. A winding alley full of trinket shops with apartments overhead. Wooden fronts, faded peeling paint and cobbles underfoot. He finds 237. It's like a grave it's so quiet but he knocks anyway. Two thuds on the old wooden door. The shop sign says *Shut* but Max hasn't come to buy anything. Well not books anyway. A pause, a long pause. People pass by, Max nods at them. He hears shuffling from inside, then a wheezy double cough and a sigh close to the door as someone sizes up Max through the spy hole. The door swings back. An ancient bell rattles. There is an instant smell of dust and burnt toast. A short, whiskery, old man looks at him, rubbing his chin. He's somewhere in his mid-70's. Everything about him appears crumpled and well worn.
'You're a bit early for business,' he says.
'Are you Blyton Gann? My name's Max Maguire. I wondered if we could talk.'
The old man thinks. 'Maybe,' he says. 'Who are you again?'
Max tells him. He fishes in his pocket and produces the journal. 'I got your address from here. Ever seen this book before?'
He narrows his eyes. Doesn't reply.
'How about Aretha Kiss? Know her?'
Two minutes later Max is following the old man into the back room of his second-hand bookshop. They get there just in time as the kettle begins whistling on a tiny range, belching steam into the little bedsit. A small bunk fills one wall and a table and two easy chairs are clustered against the opposite side.
'She in trouble? This girl – she in trouble?'
Without asking the old man fills a teapot and pours them both a thick brown brew in huge tin mugs. He hands one to Max.
'So you are Blyton Gann? It's important I see him.'
'That's me,' he says shuffling towards one of the chairs. He waves Max towards the other one.
'I don't have much to eat. Just made toast if you want.'

Max shakes his head. 'I'm fine. I'm trying to track down Aretha,' he says. 'Her boyfriend asked me.'
'You're a private detective?'
'No. I used to… find things… archaeological stuff. I gave it up, but came out of retirement for this. But I have very little to go on. Frankly just this journal and you. You're in it you see. Along with a world of stuff about the Nehushtan snake.'
The old man laughs and it sets him off coughing. He coughs for a while. Long enough to inject an intermission for sipping his tea before taking up with his hacking again. Eventually his chest settles down.
'Fancy a Weetabix?' he asks.
Blyton's hand shakes as he proffers a packet, little flakes of cereal shower the carpet. Max shakes his head. It doesn't deter Blyton. He pulls a thick biscuit from the white paper tube and sticks it straight in the hot tea. Max has seen some worrying things in his time but this has to be one of the worst. There's a terrible moment of suspense about whether the old man will get it back to his mouth before the Weetabix disintegrates in his drink. This time he proves lucky.
'Ever consider digestives?' Max says.
'Easier on the teeth,' Blyton replies through a soggy wedge of food, 'when you get to my age mush is by far the better option. Can I see that?'
He holds out his hand for the journal, his palm is covered in doodles and scribbling. The fingers too. Several layers thick.
'Forgive me for asking, but don't you ever wash, Blyton?' Max says.
'What d' you mean,' Blyton sniffs at his armpit, 'am I in trouble? Lost me sense of smell a while ago.'
'Your hands, they're covered in ink. The backs, the fingers. It's everywhere.'
Blyton examines his finger-tips as if he's noticed them before. He turns his hands and studies the endless layers of wordplay littered across the saggy skin.
'Newsprint and leaky pens,' he says happily, 'and crossword clues. Keeps the mind active. Clues and puzzles. Always loved 'em. Just never seem to have a pad nearby to doodle on.'
He leans forward and sups his tea noisily. Max does his best to join in but strong tea after strong coffee is never great.
'The journal?' Blyton says and Max hands it to him.

He flicks the pages, stops every now and then to absorb something. He chuckles and coughs from time to time. Five minutes pass. He looks up.
'Well?' asks Max.
'What did you want to know again?'
'The girl, Aretha? Why are you in her journal?'
'Probably cause she kept coming round, bending my ear. Wanted to know all about this lot.' He taps a page. 'The Nehushtan Seers. Right bunch of renegades.'
'You know them?'
'I know *about* them. Guardians of the snake.'
'Does it exist? The snake?'
'Not anymore. Not as a snake anyway. Now it's just a few bits of bronze spread across the globe. Can't see what all the fuss is about.'
'Any idea where Aretha might go if she was looking for it.'
'Yea. To me. Here.'
'Has she been here?'
Blyton shakes his head. 'Not for a while. Wherever she is, she's somewhere else. Are you sure it's about the snake? Maybe she just wanted a holiday. Maybe she argued with this boyfriend of hers.'
'Maybe. Ever come across Suzie Kruger?'
Another shake of the head.
Max leans forward. Puts his fists together and rests his chin on them. 'Suppose someone was after the snake, believing it was still powerful. Who would that be? Could it be one of the seers? Maybe one of them fell on hard times. Needed to get money by selling the pieces perhaps?'
Blyton chuckles and rubs his chin. 'No. Wouldn't happen. You don't understand. These men are dedicated. They're not just names drawn out of a hat. They're sworn to protect the snake from madmen who would want to abuse its power. This isn't just something you might find on the Antiques Roadshow. This was a means of divine power, ordained by God, then destroyed by him. It's a mystical thing. Mind you, as I'm sure you're aware, it wasn't ever really the snake that was powerful. That was only a channel.'
'Sure. Moses made it to generate faith in the people. So they'd look to their God in the desert.'

'Absolutely. The God of cloud and fire. The uncontainable deity. The God that frankly, we find it difficult to cope with nowadays, invisible, silent. Anything earthly can only be a symbol of that kind of God.'
'How many pieces are there?' Max asks.
'Of the snake? Eleven.'
'And where are they all now?'
'With the seers. As far as I can glean. Eleven pieces, eleven seers. But you have to remember this is all rumour and speculation.'
'Do you think it still has power?'
Blyton shrugs. 'Who knows? It did once.'
'But the snake got smashed around 700 BC right? That's a dramatic thing.'
Blyton pours himself more tea, stronger than ever. His hand shakes a little so he steadies it with his other one as he holds the pot.
'Yes. It had become a kind of shrine, an idol. This is a thousand years later remember. Legends expand over time. It had been somehow preserved and all kinds of mythology attached to it presumably. Ever heard of the Stone of Zoheleth?'
Max shakes his head.
'It was a place of sacrifice in Jerusalem, Zoholeth means The Crawler's Stone, or The Serpent Stone. Some scholars think the bronze snake was placed somewhere near it and that people brought offerings and worshipped it. Which was never the intention. So King Hezekiah had it broken up. He may well have given it the name of Nehushtan – it means an unclean thing. The snake was supposed to inspire worship of the God who created snakes and could heal those who got bitten by them. After all, the second commandment of Moses presses home the point – never make idols and worship them. Don't make images of animals, fish or birds and bow down to them. When people bestow authority onto a physical thing it leads to all kinds of problems. That's why Hezekiah broke up the other stuff too.'
'Hezekiah broke up other stuff?'
'Yes. Some pagan shrines and images, and the Asherah poles.'
'The what?'
'The Asherah poles, they were made of wood, and used to worship the goddess Asherah. She was a Canaanite mother-goddess and the wife of the god Baal. She represented fertility and crop-growing. The law forbade all practises associated with her. But the Israelites had let the pagan rituals

creep into their world-view. Previous kings had let it all carry on, and as a result the nation was falling apart. The snake was different. That went back to Israel's own story in the desert. That had once been a good thing. But... good things get misused.'
'And you're saying you don't believe in the power of the snake?'
Blyton shrugs and smiles. He has an impish, whiskery grin. His shoulders hunch up a little when he smiles.
'The power of God is a strange thing you know. Many people have come a cropper trying to control it and channel it and use it for their own ends. Many preachers. Many so-called prophets. The true power of God is very different. It's not spectacular or fame-ridden. You know, there are three stories around the Nehushtan snake in the Bible.'
'Three?'
Blyton nods. He's on a roll now. Slurps his tea, cradles his tin mug and continues.
'The first is about its healing power. Moses creates it in the desert. Fine. The second is about idolatry. Hezekiah smashes it in the book of Kings. Okay. But the third – the third is about sacrifice. When Jesus talks about it years later. It's as if you move from power to problem to solution.'
'Jesus talks about it?'
'Absolutely. It's the one parable he uses about his death on the cross. He predicts that he will die by Roman execution, but he cloaks it in the description of the Nehushtan snake. He says that Moses lifted up the snake in the wilderness, and he will be lifted up in a similar way. The snake was a symbol of the people's pain and problems. That's how Jesus describes his own death. A symbol for people to look to, the way they had looked to the snake in the wilderness. But when you call that the power of God it's an odd thing. A criminal's death. A wasted man. Nothing spectacular at all. Thousands of people were crucified back then. It was an appalling, offensive thing. Yet here we are centuries later with people wearing crosses in their ears and round their necks. Like sticking an electric chair on a chain and calling it jewellery.'
Max thinks for a while, takes the journal back and flicks through it.
'Is this anything to do with Hermes?' he asks. 'You know the medical symbol.'
'You mean the Rod of Asclepius?' Blyton glanced down at his graffitied fingers, as if the answer were scribbled there. 'Asclepius was associated

with healing in Greek mythology all right. And his symbol is a staff with a snake wrapped round it. It's widely used as a medical symbol so some think there may be a link. But it's not the same as Hermes staff, that's different. Has two snakes and wings and is often confused with the Asklepian Rod. Hermes was a god of boundaries and was said to move freely between this world and the next. I doubt either of them has much to do with the Nehushtan though.'
Max nods, continues flicking through the journal.
'Blyton, how do you know about the guardians of the snake?'
'I used to be a monk. I studied all this kind of thing for years. In the friary there was a huge library. Bookcases that went on forever. I prayed, I scrubbed the floors, I read up on things like this. I live in my head, Max, I always have. Look around you, I don't do well ordering the physical world. But up here,' he taps his temple, 'I have filled this world with a lot of things.'
'Why did you stop? Being a monk?'
Blyton rubs the white stubble on his chin. It makes quite a noise.
'I never did. Not really. The friary closed down and the brothers were moved to other places. But I chose to leave completely. I was over sixty by then. My sister had this shop. I love books. I can still pray wherever I am. And now I can fill my head with all this, and hopefully sell a few bits.'
Max stands up and squints into the gloom of the early morning shop. The books are piled at all angles in all places. The lucky ones get shelves. He looks back at Blyton.
'Why don't the seers just get together and reform the snake themselves?'
'Because they've sworn to protect it. They're good upright men, they don't want it used for the wrong purposes. They figure the safest thing to do is keep the pieces apart and in secret.'
'They didn't do such a great job,' Max says, waving the journal. 'This thing is full of stories about it.'
'Ah yes, but it's all conjecture. Myths, legends and theories. Ideas that have grown up overt the years. Anyone reading the Bible might wonder what became of Moses's snake when Hezekiah smashed it up. Not one of those articles will mention the seers or who they are.'
'Do you know? Have you met any of the seers?'

Blyton shakes his head. 'It's a deadly secret,' he says, 'one of those "If they told you they'd have to kill you" things.' Then he grins, 'want some more tea? Or maybe a Weetabix?'

Twenty one

She's waiting. Standing three doors down. He's been a while so she's not happy. Robbed and with sore feet.
'I trusted you, mate,' she yells, and a few passing heads turn.
'No. No one mentioned trust. You begged to get involved.'
'Ha!' she laughs. 'Like yea. Whatever. You seem to forget I paid for your bed last night.'
'If it's any consolation I didn't use it. I was hardly in the room.'
'I know.'
'You know?'
'You are officially trash at breaking and entering.'
He stares at her. Frowns. Max trash at breaking and entering? Not once upon a time. But now? She could be right.
Beluga stomps away from him, over the cobbles to the nearest bench.
'I been here hours waiting for you. Hours. Hours! You should be glad I'm still here.'
'How d'you find me?'
'Like I said, you're rubbish at the covert stuff. You came into my room, you took £200 from my shoe and you made enough noise to make the dead get up and party. I was awake before you'd even left your room. I followed you. How was your double espresso?'
Max drops down on the bench next to her. She looks at him sideways.
'Well?' She says.
'Look Beluga…'
'Blue! Call me Blue! I ain't caviar.'
'Okay, sorry. Blue… look… I can't involve you in this. It may turn out to be dangerous.'
'So?'
'Please, I can't risk that. I'm serious. This isn't a game.'
'I can help you.'
'Yea but I'd have to watch out for you.'

'No way, I can handle myself. You don't have to worry about me.'
'Believe me I would. I have mistakenly let people... die... before. I don't want to do it again.'
'Really? When?'
'I don't wanna talk about it. Let's get somewhere where we can think. I need some breakfast.'
'Well I ain't paying.'
'Of course not. I am, I've got 200 bucks.'

*

She asks for a laptop. Of course one is not forthcoming. So she asks for a pen and notebook. She has decided that if she ever gets out alive she will write about different things. About life and freedom rather than just celebrity recipes and the best soundtrack for driving the kids to school. That's all well and good, we all need some colour and entertainment in our lives, but what kind of lives? These days deprived of friends and freedom have made her wonder about reality. About why people get up in the morning. She was supposed to be interviewing Emily Blunt about her styles tips today. She's already compiled a completely different list of questions in her mind. Doing this is keeping her sane. Compiling lists and plotting that novel she has always intended to write. In her head she has written seven thousand words. It keeps the panic at a safe distance. Stops her imagination from running riot. Cordons off her fears.

Cortez comes again after having stayed away a while. He looks depressed. Bleak-eyed. Like there's some kind of corrosion going on inside of him, eating away his soul. He hands her a three inch pencil and a pocket red moleskine diary. It's out of date - three years old and none of the dates tally. But it is full of blank pages. He asks her about the snake diary. Her Nehushtan journal. It's the first time he's mentioned it. He asks her what is in it? Pictures? Prophecies? Prescriptions to make the power work again? He knows a lot about it. He pulls up a chair and asks her why she created the journal. She shrugs, mumbles something about it being her obsession. 'Why?' he asks. 'Why when it's just a few bits of old bronze?' 'Because I had a dream. When I was little. I read the story of Jesus telling Nicodemus about the snake, and I looked up the story of Moses. And I couldn't stop thinking about it. And one night I dreamt that I had the snake and I cut it

up and posted the pieces. And when I woke up I was just left with this feeling that I wanted to find them and get them back again.'
He thinks, sits in silence for a while. Gets up and leaves, limping on his cane. The movement seems a little more pronounced now.

Twenty two

'Aretha Kiss? What sort of a name is that? I mean who's called Aretha Kiss?'
'I guess the kind of girl who isn't called Beluga Odyssey.'
'Ha ha.'
The laughter falls from her lips but there is no accompanying smile.
'I think she was named after the singer,' Max says.
'Which one?'
'Which one? You're kidding me.'
'No. D'you mean the band - Kiss?'
Max laughs. 'No. I don't mean the band Kiss. Aretha Franklin. *I say a little prayer for you.*'
'Well, thanks. That's good of you but… so?' She gives the mother of all shrugs. 'Hey! I know one by Kiss - *God gave rock'n'roll to you* – neat song. Had a boyfriend once who played it all the time. He was really old though. Thirty five or something.'
Max says nothing, continues to attack his bacon, eggs and black pudding. He knows how to keep calm under these conditions. Blue sips herbal tea and studies the snake journal.
'She some kind of writer?' Blue says.
'Journalist. Writes for magazines.'
'Wow! Like *National Geographic* or something?'
'No. *Red* and *Cosmopolitan*.'
'Oh. But she loves snakes, hey?'
'Yep. Want any black pudding?'
'Pigs blood? I don't think so.' A pause, more reading from her, eating from him.
'Interesting.'
'What is?'
'Sixteen references to the serpent, twenty seven references to the snake.'

'Where?'
'In the Bible. I never knew that. The serpent seems to be the bad guy though. Did you know the ones in the desert had wings and breathed fire? Sounds more like a dragon, don't it? Check this – 'His spirit made the heavens beautiful and his power pierced the gliding snake." Job twenty six.'
'It's Joe-be, not Jobb. You're saying it wrong.'
'Well they should spell it right then. Sheez, you don't go somewhere for a *joebe* interview do ya? If it's not job like job then it shouldn't say job. Weird.'
'It's his name.'
'Whose name?'
'Job. And therefore he can say it any way he likes. A bit like turning Beluga into Blue. Ow.'
She kicks him under the table. The crimson boot packs a punch.
'So was it him that made the heavens beautiful then? This *Joebe* guy?'
'No. That was a little being known as "The Creator". Our mate Job was talking about him. He'd had a tough time and was trying to get things in perspective. That's what they do in the Bible, when things fall apart they remind themselves about the bottom line. The creator God who is compassionate in spite of the harsh realities.'
'His life fell apart? How?'
'He lost his business. His home. Pretty much a financial crash. His kids got killed too. Lost everything.'
Blue nods. 'That's tough.' A pause. 'I lost my mum.'
Max looks up, abandons his food. 'I'm sorry. Recently?'
'Long time ago. When I was little. Well, eight. Bit like this Job guy. Everything was crap. Nothing was the same anymore. I loved my dad but he wasn't like mum. He didn't know me like she did. He couldn't make my favourite drink the way she did. Didn't know what stuff I needed for school on what days. Never knew which clothes I liked. I had to teach him all those things. It was horrible.'
She stares past Max and out of the window. Goes back in time for a while. Then suddenly she looks back at Max and pulls one of her grimaces. Turns it into a wide-eyed grin.
'Still, life goes on, eh?' she looks back at the snake diary. Jabs her finger at the page. 'I could have written that book. Joebe and his troubles. "His spirit

made the heavens beautiful and his power pierced the gliding snake." Nice poetry. Can't write poetry though. I only ever wrote limericks at school. This bit here about piercing the gliding snake. Is that the snake in that old garden of Eden? The talking one that tricks people into having sex?'
'Probably. It's a reference to it. But he didn't trick them into having sex. They were already allowed to do that. He tricked them into wanting what they didn't need. The old deception that goes on today. Get more things and you'll be happy. That's how he tempted Adam and Eve.'
'I thought it was about a tree.'
'Well it was, but it boils down to the same thing. They had everything they needed. And they gave into temptation and wrecked everything.'
She snaps her fingers. 'Oscar Wilde. Remember that dude? He once said, "I can resist anything except temptation." Adam and Eve should have read some of that. Would have prepared 'em. Might have been very different.'
She pushes her head back into the book. Max finishes his breakfast. She looks up.
'And this guy you just saw, this monk dude, he knows these other guys? The Nehushtan Seers?'
'No, he knows all about them. Studied them.'
'Oh. Then why does she say this?'
'Why does she say what?'
'This. "Blyton finally came clean today. He admitted he knows all the seers. Next week I will get to see him again and force at least one address out of him, even if I have to torture him to get it." See?'
She holds up the journal. Max stares, his mouth wide. Blue grimaces.
'You have food in your mouth,' she says. 'I was always told it's not good to show it off like that. Especially to a smart, beautiful Aussie.'

*

Did he really have a daughter called Anya? Was Marty Zeus just sweet talking her or was that some kind of morbid coincidence? He was good at the sweet talking, no doubt about it. It's taking her longer than expected to get over that encounter in the lift. She's still recovering from his probing comments. She stares at her face and adjusts her grip on the scissors.
'Get it cut, girl,' Suzie Kruger had ordered as she left. Her final words before Anya began mutilating the lift. 'Change your look, and it might just change your attitude. Long hair is soft. Gets in the way. Get rid of it.'

She knows it will make her look boyish. And the hair dye won't help either. But she'll be tougher. Harder. Less like a woman. Less like Marty Zeus's daughter perhaps. She wonders what age Zeus's daughter is. Maybe fifteen? What will she be doing now? Not cutting her hair and hardening her heart. That's for sure. Probably studying hard and planning a bright future. Anya had done that, till those punks ruined her future. Anya had been like anyone else, till three guys found a way to desecrate everything. Day after day after day coming on to her with their leery comments and veiled threats. The growing despair, cutting out the light like a cloud. Other girls claimed they envied her looks, her style. Wished to be her. Joked about what doors it would open. How soon the world would fall at her feet. They knew nothing. Nothing. She lowers the scissors. Looks at the sharp blades. If only she'd had scissors like these the day they cornered her. Might never have happened. The violation. The loss of everything sweet about life. She lifts the blades again. Takes a slice of hair. Looks at it. Flings it away. It lies on the carpet, splayed like an open wound. Snip. Throw. Another gash. Snip. Throw. Another. Snip. Slash. Snip. Slash. In the end she goes shorter than she planned. But Suzie will be impressed. Just add the colour and her natural auburn beauty will be gone. That'll impress her. That's gonna make an impact. Show her Anya's for real, not some two bit amateur. Anya. Anya... maybe she's younger than fifteen. She lays down the scissors, reaches into her jeans pocket and pulls out the photo. No. Older if anything. Both kids look happy. Confident. The boy is definitely younger. Twelve. Thirteen. Doesn't look like the kind of kid who would ruin a girl's life. Marty's got his arm round his wife and the kids are either side leaning into them. For a moment her bravado evaporates. Won't be long before Mrs Marty Zeus gets the news. Maybe the shock will change them. Maybe the boy will turn into some kind of monster and it'll be her fault. Maybe the girl will never be happy again. Another Anya ruined. She shoves the photo away. Can't be looking at that too much right now. It's dangerous. She should have left it on Marty's body. Now, where's that hair dye?

Twenty three

Two thuds on the door again. The shop is still not open.

'Blyton! Blyton! It's me again. Max. Let me in. Gotta talk. Blyton!'
Shuffling from inside, another sigh on the other side of the door. People passing by give a second look towards the intrusion. Then the lock snaps, the bell rattles and the door's open.
'Can we come in. This is Belu… Blue. A friend.'
Blyton still looks as crumpled and spiky as he did two and a half hours ago.
'Shop not open yet?' Max asks as he lets them in.
'Oh I'm relaxed about that sort of thing. What you might call…' Blyton rubs his stubble and thinks, 'post-modern opening times.'
Blue laughs.
'Cool shop, sheez, look at all these books. Can I look around?'
'Be my guest young lady,' says Blyton.
'Too right,' says Blue, 'I *am* a young lady. You remember that Mr Max Maguire.'
She laughs and disappears between the precarious stacks and shelves. Max goes back shop again with Blyton.
'Still got some tea,' says the ex-monk.
It looks as if it's been there since last time. Max declines.
'Blyton, what do you know about the seers?' Max comes straight out with it. Time is moving on.
'What I told you. They're a secret collective of guardians for the snake. They each hold a part.'
'Yea, but who are they? Businessmen? Mafia? Politicians? Priests? Who? Come on. You said you studied them, you must have some idea.'
He sits, rubs his weary eyes with his inky fingers.
'You need to be careful Mr Maguire. If you ask too many questions, people hear about it. Word travels.'
'And why's that a problem? This snake is just an old broken antique. Isn't it?'
'Yes. And no. A relic of this kind is different. People think it has divine properties. That changes everything.'
'Who are they Blyton? Organised criminals? They are, aren't they?'
Blyton laughs and it sets his wheezy cough going again. Max paces while the old guy shapes up again.
'Come on Blyton, give me something,' he says.

'Pass me that mug,' the old monk says. Blyton drinks. He wipes his mouth. 'I'm a weak old man, but I'm not stupid. Information is power, so I'm careful what I pass on. You look like you can handle yourself Mr Maguire. Can you?'
'Sure,' says Max, and he nods vigorously, even though those doubts are immediately there, straightaway clinging to his psyche.
'And that girl out there? What about her? What is she - twenty? Twenty-two? Will she be caught up in this?'
'She'll be fine. Don't be fooled by the sassy, bubblegum attitude. She's got grit. Trust me.'
Blyton stares into the shop, watches Blue picking up books and smelling the covers. She glances over and gives him a broad wink. Blyton looks back to Max.
'So they're organised criminals?' Max asks.
Blyton shakes his head. 'The opposite. Just a bunch of well-intentioned, well-off men who want to do the right thing. They don't all know each other, they just know about the collective. These are good men with good jobs and kind families. And the reason it's all shrouded in secrecy is because they recognise that bad men would gladly get their hands on something like this.'
'And d'you know any of them? The seers?'
'You asked before. No.' Blyton shakes his head.
Max reaches inside his jacket, pulls out the snake diary. He flicks pages in the journal and holds one up to Blyton.
'"Blyton finally came clean today."' He recites. '"He admitted he knows all the seers. Next week I will get to see him again and force at least one address out of him, even if I have to torture him to get it."' He lowers the diary.
Blyton smiles a gap-toothed smile.
'You're very convincing you know,' says Max. 'You tell me you know nothing and I believe you. Totally. The sassy, bubblegum girl out there, she's the one to blame. She spotted this. Did Aretha get it? Did she force an address out of you?'
Blyton keeps smiling. But he says nothing.
'A benign secret organisation like this only survives because it doesn't exist. As far as you and I are concerned. The moment the news is out, no matter how secret they call themselves, people will do their best to destroy

it. Don't you know the old quote? "The light has come into the world, but men prefer darkness, because then their evil deeds don't show up."'
Max nods. 'Sure, but suppose the light is under threat from the darkness, and we can do something about it. We should do all we can, shouldn't we?'
Blyton chews on a grizzled fingernail for a moment. Then he replies. 'You told me earlier you used to find things... archaeological stuff you called it. But you gave it up. Why?'
Max takes the kettle, fills it at a sink piled with dishes and discarded food. This could take a while. He places the kettle on the tiny range. The activity gives him time to think.
'The darkness got too much,' he says eventually. 'I believe in the light. I wanted to... do what I could to dispel the darkness if you like. But in the end it started to feel like a losing battle.'
Blyton's face hardens.
'You can never give in to the darkness. Never. It only takes a little light to disperse it. Maybe you just need time to recharge those batteries of yours.'
'Maybe. But you get haunted by things. It felt as if the darkness had seeped into me. Too much of it. I was becoming part of the problem. That's why I got out.'
'But not at the moment. You're not 'out' now. Are you?'
'This is temporary. I have good reason.'
Blyton reaches out and takes the journal from Max. He takes some time reading through it. Max makes fresh tea and pours it.
'I bought you something,' Max says, and he pulls a blue tube of biscuits from his pocket.
'Easier to handle than Weetabix, way easier, and if you time it right, they're as mushy as snow.'
Blyton laughs. 'Bribery and corruption,' he says.
'Absolutely, what they call in sport, a bung. You can only have them if you give me one address. That's all. Just one. Preferably the one you gave Aretha.'
'Ah, the lovely but persistent Aretha. I miss her visits, her insistent questions and bantering. I hope she comes again soon.'
'Blyton, that's what I'm here about. I didn't come to blow the cover on this snake business. I just want to find this girl so she can come knocking on your door again giving you grief and trouble.'

He holds out the picture, the one from Ben's wallet. Blyton takes it and looks long and hard at it. Aretha looks back, still laughing. Still caught in the process of crinkling her nose and making some feisty comment. Blyton hands it back, then reaches down the side of his armchair and pulls out an old tobacco tin. He prizes it open, bits of paper and card spill out. Max helps him pick them up again. As Max holds out a folded sheet towards the old man, Blyton pushes it back at him.
'That's the one,' he says. 'That's for you. Guard it with your life. And tell no one it came from this tin.'

*

Sam Perry turns the salad with his fork. He flicks the lettuce leaf repeatedly. No matter what he does with it he can't get excited. Not about green leaves on a plate. He catches sight of his girth. It is big. There ain't no doubt about it. Matilda has a point. His long suffering girlfriend slash secretary slash life coach is right. He needs to cut back on something. And reducing the amount of lettuce he consumes will help him nothing at all. Sam forks a huge pile of nature's finest and shoves it in. It doesn't take long. A few chews and it's gone. He leans back, scowls at his diet coke and stares out of the window. London's weather is doing its best to turn the tourists off. He'd be back home right now if he wasn't on a mission. If it weren't for that call. He fights his way into a new position in his chair to give room to push his hand inside his jacket. Pulls out his iPhone. Checks his messages. Yep. There it is. Dean Amble. Code Red. He only ever had one of those before. Dean never jokes about Code Red. Last time the poor guy was being stalked by a couple of spoilt brat junkies, intent on taking him for everything he had. That wasn't too hard really. Sam's used to punks like that. But this is different. This is another country for one thing. A longhaul flight, a strange city, a covert operation. How red was this code? Sam stands up. Walks to the desk. Waves to the reception girl.
'You have any news on Dean Amble yet?' he asks.
'I'm sorry, sir. We have no updates at the moment. Until we hear more from the police all we can say is that he has gone missing.'
'What?'
'He's gone missing, sir.'
'When?'
'Overnight.'

'Overnight?'
'I thought my partner informed you, when you arrived, sir.'
'No they damn well didn't. I have an urgent meeting with the guy. I need anything you have on him.'
He flashes his fake ID. Something that makes him look official in any number of circumstances. The girl glances at it, does what so many do, gives it fleeting attention.
'Who are you with, sir?'
'The Chicago International Police Federation. CIPF. I wouldn't mess about, unless you want an international incident on your hands.'
It always works. As long as there is no one too senior in the vicinity it's the perfect tool for opening most doors. A little card, a stiff attitude and a sackload of confidence will get him most places. The girl confers with her partner. Sam drums his fingers. The reception guy comes over.
'I apologise Mr...'
'Perry. Sam Perry. CIPF.'
'Yes, I see. We are not able to disclose much I'm afraid. But if you'd like to come through.'
He lifts the desk top and waves Sam through. Takes him into an office out the back.
'There's been a terrible incident in the night. Shootings.'
'What? Here? In The Republic?'
The young man nods. 'You mean you haven't seen the papers?'
Sam shakes his head. 'Don't read 'em.'
'Oh, well... I'm sorry to have to tell you, and this really is in confidence, strictest confidence, Mr Amble is dead, sir. His next of kin have been notified but the story is not public in any way at all.'
Sam needs a whisky. He drops to a seat, his jaw flapping. The chair creaks under his weight.
'He can't be...'
'I'm afraid he is, sir.'
'I've known Dean for twenty years. He can't be gone. Can't be.'
'Can I get you anything, sir? Can I call someone?'
'No. Believe it or not, I'm the guy they've called to deal with this.'
He heaves himself up. 'I gotta go. You got any leads you can give me?'
'Leads?'
'Yea, you know, clues as to who might have done this thing?'

The young man adjust his glasses and glances to the door. Everybody is busy out there.

'This is only what I heard,' his voice changes, relaxes, drops the official tone, Sam listens up, 'and it's probably wrong. But there's been talk about snipers. All three guys shot.'

'Three guys?'

'Three, yes. Mr Amble was here with friends.'

Sam flicks his hand, encourages more.

'Well... two chaps called Marty Zeus and Stan Deal. They may have been on a business trip. The really thin guy, Mr Deal, he looked the nervous kind when I checked them in. Not much luggage between the three of them. But there was a really smart attaché case. I remember 'cause I asked Mr Zeus if he wanted us to lock it away for him. But he was adamant he was keeping that.'

'Any guesses what was in it?'

The young man shakes his head. 'No idea. Only saw it in his hand. I just know he never let go of it while he was down here. He was glued to that thing.'

'Any idea if it's still around?'

Another shake of the head.

'Any chance of looking?'

'I'm sorry. It's all cordoned off. The whole floor. The place is crawling with police. They're letting no one near right now.'

Sam thanks him and makes for the door. The young man pulls him back.

'Don't say where you got this from, please. It would be my job over. I'd be history here. Okay?'

'Sure, sure,' Sam is barely listening.

The receptionist guy opens the door and lets him out. He wanders to the bar in a daze, the diet ancient history. Orders a cold beer and a plate of fries. Dean gone? It can't be. Who would want him dead? And some kind of sniper? Here in London. What's that all about? Madness. What was going on in Dean's life that Sam had no idea about?

*

They catch the next available train from Exeter to London. Max's mind is on overdrive now.

'You know something, I got an idea.' Blue says, as she flicks through the snake diary. 'Maybe she didn't just take off. Maybe she was taken off?' She slaps his shoulder. 'By other people who want the serpent.'
'Why do you say that?'
'Well, if your woman went looking for the snake, why'd she leave her journal behind? Surely it's got everything she needs. Doesn't make sense to leave it at home.'
Max nods, staring at the age-old coffee stain on the back of the seat in front of him.
'Yea, that's what's bothering me. I don't know. I don't want you to be right. I really don't. But you may just be.'
Max sighs and shakes his head. He says nothing and pulls the copy of *Millions* from his jacket pocket. It's an easy read, and funny too. Full of money and saints. Just what he needs right now. A wistful cautionary tale.

Twenty four

By the end of the second whisky Sam is calmer. His mind is back in the tracks and he can see the future a little better. He finds a stray newspaper in the hotel bar. One left behind by someone who has attempted the crossword, given up halfway through and then tried to fill the empty squares with the names of famous serial killers. He reads the words Max scoured a few hours before. Speeds through the speculation and comment, and stumbles across that mention of the Nehushtan. The name means nothing to him. He wonders whether it's some kind of Japanese car. But it barely registers with him. He wonders about calling Dean's wife to see if she knows anything but can't face that. She will know the truth about Dean by now, but won't have recovered in any way at all. Right now he needs logic not emotion. His eyes wander back to the butchered, customised crossword. The names of those serial killers squeezed into not enough boxes. Jack the Ripper. How many did he kill? Five wasn't it? He stalked the back streets and side alleys of Whitechapel. He stops himself. Drags his minds back, the whisky was useful for bringing some calm, but it's made his head a little loose too. A hotel porter passes him. He forces a nod and a smile. The porter just raises an eyebrow. Sam stops. Side streets and back alleys. Where did that porter just come from? He swings round. A door is just closing in the far corner. Worth a try. There is no one around. Sam gets up, doesn't waste any time trying to appear nonchalant. Makes straight for the door and goes through. It's a stairwell. That's a good start. He feels his weight after one flight, and there may be many more to go. He's kicking himself for not prizing more information out of the receptionist guy. Like which floor Dean was on. Never mind, if there's half the fuss that the paper claims then it'll be pretty clear. He hears a door swing open above him, just as he reaches the second floor. He dives for a nearby doorway and slips through. The corridor beyond is narrow, and with his frame there's no way he's going to vanish from view. He crouches so that he's out of the line of sight of the little window in the door he's just come through. The footsteps trip past outside and continue on down the stairwell with all the speed of a touch typist. He relaxes, returns to the stairs and goes on up. Two, three more floors. Still no sign of action. He waits, catches his breath. The fries are sitting heavy in his stomach. He catches sight of a bathroom on the sixth floor. Takes a break. While he's in the cubicle he hears the outer door swing and voices come in.

'You seen the carnage up there? On sixteen? Unbelievable. Totally unbelievable. What a mess! What the hell was going on here last night? They think it was a Vanquish. Highly portable sniper rifle. Adjustable calibre. The boss reckons it was someone on the roof of the Cork Building next door. It's a dog leg, perfectly placed. You can shoot in the one window then skirt round and blast from the other side. Man that guy's head was a mess. D'you see him? Half his face. Blam! Clean off. Been a while since I seen that. Looks like one shot missed. Just a crater in the adjoining bedroom wall. Something weird there. Forensics found fragments of a 50p coin. Like someone used it for a clay pigeon. D'you reckon drugs? Can't be gang related surely? Can't be, can it? Man, I hope they fix the lift soon. I'm done with all this thirty nine steps lark.'

The sound of running water. No comment from the other guy. Just the monologue. The door swings, they leave. So, sixteenth floor it is then. Sam braces himself and keeps climbing. He can hear voices all the time now coming from the floors above. He has no idea what he'll do when he gets there. Be arrested probably. He doubts his CFIP card will get him far in that environment. He can't help replaying the comment he overheard about the guy's head. Was that Dean? Could it have been? No use wishing or hoping about it now. But he can't get it out of his mind. Floor sixteen.

There's yellow police tape everywhere. But no sign of anyone coming or going. He expected a guard on the door, but there isn't one at the moment. He places his hands to the little window and peers through the entrance. Nope. No one in the corridor. He could get in there. Always worth a shot, he could claim he was lost or curious. He ducks under the tape and goes through. There's a lot of noise halfway down the corridor. The door to one of the rooms is propped open. He's close but he realises immediately that it's hopeless. The place will be crawling with cops who know each other. A stranger's gonna stick out like a sore thumb. He falters, hesitates, then hears footsteps behind him in the corridor. He turns. A hotel porter is heading away from him. Either didn't see him or didn't care. Might be worth a try. He turns and picks up speed on the young guy. The boy is motoring and a lot fitter than Sam but he manages to close in. The guy is reaching the door. Sam figures he'll let him get through and catch him in the corridor where there is less danger of police intrusion. The door swings. The guy goes through. Sam follows. Their steps clatter on the stairs and Sam is breathing heavily and making a great deal of noise, but the young guy does not turn. He seems to be in a hurry. Sam speeds up, trips over his feet but grabs the rail and steadies himself. On down. Floor 15, 14, 13, Sam's happy to put some distance between himself and the cops. 12, 11, 10. Sam closes in, he's an arm stretch away, the guy slows. Sam reaches out, slaps a fat hand on his shoulder.
'Excuse me, sir.'
The young man turns. Sam, steps back.
'Oh I'm sorry.'
It's a girl. A young woman with her black hair cropped short.
'From the back I thought... I'm trying to track down a friend here. Dean Amble. D'you know him?'
The woman shakes her head. Turns to go. Sam pulls her back.
'D'you know anything about what happened here?' he asks.
The girl's face softens.
'I just work here, sir,' she says with a smile.
'Well, exactly. And I wondered if you'd heard any news about last night.'
'We're not allowed to talk about it. I'd better go.'
She turns and hurries on down the stairs. Sam watches her go. Something isn't right here.

*

The train pulls into London, Victoria, bang on midday. They head for the tube. The place is crawling with commuters. Max hates the underground. He hates the smell and the crush of the bodies, the vacant stares and the lack of humanity about it all. But they have no choice. They have to get to Heathrow airport as soon as possible and that means taking the high speed from Paddington. They head for the Circle line.

Twenty five

At the bottom of the stairs Anya leans against the wall and calms herself. That was close. She thought the sweaty guy had rumbled her for a second there. She reaches into her pocket and pulls out the smartphone. It was worth the risk, no doubt about it. The big lawyer's mobile. With that and Marty Zeus's phone they should be able to track down the next seer. Suzie's got to like this. She has to. She slips out of the door, through the bar to the kitchen and out of a side door to the alley where the hotel dumps its rubbish. She pulls a coat from behind a wheelie bin, throws it over the hotel uniform and saunters back to the street. The place is buzzing with shoppers and sightseers. She glances back, makes sure she is not being followed. She spots the tube station and wanders casually towards it. She slips the phone into her pocket and grips it tightly. There are plenty of commuters boarding the trains. That's good. Always good to have a crowd when you need it. She joins the jam of people and lets them carry her down the escalator towards the artificial lighting and the thunderous rattle of the carriages.

*

Sam sits in the Republic bar again and wonders. He wonders what a hotel employee was doing up on the sixteenth floor. And he wonders what she was trying to get away from. She seemed in a hurry, an unnatural hurry he would say. She may have visited the cops of course, brought them coffee and doughnuts or whatever The Republic's equivalent is. But she had no tray, no trolley with her. It's possible that she may have left that in the room. But there was something else missing. Something really important. Something that marked her out. A name badge. She had no name. Every single Republic employee he has met so far has the hotel and their first name inscribed across their lapels. She was anonymous. He gets up, walks around for a while. Keeps his eyes peeled for her. No sign. He goes to the desk and describes her to the reception guy who helped him out earlier. He shrugs, he's never seen her around. Sam walks to the entrance, hangs around near the steps looking up and down the street. Pedestrians push past him and he has to keep adjusting his position. She's had too long to get away. She'll be anywhere by now. There's a tube station down there, she probably took that. And she may be innocent. Just curious or lost. Though that wouldn't explain what she was doing wearing a Republic uniform. He takes a walk, tries to dodge the oncoming tide of people. It's not easy. Eventually he returns to The Republic and orders a beer.

*

Anya reaches into the other pocket of her coat. Pulls out the photo. She is squashed between a girl chewing gum who won't stop talking, and guy in a military jacket who won't start. The girl has an accent of some kind, and she's sharing it with the rest of the carriage. Anya tries to block her out, puts her head down and studies the picture. She runs a finger over the daughter's face. Wonders what she's doing now. How long she's known about her dead father. A phone rings somewhere. She keeps staring, losing herself in this shot of the happy family. Happy no more. Dad dead and kids ruined. Because of her. Because of those boys at school. The phone rings on. She feels a jolt in her ribs. It's the girl. The loud one, she has ginger hair and bright lipstick.
'You're phone's ringing, girl,' she says.
Anya realises, pulls out Dean Amble's phone, and without thinking answers it.

*

Sam's had a brainwave. He should have thought of this earlier. Try calling Dean. Try his mobile. He pulls out his phone and finds the number.
'Hi Dean, it's Sam, you okay? I heard very bad things.'
Silence.
'Dean? You there?'
Anya starts to sweat. The girl won't stop looking at her. She has to say something but the moment she speaks it'll be clear something's wrong. The voice on the other end won't give up.
'Dean? What's going on? Tell me if you got a problem.'

Anya's mouth starts to move, though she has no idea what will come out. That damn girl with the accent, she just won't stop taking an interest.
'No. No problem,' Anya blurts out, 'Everything's fine. Yea. See you soon.'
She hangs up before he can say anything else. The redhead finally looks away out of the window. Anya feels a tap on her other shoulder.
'You all right?'
It's the guy, the one in the combat jacket who's so far said nothing.
'Yea, I'm cool. Cheers. Just a friend wanted to know where I was.'

*

Sam stares at the phone. Could it be a coincidence? Was that really the girl he just met in the hotel? He dials again. In her pocket Anya feels for the off button. Too late. Dean Amble's phone rings again. She presses buttons, tries to switch it off. Can't. She pulls it out, fumbles with it. The phone clicks and flashes, continues to ring. Somehow she has switched it to camera mode. She fumbles again and finally cuts it off. The red haired girl looks at her, frowning. She smiles back.
'Hate talking in crowded trains,' she says.

*

Suzie Kruger places the attaché case on the table. She knows three of the pieces are in there, she watched the three seers bring it into The Republic. Guarding it with their lives.
Three nervous guys out of their depth. Playing with the big boys and looking for somewhere to hide. Well, they got theirs. Discovered how serious this game is. She taps the leather. She can either search Marty Zeus's phone for the combination, or she can shoot the locks. Which might just damage the pieces of snake. She doesn't care so much if the bronze bits get damaged, but she knows someone who does. She pulls out a pistol. A Colt 1911. Taps the barrel against the locks. She pulls back, steps across the room and takes aim. She feels the weight of the gun in her hand, adjust her position a little, starts to squeeze the trigger. She stops. Sighs. Too much of a risk. It would be quick and easy but she might end up with a dozen pieces of snake instead of three. And all of them covered in scraps of leather and fragments of steel cartridge.

Twenty six

He asks her if she believes the snake has power now. If she knows a way to make that power work. Then he says something chilling. He tells her that's why she is here. Because if anyone can make the snake work again she can. She must know more about it than any other single person. That scares her, though she hides it well. She doesn't know what she thinks about the snake anymore, and she certainly has no special knowledge about how to conjure up anything supernatural. She doesn't tell him this though. She nods and listens and keeps quiet. And she adopts the kind of expression which gives away nothing, but suggests she is pondering his ideas.

*

'Check this out,' she says.
'What's this?'
'A bonus. Dean Amble's phone. The lawyer guy whose face you blew off.'
'I know who he is and I know what I did.'
Suzie Kruger turns the phone in her hands. She finally smiles.
'Good girl,' she says. 'Good girl. You finally came through with something.'
'I went back to the hotel. Snuck in the room while the cops were busy.'
'You weren't seen? Identified?' Suzie's face is hard again.
Anya shakes her head, looks totally cool about it.
'Not at all.'
She doesn't mention the guy in the corridor, the fat guy with his hand on her shoulder, asking her questions. She doesn't mention him at all. It's no big deal.
Suzie switches the phone on, recoils.
'What's this?' she says.
'What? Oh that. Just a picture I took by mistake when I was messing with the phone. It's nothing.'
'Nothing? You know who that is? No, course you don't. Otherwise you would have said something.'
Kruger holds up the camera. Shows Anya the skewed shot she took inside the carriage. It's the guy in the military jacket, the one who didn't say much. His face is stretched diagonally across the screen. Must have been

looking over her shoulder when the camera went off. At least it's not the redhead with the gum and the big mouth.
'You know who that is?' Suzie says again, her face hard as bullets.
Anya shakes her head. 'Just some guy on the tube. I was standing next to him. That's all. He was just a guy.'
'Just a guy? Just a guy? That my girl is only Max freakin' Maguire.'
Anya shrugs. 'Never heard of him.'
'Well you have now. And you'd better not forget him. Remember that face. Because one day soon you may have to blow it off. Was he following you?'
'No. I got on the train and stood next to him. He was there already.'
'You sure? It wasn't a set up?'
'No.'
'He alone?'
'Yea. No. Not sure. There was this redhead. Wouldn't shut up. Kept staring at me when the phone rang.'
'The phone rang? THE PHONE RANG?'
'Yea, but I didn't answer. I just switched it off.'
Suzie eyeballs Anya, then the phone. 'You get a picture of the girl?' she asks.
'No. Just that one, it was a mistake.'
She couldn't recall Max working with a girl. She couldn't recall him working with anyone. The term lone ranger was invented for a guy like Max Maguire.
'It may work to our advantage,' she says eventually. 'If Maguire is in this somehow we may be able to take him out along with the rest of the seers. Main job now is to track down the next target. Pass me Zeus's phone. And Mack's too. They're on top of the case there. Between the lawyer and the screenwriter and the family man we should be able to get something.'
Anya passes them over, and Suzie spends time flicking between them, scrolling addresses and diary appointments. Anya watches and waits and fingers the photograph in her pocket. The lawyer and the screenwriter. Plenty more of them around. But the family man with the daughter called Anya? He was a one off and he's gone. The man with this family is just a painful memory now. Was she really called Anya?

*

Max and Blue jump off the tube at Paddington and head for the Heathrow Express. Should only take fifteen minutes now.
'D'you have a plan?' she asks him.
He moves his head a little. Is it a nod or a shake, she can't tell.
'So you do... have a plan?'
'I have something. I don't tend to work with plans. They unravel. I have options. Keeps things flexible.'
'Do I have them too?'
He's going fast now, she's struggling to keep up.
'We head for Paris. And a little place near the Pompidou centre. A café. Ever been there?'
'What? Paris or the Poppadum centre or some café?'
'Pompidou. Not *dom*. Any of them. Paris would do.'
'Nope. Just the usual, you know, Oz, Spain, Thailand and the UK.'
'You have your passport?'
'I have my life. It's all in Jason.'
He stops, she's glad, gives her time to catch her breath.
'Who's Jason? You bring some kind of stowaway? A pet or something? I told you, no passengers.'
'No, dork. My carpetbag. Jason's my carpetbag.'
'Your carpetbag? You called a bag Jason?'
'You betcha, after Jason Donovan. I got a DVD with him singing *Any Dream Will Do* in that show, you know, Joe and the Dayglow Dreamcoat. Forget the coat, Jason's my dream.'
'He's a little old for you, you know.'
'Not on my DVD he ain't. He's forever young.'
Max takes up again, walks faster than ever.
'Anyway, I like older guys,' she calls after him.
He glances back, but he says nothing. She grins and winks.
'Come on,' he barks. 'Paris!'

Twenty seven

If it's a coincidence it's a helluva one. He sees a girl running away from Dean's hotel room and when he calls Dean's phone ten minutes later someone sounding very similar answers the thing. Was she just an opportunist? A quick in-and-out, small time sneak thief? Passed the room, saw a chance and took it? But she wouldn't have been passing the room. She shouldn't have been up there at all. And not in a fake Republic uniform. This is complicated. This is more than just helping yourself to what's on offer. This is planned. This involves disguise and intent. This must be something to do with a sniper on a roof. Just what he has no idea. But he can't let this sleeping dog lie. He calls the phone again. It rings. He waits. There's an answer. But no voice. Just background noise. He doesn't speak and neither does the girl. He hangs up before they do. That will keep them curious. If they had ended the call they'd switch the phone off. There's a good chance they won't now. He dials again. The same thing. The call is answered but there's no response, he considers hanging up again but they may just tire of this game.

'I know who you are,' he says quietly, carefully, 'I saw you in the corridor. I know you were wearing a disguise and I know you're involved. If you want to find out what else I know meet me at Trafalgar Square in an hour. Wear the uniform and wait near the fountain. I'm sure you remember what I look like. Any problem with any of that just call me, you got my number now.'

*

Suzie Kruger flings the phone across the room, Anya twists sideways and it narrowly misses her.

'Who the hell was that?' Kruger screams. 'You stupid bitch! You told me no one saw you. What corridor? In The Republic? When you got the phone? Did you see this guy? Who is he?'

Anya blinks profusely and stares ahead, refusing to connect with Kruger's piercing gaze.

'He just asked me if I knew anything,' she says through gritted teeth. 'He thought I worked there. That's all,'

'It is clearly not all. What's he look like?'

'Big guy. A little sweaty. Suit. Kind of a round face. Dark hair... I think. A bit of a John Candy kind of look to him. Suzie I'm sorry.'

'Give me the phone. Give it to me! And you'd better pray it ain't broken.'

Anya stoops and scoops it up, walks across and hands it back. Suzie grabs it from and her slaps her across the face.

'You'd better not screw this up. You're already down to your last life. Give me something.'

'What?' Anya's face is stinging, she wants to rub her cheek but she daren't.

'Give me something. Start acting like a professional. Give me a next step. Give me somewhere to go with this.'

Kruger glances down and checks the phone while she waits. She presses buttons.

Anya swallows hard, her head is reeling. 'He has no idea about you,' she says quietly.

'Go on,' Suzie is texting, she presses *send*.

'He thinks I'm alone, probably some petty criminal or something. He probably wants some lead about the shooting and wants to know if I'm involved. If I meet him he won't be expecting you too.'

Suzie looks up. Smiles.

'Good,' she says breezily, 'then we got him. I just sent him a 'see you soon' and when he meets you by the fountain it'll be the last time he meets anyone ever again. You better just pray it ain't the same for you.'

*

He tells her about his suicide attempt. Perhaps that's why he has appeared more haunted recently. His weakness is making him vulnerable. He wants to end his troubles and can see only two possible ways out. One of them is with a gun. The other is with the snake. He couldn't go through with the gun. He realised he does not yet have the courage. So his need of the snake grows.

*

Trafalgar Square is jammed. Families, school groups, tourists, workers on their lunch break. And gangs of roaming, screeching teenagers, hunting in packs, looking for anything that will frustrate the adults. There's some kind of festival going on, free food is on offer, vegetarian curry served up on paper plates. People wander round attempting to eat it rather than drop it. A live theatre company performs on a makeshift stage. A band waits in the wings to spark up. A global eclectic mix, sitars, drums and panpipes. He hadn't planned any of this, it was all just seat of the pants stuff. Sam Perry doesn't do covert stuff, he's more of a 'barge in with a gun and a threat' kind of guy. A talk big and ask questions later kind of guy. He just hopes he sounded more like James Bond than Johnny English on the phone. The text is good news, she appears to have taken him seriously. Now it's the waiting game. And the 'buy a burger and eat it' game. None of this vegetable slop for Sam. Diet's officially off. You can't catch killers on cabbage soup and a cucumber sandwich. He buys the biggest burger he can find and settles himself on a bench not far from the fountain and the stone lions. He waits. He eats. He waits some more. He's still ten minutes early. Plenty of time yet.

The last few shards of beef are still in his mouth, wedged between his teeth, when he spots her. The girl with the Republic uniform. The girl with no name. She's stepped right up to the fountain and is standing on the low wall by the water. She sees him. She waves. He stands. There's a strange noise like a rock smacking through raw meat. He coughs. Catches his breath, tastes blood on his tongue. The girl has stopped waving. She has stepped off the wall and is calmly walking away. No back glance, no goodbye. He feels faint, his head swims, he looks down. It's over. Everything's over. He can't believe it. Is this what Dean felt like? Of course not. Dean had no time, Dean's brain was shut down in an instant. He sags and falls to his knees. Nearby a woman screams. Parents whisk children away. Men stare open-mouthed. So much for the James Bond tactic then. Looks like Johnny English just got gunned down in the middle of London. He falls face forward, dead before he hits the ground. No time for his life to flash before him. No time for anything now.

*

Blue's crimson boots are starting to rub a little. With less money in there they flap about when she walks. Her left heel is getting raw. She needs to play some cards, invest in their collateral reserves a little. The hotel wasn't cheap and neither were the tickets. She stares out of the window and imagines what would happen if an engine blew up. She can't help it. It just creeps into her mind. Max isn't bothered, he's got his seat back and his eyes shut already, one leg propped on the other. He's getting a power nap. He needs one. He was up all night and looks craggy for it. She pulls out her passport and wedges it in her left boot. Makes a bit of difference. She'll try it. She leans back and shuts her eyes, then remembers her gum, pulls it out and wedges it under the instep of Max's boot.

*

Suzie Kruger smiles. Two identical numbers. Six digits. Unnamed. No details. Not long enough for a phone number. Just sitting there on Dean Amble's phone and now here on Marty Zeus's. And significantly, not on Casper Mack's. Has to be the combination. Must be. She reaches for the attaché case. Flicks the dials. Pauses, flexes her long fingers, then slides the catches. There is a satisfying click and the locks fly open. Another smile. She reaches forward, takes hold of the lid and pushes it up.

Her face freezes. Her dark eyes narrow. She lets out a sudden explosion of a scream, picks up the case and hurls it across the room. Three small stone fragments fly out and scatter, clattering as they go. But they are not made of bronze and look nothing like any part of a winged, fire-breathing serpent. She stares at the mess. Cannot believe it. They swapped the snake pieces for rocks. She paces and pants and swears beneath her breath. Eventually drops onto a chair. On the table there is a leather pouch, she unwraps this. Three chunky fragments, three pieces of bronze. The first three bits of the puzzle. But she should be sitting here with six now. She should be halfway there. What did those fools do? When did they make the switch? When did they empty the case? When? While she had them pinned down with the Vanquish? They could barely blink, let alone swap three bits of bronze for some old chunks of granite. She lets out another cry, exasperation flooding from her lungs. She grabs her jet black hair and messes it up. You just get one problem solved, and another comes along to bite you. She calms herself. She has found another number in one of the phones. The big lawyer's. Anya's stupid gamble paid off in the end. They have the next move now. Maybe it's time to change tactics a little. All this killing leaves a sour taste. She needs a break. Perhaps a spot of abduction. Time for Anya to learn a new skill, let's hope she'll do better at that one.

Twenty eight

In a fresh hotel room Max thumbs through newspapers, finds a couple of articles and rips them out. He takes out his snakeskin wallet and slips them inside. Checks one he'd put in there earlier. In the en suite bathroom, Blue lies in the bath in a mountain of suds humming songs from *Joseph and his Technicolour Dreamcoat*. She has no idea death is stalking them. Max is different, he's beginning to suspect something.

*

Anya wonders if she should make alternative arrangements. Working with Suzie is hard. She's a merciless tyrant. Which is good when you're killing people but not when you're her sidekick and getting it wrong. That slap on the face is still with her. It'll be in her head for a while. And what will it be next time? Because once you've given a slap you have to build on it. A woman like Suzie Kruger looks weak if she just slaps a second time. And there will be a second time. Anya can see that now. She's too jumpy. The speed of the killings and Suzie Kruger's spiteful fury have undermined her. She thought the monitoring would ease but at the moment Suzie's watching her every move, expecting her to fail. Anya hates that. She hates being monitored. Can't do a decent job under this kind of scrutiny. And then there's the picture. Marty Zeus's Anya. Why it has got to her she doesn't now. The guy was almost certainly lying. Trying to soften her, sweeten her up, get under her radar. Well congratulations buddy, cause you succeeded. Didn't save his life but it sure screwed Anya's. She needs money so she can disappear for a while. And if she's going to disappear she needs to do it soon, before she gives Suzie another reason to hate her. Her mobile rings. She looks at it. It's Suzie. She doesn't want to answer it. But she can't refuse. Not yet anyway. She just hopes it ain't more killing.

*

Charles MacManus had lived in England all his life. So when he retired early due to a decade of unprecedented success with his haulage business he figured he could either retreat to his millionaire mansion in Surrey or open a café in Paris. He had always loved the French capital and had spent many a long holiday roaming its streets, eating its food and beating its locals at tennis. Charles was a rare kind of man, an astute business mind without the workaholic tendencies. He could happily leave his business in the hands of others and swan off to another world where he can play at being someone else entirely. His wife Sophie is happy enough, ten yours his junior and commuting between the English and French capitals on a regular basis. A life of travel, shopping and pampering. Only his children are a tad concerned that he might be in some way frittering away their sizeable inheritance on a retirement whim that could cost him everything. They needn't be worried. Charles knows what he is doing. He has everything sorted. The demure Yvette runs the refreshment side of things, the coffee and cakes and authentic French lunches. Charles does the meeting and greeting, the drinking coffee and the currying favour with the regular clientele. He has it made really. No stress, no concerns. Apart from the little matter of the bronze fragment, and that document he'd signed, pledging his allegiance to the Nehashtun Seers. But he has no need to worry about that. No one cares about a broken wing that once belonged to a replica of a flying, fire-breathing serpent. He can barely remember where he put it.

*

The sun is high and the place buzzing as the moody guy in the military jacket makes his way across the road. He is accompanied by a girl with crimson boots and a huge carpetbag. Most people sitting outside the café hear her before they see her. They are certainly an odd couple, he must be at least fifteen years older, and downright dowdy by comparison. The girl is highly animated and attempting to engage him in her own heated debate about something. He just keeps walking, making his way purposefully in the direction of the café. Charles fully expects them to pass by, or at worse stop and ask directions. They're probably here for the street theatre outside the Pompidou centre. Or maybe even performing in it. The girl could easily be a singer, she's certainly striking enough, the guy her guitar-playing manager. The only problem is, he has no guitar, just a black leather rucksack, and as big as the carpetbag is, Charles doubts you could fit an old Washburn in there.

*

'Charles MacManus?'
The girl has stopped talking and now it's the guy's turn. He steps right up to Charles as he speaks.
'I'm Charles yes. This is my café. Would you like a drink? Magnificent shoes by the way, miss.'
'Cheers, mate,' the girl says and she gives him a massive, gum-chewing smile.
'Can I talk with you privately?' The guy asks.
Charles glances down at the guy's jeans and boots, wonders if he is packing a gun perhaps.
'Please,' the stranger says, 'it's for your own good.'

Charles considers and then nods. He beckons to them. The girl doesn't follow. She just drops onto a chair.
'Hey lady, can I get a coke?' she yells across at Yvette, who is in the process of serving someone else.
Yvette gives her a tight-lipped nod. Charles leads the way to a quiet table at the back of the café.

'My name's Max Maguire. I'm trying to track down a missing woman,' Max says and he shows Charles the photo of Aretha.
'Have you ever seen her? Has she been here?'
Charles takes the picture, looks over the top of his designer glasses at it. He shakes his head.
'If she was a customer here, I might not remember. We have a lot just passing through. Visitors, tourists, you can imagine.'
'No it's not just that. She may have been looking specifically for you.'
'For me?' Charles studies the picture again. 'Beautiful girl,' he says, 'but I fear I'm a little on the old side. Probably after my millions.'
He smiles then stops when he sees Max does not.
'Somewhat serious, eh?' he says.
'Could be.'
'What's her name?'
'Aretha Kiss.'
'Really? I'd remember her with a name like that, I'm sure. Why's she looking for me?'
Max pulls the journal from an inside pocket of his combat jacket. Opens it and pulls out the sheet of folded paper.
'You're on this list,' he says and he waves the names and addresses. 'Recognise any of these?'
Charles looks over the top of his glasses again.
'Sorry. No. Not getting many right answers from me, are you?'
'You're sure? None of them? Look again.'
Charles sighs and looks closely. 'I'm afraid not.'
'You have heard of the Nehushtan snake?'
Charles leans back in his chair, ruffles his sandy hair, places his glasses on the table.
'Okay. Yes. I have come across that.'
'I believe you have a piece of it.'

'I believe so too, though don't ask me to lay my hands on it.'
Max waves the paper. 'So do these men.'
'Ah! I wondered if I'd ever meet the others.'
'How did you get the snake in the first place?'
'I inherited it. From an ancient aunt who inherited from her ancient aunt who inherited from someone else who inherited from someone else etc etc. Passed down the family line. But let me tell you, it wasn't easy. I had to practically sign my life away when I took possession. So these are the other Nehushtan Seers eh? Guardians of the snake.'
'And you and the other guys on this list don't ever get together?'
'It's not the boy scouts you know. In fact we're supposed to keep it as quiet as possible. A truly secret society is one that never meets up. And what would we do anyway? Swap Biblical snake stories? No, the best thing the Nehushtan Seers can do is keep their heads down and stay quiet. The whole purpose was to never let on there even was any snake remnants.'
'D'you believe in the power of the snake?'
Charles removes his glasses, looks off into the distance, over the heads of the mid-morning customers with their croissants and aromatic beverages. Beyond them in The Place Georges Pompidou they are setting up for a local skateboarding competition..
'My family have always been religious Mr Maguire. It's in the blood for us. I can't say I'm a card carrying believer myself though. In fact, I have to confess, I may be the least committed man on this list.'
'But you knew what you were taking on?'
'As I say I signed my life away. But it was part of a bigger inheritance. Books, scrolls, other artefacts. My family have been squirreling stuff away for years. It was a part of that. I didn't expect to ever be sitting here having this kind of conversation to be honest.'
Max flicks pages of the diary, shows Charles a detailed drawing of the winged serpent on the pole, a flash of lightning strikes the snake and smaller streaks travel towards the people surrounding it.
Max flicks the page and reads aloud, 'Then the LORD told Moses, "Make a replica of a poisonous snake and attach it to the top of a pole. Those who are bitten will live if they simply look at it." So Moses made a snake out of bronze and attached it to the top of a pole. Whenever those who were bitten looked at the bronze snake, they recovered.'

Charles nods. 'Sounds about right,' he says. He taps Blyton's paper. 'That's quite a list.' He says. 'My guess is you have more information there than any of the seers. Better keep a keen eye on it. That would be gold dust to a few people of a criminal persuasion.'
'Do any of the other family heirlooms you have relate to the snake?'
'I don't think so.'
Max nods, thinks, says nothing. Charles slaps the table.
'So? The girl. In the photo. Miss Kiss. She's not on that list?'
'No, but this is her diary, and it's jammed with stuff about the snake. I think she came looking to find out where the pieces are.'
'Why? For an antique jigsaw?'
'No, a dangerous hobby.'
'Dangerous?' Charles frowns.
Max nods, sighs and folds the paper again.
'Mr MacManus I have good reason to believe some of the men on this list are dead. Recently murdered in a hotel in London. A particularly brutal killing. A shooting. I'm not sure which ones yet. But I'm fairly sure it had something to do with the snake.'
Charles stares ahead. Blinks.
'I need a drink,' he says.
He gets up, walks to the counter, returns with a bottle of cognac and two glasses.
'You?'
Max shakes his head.
Charles makes short work of his first glass, wipes his mouth with the back of his hand.
'Are you sure?' he says.
'No. I'm not. I'm just starting to piece it all together. I think someone may want all the pieces of the snake, and that would include your bit. And my guess is they'll do whatever is required to get it. Do you really not know where your piece is hidden?'
'I've had a lot of upheaval recently. Moving from the UK, setting up the business here. To be honest I've always been a little half-hearted where the snake is concerned, it seemed a little fantastic to me. Overblown. Couldn't really see me laying my life on the line for it.'
'And yet you signed up for it.'
 My aunt was very persuasive.'

'You should find it. And soon.'
Charles picks up the journal again and stares at the hand-drawn picture. 'You know I've seen this before, or at least something very similar. Maybe there is something like it amongst the scrolls I have.'
'I'd love to see it.'
'I could try and find it. My wife is in London at the moment. I could call her, get her to have a hunt around.'
'I would do that.'
'D'you think the girl you're looking for is okay?' Charles asks.
'She's tough and resourceful, I know that. She's probably climbing mount Everest.'
Charles smiles. 'Maybe my bit of snake is up there,' he says.
Max doesn't smile back. 'Seriously, you should find it.'

Charles walks him to the street, the skateboarders are warming up out there. Blue watches them as she drains her coke.
'I'll call Sophie today, get her to do a bit of hunting high and low,' Charles says as he shakes Max's hand.
Max nods. 'Keep an eye out,' he says. 'Watch your back.'
Charles watches the odd couple walk away. The girl with the crimson shoes glances back once and waves. He returns the gesture.
Funny old thing this snake. Just when you think it's asleep it stirs and threatens to bite again. Charles yawns and stretches and stops to chat to a few regulars. They offer seats to the popular proprietor but he's got other things to do. He saunters back through the café in his chinos and deck shoes, ruffling his sandy hair as he goes. He finds himself in the back room. There's a phone but he doesn't call Sophie yet. The day's post has arrived and is lying on the desk. He throws a few bits of junk mail straight into the recycling. Opens a couple of bills. The cost of living is up yet again. No surprises there. He still doesn't call Sophie. Instead he picks up the final delivery. A small brown box. It rattles when he moves it. He turns it over, no sender address. He grabs his letter opener, slits the brown tape. Eases the top off. He stares, turns the box over, hears the thud on the table. Three bits of the Nehushtan snake. Sitting right there. Bits of body and head and wings. No letter, no explanation. Oh, wait. Yes there is, wedged inside the lid there is a postcard. A little red corvette splashed across the front. He turns it over.

Charles, you may not remember me buddy but we chatted at a business shindig in Chicago a while back. You didn't know it at the time but I was checking you out. See I'm another one of those 'Nehushtan Seers' like you. And I figure we got problems. I'm here in London with two other guys cause something big's going down and we've pooled our resources. Stashed our bits of snake in a flashy case. Too flashy for my liking. So we chatted and one of the guys Marty suggested we take 'em out, use the case as a decoy and put em somewhere a little less obvious. Which is where you come in. Marty doesn't know it but I went ahead and acted on his idea. You see a couple of the other seers got blown away recently, so I'm not in the mood for messing about. That's why I'm sending 'em to you. You seemed the least corruptible guy I ever met. So here's our three bits. Watch out, buddy, something's on the loose out there. I'm dedicated to keeping these babies safe. I trust you are too. So I'm passing them on to you in the hope you can find a quiet French corner to stash them in. Apologies for this coming out of the blue, Dean Amble

P.S. If anything bad should happen here's the number of a guy you can always call, name's Sam Perry, he's a can do kinda guy. Used to the heavy stuff. Just mention my name. D

Charles sits there for a while staring at the card and the pieces of ancient bronze. He can't believe his luck. He just cannot. He opens the top right hand drawer of the desk. Glances inside. It's still there. Of course it would be. He put it there and he's the only one who knows about it. He collects up the other three pieces in a single sweep of his hand and pushes them into the drawer. Now there are four bits of the bronze snake in there. According to Max Maguire's list that's more than a third of the whole snake. He looks at the phone, picks it up but still doesn't call his wife. His hand shakes a little. He dials, waits.
'Hi' he says as soon as he hears the response, 'Yes, it's me. I know you did but I have some good news. Yes. I have four fragments. I'm serious. You can have them all. I don't know, someone sent them to me. Is she all right? Tell me. Please. Can I speak to her? Okay, okay. Can you let her go? Can I have her back now? Please?' He waits he listens. He is no longer the popular relaxed proprietor, this call has affected his manner profoundly.

'Oh there's something else you should know. A guy came here with a list. He has all the names and address, yea, every one. Looks a bit of an action man. Max Maguire. Is that enough now? Can I see her. Where should I come?'

Twenty nine

They have brought someone else. Last night. Another female. She heard the commotion in the corridor outside. The woman didn't come quietly. Sounded like she put up a fight. There might be some hope in this. If she can signal, send a message, maybe they can plan something. She listens at the wall. Some faint shuffling and coughing in the next room. She risks a tap on the wall. Waits. Nothing. She taps again. Waits. This time there is a noise. A single muffled knock. She taps again. Same reply. Another muffled knock. There's hope.

*

A night train. Max Maguire reads a newspaper. Beluga Odyssey studies the journal. The thing is jammed with pictures and drawings and cut-outs from articles about the snake. Theories on the whereabouts of the fragments and whether the artefact has any real power.
'Maybe she's working with the bad guys,' she says suddenly. 'You know, sold out.'
'I doubt if Aretha would be up for that. She ain't that kind of girl.'
'How d'you know?'
'She wouldn't have put all that work into researching the snake just to sell out.'
'Maybe they bribed her... or brainwashed her.'
'She's tougher than that.'
'Really? D'you know her then?'
'Course not.'
'So how can you say that?'
'Okay.' Max sighs, this girl is persistent. 'I met her once or twice.'
'I didn't know that.'
'Plenty of things you don't know.'
'Which is it then?'

'What?'
'Once or twice?'
'Once. Okay? Once. I met her once.'
Blue looks back at the diary but her gaze keeps slipping sideways, studying him out of the corners of her eyes.
'You seem to know a lot about her,' she says, pretending to stare at the journal.
'I'm psychic. And you've got that page upside down. You got a phone?'
'I got everything in Jason.'
'Send a text to this number then.'
He turns the book in her hands and flicks the pages back to the inside cover. Jabs at a scribbled number with his finger.
'What do you wanna say?' she asks
'Doing okay.'
'That's it?'
'That's it.'
'Just "doing okay"?'
'That's it.'
'Whose number is it?'
'Ben Brookes. Aretha Kiss's boyfriend. I figured we should reassure him. He's probably wondering where we are.'
'He a nice guy?'
'Nicer than me.'
'That isn't difficult.' Then she laughs and slaps his shoulder. 'Come on, lighten up.'
Max folds the paper carefully and shows her the front page.
'Lighten up?' he says. 'Lighten up? A guy called Casper Mack got murdered in JFK airport.'
She shrugs, does her best to look sympathetic. 'Death happens.'
'Sure. But it seems to be happening an awful lot to the people on this paper.'
Max slaps Blyton's list of seers on her lap, and then pulls the cuttings from his wallet.
He hands them to her. 'Sanchez. Carlos Gomez. Both seers, both history. And it wasn't pretty.' He jabs the list on her lap so hard the paper gives under the pressure and tears a little.
'Ow! Careful, dude,' she says.

'No. We should *both* be careful. We're mixed up in some hailstorm here. Bullets, blades, snipers... someone's playing for keeps out there.'
She lifts the cuttings and skims them.
'If you want to go home now,' he says, 'that's fine with me.'
She grimaces then gives him a plaintive smile.
'Ain't got no home,' she replies.

*

Carlos Gomez. He's on the list. One of the Nehushtan Seers. Max shuts his eyes, tries to sleep, but in his mind he's back on Table Mountain. Standing there with Gomez overlooking Cape Town. The cable car steadily approaching. Their hands opening and closing around their guns. A couple of Glock 22's. Normally carry fifteen rounds each. The problem is Carlos and Max only have three between them. Max holds his gun inside his jacket, pressed up against his rib cage, his arms crossed as if he's trying to warm himself. The truth is he's plenty warm enough in the African sun, thanks very much. Carlos has his held behind his back. Ready for action. Max glances around. Robben Island sits in the bay behind them. Lion's Rock and Devil's Peak lurk on either side of them, ancient rocky giants, watching their every move. But the flat top of Table Mountain is quiet. Just the occasional shuffling of a rock dassie, scuttling between the boulders, maybe the hiss of a boomslang or the chirping of a ghost frog. But that's it. There are no tourists. The place is shut down for refurbishments. No one should be up there by rights. Not Max, not Carlos, no one. The cable car moves closer. Max wedges the Glock in his wasteband takes his hand out and wipes sweat from his palm on the leg of his jeans. Then he takes hold again. Carlos glances at him, gives him a reassuring nod. Are there just two of them in the car? Or three? Max can't quite make it out, his short-sighted vision lets him down again.
Carlos leans over and mutters, 'Three.'
Max nods. They wait. The cable car trundles towards them, the overhead cable groaning as it comes in to dock. The door slides back, three men get out. No two men and a woman with jet black hair cut close to her face. Max knows them all, not from attending dinner parties with them, but they've been tailing him and Carlos for three days now. Two muscular, bulky black guys. Heads shaved, hands like rocks, ribcages bulkier than

Michelin tyres. And the short, wiry woman with piercing eyes and the oddly-tattooed teeth.

'You know what we came for,' she says. 'Hand it over and no one needs any trouble.'

Carlos laughs. 'Look Miss Kruger,' he says, 'you want it you have to pay.'

The other two pull shotguns from nowhere.

'There'll be no paying,' Suzie Kruger says. 'Either you hand it over alive. Or we take it from you dead. You choose.'

Max adjust his position. Tightens his grip on the concealed gun. One of the guys motions to him with the barrel of his shotgun.

'Yea, go ahead, superman,' he says, 'try it, see how many pieces you end up in.'

Carlos waves a calming hand. 'Okay, okay,' he says, 'this doesn't have to be so confrontational.'

He holds up his hands and crouches down. The other guys tense up. He reaches slowly into his boot, as if he's adjusting his sock, and pulls out a leather pouch. He drops it in the red dust halfway between the two groups.

'That's it,' he says, 'that's what we're all haggling over.'

The woman waves a finger to one of her friends. The guy on her right steps forward and flicks at the leather with the end of his gun. He opens it up. A twisted, cylindrical piece of metal lies there, patterned and sheered at both ends.

'That's it?' The woman says.

'Sure, doesn't have to be pretty when it's three thousand years old. People'll pay for a bag of spit if it's come from the time of Moses. You know, just the other day I heard they auctioned a drop of blood from Ghandi's shooting for...'

'Shut up.'

The flat top of the mountain lies silent. Five people stare at the scrap of metal.

'Okay we're done then,' she says, moving forward to take hold of it.

'Wow, wow! Wait a minute!'

Suddenly Carlos has his gun out and Max follows. They step away and fan out a little, splitting the focus for the other guys. Two targets, not one.

'Let's talk,' says the woman, and she smiles, flashing her viper fangs.

'Yea, good idea,' says Carlos, 'what do you say Max?'

Max does what they'd agreed. Fires his gun at the shooting arm of the guy on his left. Carlos fires at the other one. Both shotguns spin in the air, both guys flinch and turn away clutching their hands to their sides. Carlos dives for the leather pouch, but the woman has her gun out now and is bringing it up to train it on Max's head.

Max pulls his trigger while she is still moving. The girl should drop, her shooting days over. But there's nothing but a click. Max's gun is spent. Carlos is on the floor, scooping up the treasure, while the woman steps towards Max and jams the gun into his chest.

'It's all over kids,' she says, 'you're playing with the grown-ups now. Daz, get what we came for. Turf, put your gun on this guy, the one they call Max.'

The other guys straighten, retrieve their shotguns and start towards them. Their wounds dripping as they come. Carlos still has his gun out but now he is torn between too many villains. He sweeps his Glock between the girl and the two wounded guys who are now moving closer. The woman jams her gun harder into Max. One of the shotgun guys joins her and places his gun against Max's temple. Carlos looks from the treasure, to his gun, to Max. He has one bullet left. One round to take out three of them. Time stands still.

'I'd drop the gun if I were you,' says Kruger, 'unless you want to go home wearing your friend here.'

Carlos tightens his grip, looks from face to face. A bead of sweat trickles down the right side of his forehead. He licks his lips.

'Okay, okay,' he says, and he suddenly loosens his grip on the Glock, he holds it out and lowers it carefully into the dust right beside the leather pouch. He lays it down and the guy called Daz laughs. Then, as soon as he's let go of the gun, Carlos grabs the treasure and hurls it across the mountain.

'No!' The woman steps away from Max, tempted to chase it down. Max grabs a fist of dirt and flings it in Turf's face. He recoils and screams. There was something moving in that dust. Max drops, rolls, twists and comes up behind him, kicking his legs from under him as he does. The bad guy drops, clutching blood on his cheek. Something green slithers down his body and away into the bushes. Turf's shotgun flies as he falls. Max catches it. Carlos's gun goes off. The woman drops. The other bad guy, Daz, stands there bewildered, swinging his gun but fixing it on no one.

Max butts Turf in the chest with the shotgun stock and points the other end at Daz. The woman with the viper teeth lies on the floor clutching her side.
'You okay Max?' Carlos asks, scooping up Suzie Kruger's discarded gun.
'Yea,' says Max.
They both train their guns on Daz, who's still swinging his gun aimlessly. Eventually the guy lowers his weapon. Max herds the three of them into a wounded huddle on the ground, and watches them while Carlos goes looking for his lost treasure. Turf has an ominous puncture wound to his face, if that green snake was a boomslang he'll be bleeding to death from every orifice fairly soon.
Max had no idea back then that Carlos was a Nehushtan Seer. No idea those guys were chasing him for that. And no idea till now that he had been standing so close to a piece of the bronze snake.

Thirty

They invent a kind of pigeon Morse code. With a series of knocks and scrapes she discovers that the woman next door is kidnapped too. Her name is Sophie and she is British and married. And scared. She has no idea what is going on or who the kidnappers are. As far as Aretha can make out the man in white does not visit her. Or at least, hasn't yet. It's comforting to know that there is someone else in her predicament, but in real terms, very little has changed. They are both prisoners with no chance of escaping. If the men choose to hurt them or kill them they will have their way. Aretha makes attempts to reassure Sophie that she has not been harmed. She thinks this message gets through, but Sophie has not replied for a while.

*

'We came all the way to Paris for nothing.'
He stirs. Opens his eyes. Blue is yawning. Yawning and talking.
'All that way and we didn't even see any street theatre at the Poppadum Centre. We got zip.'
She pulls her boot off, fishes inside for a few last notes.
'Not exactly,' he says.
'And we're nearly out of money now. What do you mean – not exactly?'

'Well, we found out Charles MacManus is not a great liar.'
'What?'
'Not sure. There was something. He was almost too nonchalant. About the snake, about the seers, about... '
Max sits up.
'His wife,' he says.
'His wife?'
'Yea. Why would he want to make me think everything was cool with his wife?'
'Maybe because everything is cool with his wife.'
'Or – because it's just the opposite. His wife's disappeared.'
'Oh not another one. I got enough with this annoying Kiss woman.'
'Why would someone abduct Sophie MacManus?'
'Cause they were bored of just killing people, wanted to branch out maybe? A new career? I'm going to get a coke.'
She slips out of the carriage.

Max stares after her. Incredible. She has a way of hitting the nail on the head without ever realising she's holding a hammer. Abduction. It could be. Kidnap the wife of one of the seers to get to all the others. Which means whoever is killing them all does not have their names yet. Which means... Max is in trouble. They're both in trouble. Because Max showed Charles MacManus his list. His precious list. The one MacManus said was gold dust. Gold dust to who exactly? And how long before they come looking for it?
Max stands up, he's been a fool. Too long out of practise, hasn't been checking to see if they are being tailed. Hasn't kept his wits about him. He glances around, scans the seats.
The carriage is almost empty. Just a couple of girls in their late teens, surrounded by cases and bags with stickers all over them. He leaves the carriage, heads off in the same direction that Blue took. Coke, she was after a coke. He steams through the next carriage and straight into the buffet car. She's not there. He doubles back to see if she was in the previous carriage. Nope, just a few sleeping strangers. All alone. None of them appear to be the armed and dangerous type. Though you can never tell. He goes back to the buffet car, asks the girl attending there if she's seen a girl with red hair. About so high. Boots as red as her lips. The girl

shakes her head. Max goes on, two more carriages, random passengers reading or sleeping or staring at laptops. No one seems that interested in him. No sign of Blue. The last carriage. There's a commotion in the corner. Doesn't sound right. One or two other passengers keep glancing round towards the noise. Max treads warily along. A group of men have their back to the rest of the carriage, grouped around a table, two of them sit in the aisle on bulging rucksacks, blocking the way through. They sound drunk, there's a lot of bragging and laughing. Max is not afraid of them. He reaches round inside his jacket, finds his pocket hunting knife and slips it into the palm of his hand. Lets his arm slip down and hang loose by his side. He moves closer. The men keep up the noise, there's no sign of Blue. He stops and watches. They have their heads down low over something. Suddenly there is a groan and they all sit up.
'Hey! What's up?'
'Yea, you looking for a bit of excitement?'
Four of the group turn and eyeball him. They look the worse for wear, all stubble and red eyes. He glances from one to the other. Can't quite make them out. Are they over-friendly drunks or up for a fight? One of them stands, starts moving towards him. He moves the knife into a usable position in his hand.
'We said, you want some excitement?'
The guy smells bad, cigarettes, sweat and alcohol. Not good, not good at all. And he's getting closer. Max contemplates backing off. It wouldn't look good, but he's not bothered about looking good these days. He wants to stay alive and find Aretha and go home. Dead faces flash across his mind. Eyes that will never see anything again stare out of bloodied skulls. He shakes his head.
'What you mean?' the drunk guy says. 'Why you shaking your head? You think I'm some loser?'
Two more of the group start to stand up. This is beginning to get ugly.
'No. I'm just looking for...'
'Max!'
A head pops up behind the guys. Red hair flicks about. A huge bubble of gum pops between glossy lips.
'Dude! Check this. I quadrupled our money!'
Blue grabs piles of cash, clambers over the table and the rucksacks, and hurls herself happily down the aisle towards him.

'Hey wait!' yells one of the drunks. 'Give us a chance to win that back!'
She turns, pouting and tracing crocodile tears down her cheeks.
'Sorry guys, wouldn't want to really take you to the cleaners. Need my beauty sleep. Cheers for the game.' She turns, then stops, looks back and tosses them a pack of cards. 'Oops! Nearly ran off with these.'
She squeezes past Max. The guys start to come after her. Max considers finally producing the knife. Instead he opts for diplomacy. Holds up both empty hands. Flat, fingers splayed, like he's under arrest.
'Look guys,' he says. 'I think we all need some rest. Seriously, she's on her way to the European Championships in Prague. She's just out for as much practise as she can get. You saw how fast she took you down. I'm just doing you a favour.'
The guys look at each other. Max backs away, makes them feel they're scaring him off. Drops his head a little, like he's capitulating to a Rottweiler. They swear and one of them laughs.
'I'm off for my beauty sleep too,' Max mutters.
'You sure need it,' says a voice from the gang.
They all laugh and the tension is dissipated. He backs away till he's at the door then turns and follows Blue towards the buffet car.

Along the way he stops by a door, opens the window and sucks in the chill night air. He's sweating, there's a slight tremor to his hand. His heart is pumping blood like there's no tomorrow. Right now he'd give anything to be back dishing out assignments, the late night Ginny giving him sly winks and wise cracks. Larry chewing his coke bottles and cracking on about Star Wars episode seven. Taking out three muggers behind the Guildford School of Theology was one thing. Not much more than a walk in the park. Out here, miles away from his bolt hole, he feels all the rigours of his breakdown coming back at him. He's opened the grave on all those spectres and they're crawling out to chase him down. What happened to him? What made him this wreck? He has his theories of course, been over it many times, played and replayed that movie in his mind repeatedly during those days when he lay on the sofa and did nothing for a month. Taking out three muggers was a good thing, it woke him up again, but maybe he has started to run before he can even crawl properly. Does he have it in him to go the distance for Aretha Kiss? He doesn't know. He won't know standing in this train with the cold wind blasting his face.

He'll only find out when the next violent crisis comes his way, and the one after that, and the one after that. If Suzie Kruger ever finds out about him taking the teaching job, man, she will laugh herself stupid. She won't believe it. He can hardly believe it sometimes. Hero to zero. He holds out his hand. It's steady now. His heart has slowed too. He walks on, finds Blue in the buffet car, leaning on the counter with a giant coke.
'I doubt they'll ever stage any Texas Holdem championships in Prague,' he says, 'but it sounded good enough for a few punch drunk poker punks in the deep of night.'
She laughs and punches his shoulder.
'You're good Max, you know that, sheez you're good.'
'You're not,' he mutters.
'Hey! Easy. I just upped our bank balance again. You should be kissing me not cussing me.'
She sips on a thick purple straw, rests her backside on a bar stool. He orders a beer and waits silently for it.
'Not kissing me then?' she says, and when he finally takes the time to glance at her she gives him one of her perfectly staged winks. He looks away.
'You were right,' he says, looking at the girl behind the bar.
'I'm always right,' Blue says. 'About what?'
He waits for the girl to move away to serve another customer then says, 'The abduction. I reckon Charles Mac's wife has been kidnapped. Which puts us in big trouble.'
'Why?'
'I showed him Blyton's list. And if he's communicating with the people who have so far blown away six of the seers and now have his wife, then you can sure as hell bet he'll drop it into the conversation sooner or later.' He drinks. 'Which means their hit list just increased by two.'
He takes a long pull on his pint. She sucks on the purple straw. It's the second time he has seen her lost for words.

Thirty one

He takes her outside, she can't believe it. The door swings open and the man is in the corridor leaning on his cane and beckoning to her. She steps

cautiously, expecting a trap. But there is no violence. He merely leads the way and she follows meekly. Sunlight. Warmth. She's being held in a villa. White walls, swimming pool, rolling hills spattered with olive trees as far as the eye can see. Not another home for miles. Just the odd shattered farmhouse here and there, dotting the skyline like rotten stone skeletons. Cadavers of buildings, walls half-gone, eaten by time and the weather. The ground everywhere is dotted with fallen olives, little black punctuation marks. The season has been good, but whoever owns the land does not care. Nothing's been picked, everything's gone to waste. They walk. Or rather, they hobble. Him because he is not mobile without his stick, and her because she has not been outside for a while and she is disoriented and unfit. Couldn't punch her way out of a paper bag right now, which is unusual for her. She could try running away, but there's nowhere to run to, and right now she'd have no speed anyway.
'Why have you let me come outside?' she asks.
He shrugs. 'Why not? Talking is better in the open air, in the beauty of the day. Stories come more quickly to mind, spill more easily from the lips.' The warmth presses against her skin, there's a breeze too and it kicks at her hair.
'I need that diary you know,' he says suddenly.
'Why?'
'I need to know everything about the snake.'
She says nothing, she learnt a while ago that if you stay quiet in certain circumstances your enemy will keep talking and give more than they intend.
'There are some who claim that the Nehushtan serpent has redemptive powers. They believe the snake inhabits a higher plane. Another reality. A mystical place with forces that can affect things in this world. I need those redemptive powers. Hell, do I need them.'
He coughs and can't stop, it takes him over for a while. She walks a few steps from him, leaves him with his trouble. She smells the air, there's the scent of rosemary and myrtle. Along with the dry soil and crushed olives. The hills slope and twist and roll away from them. Green and black with the odd burst of the dirty white cadavers of those abandoned buildings. She could lose herself in the endlessness of it, especially after staring at four walls for so long.
'Time's running out,' he says, approaching her and mopping his chin.

'For who?' she asks.
'Both of us.'

*

Mid-morning. Charles MacManus waits on the Champs de Mars at the foot of the Eiffel Tower. The wrought iron lady towers above him, puncturing the blue sky. He paces, he's normally a patient man, but this is not normal. Nothing like. This is the most extraordinary experience of his life. Waiting to swap four bits of dead bronze for the life of the woman he loves. To everyone else it's a normal day, visitors swarm, children run and scream and laugh. The fields of Mars here run amok with the sounds and sights of the normal day. The lawns of the Roman God of war. Not inappropriate as a place of exchange for this Jewish symbol of deity. Or four pieces of it. In some ways he'll be glad to be shot of the thing. He's always felt the shadow of it. Doesn't like the unknown, the mystical. Likes to keep his feet on the ground. Maybe this incident has done him a favour, or at least holds a silver lining. If he can just get Sophie back safely and the snake dispatched forever then it'll be a new start for them. He realises how much she means to him. Oh he loves her, he's loved her a long time, but love is abstract to a degree, until qualified by some kind of actions or sacrifice. The notion of never seeing her again, never laughing, walking, holding, even arguing with her has woken him up. They were made for each other. You can be married to someone for a good few years before you fall in love with them. Attraction is one thing. Loving quite another. He has had to learn that the hard way. They both have. He's under no illusion, he knows that they have both wondered about walking away. About hooking up with those strangers they call friends and hardly know. He has often heard it said that the best way to appreciate being married is to be single, and vice versa. Green grass and fences and all that. But he knows now. The grass may look greener, but underneath there are weeds everywhere. No good just upping and leaping fences every time you come across them. Might as well knuckle down and face up. Accept the lack of perfection in each other. That's the conclusion he's come to now.

A woman waves to him. Is it her? Is she there on the grass? Free and safe? Walking towards him across the green.

*

Suzie Kruger takes the backpack and unzips the pocket. She removes the Nemesis Vanquish and attaches the 308 barrel. She clips the barrel into the body of the gun and tightens the knobs. She loosens the bipod, places the rifle on the window ledge and adjusts the position. Now she can see the full length of the Champs de Mars. The God of War is about to witness a little more action. She walks away, stretches and pushes her hair well away from her face. She started shooting in school. Went to clubs, had an air rifle. Prided herself in her ability to learn quickly. The weapons felt good in her hands. Gave her confidence. Purpose. Made her feel strong, powerful, alive. Those days of lead pellets and cardboard targets are a distant memory now, but they served her well. She flexes her fingers. She may have once felt guilt over this kind of thing, had a conscience that jabbed at her mind, like a boxer pummelling the punch bag of her psyche. But the boxer grew tired, or got a new job. Now there's only a single-minded approach, almost autistic, see the job, understand the job, do it right. Any regret only comes after a job badly done, a job that should have gone better. Been cleaner, swifter, more efficient. Anya keeps pressing that particular button and Suzie is getting weary of it. She pushes the protégé out of her mind, focusses on the job in hand. This isn't like the night in The Republic. That was fish in a barrel. This is different. Exterior, daylight. Like taking out the big guy in Trafalgar square. One shot. Efficient. Clean. Pack up, get out of there and walk away as if she's just on her way to queue up for a trip up the Eiffel Tower. A blond wig covering her hair, a cheap video camera pressed to her face. She returns to the window. She can feel the adrenalin pumping. Nearly time.

*

Charles squints and waves back. The woman – is it Sophie? – waves again. She's moving quickly across the green. Coming closer. She's alone. No one with her. No one to collect the four pieces of snake. Surely that's not right. If it's Sophie they would be bringing her, not letting he roam free, surely. Charles glances down at the Macdonald's bag in his right hand. He looks around. Spins on the spot. Van Morrison's playing on a radio somewhere in the background, *Bright Side of the Road*. A little boy weaves between people, kicking a ball as he goes, the superstar of the next decade, warming up for his part on the big stage. Two teenage girls lie on the grass. There's not much sun but they are draped anyway. Men and women banter.

Teenage boys look bored. Suddenly there's an explosion and everybody freezes. A little girl screams. Her balloon has burst. She's heartbroken. People move again, the mother comforts, dad goes in search of another. Charles looks for Sophie again. It's her. It's definitely her. Well, it's her coat anyway. But the hair… the hair is wrong, it's black and cropped. Sophie has a light brown bob. Before he knows it the woman is at him, embracing him, whispering in his ear. The voice is wrong too.
'Just pass over the bag, hug me, and I'll be out of here. No one will get hurt. I'll check the pieces and we'll call you and tell you where to meet your wife. Squeeze my arm once if you've got that.'
He holds her, smells her perfume, squeezes her arm. She reaches for the bag. Takes it. Turns and walks away. He watches her go. And that's when the shot rings out.

Thirty two

They move her again. Come in the night, two guys with guns and flashlights. They move her out of the villa. Away from the tastefully furnished bedroom, with the light colours, the blues and whites. She has a feeling she may not be so lucky this time. No more hotel room, no more summer break. They blindfold her, put tape across her mouth. She panics a little, remembering the last time, and how dry her mouth became, how swallowing was almost impossible and her breathing became laboured. The claustrophobia too. The sensory deprivation from the temporary blindness. But she can't complain, there's no time. They move her quickly. Push her into a car. It's night of course, and cold. And she has to sit very still while they drive. For a long time. The road rises and falls, the bends come rapidly and repeatedly. Eventually she hears more traffic. In the rolling, olive studded hills there was little activity. This is different. This place has cars and pedestrians and bikes. Horns sound and teenagers yell. Water splashes and bubbles somewhere. And there's drumming too. They pull up, grab her, manhandle her down some steps. Lots of steps. She crashes against walls, scrapes her arms and cheek. Eventually they slow down and the sounds of the outside fade. A door slams, the sound of it echoes around. They walk her more carefully. Stop. Unlock a door. Open it and push her in. They say nothing, just tear off the blindfold and peel the tape from her mouth. She jams the back of her hand to her lips, they are as dry as an old rag. Her mouth feels like corrugated cardboard. They go. She sees a jug of water and a glass. Pours and drinks, her mouth absorbs the fluid as if it's lined with blotting paper.

*

'Where are we going now?' Blue asks as she tosses the carpetbag off the train and jumps down after it. Max scowls, he's already on the platform, pulls the list from his pocket.
'Four seers left,' he says. 'Just four.'
'Five if you count old smoothie MacManus and his little shop of coffee.'
'Maybe, but, I wouldn't count on it. Something was bang out of order there.'
'Then let's get back and save the dude.'
She's suddenly all for jumping back on the train, but Max drops his rucksack and stretches. Rubs the back of his thumb over the scar on his chin. Thirteen hours from Paris to Madrid. He's had enough of trains for a while.
'No. We go forward not back,' he says. 'Okay, listen. Number one priority now. Watch your back. Okay? They know we have the information they want.' He waves the paper. 'Which means we may well be number one on their next-target list. You see anything weird, anything strange, no matter how small, tell me immediately. Right? Anything. We can't afford to give anyone the benefit of the doubt right now.'
She shrugs, blows a bubble with her gum. He grabs her shoulders, squares up to her. She feels like a little kid being told off by her dad.
'I'm serious. This is life or death now. Remember that reason I didn't want to bring you? Well, this is it. It doesn't get any more dangerous. You want out? Say, and to be honest - I want you out. I want you back on the train and heading off towards the next stop on your world tour. But I can't be sure that even that won't get you killed. If they're watching us, and they could be, then you and I are both marked.' He sighs. She stares, eyes wide, face frozen. Silence. 'So what do you wanna do?' he says finally.
She grins. 'Catch the bad guys, stoopid!'
'You do understand what I just said, don't you?'
'No I'm a three year old - what do you think?'

He didn't say. The obvious comment would be to tell her to stop acting like one, but that would be a waste of breath. He lets go of her shoulders and straightens. Looks up and down the station. It's empty. Everyone else has gone. Wise people. He checks the list again.
'Two guys in this town.'
'Two? Two guys on that list in the same town? That's a coincidence.'
'I doubt it,' he says. 'More like safety in numbers.'
'Are they related?'
'Doubt it. Jack Carlyle and Andre Alvarez. Let's find a map.'
'There was a bombing here, wasn't there?' she says. 'I read about it at school. 11-M they call it. Don't know why.'
'11th March 2004. 191 people killed. An interconnected series of explosives. 1800 injured. All in this station.'
They walk the length of the platform.
'It's sure peaceful enough now,' she says.
'Yea, for now.'
They take the main exit out into Plaza del Emperador Carlos V, stopping just long enough to pick up a street map. The Artichoke fountain sits out in the square, shoving water into the air. Blue wanders over to it, pushes her hand in the flow, feels the water cascading on her fingers. Max points towards the Paseo del Prado and they wander down the tree-lined boulevard.
'Cool,' says Blue, nodding appreciatively like a toy dog in the back of a car. 'This place is fair dinkum, mate. It's ace. '
'Find The Siesta,' says Max.
'What?'
'We're looking for The Siesta.'
'Sounds like a tapas takeaway.'
'It's a hotel. Jack Carlyle lives there.'
'Wow! You're kidding me. He lives in a hotel? On this street? Ace! Mate, we should get to know him.'
'I intend to.'

*

'Why did you kill MacManus?'
'Because he'd given us what we want.'

'But I thought you wanted a break from the killing. Thought you said it left a bad taste.'

'It's not that simple. You don't get to choose sometimes. We abducted the wife. The man talked. He gave us four bits of snake and told us about the list. That's all we need now.'

'But why shoot him? You could have let him just live in peace now.'

'Because he wouldn't, would he? Sooner or later he'd get all guilty about being one of the seers and hire somebody to come looking for us. He swore to guard it with his life. Well, he can't complain. He's given his life.'

'That's it, is it? That's why we're killing them all.'

'Yep. And because it's tidier. And because that's the job we got paid to do. Anya, you have to learn – this isn't the movies. We're not killers with a heart of gold. We do the job and we get the cash. That's how it works. You want a conscience? Go and be a priest.'

Anya watches Suzie Kruger cleaning the Vanquish.

'You don't feel anything do you?' she says.

Suzie looks up sharply. 'And you'd better not too or this apprenticeship is over. I'm not jeopardising my future by allowing you to go all Ghandi on me. You did well with the abduction. Got that woman discreetly and effectively to Cortez. Now don't foul it up with all this caring-sharing crap.'

She crosses the room towards the younger woman and her face hardens with each step. She lifts the detached rifle barrel and presses it hard against Anya's cheek. Glimpses of her tattooed teeth flash as she hisses at Anya. 'Don't ever question me like this again. Okay? Just stay in line. You got that?'

Anya stares, eyes wide.

'I said, YOU GOT THAT?' Kruger pushes Anya's face against the wall with the side of the barrel. It hurts.

'I got it,' Anya whispers.

'Good.'

*

'Wow! Sheez. That is a hotel.'

The Siesta looms in front of them, all gleaming windows, balustrades and pristine cream facade.

'487 rooms, 7 floors, two art galleries, 523 toilets. In its time home to royalty, fascists, writers and revolutionaries.' Max rolls his eyes and holds up his map. 'So the guidebook says.'
'And now Jim Carlyle,' says Blue.
'JACK Carlyle,' he corrects her.
'Oh yea, right. That's the dude. So what's he do?'
Max jabs a finger at The Siesta. 'This. He owns it.'
For the third time Blue enters the speechless zone. Her mouth drops, the gum falls out. Max heads for the huge front entrance, trusting that she will follow.
'Can I help you, sir?'
The doorman has a strong accent but his English is perfect. He is decked out in a blue uniform with gold braid, but beneath the costume it's clear the guy can handle himself.
'We have come to book a room,' Max says.
The doorman looks him up and down, he makes no secret of it. Blue grins and pushes her hair around a bit.
'We got money,' she says and Max turns slowly and gives her the kind of look that would not be out of place on the grim reaper's face.
He beckons to the doorman and takes him to one side.
'It's a little delicate,' he mutters, 'you must have come across this before. Wealthy men don't always travel in style, attracts attention. Makes good reading in certain magazines. Especially when a wealthy man travels... in certain company.'
The doorman glances across at Blue. She grins again and pops a fresh piece of gum.
'I'm going to have to ask for more than that, sir,' he says.
Max nods. Considers. 'Are you able to get a message to Jack Carlyle for me?' he asks.
The doorman raises a single eyebrow. 'Are you serious?'
'Of course. Please tell him that one of the Nehushtan Seers has come to see him.'
He glances from Blue to Max and back again. Eventually he beckons to them both and leads them inside.
Max grabs Blue's arm and hisses in her ear.
'Say nothing!' he says. 'Whatever this place is like, act like you're used to it. Got it?'

She pulls him closer, whispers in his ear. 'Am I your lover now then?'
'Shut up.'
The Siesta is dripping with marble, silk and antique furnishings. Blue does her best but her jaw is on the floor for a while. The doorman waves them to an ornate leather couch, something from the 19th century. She strokes the polished arm and can't help smelling the thing. Max sits causally, arms folded, one leg propped on the other. He never takes his eyes off the doorman, who is now leaning across the colossal marble desk muttering to a beautifully manufactured receptionist. A flawless example of airbrushing on legs. The woman nods, glances at Max and throws him a winning smile. Her eyes crease a little as she notices Blue, but it's barely noticeable. She picks up a pearl telephone and presses buttons. She speaks, listens, speaks, waits, nods and replaces the receiver.
Blue leans across to Max. 'We should blackmail him. Or, or maybe... hey! Does he play poker?'
Max doesn't look at her, just straightens her up on the couch and puts distance between them again. Blue shrugs and sighs. Blows another bubble. The doorman crosses the glimmering floor.
'My apologies for keeping you waiting, Mr...?'
'Maguire. Max Maguire.'
'Mr Carlyle will be down in a few minutes, Mr Maguire. If you have any further enquiries, Kristy on the desk here will help you.'
He pointed to the perfectly formed receptionist. She waves back. Max nods. The doorman returns to speak to her then leaves.
Blue leans over again. 'You're good at this,' is all she says before leaning away again. They wait. Blue gives up polishing the leather and begins drumming her fingers on it instead. Max places a hand on her leg to stop her. She pauses and glances down at his hand, which he quickly pulls away. She continues drumming.

Thirty three

'Mr Maguire?'
Middle-aged, thinning sandy hair, freckled features, insanely expensive suit. Jack Carlyle smiles at them both. Somewhere in the background two

minders hover discreetly. Max glances down at a large gold cross hanging over the silk tie.

'Mr Carlyle,' Max stands as he says this, offers his hand and they shake. 'This is Beluga Odyssey, Blue to her friends.'

Blue stands and grabs Jack's hand. 'You can call me Blue,' she says quickly.

'I'm intrigued. My secretary tells me you came to book a room but then mentioned the Nehushtan Seers?'

Max nods. 'Can we talk somewhere?'

Jack Carlyle turns and indicates to Kristy behind the reception, he nods towards a door to the side of the marble desk. Kristy nods back and he leads them over to it. One of the minders follows them in. Jack indicates a couple of huge leather chairs on the near side of a mahogany desk. He takes the seat beyond it. He turns an ebony box towards them.

'Turkish Delight?' he says. 'A bit strange I know, but a weakness of mine. In the old days it would be Cuban cigars of course, but big brother won't let us smoke now. It's the genuine article, none of your cheap stuff.'

He is English, and a faint, extremely faint, Yorkshire twang still hovers there in the shadows of his delivery.

Blue dives into the perfumed confectionary. Max holds back, it's not difficult for him.

'So Mr Maguire. As I say, intriguing. Are you looking for the best hotel in Spain, or the proprietor?'

'You,' Max says, and he produces the list again. He wonders if he's going to begin to tire of this monologue. 'I have reason to believe you may be in serious danger. Someone is killing the Nehushtan Seers. Six, perhaps even seven on this list are already dead. Did you read of the recent shootings in London?'

He nods, takes the paper. 'Yes, I know The Republic. Had no idea that it was anything to do with this though.'

'Do you know any of these other men?'

Jack studies the list, shakes his head. 'Not even Andre Alvarez?'

His face lights up. 'Yes, I know Andre, well I know of him. He lives just around the corner. You mean... you're telling me he's one of the seers?'

Max doesn't answer. He takes the paper back.

'How did you come by the snake?' he asks.

Jack waves a hand towards the minder, he indicates the door. The big guy turns and slips out.

'Same way I came by everything else. I inherited it from my father.'

'He owned this hotel?'

Jack shook his head. 'No, I just got his money, but I used it to make a lot more. And now I have this hotel. My father owned land in Yorkshire. A lot of it. He also produced flour. Or rather, he got other people to do it for him. A lot of money in bread. Or there was then. When he died I took the cash and ran. This prodigal ended up here. A millionaire in Madrid. Before he died my father gave me his piece of the snake. Took me to one side on my twenty first birthday and told me all about it.'

'And do you believe in it?'

'Believe in it? Of course. What's not to believe in? I come from a God-fearing family Mr Maguire. Never had reason to question.'

'Is that 'cause you've always had loads of money?'

Jack Carlyle looked at Blue, startled by her question. Then he laughed. And his accent really came out in the belly laugh.

'Aye, although they do say it's hard to get into heaven if you're filthy rich and full of brass, you know.' He shakes his head. 'No I've been fortunate. Had a good life. Never wanted for anything. Only left home because I wanted to see the world, and without my old man around there was less reason to stay. My mother died when I was very young, you see. Don't remember her really, it was always me and my dad. We seemed to do all right.'

'Can I see your piece of the Nehushtan Snake?' Max asks.

Jack Carlyle leans back, swivels his chair and looks out of the window.

'You'll understand Mr Maguire, that I'll have to decline. I believe what you say, I think you have my best interests at heart. But I don't know you. And I swore to keep the snake from those who might abuse its power. This may be an elaborate plot on your part. Don't be offended Mr Maguire, but you may have been involved in these killings in The Republic. So as I say, I'll have to say no.'

'D'you keep it here?' Max asks.

Jack Carlyle shrugged and held up his hands. 'Again Mr Maguire, I'll have to hold back.'

Max stands up but Carlyle waves him back down again.

'I notice you're not on that list,' he says. 'Yet my assistant informed me one of the other seers was here. What exactly is your involvement in this? And Miss Odyssey here?'
'I've been asked to track down a missing girl. Aretha Kiss? You don't know her?'
He shakes his head, pushes a piece of Turkish Delight into his mouth. Max pulls the Nehushtan diary from his rucksack.
'She has been researching the snake for years, she's a journalist. Been keeping a book on it.'
'May I?' Carlyle takes it and flicks the pages. He sniffs and nods.
'Dedicated lass,' he says. 'Any clues to what's going on in here?'
'Perhaps, I'm not sure. Blue has been scouring it more than me.'
Carlyle swivels his chair towards her. She grins and chews on Turkish Delight.
Max continues. 'I think she's either trailing the bad guys or been kidnapped for what she knows.'
'And what does she know?'
Blue stands, takes the diary and manhandles the pages till she finds something.
'This,' she stabs a finger at a pencil drawing. 'That's how the pieces fit together. Now, jeepers, how'd she find that out? I think whichever seer she went to knew somehow. If it wasn't you, then it was one of the others.'
Carlyle takes the book again, studies the picture.
'Just help us with one thing,' Blue says, adopting her best smile, 'can you see the piece of snake you have in that picture there.'
He glances down at the drawing of the snake, the sketchy fragments fitting neatly together. A jigsaw of the reptile.
He nods. 'Yes, and it's not a bad likeness. I'll even show you which.'
He taps at the paper.
'You have the head?'
'I do. The front half of it. Though again I have to say I can't reveal where it is.'
Blue grins at Max. Max frowns back.
'You didn't mention this before,' he says, grey eyes boring into her.
'Spotted it on the plane,' she says. 'Look, this is what the pieces look like, somehow she figured it.'
Max takes the book from Carlyle.

'One of the seers must have the same picture. And that must be the guy she went to after Blyton showed her the list.'
'Blyton?' Carlyle sits forward in his chair.
'An old monk we met. He knew a thing or two about the snake.'
Carlyle's eyes narrow for a moment.
'You met him?' asks Blue.
Carlyle thinks then shakes his head. 'No,' he says slowly, 'I don't think so.'
Max stands up again and picks up his rucksack. Blue follows him.
'You'll be staying for a few days?' Carlyle asks.
Max nods. 'For one night, at least.'
'I'll take care of that,' Carlyle says, 'I have to be cautious about the snake, but I can at least give you a bed for the night in the best Hotel in Spain.'
Blue pointed towards the ebony box of sweets.
'Do the rooms come with those?'
Jack Carlyle laughs. 'I'll see to it personally,' he says.

Thirty four

Suzie Kruger runs her finger over the scar on her side. Max Maguire. He was responsible for this. Max and Carlos on that mountain. She forever has their fingerprints on her body. The only time she's ever been sick in her life. The only time she's ever been injured on an assignment. Well, it's payback time now. 'I will find you Mr Maguire and you will give me what I need and I will get my retribution.'
She stares at herself in the full length mirror as she speaks. Watches her dark lips moving.
'It won't be easy, won't be like Charles MacManus or Sam Perry. But that will make it all the more satisfying. I got Carlos and I will get you.'
'Who you talking to?'
It's Anya, her head poking through the cracked door.
'What do you want? Don't you knock?'
'I heard voices, thought you might be in trouble.'
Suzie laughs, a real derisory snort. 'Me? In trouble? From Max Maguire? I don't think so. Now get out.'

Anya goes, returns to her own hotel room, next door. She sits down at the dressing table, glances up to see the photo of Marty Zeus's family, stuck on her mirror. They're all smiling at her. Even the dead Marty. Better not leave that there, if Kruger catches her with it she'll be finished. She peels the tape off the mirror and pulls down the photo. Anya Zeus. Nice name. Better than Anya Barlowe.

She leaves the hotel room. Decides not to tell Suzie, strolls down to the hotel restaurant, orders food. A green salad and a mushroom omelette. She places two photos on the table. Marty's family and Aretha Kiss. Her phone rings.
'In future don't go anywhere without informing me. Understand? The idea that we're a team right now is laughable. Now listen, get out of that restaurant and do some homework on Maguire. I want to know what he's been up to in the last six months, who his mates are, what toilet paper he uses and where he is right now. Got it?'
Anya stands up, keeps the phone to her ear as she scans the restaurant and the corridor beyond the glass wall.
'I said, have you got it?'
'Yes, sure, how did you…'
'And the bits of snake, you secured them, yes?'
'Of course. You don't have to keep checking up on…'
Dead. Suzie's gone. Anya looks around again. No sign of her. Just suited business women holding working lunches, picking at their food like they're trying to extricate calories before they push it into their system. She sits down. Her food arrives. She stares at it, studies the two photos. She picks up her fork slowly and eats. She will do some detective work on Max Maguire. She'll be happy to. But not as soon as possible, right now she's hungry and the omelette is good. She'll go when she's good and ready.

*

Meet me at Aretha's flat at 7.00pm tonight if you value her life.

Ben Brooks stares at the hastily scribbled note. No signature. No clue, just half an A4 sheet, torn from a pad and shoved on the reception desk at work. He looks over at the guy behind the desk. Duncan. Been there twelve years. Never fails to smile.

'Dunc, who left this?' he asks.

He shrugs.

'Been busy this morning,' he says, 'lots of people coming and going. Probably someone who slipped in the foyer and just left it.'

'You signed everyone in as normal?'

'Sure, but if they just did a quick in-and-out I wouldn't have clocked them.'

Ben grabs the signing-in book, scans the pages. Usual kind of thing, some regular visitors, a few business colleagues, a smattering of unknowns. Hardly worth the effort of chasing them all down.

'Bad news?' asks Duncan over the top of his John Lennon glasses.

Ben shrugs. 'I honestly don't know. Could be good or bad. I just hope it isn't very bad.'

*

Blue is back in Aretha's journal, lying on the pile carpet, her feet crossed and sticking up behind her, overlapping back and forth as she reads.

'Why were the Israelites in the desert anyway?' she ask, twirling gum from her mouth on her finger.

'Moses led them out of slavery in Egypt.'

'Why were they slaves?'

'Long story. It all began with Joe's family.'

'Joe who?'

'Your Joe – Joe and his Dreamcoat.'

She spins round to look at him. 'You're kidding me! Joseph was mates with Moses?'

'Not exactly, they were a couple of hundred years apart. But Joe and his brothers lived in Canaan. They'd settled there with their old man Jacob when he came back from his walkabout years. Joe was kinda naïve, had big dreams and an even bigger mouth, started telling his brothers how he'd dreamt about being top dog one day. The brothers didn't like it. Plotted to get rid of him.'

'They threw him in a well right? I remember that. They nicked his coat.'

'Yea, but then they saw some slave traders and decided to sell him instead. The slave traders took Joe to Egypt and after a long and winding road Joe became Prime Minster. Of a superpower. Not bad for boy who got hurled down a well and ended up in prison.'

'Close every door to me.'
'What?'
'That's the song that Jason sings when he's in prison and his life's in the dunny.'
'Okay.'
'So when does Moses turn up?'
'Years later when Jacob's family has grown so much that it's become a nation in Egypt and the locals get all uptight about it and decide to subdue them by making them work long and hard. It's a typical story of brutality and oppression.'
'That's unfair.'
'Well, the Israelites had multiplied pretty well over the years and by the time of Moses they were a healthy, strong breed of people. No one's exactly sure which Pharaoh was in charge when the persecution kicked in but it could have been Rameses 2nd. He loved his building projects and he needed a huge workface to complete them. It was a useful way to suppress a bunch of aliens. Come on, let's go for a walk.'
He reaches the door, stops and glances back. 'Oh and by the way, next time you make a useful discovery, keep me in the loop, right?'
'What?'
'The picture of the snake pieces, would have been useful to know about it before you told Carlyle.'
'Thought I'd mentioned it…'
He shakes his head, turns away and opens the door.
'Jeepers,' she says, 'it's just a picture. No need to get steamed up. Wasn't like I snuck into your bedroom and stole £200 from your shoe.'
He levels his eyes at her. She grins. Winks. Blows him a kiss. He turns away, supressing a smile.

Thirty five

Outside on the Plaza del Emperador Carlos V the road is jammed with the evening city traffic. Blue weaves her way through like a pinball in a machine, arriving at the Artichoke fountain and leaping up to walk its circumference, getting her crimson boots well and truly splashed. Max waves her back, points on down a nearby boulevard, the Paseo del Prado,

quieter, thick with leafy trees and broad pavements. Max makes his way down there. Blue stops, salutes some great stone politician in the square and jumps down to weave her way back towards him through the cars and buses.
'So,' she says, catching him up, kicking water off her boots as she goes, 'tell me about big Mo – does he kill the dirty 'gyptians? Deck Rameses with a drop-kick?'
Max manages a quiet grunt of a laugh. 'Hardly. Rameses II, or Rameses the Great as he's also known was one of the top Egyptian kings. There's a colossal statue of him in Cairo. Three thousand years old. He took the empire into great days, battled with the likes of Libya and Syria and Turkey and won. Reigned for sixty odd years, built cities and temple complexes and tombs and mausoleums. Went down in history so much that nine future kings took his name. So no, Moses didn't drop-kick him. Moses didn't even want the job. He was heading for retirement, shepherding in the Arabian Peninsula. He had the granddaddy of all arguments with God about going back to Egypt. That's the thing about the Biblical heroes. They are none of them Supermen you know. Heroes in the Bible aren't like heroes in the movies. They don't have capes and the ability to fly or spin webs. To hear some people speak you'd think the Bible was a Marvel comic.'
He's frowning as he talks now, his forehead ribbed with cramped furrows. She comes close, takes a good look at him, he's not happy. 'Woah there tiger!' she says. 'Who rattled your cage?'
'No one, I'm just clearing up a point here. My students always come with this idea that the Biblical heroes are gleaming saints with Harry Potter wands and the strength of Achilles. Never was like that, never. Never. The Bible's pretty plain about the peoples' flaws and misdemeanours. They're as imperfect as you.'
'First off here, mate, I ain't one of your students. And secondly, who told you I'm imperfect. That's just a damn lie.'
She slaps his shoulder and pushes him to walk on. He sets a good pace. She jumps on the low wall and keeps up with him, balancing as she goes. 'So? Tell me about brother Mo?'
'Moses? Well, Rameses puts the Israelites in chains, comes on real heavy. Cuts back on their supplies and yet demands they make twice as many bricks. Like I say, typical of the kind of madness that comes with power

and tyranny. Moses goes down, sees what's happening and decides he wants to do something to help his brothers and sisters.'

'What do you mean? His brothers and sisters?'

'Moses is an Israelite.'

'Why isn't he building pyramids like the rest of them?'

'Ah, well, because he was taken to the palace as a baby and raised as a son of the Pharaoh. Sort of like Rameses little brother. It's complicated, but it's all a part of the guy being chosen from birth to save the people. Ever hear of the bulrushes story, the baby in the basket?'

'Wasn't that Jonah? Or maybe Noah?'

'No, Jonah ended up in a whale. Noah in a boat. Moses found himself in a basket. All the Israelite baby boys were under threat when Moses was born so his mother put him in a basket and hid him in the reeds. Pharaoh's daughter found the baby and rescued him. As a result Moses got raised in the royal court, which I hasten to add turned out pretty useful later on, when he had to haggle with Pharaoh. But in the meantime he went down one day to check out the action with the building force. He saw an Egyptian beat an Israelite and figured he'd do something about it. So he grabbed a spade, pummelled the Egyptian and buried the body, presumably with the same spade. The murder leaked out and Moses ran for his life. Went to a place called Midian. Downgraded from prince to shepherd overnight, got married, settled down and thought that was the end of it. Till he was out tending sheep one day and a bush caught fire. Now that wasn't unusual in the desert heat, but the voice coming out of it certainly was. God had showed up with an offer he couldn't refuse and the rest as they say is history. Want some squid in a bap?'

They stop at a street vendor, buy some food and Spanish beer and sit on the wall swallowing it down.

'It's a lot to take in, ain't it?' she says. 'You know - bushes burning and babies in baskets, not to mention people doing miracles and having weird dreams.'

'Sure, and we ain't even got to the plagues and the Red Sea yet.'

'D'you believe it all?'

Max stares ahead, wipes a drop of beer from his chin with the back of his hand.

'Everyone believes stuff,' he says eventually, 'if I decide to trust these age old stories then, in the belief stakes, it's no difference to someone deciding to read their horoscope. We all trust in things we can't prove or see.'
'That's a copout.'
'Of course it is. But maybe I don't want to waste my energy trying to argue for something that I can never prove. Faith is faith. You believe things, I believe things. You have to make your choices.'
'Why are you so defensive? I ain't saying I don't believe it. I'm just not sure. It does seem a heck of a weird thing that this ancient bit of history about some people in Egypt is supposed to somehow affect an Aussie girl now.'
'Yea but that would be the same with reading the stars, or worshipping stones. It all goes back to ancient stories and distant civilisations. People love old stuff. Except the Bible, then they just have this blind spot.'
She bites and chews, thinks for a while, then stops and turns to him.
'Why d'you teach the Bible?'
'It's a temporary job. Pays a few bills.' A pause. He sighs. 'No, all right, I do it 'cause I think it matters. It's in my blood. Got the gene from my old man. Plus it freaks me out that so few people bother to read it or try to understand it. All those myths about how it's just full of violence and totally contradictory. Get a life. Makes me wanna punch a wall.'
'I ain't never seen you angry like this,' Blue says.
'You ain't seen much. I need another beer.'
'No you don't you need to tell me how Moses ends up making a bronze snake.'
'Some other time.'
'I made you mad didn't I?'
'Nope.'
He gets up, walks on. She follows. Says nothing for a while.
She can't keep her mouth closed forever though. 'We could have just stayed in Paris and called him,' she says.
'Who?'
'Jim Carlyle.'
'JACK Carlyle.'
'Oh yea, Jack. Would have been cheaper. Plus we could have then checked on Charlie MacManus, made sure he was still breathing.'
'Yea well, I made a bad choice. I hate making decisions.'

'And you're short-sighted.'
'Bang on. What about you?'
'20/20 vision.'
'I didn't mean that. I meant your faults.'
'I told you, I don't have any imperfections.'
'And there we have it. Right there. The first one. Glaring as daylight.'
'What?'
'You're just too darn humble.'

Thirty six

Anya's tempted to break in. She has an old credit card and she's pretty sure there's no deadlock on the door. With a little manipulation, and a quick slide and push technique with the card, she'll be in Aretha's flat in seconds. Failing that she has a small tension wrench and a rake made from a couple of large twisted paper clips which, with a little careful handling, will pick the lock anyway. But either way she'll be making trouble. And she doesn't need that. She doesn't need to break in. She needs to meet Ben Brooks. So she can wait. There is no one coming or going in the corridor. No witnesses. She takes out her phone, checks again that no one else is around and then presses buttons.
'Suzie? Anya. I know but listen, this is important. You're gonna like this. That journalist bitch that Cortez has? She could be more valuable than we thought.'

*

'We have no idea that this treasure hunt will lead us to your lady Kiss Kiss Bang Bang, do we?'
'Don't call her that, Blue.'
'Why? What's she to you?'
'Just a friend.'
'Just a friend? I thought you didn't know her.'
'I told you, we…'
'Yea, yea, met once or twice, yadda yadda yadda…'

*

Anya strolls around Aretha's room, picking up objects and putting them down again. She has a feline way about her, like a large, sleek cat. She does this for a full two minutes. Ben watches, neither says anything.

*

'So, wasn't that a heck of a coincidence? I mean you must have got a shock.'
'What d'you mean?'
'When Ben Brooks told you she was his girlfriend.'
'He didn't tell me, he showed me a picture.'
He pulls the shot from his pocket. Looks at it, as if it might have suddenly faded. Shows it to her.
Blue laughs, a good-natured, knowing kind of laugh.
'What?' he asks.
'Ben Brookes may have been fooled, but I'm a girl, you can't fool me.'

*

'I did some research,' Anya says softly. Her voice almost a purr. 'I spent a long time looking at web pages and asking around and following up leads and looking up stories. Nothing's private anymore you know, everything's out there somewhere.'
She holds up a copy of *The Hunger Games*, twists it in her hands. Ben frowns, turns away and stares at the picture of the winged serpent. It has piercing red eyes, flickers of flame in them. Unnaturally large, but then the whole picture's a caricature.
'This friend of yours, this guy you sent looking for your girlfriend, what was his name again…'
Ben says nothing, intends to give nothing away here.
'Oh yes,' she says, holding up a long finger, 'Max Maguire. Interesting guy. How long you known him?'
He says nothing. At least nothing in answer to that question.
'You said you wanted to meet me about Aretha,' he says, tight-lipped.
'Just tell me what you want so we can get this out of the way.' Then he stops. Turns and stares at her, his eyes narrow behind his glasses. 'He's not dead is he? Max? He hasn't been killed?'
She can't resist a smile. 'Not yet. No. Not yet, Mr Brooks.' She puts down the book and picks up a pair of discarded jeans. She's enjoying this,

starting to feel like Suzie Kruger. She folds the jeans and lays them on the bed.

'Not that tidy is she? Your girlfriend.'

'What do you want from me?'

Anya holds out her hands. 'This,' she says, looking around, 'this conversation.'

She picks up copies of *Red* and *Cosmopolitan*. 'D'you know where she is? Your girlfriend? What's her name by the way, Anita?'

'Aretha.'

'Oh yes. Aretha. Aretha Franklin. *Say a Little Prayer*... maybe you should say a little prayer for your girlfriend. Have you done that?'

He doesn't reply. Of course he has, every hour of every day since she went missing.

'Do you know where she is?' he asks.

It's Anya's turn to keep schtum.

'Where is Max Maguire now?' she says instead. 'Do you know?'

'He works in a theological college, he's a teacher,' he says.

'Yes I know. Must have been a slap in the face. International adventurer ends up marking homework and giving out detention.' She laughs.

He says, 'I don't know what he did before.'

'Really? So you had no idea about the tales of derring-do and the missions to save the world?'

He shakes his head. 'I told you, I don't know anything about that.'

'Did you know he has history with your girlfriend?'

*

Max is saying nothing. He's sitting on the fence. It hurts more than he thought.

'That's why you took the job, wasn't it?' says Blue. 'Ben showed you this picture and you're still in love with her.'

'I'm not in love with her.'

'But that's why you took it, wasn't it? If his girlfriend was Aretha Franklin you wouldn't be doing this.'

'If his girlfriend was Aretha Franklin I'd be very surprised. She's seventy.'

'You know what I'm saying.'

*

'You'd have thought he would have tired of it now,' Anya purrs on.

'Tired of what?' says Ben.
'Rescuing her.'
'What do you mean?'
'He saved her life once already. Oh! Didn't you know that?'

*

'You saved her life already? How many chances does this girl need?'
Max shakes his head. 'Wasn't like that.'
'Oh it wasn't like that? So what was it like then?'
Max stops walking, he does it so abruptly she bumps into him. He points to an apartment way up on the fifth floor.
'That's it,' he says. 'Andre Alvarez's flat. Seer number nine.'
'Sheez, you'll do anything to avoid answering eh?'
Max points again.
'We should see if he's in.'

*

Ben Brooks drops onto Aretha's bed. He stares at the carpet tiles. There's a dark stain that pools at the junction where four blue tiles meet. Red wine probably. Aretha drinks a lot of it. Ben creases his eyes as he stares at it, as if it's a magic eye picture and if he looks long enough at it all will become clear. He hadn't seen this coming. Not at all. Anya can't resist a sly smile, but she doesn't show it to him.
'You see Ben, you're too trusting. You thought the guy was just going after your girlfriend for you. Maybe he's going after her for something else. Maybe you'll never see either of them again.'
'But I started it. He didn't want to help. I got him involved. He had no idea who she was…'
'What changed his mind? If he didn't want to help. Why did he suddenly do a u turn?'
Ben frowns, thinks. Says slowly, 'I showed him a picture.'
Anya snapped her fingers. 'And there you have it.'
She sits beside him on the bed, becomes far more understanding. Her voice softens.
'It's a bad world, Ben. A bad world. I'm sorry this has happened to you. That's why I wanted to talk to you. I can get to Max, I can get Aretha back to you. But you gotta help me here. I need some clues as to where he might be.'

Ben stares into space. What to do? Who to trust? Who is this woman anyway?

*

He stops on the steps of the white apartment building, pulls Blue back. 'Hang on,' he says. 'I meant to do this earlier. Got your phone there?'
She tuts and pulls it out, hands it to him.
'Can you do it? Just message Ben Brooks again, tell him… whatever you want. Not too much though. Just say we're narrowing the options, something like that.'

*

Somewhere in the background *Only The Horses* by Scissor Sisters is playing. A distant tinny sound. As if they're encased in a steel box that isn't quite soundproofed.
Ben licks his lips. This has thrown him, this woman can't be trusted he's sure, but she knows so much about Max, way more than he knows. Why did he trust that guy? Because he threw a bin bag of trash at three muggers? Was that enough? The Scissor Sisters song plays on. She nudges him.
'Ben,' Anya says softly, he looks at her.
She nods towards his jacket pocket.
'I think that's your phone. Might be important.'
He snaps out of it and pulls it from his pocket. *Only The Horses* get a little louder. It's a text. He presses buttons and cuts off the music. He gives a wry snort of a laugh.
'It's him,' he says.
Her eyes light up. 'Really? Good timing,' she says, all friendly like. 'What's he say?'
Ben reads the message. Licks his lips again.
'He's in Madrid. Looking for some guy called Andre Alvarez. Ever heard of him?'
'Nope, but it'll be good to meet him.' She stands up. 'Ben, look after yourself mate. I got to go. Here.' She grabs a magazine and rips off a corner, scribbles her number on the torn strip. 'If you want to talk more. Call that. Remember, I'm here to help.'
'Where are you going now?'

'Where d'you think? Madrid. I'm gonna find Max for you. And sort out this whole mess.'

Thirty seven

'Andre Alvarez? Do you have a few minutes? We need to talk to.'
The little man in front of him looks uncertain. His flitting green eyes, his nervous cough, the arms folded and shoulders hunched.
'I'm busy at the moment. Who are you? I don't know you do I?'
'No, we've not met. But I'm trying to find someone and the search has led me here.'
His green eyes burst wide. 'Here? What... why?'
'Can I come in?'
He looks at Max, then past him to Blue, who's loitering at Max's elbow. She throws him one of her grins but it doesn't work, she might as well have handed him a severed head.
'I don't think so...'
Max turns to Blue, mutters in her ear. She purses her lips, kicks at the floor.
'I suppose,' she says.
Max gestures with his head back along the corridor.
She saunters off, not even giving Alvarez one of her goodbye waves.
'I know this may be delicate Mr Alvarez...'
'I don't know what you mean.'
'I believe this has something to do with the Nehushtan snake.'
'Pardon?'
'The bronze serpent. You have a piece of it?'
Alvarez frowns, scratches his head.
'I've never heard of the... what d'you call it?'
'The Nehushtan snake.'
He grimaces and shakes his head. 'Some old relic... not my kind of thing Mr Maguire.
'Then why are you on a list of the Nehushtan Seers?'
'The what? Seers? I'm not any kind of seer. I think you have the wrong man.'
'Look, can I come in?'

Alvarez looks as if he is going to say anything but yes. He glances back into his own apartment. It is dark in there.
'Why can't we talk here?'
'Because I think you're gonna die.'
Alvarez's face is already white, but it manages to blanche a little more.
'Your life is in danger. This list I have, it's like a hit list. If you don't talk to me you're gonna die. It's up to you.'
Alvarez looks back into the gloom of his apartment again. Max waits. The other man steps back and makes room for him to walk in. The air is thick with smoke and the room inside dimly lit by red bulbs. Whatever the walls are painted it's dark. The place is tidy though. Sparsely furnished with a huge flat screen television on one wall.
Alvarez waves him to a leather couch.
'Do you know Jack Carlyle?' Max asks him.
'Why?'
'Cause he knows you.'
Silence. Alvarez lights up a cigarette. The odour's pungent, fills the air in the apartment quickly with its own trademark smell. Max never really smoked. A few ciggies with the lads at school but it never caught on for him, peer pressure was never a big thing - he didn't spend enough time with his peers. Alvarez offers him the packet but he shakes his head.
'Why am I in danger?' Alvarez asks, the words spilling out reluctantly.
'Because of this snake you claim to know nothing about. Whether or not you do in one sense is immaterial. There is a certain group of people with violence on their minds. They intend to get the pieces of the snake back together, whatever it takes. And if you're on this list, sooner or later they'll come looking for you.'
Max takes time to glance around the room. As he grows accustomed to the light he sees that much of the red glow emanates from one corner of the room. A table with photographs, cards and letters carefully arranged on it. One or two items of clothing too, a scarf, some shoes, a folded top. A string of lights traces a line around the items and some red candles punctuate the display. Alvarez notices Max's interest.
'Someone I cared about,' he says.
Max walks over to it.
'Please, don't touch anything.'

A woman in her thirties, framed shots of her, cards and notes signed by *Carmen*. Ornate handwriting, letters formed lovingly, not scrawled like his own. In the flickering light the images in the photos almost look as if they are moving.
'I cannot go anywhere,' Alvarez says.
His accent is local.
'Because of her?'
'No. Because of me. I just don't go out.'
'So you'll stay here and wait for them to come.'
He shrugs. 'They may not come. You may be lying.'
'And the snake? Am I lying about that?'

Thirty eight

A knock at the door. Blue's back.
'Sorry,' Max mutters, 'she's not the most patient of women.'
Anders is agitated. 'I don't want her in here, she might mess things up.'
Max considers, 'I'll tell her to take a walk,' he says.
A second knock. He's not wrong about the lack of patience.
He reaches for the latch, notices there are five locks on the door. He swings it back, gets that feeling you get when you see someone you never expected to see in that place at that time. A certain disorientation. Familiarity because you know them, bewilderment because they shouldn't be in front of you right now. She smiles. The cold eyes, the black hair, the viper teeth. He does the obvious. Drops straight onto his haunches, twists, rolls and slams the door as he goes. There's an almighty explosion as the bullet smashes through the wood. Somewhere behind him Andre Alvarez screams. Is it pain or just anguish? He can't tell. A second bullet slams through the wood and over Max's head. He reaches up, pushes home three of the locks before her foot connects with the door. When it does the thing is tight and bolted. A little give in it but it's holding. He jams home the other two locks and, crawling low, makes his way back inside Alvarez's apartment. The little guy is as pale as hell. He's pressing himself against the far wall, his eyes wide. Like a nocturnal Tarsier. He has dread etched all over his bleached face. Max indicates with the flat of his hand for him to drop to the floor. Alvarez inches down the wall. There is another thud as

Suzie Kruger's boot connects with the door again. Then another. The kicks speed up into a quick rhythm and Max figures the door won't stand too much more.
'You got a back door?' he asks.
Alvarez nods, his eyes still wide to bursting. 'I ain't leaving though.'
Max grabs his hand and peels him off the wall like a piece of flung spaghetti. He hauls him back through the flat. There is a kitchen with spotless surfaces and shiny pans hanging from ceiling racks. Not a dish out of place. No stains, no sign that anyone ever cooks in there. At the far end there is another door. Heavily bolted. Max props Alvarez against the wall and starts sliding bolts. The Spaniard stands there cowering and shaking his head repeatedly.
'Key,' says Max, 'I need a key for this mortise lock.'
Thud. Crack. The rhythmic kicking reaches its climax, the front door splinters. Alvarez looks past Max back towards the red-lit lounge and the shrine to his lost love.
'Key!' yells Max, shaking him by the shoulder.
Alvarez raises his arm stiffly and points like Frankenstein's monster towards a slot in the white brick wall, just past Max's shoulder. Max slides his hand in, pulls out a ring with a single key on it. Pushes it into the slot and twists. Crack. A second splintering sound and another thud as the front door bursts open. At the same time the back door swings back. Max grabs Alvarez, but the guy keeps shaking his head and hugging the wall.
'I can't go out there,' he pleads.
'You can, you have to.'
'I can't.'
'You have no idea what that woman will do to you,' says Max.
'It's a woman?'
Max grabs him while he's wrong-footed. Tears him from the spot and shoves him ahead through the door. There are footsteps coming at them and a third shot rings out. Wooden fragments spit at Max from the doorframe, splinters shower his right eye. Alvarez yelps. Turns back, staring and frozen to the spot.
'Move!' Max barks. 'Now.' But he won't.
'Move!' he yells again.
Suzie Kruger's in the kitchen, her boots clattering on the slate tiled floor.
'I wouldn't,' she says. 'Not if you want to keep breathing.'

Three shots, she got three shots off earlier, whatever she's firing there's most likely two rounds, maybe even three left. If it's a Glock then more. Either way it's enough to finish them both.

'How did you find us?' Max asks quietly, without turning to face her.

'No, no. I ask the questions,' Suzie purrs. 'Now turn around and come back in.'

Max turns to face her. Alvarez doesn't need to, he's already staring back into the room, his green bug eyes practically out on stalks. The problem is he can't do more than that. He's going nowhere, in or out. He's stuck to the spot, all his demons colliding in his head all at once, rendering him impotent.

'I said, come back in.' The tone just a little more sinister.

No dice. Alvarez stares at her and the gun. It's a Glock 22, which means she has another twelve rounds left, but Alvarez doesn't know that. He just knows it's the kind of thing that will end his life. She lowers the pistol and aims at Max's knee. Problem. If she threatens to cripple him it'll mean nothing to Alvarez.

'One last chance, boys, back inside or Maguire sees out his days in a wheelchair.'

*

Blue nods at the doorman. No questions this time. Doesn't matter how inappropriately she's dressed, she's going in. Breezes into The Siesta like she owns the place. After all, she's now well in with the guy who does. She grins at the big guy. He nods back, no smile, just the nod. She winks and goes on in. The foyer's full of the rich and, she hopes, famous. The great and the good, a few of them ugly. But all dressed like movie stars. The women glide, the younger men strut, the older ones parade as if every one of them owns the place. Whilst they are there they do, at least in their own minds. Blue leans against a column and watches this world go by. She's the only one chewing gum, but not the only one eyeing up the guys. Plenty of the woman are doing that, with just a little more subtlety. Sidelong glances at the suits and the shirts and the chinos. Or the bodies inside. Smiling at one guy while sneak-peaking another. There's plenty of jewellery on show too, plunging necklines dotted with all kinds of glittering stones. Rolex watches, diamond bracelets, fingers dripping with rings. And all headed through the foyer to somewhere deep within the building. Which makes her wonder, does this place have a casino? A pretty little poker table somewhere? She spots a group of glittering thirty-somethings, slips in step with them and shadows them as they make their way through the foyer.

*

The gun goes off. Max drops to the floor. But he does it a second before she fires, pre-empts the strike. He twists too, away from her line of fire. His reactions are good, the bullet slips out through the door, finds some other target, hopefully not human. He shoulders Alvarez and topples him backwards, out onto the iron fire escape. He slams the door and hurls the Spaniard down the steep stairwell of narrow steps. Alvarez is moaning, making scrambling attempts to fight back, but Max is on top of his game now, he'll rugby tackle the guy all the way down to the ground floor if necessary. Not far above them the door flies open again. The stairs are all wrought-iron, so no protection, plenty of sight-lines. All he can do is keep moving, just not in the way she might expect. He staggers drunkenly from side to side, picks up Alvarez by the shoulder and bowls him down further. They're falling like drunken men, their feet barely connecting with the steps, but hopefully it makes them impossible targets. He doesn't stop to find out, any hesitation, any momentary glance upwards and either one of them will be dead. Best just to keep on staggering like fools, and when the ground comes close enough to abandon the steps altogether and throw themselves over the rail. He hears feet above him. That's good, a hopeful sign. If she's running she's not aiming. No matter how practised she is to have any chance of bringing them down she needs a steady hand. Max is guessing she'll want to take him out. Alvarez is a soft target anyway, it's only Max driving this thing forward right now. He pushes on, bounces off the rails left and right, the bruises building up as he goes, he reaches Alvarez and bats him on again. The guy hunches and falls and rolls. Hopefully he won't break his neck before the bottom. The ground is close enough now, if he can hoist Alvarez over the handrail and push him down then he can jump and follow and they'll be on solid ground. The feet above him have stopped running. Not so good. Maybe she's figured it too, waiting for him to jump off, gun poised, so she can wing him as he goes.

Thirty nine

The Gran Casino Siesta. It announces itself as they emerge from the broad, swooping corridor into the lights and the music and the noise of the slot machines. Astonishing. Like a piece of Vegas tucked away here in Madrid. There are croupiers everywhere, waitresses with trays of drinks, and men and women pouring good money after bad around the roulette, black jack and poker tables.
Poker is not really about the cards. It's about the people. And the bluffing. The ability to lie well with an honest face. A poke face. But mostly it's about the people. Learning to read them quickly after only having played a couple of hands with them. The beauty of the game is that you can bluff like hell and still get away with it, even if you lose. Because you can throw in a hand and have your opponent never know whether you had anything good at all. And if you do that for three successive hands, whatever your cards, you begin to feel powerful. Blue does anyway. She'll lull them into a false sense of security. Throw away money doing it, and get a kick out of the experience. That's her secret. She's young, bulletproof and loves every second. She never gets scared and her skyscraper confidence wins her money time after time. Very few people get flushes or straights. And certainly not three or four players in the same hand. Most hands are won with a couple of jacks, ace high if you're lucky, or maybe three tens, or two pairs. But you don't need a handful of royalty to win out. You just need to be better than your opponent, and unless they're playing in a movie the chances are they have a couple of twos and a stray king. And all you have to do is make them believe that's not good enough. Then they'll throw in, and you collect big time without ever having to show your hand. She's won with nothing at all on many occasions, just scared the hell out of the opposition, that's what she was doing on the train, admittedly it was easier with half-cut guys who had barely lifted a deck of cards before. These folks might be rich and glamorous, but the principal remains the same. Bluff, bluff, bluff. She has a good face for that. Pretty enough to be disarming, bright, confident eyes, and a well-practised steady expression. To Blue the bluffing is everything, and knowing when your opponent is likely to be doing it. Knowing how far their nerves will take them. Grasp that and you're onto a winner.

She stands and surveys the casino, she can barely resist rubbing her hands. This won't be easy, these people play a lot, but that's what makes it so appealing.

She weaves her way through the bodies, gets some looks from the elegant and beautiful, till eventually a suited croupier steps in her path. He's incredibly goodlooking, and even more so when he smiles. He smiles now but he's built like Hadrian's Wall and is going nowhere. He leans forward, places his lips close to her ear.
'Madam, you're very welcome. I know you're a guest of Mr Carlyle. You might just want to reconsider your dress, we do have a code here.'
Blue glances deliberately down at her jeans and boots. She doesn't need to look, she knows exactly what she's wearing but she might as well make a point of doing it. She beckons to him and places her lips so close to his cheek they brush it as she moves them.
'I don't have a posh frock,' she says slowly, her accent at its drawling best. He smiles and straightens. 'We do,' he says and he beckons to a waitress.

*

Max presses himself and Alvarez into the one place on the stairwell that could be called a blind spot. As it is he can still see her, hovering there, the Glock extended over the rail, waiting for him to jump onto the open ground. The moment he drops she'll take him out. Then she'll search his pockets, get the list of seers, kill Alvarez and take his piece of the snake. So he does the one thing that often comes to mind in these situations – the opposite of what is expected. He abandons Alvarez and hurls himself back up the stairs towards her. He takes the steps five at a time in a series of running leaps. He's on her and punching the Glock out of her hand and over the rail before she knows he's hit her. Then he hooks his foot behind her knee and pushes her backwards. He has no idea which part of her body cracks against the iron stairs but he doesn't care. He just hears it happen as he turns and heads off back down again, scooping up Alvarez on the way, and tipping him over the rail at last. Max jumps after him, scoops up Kruger's Glock on the way and then runs him down the path, along the side of the apartment block and back out to the street and the safety they'll find amongst the crowd. As they go his mind is busy. How did she track him down? Who told her? Who even knew where he was?

*

She would not have picked it, though it fits remarkably well, and may be the most expensive item of clothing she ever wears. A Roland Mouret number. Red. Makes her look like some scarlet mermaid, sleek at the waist, with the 'tail' flaring around her ankles. She insisted on the red one. If she was leaving her crimson boots behind then she wanted compensation. It's most likely a little much with her fiery hair but no way was she going for the black. She didn't want to look like cat woman out there, thanks very much. These heels are killers but if they get her to the right table for a winning streak, who cares. She perches on the seat. Calls for a glass of coke and eyes the competition. Some guy with a huge beard, a red nose and a habit of not blinking. A woman with a world of freckles in a silver dress a size too small, hoping no doubt to distract the others with her chest area. Late thirties maybe, still doing well on it, but pushing her luck with that dress.
Next to her a thin-faced nervous guy, tiny square glasses, with cropped hair in a carefully waxed designer mess. And this guy, now approaching, a guy with a cane, distinguished, lean, with the kind of expression that could veer between savagery and benevolence. His white suit is immaculate. He moves slowly, seats himself carefully at the table. A minder hovers a few feet behind, but doesn't dare to interfere with his struggle to sit down. The drinks arrive, champagne for Ms Freckles in the silver dress, Jack Daniels for the guy with the tiny square glasses, a beer for non-blinking big beard, Perrier for the guy with cane. The croupier deals. Burns the first card. Discards it and deals two cards to each of the players. Blue can feel the surge of adrenalin. Win or lose, she'll never forget tonight.

*

It's difficult to keep moving because Alvarez won't straighten or look up, in fact he won't face front. Keeps insisting on shading his eyes and turning his body away from the crush of people. Max has a serious dilemma. The guy clearly hates the great outdoors and the crowds that go with it. But if he takes him somewhere secluded and Suzie Kruger follows them she'll finish them off. Right now people are their salvation. He pushes him on in the direction of The Siesta. He has no idea whether Alvarez will be allowed in, but if Jack Carlyle is his buddy and they're both Nehushtan Seers then it's his best bet. And they'll be inside, away from the crowd, but

still have plenty of witnesses around. Max glances back. Between the faces of the partygoers, tourists and late night commuters, he can see her. Kruger. Her head darting left to right, clearly not sure if she is heading in the right direction, but pushing on anyway, and by some dark coincidence, getting it right. Max turn to Alvarez, pulls his face up to his own.
'Listen to me, we're going to Jack Carlyle's hotel. Okay? You'll feel better inside, but you have to move faster. That woman, the one with gun, she's still on our tail, and she's not a quitter. Believe me. But if we make it to the hotel I can find you a quiet corner where you can hide all night. But you gotta move faster. Okay?'
Alvarez blinks at him. There is sweat all over his face.
'Okay?' Max says again.
The other man clears his throat, it sounds as if its thick with phlegm, his breath is rattling as its fights its way through the clogged oesophagus. He still says nothing, but doesn't drop his head or twist away. Max turns him in the right direction and hurries him on. It was worth the pause and the lost time. They're making better progress. They keep bumping bodies but that's a good thing. Another glance back. Kruger is still coming, still craning her neck to spot them. Max pushes on.

*

They all throw in chips. The guy with the tiny square glasses folds, but the rest are in. The dealer burns another card and places 'the flop' in the middle of the table. That's three cards face up. A ten, a two and a seven. Blue checks her hand again. It's as it was before. A nine and a six. She wonders about folding. If an eight appears on the table she'll have a straight. Six through to ten. She's never had a straight, might be worth the risk. The dealer burns another card and deals 'the turn'. A fourth card face up alongside the other three. It's another seven.

*

She'll see them when they mount the steps to The Siesta, there's no way of avoiding that. They'll be elevated and it'll take too long to get through the doors, especially if the hulk on the doorway stops them for an interview. But they have no choice, Alvarez is a liability outside. He hauls him on, reminding himself of the time he was dragged by the scruff of the neck to the headmaster's office. Somehow it's just like that, manhandling Alvarez all the way to the best Hotel in Spain. They make the steps, Max glances back. Kruger's still on their tale. He starts up the broad sweeping marble steps. The big guy on the door has spotted them and is making towards them. Max looks back. Kruger's surely seen them, but something is distracting her, taking her attention towards the ground. She's looking down, searching for something. Max pushes on up, surprises the doorman with the speed he is going, slams a hand on his chest and swings him out of the way like he's a huge door on a hinge. They're at the entrance, the big doorman calling after them, Max looks back. Kruger's in the crowd, fumbling with something. She's not watching them. They go in.

*

Suzie's phone is ringing. Here, now, on the verge of catching Maguire someone is calling her. She tears it from her pocket, looks at the name, gets ready to blast the caller.
'Anya! What the hell...'
'I got news. Did you get my text?'
'Not really. I'm a little busy right now.'
'Well drop what you're doing because he's in Madrid.'
'Who?'
'Maguire. I've been trying to tell you.'
'I know.'
'What?'
'I know. I'm after him right now. Get off the damn phone.'

*

Anya stares at her mobile. Then she turns and stares at the departure board. Then she turns and stares at her airport cappuccino. Then she stares at the photo on the table.
She doesn't have to go back. She could stay in the UK. Miss the flight and disappear into the darkness. Find a new life and open a manicure shop in Wales. Date the local guys, get a German shepherd and join *lovefilm*. What's the alternative? More abuse from Suzie Kruger. More killing. Further attempts to exorcise her past by destroying someone else's future. Does she want that? Does she want to be another Suzie Kruger? She did once. She thought that vicious ambition and cold blooded murder could somehow expurgate her demons. Now she's not so sure. She sits there for a long time, letting her coffee go cold and staring at the picture of Anya Zeus.

Forty

The old guy with the cane sits there like a granite statue. No emotion, no reaction. Nothing. She wonders why he's even bothering to play, he seems to get so little from the experience. And he's clearly filthy rich already. Maybe too much excitement would kill him. He's certainly frail. The dealer burns another card, slips it to one side and reaches for the fifth card, 'the river.' If this is an eight she's laughing. First ever straight she's had in a game. He's turning the card slowly, too slowly. Come on. Be an eight. Be an eight. Be an eight. It's a six. The croupier places it beside the other four. The non-blinking beard guy drops out. That leaves just Blue, the cane guy and Ms Freckles. The woman throws in a couple more chips, Blue hesitates. She has two pairs now with the sevens in the middle and her own six to add to the one on the table. That's two pairs, sixes and sevens, ten high. Not great. And everyone gets the pair of sevens anyway, they're right there for the taking on the table, so she's only bringing a six. That's it. So the question now is, does Ms Freckles have something better, or is she just confident that this girl in the mermaid dress will fold and give up? The croupier clears his throat politely. Blue takes a sip of coke. She thinks, winks at the croupier and folds. Tosses away her cards, face down. The guy with the cane throws in more chips to see the woman. Time for the showdown. The woman lays down her hand and pulls three cards out of the five community cards in the middle. Blue smiles. She has a two and a jack. With the sevens and the two on the table that's a couple of pairs, jack high. But Blue's sixes would have shot her twos down no problem. The guy with the cane nods. Lays down his hand. He has two eights. He's cleaning up. No argument there, his eights would have kicked Blue's sixes into touch. Blue's beginning to get the lie of the land. They play four more hands. Blue doesn't gamble much and folds each time, watches the others. The woman is a real trier, nerves of steel, but her face is animated. She's enjoying herself and that's fine by Blue. Let it all out lady, it tells Blue plenty. The bearded guy looks like he's never come across the word bluff. He's either got a good hand or he's throwing in. The guy with the steel glasses is more complex. Sometimes he's bluffing big style, others he's taking no chances. The dealer deals another hand. Blue picks up, two kings. A no brainer. She's in. The flop goes down, the first three community cards. Nothing interesting. A four, a six and a two. They all throw in a few more chips. Apart from big beard who folds and drops out. Steel glasses doesn't, he's up for winning this one. The woman in the silver dress too. The guy with the cane, for the first time, folds. More chips go down, the fourth card appears. An eight. No problem. Blue's staying right there. More chips. No one's folding. The final card. Bingo. A king. She can't believe it. Another king. That gives her three. Blue's laughing. No one out there can have three aces now. And she'll be the only one with three kings. She piles in more chips. Half her stash. Ms Freckles takes one look and drops out. Her face says it all. But not steel glasses. He's up for the showdown, pistols at dawn. If Blue wins, she's getting out of there. She's no sucker for gambling, in a place like this you quit while you're ahead. Max will be dead pleased.

*

'Sit there. You can do that can't you?'
Alvarez looks around, his face clammy, his eyes furtive. He nods. He's tucked away in a corner, surrounded by high-backed chairs. Max moves them in a little closer, making a protective wall. It's public enough. There are plenty of people passing by and so far no sign of Suzie Kruger. Max finds his way back to reception, glancing ever so often towards the door. The doorman appears, looking left and right, trying to track them down. No point fighting that battle. Max indicates to him. The big guy is not happy, he starts coming over. The girl behind the desk gives him her attention.
'Is Jack Carlyle around please?' says Max. 'I really need to talk to him.'
She hesitates.
'One moment, sir.'
He feels a hand on his shoulder, the doorman is there.
'Who d'you bring in?' he hisses, making attempts to keep his simmering voice down. 'And don't ever push me around like that again.'
'A friend of Mr Carlyle's. He needs to see your boss.'
The big guy scans the room. Can't see Alvarez because of the mess of bodies and furniture.
'Where is he?'
Max considers. He doesn't need to make more trouble for any of them. But right now he'd prefer to keep Andre Alvarez under wraps.
'What will you do?' he asks.

'What?'
'If I show you where he is, are you going to evict him?'
The doorman shrugs with a grimace. 'Maybe. I need to talk to him. Check he is acceptable for The Siesta.'
'Trust me, your boss is gonna want to see him.'
'No doubt, but...'
Suzie Kruger's at the door. Max taps the doorman's shoulder, points.
'She acceptable?' he asks.

*

The showdown. Blue lays down her kings. Three kings. Three sweet kings. Just like Christmas. She grins and winks at the steel glasses guy. He doesn't smile back. He lays down his cards, frowning as he goes. A seven and a five. Doesn't look like much. Doesn't look like much at all. Blue's smile starts to fade, she swaps it for the guy's frown. A seven and a five. Add that to the four, six and eight on the table and you got a straight. No one ever gets straights. Not often anyway. Not in the smoky backrooms where she normally plays. Not against a bunch of drunk guys in the last carriage of a night train. The guy leans forward and scoops chips. She can't believe it, she had a sure winner and she lost. Blue's down to half her money. No one else takes much notice. The croupier is dealing again. The machine goes on. Damn. That wasn't supposed to happen. She was supposed to be up and out of there now, cashing those chips and off to find Max. Not now though, now she needs to keep playing. More chips go down. Here we go again. Time to raise the bar a little.

*

There is just one problem. Anya knows where the pieces of the fiery serpent are. Suzie does not. Kruger gave them to her, and she hid them. If she doesn't go back Kruger has every reason to come looking for her. And if she texts her to tell her where the pieces are stashed Kruger will suspect she's running out on her. On the other hand, it's a bargaining chip. As long as Anya is the only one who knows their whereabouts she has a weapon.

*

Blue wins the next hand. Easy. Too easy really. She has two queens and combines them with a third on the table. She collects the chips, not a huge pile, no one was risking that much and big beard and square glasses dropped out pretty quick. Another three hands go by. The guy with the cane wins them all. Though no one has any idea what he had in his hand. He raises the stakes and scares the others, pushing the bets up so high that they all fold. Any one of them might have won in a showdown, but there isn't one. The guy has nerves of steel. Blue's getting low on cash now. She has to start winning. Dig deep girl, dig deep. Find that place of power. The croupier deals. She has a seven and a two. Both diamonds. She bets. The others follow. The flop goes down. Three cards, all low, three, six, eight. No pictures. A diamond and two hearts. Not looking good. Blue stays in. Big beard drops out. Ms Freckles is in though and square glasses too. And of course the unflinching guy with the cane. The fourth card goes down. Blue's heart rate picks up. Ms Freckles frowns. Square glasses raises his eyebrows. Is he suppressing a smile? Suddenly this is looking good for Blue. It's a four. But more importantly, it's a diamond. With the two cards in her hand and the other diamond on the table she's one card from cleaning up. She raises the stakes. She has a good feeling about this. Ms Freckles stays in. Square glasses folds. The guy with the cane stays in too. Blue holds her breath. Time for the fifth card. The river. The croupier is peeling it back. It's red. Definitely red. He lays it down, his hand masking it for a second. Blue's stopped breathing. She realises this when he takes his hand away. She sighs. It's a heart. So close. So very close. No, hang on. It's not. It's a diamond. A nine. She's got a flush. Five diamonds. Two in her hand, three on the table. Two, three, four, seven and this nine. She's laughing. She pushes half her pile of chips into the middle. Ms Freckles pulls out. So it's just Blue and the guy with the cane. He matches her bet. Then raises it. It's not difficult for him. Small change really. She matches him, pushing everything she's got into the middle. Every last chip she has. If this comes off she'll be back in the money. She glances up, catches his eyes for the first time. He looks weary. And sad. Not really a worthy opponent somehow. But there's something else – his eyes are hiding something. Like there's another man behind this impassive poker player, an unscrupulous shadowy figure, darkness lurking behind the mask. She shivers, forgets the cards for a second. The croupier clears his throat again, he's good at that. Used to reminding his players that there's a game on.

*

Suzie Kruger has entered The Siesta and is walking towards Max. There's no sign of the Glock but that doesn't mean trouble is not brewing. Her face is hard and glistening from the chase. Her black hair flaring slightly as a result of the speed she's moving. She's within six steps when the doorman steps between them, hand on her shoulder. He leans forward and speaks softly to her. She doesn't take her eyes off Max for a second. She stands her ground, stares at him and eventually gives a barely perceptible nod. Then she turns on her heel and takes off. Max breaths out. Stays there watching, making sure she leaves. He walks to the huge glass doors after she has slithered through them. Watches her melt away into the evening crowd. When he turns back the doorman is right there, within an inch of his face.

'We don't want any trouble here, sir,' he says, 'now I need to see the man you brought in.'

Max nods and walks back to the corner, the high-backed chairs are still there, hemming Alvarez in. But as he walks Max is thinking, there's something gnawing at his mind, something about that exchange between the doorman and Suzie Kruger. He has no idea what was said, too far away, but it was the body language. Like the big guy wasn't talking to a disruptive stranger. Like they'd met before and exchanged whispered words on previous occasions. Max slows down, wants to give himself more time.

*

Blue licks her lips. She's not normally this obvious about a good hand, but then she doesn't normally play in a glitzy casino like this. Normally she gets winning hands in surroundings far more shabby. The guy with the cane is as neutral as ever. The others look disinterested, biding their time, waiting for their chance to scoop some cash. The guy with the cane hasn't moved. He's looking across the table at her, as if he's making a mental note. Reserving the right to stretch her nerves to the maximum. Taking in every detail of his opponent, storing the information away for use at a later date.

*

The doorman is talking to himself, muttering into his headset. Max stops, looks at him.

'I have just spoken to Mr Carlyle,' he says, his hand covering the tiny dot of a microphone, 'he wants you both to see him. Now.'
Max nods. Walks on. For a moment he half expects Alvarez to have passed out from the shock. Or worse, have disappeared altogether. But he's there. Clammy, wide-eyed, his hands clutching the arms of the chair so firmly his knuckles are white. Max leans into him.
'We have a quiet room for you,' he says, 'I'll stick with you but this guy has to show us the way. You can do that? You can manage that?'
Alvarez nods repeatedly, making little stiff movements, his neck taught with tension. Max helps him up. The doorman says something else into his headset, turns and leads the way. Max doesn't like this but there is no choice.

Forty one

The showdown. Blue lays down her cards first. A seven and a two to go with the three four and nine on the table. All diamonds. Perfect. A glorious red flush. Match that mister. He stares at her, glances once at her hand, then back up to hold her gaze. She's tempted to wink but something about the hint of cruelty there stops her. He lifts the cards in his hand, tears his eyes away from her to study them. Smiles, pauses and takes hold of the first card. A chill grips her heart. He's got a five and seven. That's all he needs – a straight to beat her and take all her money. Max'll kill her. He lifts his cards, prepares to lay them down and destroy her naïve hopes. How could she ever think she'd win in a place like this? She's way out of her league. Everything slows down, he places his cards on the table one at a time and she watches it all in slow motion, her poker face long since discarded. He lays them down, his two cards. But something's not right. They're the wrong way up. Just showing the backs. He's throwing down. He's folding. Pulling out. She can't believe it. Looks up, directly at him, he shakes his head and gives her a slight nod of defeat. Capitulating. Her mouth drops. Ms Freckles nods towards the pile of chips, urging her to clear the winnings. She reaches in and does so. Grabs the handful and stands up. She gives the croupier the biggest grin and nods at the other players. Suddenly she's very happy to be out of there.

*

Another office. Carlyle appears to have dozens of them scattered about the best hotel in Spain. He has a chair prepared for Alvarez, carefully positions it for him to sit in. Max stays close, hovers within inches of the wreck of a man.

'How long have you been agoraphobic, Andre?' Carlyle asks, offering him confectionary from another box of Turkish Delight.

Alvarez stares at the box as if it contains explosives. Eventually he reaches for it and grips a handful of the white dusted chunks.

'Since she went,' he says through a mouthful of goo. He inhales the sugar as he speaks and it makes him cough a little.

'Since who went?'

'My wife. You love something and you lose it. You can never rely on anything again. Nothing is solid. Everything shifts. Keep your world small and at least you can see when it shakes a little.'

Alvarez glances around at this new world, this huge world, this vast place of expensive wood and opulent decors, jammed with music and people and money and noise. So many unreliable variables. So many dangerous possibilities. How could you ever sit in a place like this and feel at home?

Carlyle watches him, nods slowly. Max gestures to Carlyle, approaches him, slipping around another vast desktop. The doorman is still there, immobile by the door. Big hands crossed in front of him, face looking like it just solidified out of a bronze cast.

Max pushes his face close to Carlyle's. Speaks quietly.

'How well do you know this guy then?' he asks.

Carlyle shakes his head. 'I know of most people around here. It's my job to keep an ear to the ground, Mr Maguire, very good for business. But he and I have never really shared the time of day.'

'Then how do you know he's agoraphobic?'

Carlyle smiles, but there's little warmth in it.

'Because I meet a lot of people in The Siesta. Not all of them are glamorous and successful, Mr Maguire. Some of them have these kind of… problems. And if I might say – go careful Mr Maguire, your questions are taking an accusatory tone. Remember, you are here as my guest, as is Mr Alvarez right now.'

Max sighs, shakes his head. 'I apologise, I'm not threatening you, but you have to understand, you're both in great danger at the moment. I don't think you realise. You are dealing with professional killers here. They approach their work as you do. I'm not overstating it when I say that right at this moment either of you could end up dead.'

The sound that follows is not the kind of blast that spatters concrete and makes walls explode. It's a lot more precise. Clean. Less disruptive. Not some movie moment of planet shuddering consequence. There's no rock'n'roll score or some Bernard Herman strings to announce its coming. One moment Max is muttering to Jack Carlyle, the next there's the crack of glass and the sudden groaning sigh of a man pitching forward, folding over himself. There's a thud as the doorman dives for cover, shouldering a nearby bookcase on his way down. There's a grunt as Carlyle drops too, but Max makes no sound. He slips quietly to his haunches and stares across the plush office. The decor is not as it once was, not quite so ornate anymore. There are flecks of flesh and bone and chair-back on the wall now, along with a burst of blood and a bullet hole. A second shot rings out as the men shield their heads. Only Andre Alvarez does not move. It's pointless for him, he's already dead. The second 223 round simply slams into his exposed upper back as he slumps forward, no longer worried about the insecurity of his new surroundings, or the strange discomfort of the outside world. He has at last re-joined his wife. No need for the shrine now.

Forty two

The office window opens easily. Across the grand expanse of open grounds and gardens there are any number of trees and outbuildings. The shooter could have been anywhere, and presumably by now, nowhere. Max surveys the scene then jumps through the open window and down onto the lawn below. It's perfectly manicured. His boots leave indents in the turf as he zigzags his way across the grass, probably looks like a fool, but he wants to be a living fool by the time he reaches the other side. He hugs oak trees and ducks behind bushes, but there's no further shooting. If it was Suzie Kruger out there she only came for Andre Alvarez and having got her prize there's nothing left of the woman but blood on an office wall and a cracked window. He meanders around, looking for clues. Kicks at the grass for the cartridge shells. Nothing. Suzie Kruger knows what she's

doing. Probably uses a Vanquish. The best kind of versatile sniper rifle. Portable, simple to carry, multi-calibre. Easy to buffer it up against a tree trunk then swivel and nuzzle the bipod hard against the bark for a crack shot. Bang. One less Nehushtan Seer. There are imprints in the grass by a gleaming gazebo, could have been left there by kids or lovers, or possibly a hired assassin. Possibly. The place is quiet now. He strolls back to the hotel, doesn't duck or dive on his way, no point, other than looking an idiot for the few guests happening to peer out of their satin-draped windows.
'No joy?' Jack Carlyle says, coming around the building to meet him. He's alone, there's no sign of the doorman, or any other kind of minder.
Max shakes his head.
'We'd better get this cleared up,' he says, 'you called the cops?'
Carlyle nods. 'I'll take care of all of that. Don't you worry. I've got people on it.' He sighs and shakes his head. 'Can't quite believe someone like Alvarez was one of the seers. Doesn't match up somehow.'
'Someone figured it did. Ever come across a woman called Kruger? Suzie Kriger?'
Carlyle thinks.
'Doesn't ring a bell.'
'Well, you should check out your door guy. The one who was with us in the room. He knows her, damn sure of it. The way they were whispering sweet nothings they had some kind of history. Certain of it.'
'Did you find Alvarez's piece of the snake?'
'He never admitted having any of it. Denied being a seer.'
'Maybe he was telling the truth.'
'Why? Why wouldn't he be a seer? Cause he wasn't rich and successful, cause his life had fallen apart?'
Max sounds bitter. Carlyle presses a hand to his shoulder.
'You need a drink, my friend,' he says.
'No I don't. I need to go home and forget all this. But I can't, can I? No chance. Which reminds me, what happened to Blue, you seen her? The redhead I came here with.'
'Last I heard she was losing a fortune on the poker table.'
'Oh no. Don't say...'
'I'm sure she'll be fine. You want me to take you to the casino?'
Max shakes his head.

'I'll find my way. Look, this business with the cops, I can't waste my time embroiled in that…'
Carlyle raises a hand.
'Like I say, I have people on it. It's messy, there's no denying, but I have friends in high places here. The Siesta doesn't need a contract killing on its carpet right now. This thing will melt away. After all, whose gonna come looking for Andre Alvarez?'
Max walks away. He isn't sure he really likes that. It might be neat and tidy for them, the way an awkward wreck like Alvarez can just disappear, but it doesn't feel right. Not at all. Broke or not the guy was still flesh and blood and deserved the same kind of respect as anyone else. Max circumnavigates the building, it takes a while, which is good because it straightens him out a little, calms his mind. Then he makes for the main entrance of The Siesta again, there is a new doorman on there. Max is about to stride the steps when he changes his mind. Losing or not Blue would have to handle herself just a little longer. If there is ever going to be a good time to revisit Alvarez's apartment then now is it. No cops yet, Kruger hopefully keeping her head down for a while. He can be alone and take a proper look round. Maybe even get his hands on a piece of the snake. A snatch of the brief conversation they held on Alvarez doorstep saunters back into his mind.
'Some old relic…'
A throwaway comment by Alvarez when Max mentioned the snake, yet it showed he knew something, it clearly wasn't the first time someone had spoken to him recently about the Nehushtan serpent.

*

He takes the fire escape, the one they clambered down when Kruger was after them with the Glock, and Alvarez was still alive and struggling. Less than an hour ago. As his boots clang against the wrought iron Max ponders the last sixty minutes. His old self is kicking in, he can feel it. The thick skin creeping back over his body like an old wet suit. Clammy in places and cracked here and there, but a reliable covering all the same. He's not worn it in a long while. But the thick skin is certainly back. He put it on time and again when he needed to in the past. Under threat of death or torture, when the demons closed in, when failure looked imminent. And when men close by had their brains blown out. Particularly when men close by had their brains blown out. You had to keep going when that kind of thing happened, that was the one time when nothing could be allowed to blur his vision, not if he was to stay alive. Later in the dark he might sweat and shiver and swallow hard. Feel sick to his stomach. But not now. Now it's time to cover up and keep going.

Back through the kitchen, back to the red-lit lounge. The candles still burning at the shrine, some of them nothing but wicks floating in dead wax without Andre to revive them. Max reaches for the nearest switch, bathes the room in yellow light. How long has it been since that happened? He puts out the rest of the candles, stubs the flames with his fingers whilst clocking the pictures of Alvarez's long lost love. The place is pristine, Andre may not have seen much daylight lately but he hasn't wasted time, agoraphobia didn't come alone. Brought some close obsessive relatives. Max never liked this part, turning out other people's lives, peeling back the private layers under the guise of detective work. But if he doesn't do it Suzie Kruger will, and she'll be one step closer to completing her serpent jigsaw. How many pieces does she have now? He stops to check his list. Casper Mack at the airport, Gomez in Greece, the three guys at The Republic, Sanchez in his shack, Charles in Paris, that's seven and it may well be more. She's nearly there, and then what? He doubts the world will end because all the pieces are back in one place, but he's seen killers like Kruger driven to much further extremes when they think God's on their side. The fall is not far. A person can turn into the devil overnight once they start believing they have some kind of divine power in their fist.

The cupboards are easily searched, they're as ordered and tidy as the rest of the place. The drawers too, minimal clothes, few books, barely any ornaments around. Just a colossal DVD collection to compliment the flat screen TV. Movies from a century back, when dialogue appeared on shaky cards punctuating the flickering black and white footage. Classics from the thirties and forties, and on into the more memorable decades and the advent of Spielberg and Lucas and the omnipresent blockbuster. He had everything, everything from *The Battleship Potemkin* and *Metropolis* to *Schindler's List* and *The Artist*. From silent black and white all the way through talkies and Technicolor to silent black and white again. When Jack Carlyle looked at Andre Alvarez he saw nothing but the wreckage of a life, but there's always more to people than that. Max has learnt that. Most people put out a two dimensional version of themselves, they learn through the bad times that three dimensions are too much, too dangerous. Three dimensions only invite ridicule and manipulation. Best to save that reality for lovers and soul-mates, and even then only a diluted version. Alvarez may not have seemed the best bet to guard a sacred artefact but perhaps that was the perfect thing about him. Who suspects the grubby, homeless girl busking outside the job centre of being a genius? No one. Beautiful people are the ones to watch. No doubt Andre didn't concoct his disguise, life hurled it his way, but it was not a bad one for keeping out of trouble. Literally. An agoraphobic Nehushtan Seer, locked behind closed doors. It was a sure way of keeping the snake out of the limelight. So where is it? Where did he secrete the deadly serpent? The snake that killed him. Max peels back the rugs, tears open DVD cases, unzips sofa cushions. Nothing. Every so often he stops to listen for other intruders. Checks outside for any sign of Kruger coming back. But there's none. In Alvarez's bedroom the mattress is a sealed, stitched unit. He could take a knife to it, and he has one that will open it up, but he isn't convinced. He leaves the bedroom and returns to the lounge, sits down in front of the TV in a swivelling armchair. He kicks at the carpet, spins round gently as he surveys the corners of the room. And then it hits him. Obvious really. It seems barbaric to dismantle it with Alvarez himself still warm, but there is no choice. Time is short. He stands up and walks over to the shrine. Pictures, candles, scarves, ornaments, trinkets, jewellery, all those things that are absent from the rest of the apartment. It's as if Alvarez had poured that part of his life into one corner of the room. His attempt to keep his woman alive. His beloved Carmen, jammed into a few feet of crimson candles and gathered trinkets. Max begins gingerly collecting the sacramental reminders together. It's a busy landscape and takes a while to clear but there, at the heart of it all, once the layers have been peeled back, he finds a tiny chest. Complete with a padlock and a miniscule chain. A foray into the jewellery unearths a bracelet laden with charms and hearts and silver stars. And one single key. It takes some time, Max's fingers are about as dextrous as a drunken giant's, but eventually he slips it into the slot and turns it. A click and the chain falls back and the top slews open. And Max lays his eyes on a piece of Nehushtan snake. Only the second he has ever seen after that chunk on Table Mountain. He's close enough to touch this one. Not for long though.

Forty three

Maybe he is out of practice. Maybe he just isn't used to wearing that thick skin anymore. Maybe he's just getting old. Either way he never heard her approach. He has no idea how she was able to time it like that. How she was able to choose that specific moment to step up behind him, just as he was revealing the snake inside the silver chest. But there she is. A footfall, a tap on the shoulder with the muzzle of her gun, a whispered command. Two words.
'Turn around.'
Max sighs audibly. He feels like he's turning into a joke. An action has-been. How can he ever hope to win against this?
'Candy from a baby, Maguire,' she mutters. 'Candy from a baby.'
And she reaches over and takes the chest from him.
'What happened to you?' she asks.
He stares her full in the face. Suzie Kruger. The bobbed black hair, the cold eyes, the lean figure, and there it is, the cruel smile revealing the viper teeth. She hasn't changed. And that should help him. She's predictable. And it shouldn't be an advantage for her. She's the same cold, intentional killer. Ruthless, efficient. The problem is, as she has spotted, he is out of practice. He is tired and haunted. She is not, she is at the top of her game. And he will soon be dead.
She eyes him over the top of her Glock. Didn't he recently steal that from her? How did she get another so quickly? This woman is really starting to get him down.
'What happened to you?' she asks again.
Max shrugs. 'I retired,' he says.
She laughs, a harsh snort of a laugh that doesn't become her at all.
'You fool,' she says, 'you loser. How can you retire? What you gonna do, become a car park attendant? A lollipop man? Showing the kids and the old ladies across the road? I'm here to do you a favour Max, give you a noble end. If you're gonna call time on saving the world, then the best way to do it is by dying for the world. Don't you reckon? A big funeral, full honours and all that. A retrospective documentary, newspaper headlines. "How could it happen to such a nice guy?" An irreplaceable hero. What do you reckon? Ready for the afterlife?'

Max smiles, glances down at his feet. Old lessons come back to him. Don't rush a moment like this. Don't play to her rules. Keep control. He glances up and smiles wistfully.
'I've been ready for a while now,' he says, which is perfectly true.
'Not even scared a little bit?'
'Disappointed. But not scared. What's to fear?'
Her gaze never flickers, if she is afraid of death, she isn't showing it. But then, she is the one with the gun.
'Yea, I guess you've done your time,' she purrs, 'had your best shot. A bullet through the heart is better than one in the back.' She pauses, thinks. 'Isn't that in the book of Proverbs?'
That's the moment. He still has the instinct. You wait for that fraction of a second when a woman like Kruger just gets too clever, too witty. It's only a moment and easily missed, but if you catch it right you can't lose. For a splinter of time she is not quite as focussed, too impressed with herself. That's when you make a small movement with the back of the hand, nothing melodramatic, nothing that will telegraph an attack, a barely perceptible strike. But before she knows what's happened Suzie's gun is in the air and she's no longer in control. She's grabbing at space, flailing like a harpist with no instrument, and meanwhile Max is out of there, clattering down the fire escape for the second time that day, only this time he's alone and taking the steps five at a time. By the time Kruger has regained the Glock and appears at the door he is back out in the street, slipping through the crowd, using the mass of people like one seething, invisibility shield.

*

Thankfully Blue is sitting on the steps of The Siesta. He waves to her as he passes by but he doesn't stop, right now he needs to keep moving, head somewhere new, somewhere Kruger can't find him. Blue's face is a picture, grinning like a Cheshire cat. She leaps down to the street and grabs his shoulder.
'Guess what? I have so much money… I beat 'em all.'
Max doesn't smile. 'Great, let's keep moving.'
Blue stops, stands still.
'Well you could be happier, I risked everything.'
'Exactly. You risked everything. Is that wise? By the way, keep moving.'
'I won, course it's wise.'

Max scowls, keeps walking. She squeezes his shoulder as she works hard to keep up.

'Where are we going? What's happening?'

'Plenty. Andre Alvarez is dead, Kruger's in town, she nearly killed me. There are only two seers left alive. And we're no closer to finding Aretha.'

Max looks bad, his face is grey, his lips close tightly and stay clamped. She gets the feeling his worst nightmares are not far behind them.

'Don't give up,' she says, 'we can win, we have right on our side. Be cool.'

He stops, turns his head, just his head.

'What?'

'We're fighting for what's right. We're the good guys.'

'Beluga – good guys die every day. Every day! You wanna be a good guy? Get ready for the worst. Right now good guys are being tortured and beaten, they are having their houses bombed, their kids stolen, their lives ripped apart. Being in the right does not mean you ride off into the sunset. For most people it either means keeping your head down and not rocking the boat, or standing up and getting knocked down. Being in the right can cost everything. It can leave you ruined. This is not about Superman coming to save the world in his bright red pants. The bad guys can win. Right now, they are winning. Do you get it?'

She wants to say yes, she wants to nod quietly, but she has her pride. It's not in her nature.

'Is this about her?' she says.

'What?'

'Is this about your history with Little Miss Kiss Kiss?'

He looks like he might punch her lights out, he looks as if he'll be the one to knock her down right now. She forces a big grin.

'It's about everything,' he says quietly, and he turns and keeps walking.

'Well tell me about it,' she calls after him, and passers-by turn to look. 'Don't just bottle it up.'

He doesn't look back so she lets him go. If Max Maguire wants her she'll be back at The Siesta, let him come looking for her.

Forty four

Anya watches her phone buzz and shimmy across the table for the third time. She clamps a hand on it to stop it moving. It's Suzie again. She switches it off. Sooner or later she'll have to answer it. Sooner or later she'll have to bite the bullet on this one. But not yet.
People pass her by, on their way in and out of Heathrow. Oblivious to the wretched struggle going on in her mind.
The flight announcer's voice breaks across the foyer. The next flight to Washington is boarding. She takes out the picture again. Anya Zeus, still there with her, well soon she'll see her face to face, knock on the door of that huge log residence they appear to live in, find out if the reality is the same as the picture, find out if this smiling girl is really called Anya. She feels a strange kind of glow about it all as she pictures it in her mind. Oh she'll have to make up some excuse of course, can't tell the truth about killing the girl's father in a lift. Can't admit she was the one who ended that happiness. But she'll think of something.

*

She wonders if anyone is coming for her. Will Ben do anything? He's not the action man type really. Better with a laptop than a handgun, prefers walking to running, lives in his head really. There have been a few occasions when she still wishes Max were part of the picture, and right now is one of them. The man with the cane comes to see her again. He talks for a while, asks her about the snake. He stays for quite some time, for hours even. She sees little reason to hide what she knows. He asks her about her journal. Where it is. She says she lost it. It's the one lie she clings to, something about the question makes her cautious, guarded. She play's it deliberately vague, skirts around the subject. She knows plenty, and she figures that he knows that she knows plenty, but they carry on the game . Then suddenly he changes tack, forgets the bronze serpent. Suddenly he's telling her his story, the petty crime and big business. The wave of misdemeanours that has carried him here today. He wants to know something, would she ever consider writing his story? And that's when she realises something. She's in dangerous territory. If he trusts her with his tales of true crime it can mean only one of two things. Either he sees her as a potential criminal too, or he knows she'll be dead before too long anyway.

*

Max stares ahead as he walks, his shoulders bumping against the thinning tide of evening travellers. There are two seers left. Just two. And no guarantee that either of them will be much good for leading them to Aretha. If he goes hunting for them the chances are he'll only lead Suzie Kruger to them and get them killed anyway. What good did he do Andre Alvarez? None. Except to cure him permanently of his agoraphobia. And any minute now, for all his minders and glamorous lifestyle, Jack Carlyle could well find himself lying in a pool of his own blood. The mission is turning into a massacre. He's being played for a fool. He breaks away from the stream of people and slips into the Retiro Park. A couple of human statues stand in his way, top hat on the ground, waiting for paid permission to move. He drops a couple of euros in the hat, the statues shudder, two grey faces stir and click and rotate in his direction, one eye winks. On a better day he'd smile at that. Drumming, somewhere in the background there is drumming. He walks on, the boom of it grows louder. At the Alfonso VI monument young guys sit in front of the colonnade and beat their djembes fast fast fast. One or two men and women dance, bodies swivelling in time with the drums and each other. He stands and watches the guys and girls move, fighting off the rigours and disappointments of adulthood, holding the inevitable at bay by staying out late and dancing in the street. He's never been a dancer but danger was the same kind of thing to him, the vehicle he used for staving off normality, and not too long ago either. Now the past is catching up with him. Or so it seems. He walks on by the lake, comes to the Fountain of the Fallen Angel. Another bronze statue, this one firmly in place and still in once piece. The body intentionally buckled as the angel falls and attempts to twist away, face shielded with a bronze palm, recoiling from some kind of danger. He stares at it for a long time. Finds comfort in the timeless pose, he's been there, done that. Contorted his way out of trouble. The drummers drum on and he listens and stares and thinks about giving up. Contemplates twisting and turning himself from the danger, jumping on a plane, not even returning to find Beluga and her carpetbag. He pictures Ben Brookes's face in his mind, the disappointment, the anger, the disbelief if Max should return without

Aretha. He pulls Blyton's list from his pocket. Two names remain. Brecht Nobel and Kurt Danby. He has no full addresses for either. Just the home country and their cell phone numbers. Maybe he should have called them days ago, alerted them, told them to go into hiding, protect their families. Brecht Nobel is in Holland, Danby's in Canada. Max needs a phone and Blue has one. So he has no choice. He has to go back and find her. He couldn't leave her here anyway. Not with Kruger on the prowl and Carlyle still in danger. Money can make a man like him powerful but it can't make him bulletproof. Sooner or later someone like Kruger gets to you. She got to the doorman, knew him all right, and that makes him an inside man, and, with an organisation as big as Carlyle's, if there's one inside man then there might well be plenty more. This is good. This is distracting him, his brain is starting to work again, operating like the old days, thinking strategically. The drums continue in the background, the dancers dance, the fallen angel still twists and cringes. But Max is on the rise. He can do this. If it kills him it kills him. But he'll keep going till it does. Or until the next time his confidence dips and the depression claws at his courage again. And those monstrous voices from the past drown out the sound of his calling.

*

It's disconcerting, she can't quite come up with the goods, can't think what she'll say when Anya Zeus stands there on the doorstep of that colossal log cabin. Where is it anyway? Doesn't exactly look like Washington, more like Oregon or Idaho. There are mountains in the distance, probably the Rockies or the Blue Mountains. The place looks well off the beaten track, far from the gleaming white monuments to Lincoln, Jefferson and Washington himself. A long, long way from the Bill of Rights and the Constitution. She'll fly to Washington and work it out from there. No problem. Marty's daughter must go to some kind of boarding school, no way you could live in the sticks like that and hop on a bus every day. No doubt it's a good school. The kind of school where boys don't molest you and the teachers don't turn a blind eye. Anya Zeus may have lost her father but she'll come out of her education with a future, not a plan B. Not a scheme to get back at the world for everything it's yanked from the back of the closet and hurled all over her. How long might they be friends? Could they know each other for years without the girl ever discovering the truth?

How macabre would that be? New Aunt Anya becoming a favourite friend, her dark secret hidden. Days out, weekends away, holidays abroad, young Anya showing her America, aunt Anya taking her round Europe, backpacking, jumping trains and sleeping in hostels. Seeing the sights and getting a higher education. Some kind of atonement for putting a gun to her dad's head. She shivers, picks up her coffee cup then recoils from it, realising the remnant liquid is cold and coated in a slick of coagulated cream.

*

Blue waits. The biggest challenge in the world to her. She was never good at it. Born prematurely, moved up a year at school, never finished college. Left home at sixteen, engaged at eighteen, broke it off at nineteen. Life was just too short for her, can't be left hanging about waiting for the next thing, the next thing is now. Now, now, now. Live light, travel easy. The Siesta is a hell of a grand hotel, but even a glitzy palace like this is starting to get her down, she can feel the dust settling, the wet cement pooling in her soul, her life filling with ballast. Where's Max? Why doesn't he just come back so they can solve this thing and move on? She waves to the barman, orders another coke, glances towards the doors again. Will he look in here? When he's checked the room and found her missing, will he figure this is the best place to start looking? She strikes a pose, imagines him strutting through the door now with his combat jacket, and his 'these-have-sure-seen-some-action' jeans and boots. His hair suitably messy and his chin flecked with just enough stubble. How does a man like Max become a man like Max? Where did he go to end up like that? There's hardly a finishing school for action heroes. A place where you can learn the finer points of choke-holding villains and wrestling crocodiles. There's surely no course you can take to learn the full gamut of smart quips and casual violence that go with the territory. A figure steps through the door, jeans, jacket, something about them screaming 'action'. But it's not Max, too small, too lean, too pale. The outfit way too dark. Plus it's a woman. It's the girl with the gun and the viper teeth. What's she doing here? How did she get in? She hovers like a virus, eyes narrowed, scanning the bar, looking for Max no doubt. So that makes two of them then. It's difficult for Blue to remain inconspicuous now she's ditched the requisite designer dress. With her red hair and crimson boots she's nothing short of a beacon, but she slinks a little lower against the bar, nurses her coke as if it's a piece of camouflage. If Kruger notices her she doesn't show it. Keeps looking, keeps scouring the place for mad Max. She turns, an efficient, sharp movement and immediately Blue is up and after her, no time wasting, no messing about, Max will have to wait. This is a golden opportunity. Let the predator discover what it feels like to be hunted down. If Blue can unearth Suzie Kruger's nest then there might be rich pickings on offer. You go girl, better than sitting in that bar sipping chemicals and waiting to get old. Time to find that witch's lair.

*

The bedroom is empty. The casino too. And by the time he makes it to the bar Blue's stool is occupied by a demure girl in silver, sipping cocktails with a man twice her age and three times her size. Max stalks a few corridors, past the drapes and silks, the marble and oak, the facades and decors. The place is awash with bodies in suits and gowns but no sign of Blue. Eventually he winds up back at the reception desk, asks for Carlyle and waits. He notices something. There is a distinct lack of uniforms about the place. No flashing lights in the street outside, no crackle of two way radios, no flint-faced cops in their element, striding about the hotel cordoning everything off. Max notes this, as sure as if he was scribbling it on the back of his hand. When Carlyle appears he'll check it out.

*

Suzie Kruger can move, she's like a cheetah in the wild, limbs pumping, body gliding as she veers from place to place. Barely breaking a sweat, effortless efficiency. Blue has to work hard to keep up, concealing herself every so often when the woman pauses to look around. She takes a stairwell and Blue follows. The decors begins to change, the chandeliers and flawless artwork are replaced by harsh yellow lighting and plain white walls. This is backstage, and it smells like it. Blue smiles to herself, this is looking good, very good. This is what they want, cut through the crap and the glamour and the posh frocks. Let's see how the place really functions. And let's see what the hell Kruger thinks she's doing creeping down the back stairs.

Forty five

Down, further down. A floor beneath basement level. Deep in the ground. A corridor. Grey cement walls, flickering lights, just like something out of one of those grim torture porn movies. She can't get the images of barechested men in bondage masks out of her head. A line of doors set in the drab wall, every ten feet or so. Kruger walks silently past them, no noise, no crunch or shuffle as her feet connect with the concrete and peel off again. She's moving with no friction whatsoever. Kruger suddenly stops and Blue pulls back into the shadows. Waits for Kruger to make some decision about where she's going next, pleads with the heavens for the other woman not to glance back. Blue's red hair is just sitting there like a target, a blazing 'You are being followed' sign. Kruger stands still, glances left then suddenly melts into the wall. No sound of a door, or creaking hinges, no swish of a lift opening. She's just gone. Then Blue hears another sound, a faint cough. She listens, strains to catch where the noise came from. Behind her? In front? Another cough. Close yet distant, muffled by wood and walls. She moves forward. Looks up and down the grey corridor. Any number of doors, any number of possibilities. Nothing more, at least not for now anyway. She listens again. Silence.

*

The Siesta has approximately fifteen hundred guests each year. With 567 rooms that's a steady flow of people over the carpets, in the beds, through the bathrooms, at the bars, in the restaurants and around the casinos. Not many have flaming red hair and the kind of attitude that Beluga Odyssey brings to town. She should stand out, even amongst so many other guests. 'No one's seen her,' says Carlyle, replacing the phone in yet another of his ubiquitous offices. This one's on the second floor.
Max walks to the window, ponders the fading light and the restless traffic. 'Where are the cops?' he asks.
'What?'
'The police,' he doesn't turn around, keeps his back to Carlyle. 'Why aren't they here?'
Carlyle clears his throat, even in that small guttural sound there is an apologetic note. 'I mentioned that I have friends,' he says. 'Friends who can allow me to report a gruesome occurrence without the requirement of

state intervention. Friends who have 'cleaners' who will for a fee straighten everything out. The glass has already been replaced in the office window downstairs. The carpet cleaned. The bullet hole in the wall will take longer. For now there is an extra picture on the wall. A painting by Goya. One of his less expansive affairs.'

Max finally turns. 'Can I borrow your phone?'

Carlyle shrugs. 'Be my guest. You're not... you're not intending to call the police yourself? Only I'd like to protect The Siesta from unnecessary scandal...'

Max snorts. 'No. But there are two men I need to contact immediately. And then I need to talk to you about your piece of the snake.' He stops. 'Unnecessary scandal? Is that all Alvarez is to you? An awkward intrusion? A business glitch? His heart gave out in front of you. It could be you next Carlyle. You may feel protected by your empire, but...' words fail him. He shakes his head. 'Which phone should I use?'

Carlyle hands him a cordless receiver. Max flips it over, pulls out the list and punches numbers.

'I built this business from the ground up,' Carlyle says quietly. 'It wasn't always the most successful hotel in Madrid. Others held that accolade. Had held it for a long time in fact. I upset people. Powerful people. There were threats, failed arson attacks, a couple of letter bombs, discrediting lies and slander. Money talks Mr Maguire and I had to learn the hard way who was going to shout loudest, who was going to badmouth me, and who was attempting to spit poison. I survived all the attacks. More than survived. I wooed or subdued the various enemies. I charmed my way through the carnage and the barrage of business shrapnel. I built carefully and thoroughly. Today I can discreetly dispose of an unfortunate event because I have a carefully constructed machine in place. I care about people like Alvarez, but I won't be cowed by those who threaten me with any kind of violence or bodily harm. I've been around the block so many times I own it. Every brick and paving slab.'

Jack Carlyle stopped. Poured himself a whiskey. Waited for Max to finish his call. The phone was ringing on the other end of the line. A click.

'Hello?'

'Is that Kurt Danby?'

'Yes.'

'Hello Mr Danby, my name is Maguire. I believe your life may be in danger. Have you ever heard of the Nehushtan snake?'
It wasn't the most subtle of conversation starters but then this was no time for pleasantries. There was silence on the end, understandably Kurt Danby was not going to disclose information to a total stranger. Max went on.
'I am calling you now because so far two of the other Nehushtan Seers have been gunned down in front of me. As far as I am aware six others are also dead. There are not many left Mr Danby. If you are one of that diminishing bunch I suggest you do everything you can to get yourself to safety. Do you have a computer to hand?'
A pause, a clearing of the throat. 'Yes.'
'Then I suggest you look up the following names. Casper Mack, Carlos Gomez, Marty Zeus, Dean Amble and Stan Deal. News on them will vary but I think you will find that all of them are dead. If you have family get them somewhere safe too. Someone is hunting down the seers and killing them to get to the snake. I have to call one other member of the collective. Did you get all that Mr Danby?'
'I think so.'
'Good, and you understand?'
'Yes.'
'You realise this is a grave situation?'
'Yes.'
'Good. All the best. Goodbye.'
Danby is halfway through his farewell when Max hangs up and dials again. This time an answering service kicks in. First in Dutch, then English.
'Hello! Congratulations - you are speaking to the phone of Brecht Nobel. I am unable to speak to you right now, but am very interested in your call. Please leave your message and your number and I'll get right back to you very soon. Thank you and goodbye. Have a good day.'
Incongruously cheery. Max scowls. He hangs up. No way can he leave a message – the answerphone might well be on because Brecht and Brigitta are sitting near the other end of that line, masking-taped to a couple of chairs, a guy with a gun just waiting for this kind of call.

Forty six

The silence is broken and Blue is listening again, with every step she takes the coughing beyond the string of doors grows louder. It's always just ahead of her and she has to keep taking another footstep. She paces the corridor, hovering by each door, the muffled coughs continue, not here, nor here, but soon. She walks, listens, walks, listens.
She listen for the longest time at one door and eventually is rewarded. A single cough comes from beyond the wood and cement. This is it, whoever is down here is a few feet away. Another cough, there is something plaintive about it, something desperate and lost, something that tears at her, snags her soul, like the sound of protracted death. She places a hand on the plain wooden doorknob, it hasn't even been sanded, nobody cares about the rooms down here. Maybe nobody cares about the people that get placed here too. It's another world from the opulence two floors up. She tenses her hand, squeezes her fingers around the wooden sphere handle, hugs it to her palm, begins to turn. It's locked. Instinctively she reaches up, runs fingers along the top of the frame, feels the caked dust and the dead flies. Then feels something else. A stray key. She smiles and hooks it down, blows the dirt from her fingers and eases it into the lock. She listens again. No movement from inside. She turns the key, the lock gives easily. She grips the handle and turns it again. There is the smallest of scrapes and a faint creak. The door gives, opens a crack. She pushes on it, another cough, this one much louder now. She stops abruptly wondering what she'll say. When she encounters the shadowy cougher, what's her excuse for intruding? Lost. The easiest thing, obvious too. Anyone could lose their way down here in this alternate sterile reality, without so much as a sweet wrapper for a landmark.

*

'I don't suppose you know either of these guys? Met them ever? Kurt Danby and Brecht Nobel?'
Carlyle shakes his head. 'I told you earlier I have no idea about any of the others. It's not a gentleman's club.'
Max nods. 'Carlyle – I have a problem now.'
'If I can help...'

'The reverse. It's whether I can help. So far I seem to keep leading the killers straight to the seers. This list is turning into a hit list and I'm turning into the courier.'

Carlyle laughs. 'Don't fret yourself Maguire. You overstate your importance. I'll be fine. These guys you've called – just stay away from them and they'll be fine.'

'Maybe, but I have a missing woman to find. To be honest the seers and the snake don't matter at all to me. They're just a means to an end. But I'm not like you Carlyle, I see Andre Alvarez assassinated and I get kickback. There was a time I wouldn't bat an eyelid, all part of the job, another hour in the day. Not now. Now I'm in trouble. Now I just want to find this woman and go home.'

'She mean something to you? This girl?'

He pours Max a similar drink to his own, passes over the crystal tumbler. Max drinks, recalls the nights when a measure like this would have been merely the cork in the bottle.

'She did once,' he says. 'Wouldn't be here if it was someone else.'

Carlyle smiles.

'So what does she have to do with the snake?'

Max pulls the diary from his jacket pocket. Hands it to Carlyle. The other man flicks pages, gives the passing sheets a cursory glance.

'This is what, exactly?'

'It may be the reason she disappeared. It's her writings about the snake. Full of juicy information that might appeal to someone trying to piece the Nehushtan serpent back together.'

'Why would anyone do that?'

Max sighs, he's growing tired of the story but he tells it again. About the power and the idolatry and the scattered snake fragments.

'But then you know all this,' he concluded. 'That's what the seers exist for, to keep the pieces apart, to prevent the abuse of its power. Isn't it?'

Carlyle smiles. 'You don't really think the snake has any power do you Maguire?'

Max shakes his head. 'But I know that people motivated by a belief in the supernatural can do dangerous things. The snake may be harmless, but in the wrong hands it could be deadly. In some ways its too late anyway. Too late for Andre Alvarez.'

*

The door swings wide, tired of the hesitance and the dawdling she pushes it hard. It's dark and there's a figure on the bed. She clicks a switch on the wall, lighting up the room. The figure on the bed doesn't stir. Doesn't look up or react. Just lies there, head cranked to one side, breath coming slowly, rhythmically. Dirty blonde hair spewing across the cheap blanket. The dress is crumpled and soiled, and there is no way she would dress like that for a night in the casino. Or even for a night in the basement of a casino. There is cement dust on her face and shoulders. Blood on the knuckles of her right hand as if she scraped the wall at some point. Blue jumps as the woman coughs and her body rises and falls violently. Blue braces herself with her hastily assembled excuse, but she doesn't need it. The other woman doesn't stir or look up. She's asleep, and her intermittent coughing is just dry-throated punctuation to her otherwise rhythmic breathing. Blue ventures closer. There are no ropes, no cuffs or carpet tape. She's a free woman, not some prisoner held captive due to poor conduct or illegal behaviour in the casino. But she's heavily unconscious, either drugged, drunk or just plain dog-tired from life.

*

'Where is your piece of the snake Carlyle?'
Max is tired of trying to get through to this guy. This self-made millionaire, if he wants to put himself in the firing line then fine. But if Max can get just one piece of the snake then all may not be lost. It would be a bargaining tool if nothing else.
'Let me have it for forty eight hours,' he pleads.
'I'll swap it,' Carlyle says.
'For what?'
'For a copy of this diary.'
'There isn't a copy. That's the only one.'
'Then let me make one.'
'Why?'
'Because I'm a Nehushtan Seer. One of us should have a copy.'
'Can't let you do that, not without Aretha's permission. Maybe afterwards, when she's free and it's all over I could get a copy for you then.'
Carlyle turns it in his hands.
'It's in the basement,' he says. 'The serpent fragment, it's in the basement.'
'I can have it?' asks Max.

Carlyle nods, says nothing. Max tries calling Brecht Nobel one more time. Still the answering service. Brecht and Brigitta, still indisposed, but really keen for his call. He hangs up.

*

Suzie Kruger picks up her phone, glances at it and says, 'Yea?'
'Two numbers for ya. Holland and Canada. I'll text 'em over.'
Kruger bites her lip and pushes hair from her cheek. 'These the last two?'
'Absolutely.'
'I presume the boss wants the same thing. Snake and dead?'
She listens, nods, hangs up.
She'll be out of a job soon, this has been quicker, easier than she anticipated, good old Maguire, he's led them to the last four. Best to finish this one then finish Maguire. Then maybe a holiday. Somewhere hot. Somewhere unsafe. Somewhere untraceable. Afghanistan maybe.

Forty seven

Blue can't resist coming close, taking a good look at the woman with the dirty blonde hair and soiled white dress. Who would crash out down here? And looking like that? She looks for a pocket to see if there's a purse or a phone. Nothing. She leaps back as the woman stirs again, then closes in again when she still doesn't wake. Something catches her eye, something in the shadows under the small, circular, antique table by the bed. A ball of paper, screwed up and discarded. She picks it up. Unfolds it. Oh! It's a photo. It's that girl, Ben's and Max's. Aretha Kiss. Not the same shot Max has been showing around, the hair is shorter and the expression on that pretty face a little more sombre. No crinkled nose. But it's her okay. She slips it into her pocket. Why does a sleeping woman in a basement have a photo of Lady Kiss Kiss? Is everyone round here obsessed with her? What is it with this girl? She turns to inspect the rest of the room and as she moves her foot kicks against something.

*

In the stairwell Max waits. Jack Carlyle is on his way, delayed by business. Max gets impatient, starts to move on down. Cement walls, grey,

stretching on forever. He listens hard. A cough, and the jangling of keys, way down there somewhere. He steels himself and makes his way down. Without Carlyle he has no idea what he's looking for, all he knows is that there's a piece of bronze snake down here, probably embedded in a wall safe or under the floor in a little chest, not unlike Alvarez's tiny strongbox. Another cough, more jangling. Max is getting close to the source of the sound. He doesn't hang about. Listens at the door, wraps his fist around the handle, turns and presses his shoulder to it.
'Not that one!' as the door begins to swing open he hears a shout from behind him along the corridor. He looks back, it's Carlyle. He's finally made it down here.
'It's not there!' he barks. 'Leave that.'
Max pulls the door to, closes it softly. He doesn't like Jack Carlyle telling him what to do but it's not worth the trouble. He's come for the snake, whatever's going on in the room with the keys and coughing it can play out in its own time. He can always come back later now he knows about it. Carlyle catches him up.
'It's down here, at the far end. I think you'll agree it's ingeniously hidden.'
'What is this down here?'
'Failed experiment,' says Carlyle. 'Was going to put in extra rooms, cheaper options, sort of high class student hostel kind of thing. Came to nothing, couldn't get planning permission, something to do with fire exits and the like.'
'Not to mention a distinct lack of fresh air and daylight,' says Max.
'I guess so. Though I've seen a lot of student accommodation in my time, it doesn't appear to be an issue for some of them. Still, it's useful for storage though. As you're about to see.'
Max follows him until they reach the final door. It isn't locked. Carlyle shoulders it gently in the style Max had used on the other door. The room is plain, undecorated, which is incongruous because it's piled with paint cans, wallpaper rolls, brushes and ladders.

*

Blue stays frozen, kneeling there, rooted to the spot. Someone came through the door. Or rather, someone made an attempt then pulled back. That was close. She pushes her hand under the bed, feels around. There it is. The thing her foot kicked against. Something hard and flat. She pushes both hands under the bed and grabs for it. She slides it out. It's a black attaché case. Probably locked. Is locked. But taped to the side there are two flat keys, a couple of thin slivers of steel. Whoever left it here wants it opened. She does a quick sweep of the room. Nothing much else to see. No windows or other exits. Just the bed, the table, and an antique armchair. Time to get out of there.

*

Carlyle pulls a toolbox from the pile of DIY detritus. He cranks open the cantilever lid, splits it apart likes he's peeling back an orange. It's full of metal accessories, brass door handles, stainless steel wall brackets, chrome hooks. Some of them more decorative than useful. He jabs his fingers in, shoves the pieces around and hooks out a small piece of bronze.
'See what I mean? Buried treasure.'
He holds up his piece of the Nehushtan snake. Max takes it, feels the weight, turns it in his fingers. A pointed chunk of cold, metal face peers at him, a dart of fire protruding from the carved slit of a mouth.
'The head end of all this trouble,' Carlyle says. 'Can you believe that Moses fingers were once clutching that? Can you believe people looked at it and recovered from snake bites?'
Max nods. Frowns a little. 'I guess faith has brought about all kinds of strange things.'
'I heard it's a winged fiery serpent,' Carlyle says, 'what do you think?'
'There were tales of flying snakes in the Arabian desert. The Israelites were terrified of them. Most venomous snakes just hid in the sand, and a bite would bring on a tortuous, painful death. Easy to step on them and be caught napping. The story goes that the people complained about the manna, and unleashed a world of snake-bite trouble. I guess you know this?'
'Sure. Bread from heaven. Free food. But they got fed up of the same menu every day. And as a result of the moaning, a plague of snakes emerged and did their worst.'
Max holds it up, 'Plainer than I expected,' he says, 'doesn't look like anything at all. You could easily sift through a tool box like that and miss it. But I guess we always imagine the significant things to be the most glamorous. Often the opposite.'

'Not much to it really is there? But then, they made it in a hurry, and no one expected that they'd keep it around and put it in a glass case for posterity. Not with people dropping dead right, left and centre.'
'A healing snake after a poisonous one,' Max mutters.
'A whole raft of poisonous ones...'
'I was thinking further back. The Genesis poem. The snake that caused the whole of humanity to drift away from their creator, break free from the source of life itself.'
'Oh that one. The talking one. One snake destroys, another rebuilds.'
'And Jesus referenced them both. You know this snake is the one picture that he used to sum up his slow death at the hands of the Roman Empire. Can you believe that? He referenced this snake we're looking at now. This relic. How about that for a link to God?'
'You think that's why these guys are after it?'
'Probably. They believe it has enough power to make it worth killing every one of the Nehushtan Seers, which is why I want you to get out of Madrid for a while. That woman, Suzie Kruger, she's an assassin. She's here looking for you. She won't rest until she holds this piece of snake and you are lying in your own blood. I'm serious Carlyle. You should consider getting out. Look what happened to Alvarez, I brought him here to keep him safe and he was cut down right in your office. She could get you in the same way within an hour.'

Forty eight

Blue cracks the door, listens. The corridor is quiet. She eases the attaché case through the door and follows it out. The thing is heavy, and moving it quietly is not easy. The air is pungent with cement dust, kicked up by footsteps down there. Someone is moving about in a room at the end of the corridor, she can hear it now. Voices and furniture being shifted. Best get out of there now girl, before her plan collapses. She turns and runs, not caring about the thumping of her boots. She bends round into the stairwell, ignores the sound of steps coming down towards her. She's clattering as she runs, the approaching feet are light, glancing quickly over the surface. There's no way out of this but confrontation. But she's prepared, whoever it is she'll just wink, flash a smile and run on. Hotel staff, police, whatever,

confidence will get her through the encounter and back to the safety of civilisation up there. Then it's back to the room, wait for Max and hike out of there as fast as possible. The stairwell continues to curve round, like something out of a medieval castle, the approaching steps are so close now she knows they'll meet in the next six strides. She miscalculated. It's just three, and in spite of the mental preparation she's taken by surprise. The figure in black recoils as Blue comes face to face and their bodies barely avoid collision. The steely eyes pierce hers. She nods, pulls out the grin and the wink and ducks round her. Kruger's reaching for something as she squeezes past. Knowing her it's a gun, and knowing her there's a bullet with Blue's name on it. Too late, sucker. Blue speeds up and runs the last few steps, shoulders the door and bursts out into the hotel foyer. She slips along the wall and presses herself behind a couple of palm plants. The door opens a little, hovers halfway and jams shut again. No one emerges. She relaxes, steps out of the cover. She makes it over to the reception desk.
''Scuse me? Seen Max Maguire?'
The receptionist's expression creases a little.
'We're like, here as guests... of Jim Carlyle.'
'You mean Mr Jack Carlyle, the owner?'
'That's the dude. Max might be with him.'
The receptionist shakes his head. 'They haven't been around here in a while,' he says, 'I can try messaging Mr Carlyle's P.A.'
She shakes her head, turns and sees the door to the basement stairs swing wide. She freezes. A foot appears and a hand comes round the door. Then a face. She breathes again. It's Carlyle, and he's with Max. They were down there all the time.
'Max!' she yells. 'Where you been?'
He sees her and nods, Carlyle says something to him and they separate.

*

Before Max can say anything she grabs him by the arm and steers him towards the lift.
'Let's get to the room,' she says, unusually quietly.
They ride up a few floors, make straight for the room and lock the door. When Blue turns she has a grin a mile wide.
'Mr Maguire you are gonna love me.'
'Why?'

'Not only have I won us a whole stash of new money. Yea. No kidding. Straight up, in the Casino tonight. And that would be the best news, except it ain't. I been busy. You know who was here tonight? You know who came looking for you? The woman in black! Yea, she was snooping around, old viper teeth. She was sneaking about down there. Breezed into the bar where I was waiting for you and just started wandering around like she owns the place.'
'Where did she go?'
She jabs her finger at the pile carpet.
'The basement. I followed her.'
'That was stupid.'
'What?'
Max is shaking his head. 'Do you realise how dangerous she is? She killed another seer tonight. Right here in this hotel.'
'What? Not Carlyle?'
'No of course not, he's alive, you just saw him come up the stairs with me.'
'Yea,' she frowns, 'what were you guys doing down there?'
Max finally smiles. 'You think *you* did well. Take a look at this.'
He reaches into his pocket, closes his hand and pulls out his fist, opens it for her to see. The bronze head sits in his palm.
'That is the face of the Nehushtan snake.'
'He just gave that to you? Just like that?'
Max nods. 'Took some persuading. He wanted the snake diary. I promised him I'd make him a copy in exchange for it.'
She stepped over and lifted the piece of bronze. Twisted it, sniffed it even.
'Not much really,' she says.
'Yea I know, you'd expect something a little more ornate.'
'No I don't mean that,' says Blue.
He frowns. 'Then what?'
She places the pieces of snake back in his palm.
'I mean this,' and the mile-wide grin is back.
She slaps the attaché case on the bed. There is a clatter and a thud as it lands.
'You think that's good? Wait till you see this.'
She slips the catches and throws the lid. Max can't believe his eyes.

*

Anya's phone buzzes again. She picks it up. Suzie Kruger. She answers it.
'Yea?'
'What's going on?'
'What do you mean?'
'You know what I mean, why aren't you here? Where the hell are you and where the hell is the snake?'
Silence. Anya chews the side of her cheek as she thinks.
'Tell me!' Kruger barks.
Anya waits.
'All right,' she says eventually. 'I'm taking some time.'
'Taking some... what the hell are you talking about? We're in the middle of an assignment. You don't take time out till I say you take time out. You are fast becoming a liability, girl. Get back here now.'
'I can't I'm flying, any minute now. Listen...'
'Don't ever tell me to listen. I tell you. You got it?'
Anya says nothing. A charged silence on the line. Kruger will go on, she won't be able to shut up for too long.
'Okay, you get on a plane and get out of London and get back here. Got it?' Silence. 'Okay. Fine,' says Kruger. 'I don't care if you got it or not. Just do it. Now, where are the pieces of snake?'
If it gets Kruger off her back and buys her some time then it'll be worth giving them up.
'Under The Siesta.'
'What do you mean?'
'There are dozens of unused rooms in the basement. I stashed the attaché case in a room down there. There's an undecorated corridor, goes on forever. One of the middle rooms. Under the bed. No one'll look down there.'
'You know we've moved them to The Siesta?'
'So?'
'So right now there's a lot of action going on down there. That case'd still better be there. Now listen, we got two more names to...'
Anya doesn't hear whatever Suzie Kruger says next. She hangs up. She hangs up, walks to the nearest litter bin, places the phone on the floor and crushes it beneath her heel. She does it as much damage as possible then drops the remnants in the bin. Then she heads for the boarding gate for the flight to Washington. As she walks she reaches into her shoulder bag, she

has a new smartphone in there. She has considered this moment for a while. She planned ahead.

Forty nine

Max stares. Blue stares. Then they both laugh, admittedly Max is way more restrained about it than Blue, but they both laugh.
'Seven pieces,' she says.
'Eight now,' and Max drops the head into the case.
She sits beside the open case and begins arranging the bronze fragments.
'Where did you find this?' he asks.
'In the basement. One of those rooms down there. When I followed Kruger I heard this coughing. Found a woman asleep in a room. It was under her bed. Oh. There was something else too.'
'What?'
'This was on the floor, screwed up. A picture of your missus.'
'My missus?'
'Yep. Cute as ever. Lady Kiss Kiss. Everyone's sweet on her aren't they?'
Max stares at the photo. There is no laughing now. He flips it over. Reads the line of writing scrawled on the back.
'AK. 5.15. SB. SD.'
'I didn't see that,' says Blue.
'Take me back down there,' he says. 'I want to see the room.'
'Now? But you said yourself Kruger's dangerous, and we both know she's still skulking around...'
'I don't care. Come on.'
Max is at the door waiting. Blue sighs. The kind of heavy, vocal sigh that's worth a thousand words. Max isn't listening though. As far as he's concerned there's only one place to go right now. Blue shoves her money in the carpetbag and pushes it under the bed, along with the attaché case.
'If this gets us killed I'll be really mad with you.'
Max drums his fingers against the door.
'Okay, okay,' she says, 'I'm coming. So who did Kruger wipe out?'
'Alvarez. I brought him back here, Took him to Carlyle's office. Thought he'd be safe. She shot him through the window.'
Blue whistles. Long and low.

'You can still go home,' he says.
'No I can't. I've got to show you this woman.'

*

When Sir Walter Raleigh sent two ships to claim American land for Queen Elizabeth in 1584 they landed on Roanoke Island and founded a colony there. It was a place of peace, abundance and welcome and the locals were gentle and faithful. According to one of the ship's captains, Arthur Barlowe, the people treated them with hospitality and generosity. Strange then that the settlers vanished completely and the fate of the Lost Colony of Roanoke turned into an unsolved mystery. The colony produced the first English child born on American soil, and conflicting theories abound about what became of the settlers. Not so many people think about the lost colony these days, but Anya Barlowe does. Her distant uncle Arthur was always a hero to her. And not least because he went into the unknown and never returned. Something mythical and mysterious about this man. A pioneer, a keen adventurer. When she's done with Washington and Anya Zeus and her house on the hill, she may well venture to Roanoke Island and, like her long lost uncle, she may well never return.

*

Voices. And footsteps. There's been a lot tonight. More activity than she's heard in for some time. She hasn't seen the man in white for a while. She listens at the door, her ear pressed hard against the rough wood. There's something familiar about one of those voices.

*

Max reaches the foot of the stairwell first and has to wait for Blue to catch up and lead the way.
'Which one?' he asks.
Blue surveys the corridor. Too many doors and they all look alike. Still not so much as a sweet wrapper for guidance.
'I know it's not the first three or four,' she says.
Max sighs, pushes her on.
'Come on, time is short,' he says.
She starts pacing again, gets déjà vu as she listens at those doors. There is no coughing now. No noise at all. No noise that is except the distant creak of the door at the top of the stairwell.

'Wait,' Max says.
'Make up your mind will ya mate. Stop, go. Which one is it?'
There are light footsteps descending the stairs. Soon they will not be alone.
'Hurry, just try the doors.'
He moves ahead of her and shoulders the next door along. The rooms are dark and empty, a few bits of furniture, some old bedding, rubbish sacks, packing cases. They move on, check the next doors. And all the time the steps approach, growing louder as they reach the ground level. Max is pretty sure he knows what's coming now. He's heard those feet before.
'It's this one.'
Blue is standing outside a door halfway down the corridor.
'You're kidding,' says Max.
'Nope.'
'I nearly went into that room!'
'You mean it was you! You opened the door!'
The footsteps stop. They turn. Suzie Kruger stands in the corridor.
'Well, well,' she says, 'we meet again, as they say in all the best movies.'
Max is about to open his mouth when another voice calls out. From one of the rooms.
'Max!'
A fist beats against one of the doors. It wrong foots them all.
'Max!'
Kruger moves first. Hurls herself at Max. She has quickly sized up the situation and figures he is the best target. The fist continues to beat on the distant door. Blue runs towards the sound of it. The voice shouts again.
'Max! Max!'
Kruger hits Max once, but it's a powerful blow. A single punch to his jaw. He twists backwards and towards the wall, catches his head against the hard cement as he stumbles. She raises her fist to punch him out properly but he grabs her hand in his and starts to twist it at the wrist, bending it backwards. Kruger grimaces but makes no sound. Blue rattles a door handle in the background, but she's getting nowhere. The door's obviously locked.
'Try the top of the doorframe! Might be a key!' Max shouts.
'I know, I know,' Blue yells back.
Distracted by Blue, Max relaxes, only for a fraction of a second, but it's enough. Kruger twists her fist free and slams it into Max's stomach, a

sledgehammer blow that sends him staggering backwards, gasping for breath. This gives her time to pull her Glock from the back of her waistband. She lifts it and takes aim. Squeezes the trigger. Max twists and presses himself against the wall, but he needn't have bothered, the bullet was never meant for him. An explosion as the gun goes off. A ricochet and yelp from down the corridor. Rage engulfs Max and in an instant he's on Kruger, ripping the Glock from her hand and punching her once so hard that it knocks her on her back. He turns with the gun and tears down the corridor. He's yelling at Blue but the sudden gunshot has deafened him temporarily. He can see she is still trying to open the door but he can't hear the voices anymore or hear the fist pounding on the wood. Suddenly a door flies open as he passes it and the next thing he knows he's waking up in darkness.

Fifty

It was Max. She knows it. That voice so close could only mean one thing. He had come for her. Some kind of rescue operation. By the sound of it, bungled. Not like Max at all. Is he losing his grip? She doesn't have long to think about this. An hour at most. Then the man with the gun is back, with his blindfold and masking tape.

They move her again. Blindfolded and gagged as before. But not far. And not outside. There are no car journeys and no sounds of the street. Just stairs. Flights and flights of them, and eventually, when she is able to open her eyes she finds herself in extraordinary surroundings. Marble, mahogany and silk everywhere. The antithesis of the room she has left behind. She even has a window and can look out over the city. It's dark out there but she recognises the fountains and statues and the stretches of parks and boulevards. She knows its Madrid. Unmistakable. She once did a feature on the place. Third largest city in Europe. And home of course to Real Madrid, tapas, flamenco and sangria. City of bohemian culture and bullfighting. The Museo del Prado with its collection of colossal, widescreen Goyas. Good old Goya. The Imax of the art world she once called him. She catches the drumming from the Retiro Park and can picture the dancers now. She hears another sound, closer, guttural. And she realises she is not alone. A woman with blonde hair and bruises and scuffs sits across the room in the shadows, hunched and asleep in an armchair. Perhaps the woman she heard in the room next door. She is not stupid. This is not a secure set up, and two heads together are more dangerous than one. Clearly this is close to the end now. They no longer seem to care about keeping her concealed, soon there will be an exchange of some kind. Or an execution. She's sure of it.

*

When he wakes the first thing Max thinks of is the diary. The first thing Blue thinks of is the money. They sit up, their heads swimming.
'Where are we?' she says her voice dry and husky as hell.
'And why aren't we dead?' he mutters.
It's still dark, just beginning to get light. She shivers. And she notices the ropes.
'We're tied up.'
'Yea I know. This could be bad. Don't suppose you have a knife concealed somewhere?'
'Oh yea sure. I have a machete concealed in my bra strap, I'll just get it.'
Max says nothing. He is backed against her, their arms tied to each other at the elbows. She can feel him moving around back there, shuffling his hips, manipulating his arms and shoulders. There is a loud crack and she winces.
'What was that? You break a bone?'
'Be quiet. Just make sure you don't fall off.'
'Fall off?'
She looks around, with the light creeping in she catches her first sight of the dawn sky, they are high up here. Very high up. He groans and yanks his shoulder then suddenly the ropes around them fall slack. She pulls her arm free and uses it to tear the rest of the ropes from them both. Max nurses his shoulder, manipulates it again. There is another sickening crack. He groans.
'What are you doing?' she says. 'Stop it. It's horrible.'
'It's the price of freedom. I dislocated my shoulder years ago. It taught me a trick that often comes in handy in situations like this. See. A little manipulation and we're free.'
'Yea, and feeling nauseous.'
'You're welcome.'

He stands, massages his arms. Swings his right arm and clutches the shoulder.
'What happened to us?' she says, still sitting. 'How did we get here?'
His head is cloudy but images start emerging from the fog. The attack in the corridor. The fist fight. The gun going off. That was it. He blacked out after that.
'Didn't you get shot?' he says. 'Kruger fired at you. I remember.'
She suddenly recalls it too, grabs her arm.
'Ow!'
'You're wounded?'
She peels back the torn sleeve.
'No, lucky. Just a hell of a bruise and a scrape. Oh… I remember now. Heard the shot and the wall exploded. The bullet must have missed me and dug a chunk of concrete out of the wall or something. Guess it must have hit me. Ow! Don't know what happened after that.' She presses her fingers to the side of her head. 'Ow! Yes I do.
Wasn't just my arm got crunched by concrete. Feel this lump under my hair. Go on, feel it. It's massive.'
'Not right now. As long as you ain't bleeding to death I'm fine.'
She huffs, rubs the spot tenderly and looks around. There's a city sprawling there, dull and quiet below her feet. A sand-coloured cathedral towers above everything else, looking like something out of a Star Wars movie. Beyond it the distant mountains are dwarfed by its size. The old streets lie empty. The place is yet to wake up.
'Where are we?'
'By the looks of it I'd say Segovia – about an hour from Madrid. In fact I know it's Segovia. You don't get an old aqueduct of this size in every Spanish city.'
She stands up, staggers a little.
'Careful,' he says, 'this old bridge ain't wide enough for stumbling about.'
'Wow! Look at it, stretches on forever. This is amazing.'
'Built by the Romans sometime around the first century AD. Something in the region of 160 arches to the thing.'
She strikes out across the aqueduct. Stares into the distance. The light is coming fast now.
Around them Segovia crouches quiet and still. The occasional pedestrian strolls somewhere but no one takes much notice of a couple of early

morning strangers wandering the aqueduct. She sees something. Squeals happily.
'Hey, I can't believe it. They brought my bag! Yours too. Look. We're in luck. Crazy. Sheez.'
She runs and crouches by her carpetbag. She stands and throws Max's rucksack over to him, then kneels again and pulls her own bag open. There is a pause as she shoves her fists in. Then, 'Damn! Damn! Damn!'
She kicks it and stomps away.
'They took it,' she says and then she screams, a gut-felt, searing shriek. Total frustration.
'The diary's gone. The money's gone. All that money I got from the game. I can't believe it. They took everything.'
'And I guess there's no sign of the case with the snake fragments in it either. Just when we were getting close. Hell, I'm getting rusty. Completely out of practice. Idiot.'
She slumps to sitting again. Clutches the bag like it's a comfort blanket.
'What the hell was going on down there?' she says.
'Where? What do you mean?' Max is looking off into the distance. Back along the aqueduct. Something's bothering him.
'You know. Under The Siesta,' she says, 'Something weird was going down. All those locked doors… the snake pieces… the voices and coughing… that woman…'
Max is pointing.
'What's wrong?' she says. 'What are you looking at?'
'That woman.'
Max starts to run, Blue leans left and peers round his moving body. She catches a glimpse of something, maybe an arm at the far end of the bridge. Max speeds up, Blue grabs her carpetbag and throws it over her shoulder. Most of the valuable stuff is gone but she's not letting it out of her sight again.
'Come on Jason,' she mutters, and she pats it wistfully.
She limps along. She's in no rush to catch Max up, this can't be good. There's no way that this is a day with any good news coming. Her vision is still a little blurred, they must have drugged her, knocked them both out so they could dump them here. Her head feels like it's in a fish tank, may take a while to clear. She needs an inordinately long soak in a very large bath if she's ever going to feel human again. She keeps walking.

The figure's lying face down, but even that way up, she's all too familiar. Way too familiar. The dirty blond hair, the scuffs and scrapes. The soiled white dress.
'Sheez it's her. It's her! How'd she get here?'
Max is leaning over the body, checking for a pulse. There is no movement, no sign of the body rising and falling. There is a note though, pinned through the woman's upper arm with a large safety pin. That can't be good. They could have attached it to the crumpled white dress. No need for that. Max looks up.
'What d'you mean, it's her? Is this the woman you saw in the basement at The Siesta?'
'Yea, well I think so. It's the same dress. And the hair, and those scrapes on the arm. Why did they put a pin through her arm? That's disgusting, why did they do that?'
'Look away,' he says.
'What?'
'Take a walk, go look at the view. I'm gonna turn her over and if the pin looks bad to you I don't want you seeing the rest of her.'
'Why?'
Max sighs. He's been here too many times before, trying to protect innocent people from the machinations of the evil and depraved.
'Because I don't want you throwing up and having an image that you see every time you try and sleep in the next fortnight.'
Blue grins, it's an unexpected response. 'What are you being so melodramatic for?' she says.
'I'm trying to protect you. The pin through the arm is nothing.'
Max stands up. 'Look, we're talking about a group of people for whom killing is nothing. It's a means to an end. We got too close, and for some reason we survived. So my guess is, they don't want us getting any closer. This is intended to scare us off. Which means they may have put a bullet through her heart, but after that they probably took a chair leg to her face. D'you wanna see that? Really?'
'You're kidding.'
'No. I'm not kidding. History is littered with this stuff. Kings and tyrants and drug barons and small time thugs who do not care about people. They only care about themselves. They cut off arms and legs and toes and ears and all manner of things to get what they want. Right now we are in that

zone.' He pauses, clears his throat.' Now I have to turn her over, I have to make sure she is dead. And I need to see if there are any clues on her. I don't think you wanna be here when I do that. And this is nothing do with the weaker sex crap, if you were a guy I'd say the same thing. I've seen plenty of gore in my time. I can live with that, but you don't have to. Now go away.'
Blue opens her mouth but Max just shakes his head. She slings the carpetbag over her other shoulder and walks back to the centre of the bridge.
'Call me when you're done,' she says, if only so she can have the last word.
He waits for her to dawdle away. Gives her plenty of time, then turns and kneels with his back to her, shielding the body from any backward glance Blue may be tempted to throw. He grabs the corpse by the shoulders and manhandles it over. His stomach turns, the bile rises in his throat. He gags but keeps it down. Turns his head to one side and breathes in and out deeply. Waits for a moment then looks back. It may not have been a chair leg but they took something to her face, and when they'd done that they took something else to her stomach. The dress is flayed and matted with blood and bodily fluids. Turning her over has released the smell. He gags again. There's nothing useful here, just a barbarous message from a people who will stop at nothing. He snatches at the note attached to the flesh on her arm. As he rips it free from the pin a little drop of blood flicks up and catches him on the cheek. He smears it away then opens the paper. Reads it quickly.

Don't worry, Charles MacManus won't miss her. He's too dead to notice anyway. And you will be too if you don't back off. You cannot win this and you do not want to lose it in the same way that Sophie MacManus did. Let this be an end to it all now.

'Oh my....'
Max spins round. Blue's behind him. Standing there. She came back.
'What are you doing?' he snarls I told you to…'
Blue turns and throws up.
'What did I say?' he shouts. 'What did I say?'
Blue wipes her chin and doesn't look at him.

'You said I'd throw up.'
'Well, there you go then.'
He stands and shields her from looking again, uses his body to push her away. He walks her all the way back to the centre of the bridge.
'Who is she?' Blue asks eventually, her face grey.
'Sophie MacManus. Charles's wife. Though you wouldn't know it. Not even Charles would recognise her now. No way. You okay?'
She shakes her head. Throws up again. He holds her hair back.
'She was so pretty,' Blue says when her mouth is clean and she can speak again.
'Was she?'
Blue nods. She sniffs and suddenly breaks down, collapsing in Max's arms.
They stand on the bridge for a while. Eventually she stops sobbing.
'We have to go home,' she says. 'We have to do ordinary things. Play cards, drink in a café, watch TV. I need... I need something normal.'
He nods. He knows that feeling. Whenever the world has fallen apart a little too much he has needed that. When he watched a man beaten to death on a railway station he was exactly the same. When he went to Toul Sleng, the torture centre in Phnom Penh, saw the pictures and read the records. You need to know that normal people, nice people, regular people, are still around. Something to redress the balance, something to weigh against the horrors.

Fifty one

Washington is wet. This is not what she planned at all. She wanted blue skies and sunshine and the feeling of freedom. A new bright start. The end of everything dark in her life. Instead there are clouds everywhere and people hurry along under umbrellas and waterproofs. She can't imagine her long lost uncle Arthur Barlowe arriving to this kind of welcome, forging a new life at the Roanoke Colony in the rain. Landing on the island with the other hundred and seventeen settlers must have been more hopeful. Surely. She makes her way through the arrivals and baggage processes. Collapses in the lounge and watches the Washington world go by. She pulls out her picture of Marty Zeus's family. There's Anya again.

She takes out her new smartphone and Googles the Zeus's. There are news reports, Facebook pages and some YouTube footage. It shouldn't take much surfing to track down the dream house in the hills. But before that she takes some time to track down an airport locker registered under Suzie Kruger's name. There is something in there she might need.

*

'Why do they want to scare us off?'
'I told you. We got close. Very close. In that basement we were probably on the verge of something.'
'Then let's go back!'
'No. They're not stupid. There won't be anything in that basement anymore. They're probably not even in Spain anymore. We have to find another way to get to them.'
'Why did Sophie MacManus have a picture of your woman?'
'My guess is she didn't. It was the people who took her there. Whoever dumped her in that room threw it away and didn't figure she'd be getting any visitors. D'you remember what was on the back?'
Blue shuts her eyes. Her heads throbbing. 'Some letters and numbers. AK. SB. SG and 5 something, 15 I think.'
Max nods. 'It was SB and SD. Maybe a planned meet up. AK are Aretha's initials so SB could be something like Starbucks at 5.15.'
'And SD?'
'On the back of a photo of Aretha – would have to be... snake diary? Maybe that was the trap they set to get her. Fixed a meeting with her and kidnapped her.'
'But she didn't take the diary along.'
'No. Maybe she got wise to something.'
Max grimaces, manipulates his recently dislocated shoulder. 'You know we could have been that close to Aretha. Maybe one room away from finding her.'
He snaps his fingers again. Other things are coming back to him now.
'That shouting, that beating on the door. I'd forgotten! Remember? That was her. I'd bet my life on it. She was in that basement all the time. Must have heard us down there. Recognised my voice maybe. Damn. We were so close.'
He turns and looks back towards the body on the bridge.

'It'll be daylight soon. We have to do something about that body,' he says.
'We can't take it with us,' says Blue, 'I don't want to go near it again.'
The city is starting to wake. Cars appear on the old roads, people weave their way to work down the narrow backstreets and twisting alleys.
'Well, it's too late now to try and bury it somewhere. Stay here.'
Max walks back to the end of the aqueduct. Blue doesn't move, just watches him go. He is scribbling something on a piece of paper as he walks. He kneels down, heaves the body back over so that Sophie MacManus is face down again. Then he pins something to the back of her dress. He places a hand over his eyes, mutters something quietly, crosses himself and stands. He walks back quickly, doesn't stop when he reaches Blue, just grabs her arm and walks her along the bridge away from the body.
'Where are we going?'
'To get some breakfast. And to think. We need a plan b.'

*

Blue orders churros and porras, sweet, crisp-fried fingers of dough with thick hot chocolate. Max has an omelette. He is amazed she can face the substantial, sweet breakfast after the bridge experience, but he's learning that Blue's the type to live fast and move on. Max's omelette arrives, a thick wedge of potatoes and eggs fried in olive oil. They sit outside in the morning sun. At a café well away from the aqueduct. The warmth and the food pushes the spectre of death a little further away.
'What did you put on her body?' Blue asks, plugging her huge cup of hot chocolate with churros sticks.
'I left the note they sent us, along with the address of The Siesta on it. I figured it might cause some disruption if nothing else.'
'What was Kruger doing there? In The Siesta?'
'Well, clearly she was working with whoever abducted Sophie MacManus and most likely Aretha too.'
Blue chews on one of the churros. There is a lot of chocolate on it.
'So what next? More seers?'
Max shakes his head. 'No. I called them and warned them. I figured I've done enough damage. The seers die when I go looking for them.'
She laughs. 'It ain't supposed to work that way. How many we got left?'
'Two.'

'Two?'
'Kurt Danby in Canada and Brecht Nobel in Holland.'
'So...' she frowns. 'How many we got so far?'
'Well, Carlos Gomez died in Iran. Sanchez in the hills of Texas. Casper Mack stabbed at JFK airport. Then there's the three who got gunned down at The Republic, Marty Zeus, Dean Amble and Stan Deal. Sophie's husband Charles was in Paris, Andre Alvarez died in The Siesta and, as far as we know, Jack Carlyle is still alive and kicking. But don't count on it with Kruger in Madrid. That leaves Danby and Nobel.'
Blue stops, a porras sliver hovering between her mouth and the cup. Spots of dark chocolate leak from it onto the table.
'No,' she says eventually.
'What d'you mean?'
'You missed one.'
He reaches into his pocket for the list. Stops. Tries his other pockets. Sighs.
'I don't believe it. They took that as well. The list, Blyton's list, it's gone. Man they were nothing if not thorough.'
Blue isn't listening, she's dumped the dough and is counting on her fingers, mouthing the names as she goes.
'You missed one,' she says again.
'I didn't. Trust me. I looked at that list enough times. There were eleven names on it.'
She nods. 'That's what I mean.'
He forks potato into his mouth and shakes his head. 'I don't know what you're saying,' he says out of the side of his mouth.
'I remember it clearly. I looked at that journal enough times too, you know,' she says.
'The list wasn't in the journal.'
'No. But there was a number. You probably never saw it, you didn't look close enough. Your Lady Kiss Kiss knew the number of seers. Don't know how. There are no details in there. But she knew. And she wrote it in there.'
'So?'
'So she didn't write down eleven. No way. She wrote down twelve. I remember. Twelve! Someone must have told her. Your list was wrong. It was a name down.'
Max shoves more omelette in and counts on his fingers as he chews.

'You sure?' he says.
She punches his shoulder and grins.
'You bet. Sheez. How could we miss that? We've had that list and the diary for days.'
'Doesn't matter. Only one thing matters now.'
'What?'
'Who's the twelfth seer?'

Fifty two

The Zeus family live in Shire Road, Port Ludlow, Washington. According to Anya's phone and the plethora of internet information. Looks nothing like the huge, log-cabin villa in the picture, that mountain mansion in the photo. This isn't going according to plan. She'd got her mind set on meeting Anya there. And in the sun. But it's still raining. It's a big place, all green lawns and well-manicured flowerbeds. But disappointing in comparison with the grandeur of that mountain mansion. A waterfall pond features in the five acre garden along with scenic views of the hills and canals. Two garages and a workshop. Doesn't look like they'd sell many copies of the Big Issue round this way. Looks like the neighbours are miles away too, not living on the other side of paper thin walls, pumping rock'n'roll through the cracks into the small hours. Not the kind of place where kids throw litter and crap in your garden, and dump their leftover fast food through your letter box. Not the kind of place Anya grew up in. Not at all. She stands outside and stares. Wonders what life is like for a kid who grows up here. Suddenly she can't remember what she's doing here. She wanted to make amends for killing Anya Zeus's father, but now she's here that seems hollow. She's getting soaked but she daren't move. A girl's face appears at the window. It's her. The other Anya. She calls to someone. A boy joins her. Looks like her brother. Marty Zeus's only son. So this is the place. And now is the time. She starts to walk across the massive lawn.

*

'We're going back to London.'
Max announces this and then refuses to add details. Blue badgers him but he's retreated into himself. She plays a couple of Russian guys in a

Segovian bar and does her best to scrape enough for the train ride back to Madrid and a couple of cheap air tickets. With all her money stolen she has to start by betting her crimson boots and her carpetbag. Worrying times. The guys are good and she's not in the best of spirits. Her fortunes rise and fall but she comes out of the game with her boots and bag intact and just about enough money. They catch an evening train and ride it to the Madrid Atocha station, then take the underground to the airport. Blue tries to talk on the plane but Max keeps his eyes shut. She's sure he's not sleeping, but he's as stubborn as hell so eventually she shuts up and dozes off herself. As he predicted, it's Sophie MacManus's body she sees before she drifts off.

*

The girl comes out to meet her, she looks younger in the flesh than in the photo.
Anya suddenly feels a surge of adrenalin as she holds out her hand to her. All very British but it seems somehow appropriate. The girl looks cautious.
'Hi, you don't know me, but I'm from England.'
Anya stands there with her hand extended. The girls has not taken it yet.
'Hello,' she says shyly.
The boy appears. 'What do you want?' he asks, his voice hard.
'It's about your dad,' Anya says, surprised at her own sudden confidence.
He flinches, the girl looks away. This is the right house, no doubt about it.
A voice calls from inside the house.
'Is that your mum?'
The boy nods.
'D'you know what happened to him?' he asks.
Anya nods.
'Really? Cause no one seems very clear on it.'
'Oh I'm very clear,' she says.
'You'd better come in,' says the boy.
The girls sniffs and doesn't look up, she rubs her eyes and goes inside.
Anya follows them.

*

They arrive at Heathrow with no plan b. Or at least, without one that Blue is aware of. She follows Max out into the night.
'Any money left?' he asks.

She has five euros and some change. Max has a ten pound note.
'I won so much in that game in The Siesta. We should be in The Ritz. Life sucks.'
'Well, as someone once said, "in this world you get trouble."'
'Who said?'
'The man from Nazareth. And he should know. He had nowhere to lay his head either. I suggest we crash in the airport lounge and get a train tomorrow.'
'A train to where?'
'To The Old Bookcase.'
'Where?'
'Blyton's shop. I want words with him.'
They snuck back inside.
'I don't suppose we could try the business class lounge?'
'Good luck,' says Max and he slings his rucksack onto an empty row of seats and lays his head on it.

*

He wakes to see Blue grinning. Looks like she's cleaned up a little too.
'D'you want the good news or the good news?' she says.
He sits up and tries to swallow, his mouth feels like a dirt path.
'Some water would do,' he growls.
She holds out a new bottle.
'Where d'you get that?'
She winks. 'All part of the good news.'
He drinks most of it down.
'What time is it?'
'Seven o'clock. D'you get some sleep old man?'
He nods. 'Some,' he mutters between gulping water.
'I didn't' she says, and she's cheery about it. 'I did what I'm good at.'
And she holds up a fistful of cash, fans the notes like a pack of cards.
'You found a poker game here?'
'Nope. I made a poker game here. Bought a cheap pack of cards from the shop and preyed on a few cocky Englishmen. Couldn't have gone better. To be honest, I was worried in Segovia last night. Thought I was losing my mojo. But not today. Today I cleaned up big time. Big time! How about a cooked breakfast?'

Max considers. Nods. 'Why not?' he says. 'But first - what was the other good news?'
She taps the side of her nose. 'Tell you later. But you'll be impressed. I'm on a roll.'

*

An hour later she slings the carpetbag into a taxi and they climb in. Max mutters the request to get to Waterloo and they pull away. Blue is grinning like she has a hanger in her mouth.
'Gonna tell me now?' Max asks.
She shakes her head. 'Soon,' she says.

*

Suzie Kruger lays out the pieces on the desk in front of her. Nine bronze fragments. She has half of the head and all of the tail now and most of the pieces in between. Just two to go. The other half of the head and one wing. And trips to Canada and Holland will settle the matter. She is gutted that she was not able to finish Max Maguire once and for all. They were too lenient. When you get a man like Max in your hands you don't mess about. No need for compassion. You kill him and kill him good. But that's by the by for now. She has a ticket to Montreal in her pocket and she must stick to the schedule. She studies the bronze jigsaw again. The winged serpent with the fire in its mouth. No great work of art but then, no one's collecting it to put in a glass case. This thing has a job to do, the same kind of job it did thousands of years ago. She scoops up the pieces, places them back in the case. Time to go to Canada. Time to lay another seer in the ground.

Fifty three

The Zeus family home takes her breath away. Marty certainly knew how to live. The youngsters lead her through the spacious rooms, across the pile carpets and hardwood floors, past the rare works of art and granite fire places. Marty's wife sits on the massive leather couch in the vast lounge. She looks as if she has been sitting there for a while, waiting in that room just to receive Anya into her life. She looks sad, heartbroken. She forces a smile, but it looks like work to do it.

'I'm Anya Barlowe,' she says, turning her charm on full.

Marty's wife nods. 'I'm Linda,' she says. 'I'm sorry to rush you, but what were you saying to my family? You mentioned my husband?'

Anya nods solemnly, perches on the far end of the couch.

'Your husband died in a terrible accident,' she says, and she can see Linda well up as the words escape her lips. 'I'm sorry to have to tell you this. But I thought I should do my best to find you. You see I was with him when he died.'

'They told us he was shot.'

Anya glances around at the rest of the family.

'Oh don't worry,' Linda reassures her, 'we all want to know, as painful as it is.'

Anya nods. 'He was in a lift, an elevator. Shot at close range. By a gunman.'

Linda Zeus gasps and presses her hand to her mouth. Her daughter sits down beside her. Her son steps close to them. The family suddenly looks very small.

'Why?' the son asks.

Anya thinks. Why indeed? Should she mention the snake?

'Did you know your husband was part of a secret collective? A group of men guarding an ancient artefact known as the Nehushtan snake?'

They all shake their heads.

'He was killed for that?' says the son.

'I'm afraid so. Such a waste. A trained assassin is hunting the group down. A woman called Suzie Kruger.'

'I thought you said it was a gunman?' says the boy.

'Did I? Yes... sorry, I wasn't thinking straight. I meant a woman. Suzie Kruger shot him and then stole his piece of the snake.'

'And you were there?'

'Yes, I tried to stop her, I... I tried to get the gun off her... but I'm no fighter I'm afraid. I couldn't do anything.'

Anya looks down, doesn't know what else to say.

Linda Zeus turns to her daughter.

'Amanda, bring us some iced tea will you please?'

Anya looks up. Looks around. There's no one else in the room. Just the family. She looks back at them, her mind suddenly frozen. Her heart skips a beat.

'Amanda?' she says, barely comprehending.
'Yes, my daughter. I'm sorry did they not introduce themselves? This is my son Steve and this is Amanda.'

*

He finishes *Millions* on the Waterloo train back to Exeter. It's crowded and unpleasant. She drums her fingers, sighs, tries to make him talk and ends up making conversation with a four year old across the aisle. They spill out of the train at Exeter and get another taxi.
'Want to tell me your genius idea now?' he says.
'You're kidding! After you just ignored me for three hours on that train?'
They sit in silence but he can tell she's busting to talk.
Thirty minutes later, down the side street with the cobbles and the trinket shops, Max thumps on the old door. They wait. And finally Blue starts talking.
'Okay,' she says, 'I worked it out. Last night, about four in the morning, when the poker was slow, I sat there thinking. Schemed it all through. I know who the twelfth seer is. I nailed it. Think about it. How would Aretha Kiss know there were twelve seers? How did she find out most things? By talking to Blyton. And how would Blyton know that? How come Blyton knows so much about everything anyway? How come he has a list of all the other seers? The only person to have that? Because he is one. He's the twelfth seer.'
The door opens. That familiar toast smell. Blyton Gann stands there. Crumpled and whiskery. He looks at first shocked, then pleasantly surprised.
'You came back,' he says, 'did you find them?'
Max gives him a knowing look, head lowered a little, eyes narrow. Blyton reads it well.
'You'd better come in,' he says cautiously. Then more cheerfully, 'You're looking good Miss Odyssey.'
'I am good,' she says, 'very good.'

*

'Amanda?'
Anya stares at the girl. She knows it looks odd, but she can't help herself.
'Yes.'

Anya pulls out the photograph. Looks at the girl in it. Not Anya at all then. He was lying. Marty Zeus was lying. Trying to trick her. Deception. Wasn't her friend at all.

'Where did you get that photo?'

Anya looks up at Linda. Says nothing. Linda Zeus encourages her daughter to stand.

'Amanda, the tea, darling, please. You go with her Steve, make sure she's okay.'

They leave slowly, confused by this latest turn of events. When they have gone Linda Zeus moves closer to Anya.

'Did you get that off my husband? What's going on? Why would you have that?'

'He told me she was called Anya,' she says in the softest of voices. 'I believed him.'

'Who was called Anya? Amanda?' Linda frowns. 'How well did you know my husband?'

Anya stares at the pile carpet. Must be worth thousands, it stretches on forever. Marty Zeus with his rich family and wealthy lifestyle and his lies in that lift.

'Where was this taken?' Anya asks, holding up the photograph.

'On holiday, in Idaho. Can I have it please? I'm wondering if I should call someone for you, Anya. Did this ordeal disturb you?'

'Don't call anyone,' she raises her voice and stands up. 'Don't involve anyone else.'

She's suddenly the professional again.

'This has been an awful week for us all, Anya,' Linda's voice is calm, has a soothing quality to it, but Anya has seen this approach many times before. Point a gun at a few people and sooner or later someone will adopt that tone.

'That experience in the lift must haunt you...' she is saying.

Anya nods. 'It does. I think about it every day. Does she have a middle name?'

'Sorry?'

'Your daughter.'

'Yes, She has two.'

'What are they?'

'Kate and Danni.'

Anya lashes out, kicks at a nearby armchair. Leaves scuffmarks on the soft pale leather.

'Why isn't she called Anya?' she hisses.

'Please don't do that. You're scaring me, I don't understand what this is about.'

'You should be scared. Your husband lied to me. Maybe he lied to you too. I thought he wanted to help me.'

She kicks again, the chair recoils a little. Amanda and Steve come back in, Amanda carrying a tray.

'Kids, stay out will you,' their mother says, her voice still quiet, still laced with that soothing tone.

'No,' says Anya. And suddenly her hand is full of something. An olive coloured handgun. Another Glock. Suzie Kruger has them spattered all over the globe in lockers and bank vaults, ready for whenever she needs them. Next time she comes to Washington she'll find one missing. Anya waves it around. Feels a little drunk, like she's standing on the edge of a precipice and the height has gone to her head. Amanda screams. Anya swings the gun on her.

'He told me you were called Anya too, when I had the gun on him in the elevator, he told me that. I thought it was true.'

'Oh my... It was you. You shot my husband, didn't you?'

'Had to. Though he tried to talk me out of it.'

She waves the photograph. 'I thought this would save me. Instead it's all a lie.'

And the gun goes off. Just seconds after she presses it to her temple and she pulls the trigger. Glocks have no safety catch, so pulling the trigger always fires a round. It fires one now. And Anya is finally out of her misery.

Fifty four

'What happened to Sophie?'

Her voice has a desperate edge to it, her eyes plead as she looks at him. Cortez leans on his cane. Says nothing. Slowly he lowers himself into the chair, the same chair Sophie had been sitting in before they took her away. He speaks.

'You do know how to make the snake work, don't you? You know I'm relying on that? You can do it, can't you?'
She nods. Terrified.
'Only, you're here and Mrs MacManus isn't because of your knowledge about the snake. So don't let me down.'

*

'It's true isn't it?' says Blue, having waded straight in with her deductions. 'I got it didn't I?'
Max can't help thinking she's more impressed with her ability to identify Blyton than with what this might mean for everything else.
Blyton looks from Max to Blue, back to Max again. He holds up his hands as if they have an AK47 on him.
'All right,' he sighs. 'But I hope you appreciate what you're doing here. This is completely against protocol. Against everything I swore to protect.'
'The protocol is gone, Blyton. There are only three seers left. For all we know Suzie Kruger has most of the snake, and we're no closer to finding Aretha.'
'So what do you propose? I'm not saying I'll comply, mind you.'
'It's simple. I need your piece of the snake. The last bit of the jigsaw. I need it as a bargaining chip. The advantage we have is that Kruger must still think she only needs eleven pieces. We will have the advantage, track her down, and offer your final piece of the snake for the life and whereabouts of Aretha. It's a long shot, but it's still a shot.'
Blyton coughs and wheezes, sighs as he shuffles around his little musty shop, touching books on the shelves as he goes. Blue opens her mouth to speak but Max silences her with a simple wave of his hand.
'I knew it would come to this one day,' he says. 'When men mess with God for their own ends it always ends badly. I wish Hezekiah had melted the thing down and turned it into a toilet seat.'
'Then we'd probably be looking for that right now,' says Max. 'People want power, they want quick fixes and easy magic. Doesn't matter whether it's a loo seat or the Ark of the Covenant. If they think something has the power of another world about it they'll go to the ends of the earth chasing it.'
'I don't get it, what's so bad about bringing the pieces back together anyway? Why couldn't the seers just have a barbie and swap stories and

put the ol' fiery serpent back together for old times sake, use it for science or something. Put it in a museum. People would pay sackloads to see it.'
'Yes,' Blyton says, 'And sooner or later it would get stolen. This isn't just the Mona Lisa, Miss Odyssey, this is a snake that beat death in the desert. Whether or not it can still do it now is irrelevant. People will still look to it for answers. That's where it all went wrong when Hezekiah was king. People turned a bit of bronze into an idol. The seers don't want that. That's why we keep it apart. Hezekiah smashed it because people misused it then and they'll misuse it now. The seers are good men, were good men, dedicated to keeping it hidden. Out of the limelight, away from abuse.'
'I don't know, seems kind of whack to me.'
'We're just trying to learn from the past,' says Blyton, 'stop history repeating itself.'
'But Jesus said the snake had power though,' says Blue, 'he said it could heal the world. I read it in here.'
She grabs a fat brown book from a shelf, dust flies off it and a dead moth spirals to the ground.
'Must do some cleaning,' Blyton mutters but she's not listening.
'Look, the gospel of John chapter 4 in the Bible,' she flicks at the pages, can't find it.
'You're thinking of John chapter 3,' Blyton eases the old book from her and finds the page. 'But he doesn't say the snake has any power. This is what a lot of people get confused about. Jesus speaks in parables all the time, it's what the rabbis did. They used picture stories, little cartoon doodlings that are layered with meaning. Jesus doesn't say the snake has power anymore, he says this, look – "just as the snake was lifted up in the desert, I will be lifted up". Imagine two cartoons, Moses holding up the Nehushtan snake on a pole and beside it Jesus being held up on a cross by the Roman army. Both pictures are about changing things for the better. Healing, if you like. But it's not about the snake, the serpent was a one-time incident for a group of desert pilgrims. That's the difference, the man on the cross is a much bigger means of healing or cure.'
Her faces creases in a frown as she squints at the tiny black text. 'Then why bother confusing us with the snake at all? Surely it's this that motivates someone like Kruger.'
'Because the snake is a good picture to use. Today Jesus might use other metaphors, like the way an aspirin can fix a headache, or antibiotics can

cure various illnesses. Back then the snake story was well known, so Jesus used it as a useful analogy for what he was doing. It's not his fault if people twist his words. History's littered with that sort of thing.'
Blue chews on this. Then shouts, 'The picture!'
'What?' Blyton stares, eyes wide.
'You showed her the picture didn't you?' Blue says. 'The sketch of the snake that she copied into her diary. You have it don't you?'
He snorts. 'Ah that. She was so persistent.' He drops into his easy chair, pulls the tin from its hiding place down the side of the cushion. He fishes out the drawing of the snake pieces, shows it to her. 'I had no idea it would lead to all this.'
'How did you get all this stuff?'
Blyton leans back in his chair, closes his eyes. Says nothing for a moment. Blue looks to Max.
'Before I left the friary, when it was closing down, a wise, wiry haired old monk known as Father Tom called me into his study. He had this tin and a piece of the snake. He had been guarding it for years. Most of the time around Europe. Spain Italy, a few other places. He was a great character Father Tom, had lived through some things, seen a bit of life and was a great story teller. You'd have liked him. Loved the old Bible stories if I remember rightly, especially that one about the rich fool. Anyway, last time I saw him he was dying, and knew it. A mixture of some rare disease and old age. He was ancient to be honest. Anyway, he told me about the seers and said that he was concerned about what would become of his piece of the snake. Apparently he was worried he'd not always been as discreet as he might have been about it. Enjoyed the odd shot of Bourbon and that loosed his tongue. He knew I was leaving the brotherhood, giving up the friary, so he asked me to take what he had. His piece of the snake and this old tin full of bits and pieces about it. Wouldn't tell me where he got it all, just said I should guard it with everything I had. So I promised I would and I took it all from him. And I have had it ever since.' Blyton looked down at the tin. Drummed his fingers across the top. 'Ever since.'
Max clears his throat. They look to him.
'Blyton, time is short, we need your help. Aretha needs it. Otherwise I'm sure she'll die.'
'And how many will die if the snake falls into the wrong hands?'
'But the snake doesn't kill people,' Max says.

'No, but it seems to motivate some people to wield power.'
Max stares at Blyton willing him to respond. As he scrutinises the old man other images flood his mind. Other deaths and failed assignments. He doesn't want more of that. He doesn't need another dead woman. Time stands still. Blyton looks down at his sandaled feet. He shuffles again. Walks past Max into the heart of his shop, running his fingers over the spines of the books as he passes them.
'There is no guarantee this will work,' he says.
'No,' says Max. 'But I have to do something.'

Fifty five

Kurt Danby lies dead. It wasn't difficult. Kruger just did what she's been doing so well. Taking the life from stupid, ill-advised men who thought it was worth risking everything for a chunk of old bronze. The hardest thing was the flight. It takes eight hours to fly from Heathrow to Toronto Pearson Airport, not to mention the time wasted in the airport waiting to check in, sort out baggage and get through passport control. And it's all stupidly protracted these days because of the damn terrorism threat. Too many killers trying to fly. So what does an assassin like Kruger do to pass the time? Small talk is a joke as far as she is concerned. She bought an e-reader at Heathrow and read The Da Vinci Code, tried to get lost in it, but somehow she couldn't quite imagine an assassin walking around leaving a self-inflicted trail of dripping blood. Surely you'd draw attention to yourself? Not easy in any case for an albino monk to disappear into a crowd...

She found Danby at his place of work. At the oldest operating cemetery in the city, the green spire rising out of St James's Crematorium on the Cathedral site. She called ahead and arranged to meet him in the grounds there, seemed appropriate to take him out surrounded by death. He was obliging, even told her that Maguire had tried to warn him into hiding but he had too much gumption for that. Suzie had commended him on the phone, smiled to herself as she promised to do everything in her power to sort the problem out. They arranged to meet at one o'clock and by five past he was dead, his head striking a tomb stone as he fell, the grim hollow sound being the only distasteful aspect of the meeting as far as Suzie was concerned. She was never one for drawing the thing out. Long explanations and self-indulgent speeches were best left to the likes of Quentin Tarantino. Just go in, do the job and clean up. Like changing a tyre. She leans over him now and checks his pocket. He's been as good as his word, kept the precious snake fragment close to his heart. She removes the piece of wing and examines it. This is the one. Only the last piece of head left and the old reptile will be reformed. Then the job will done and she can forget it all. Take the money and leave the men to get on with it. She slips it inside her coat, into a pocket secreted in the lining. A flight from Toronto to Amsterdam will take her another seven and a half hours, and that's without the sitting around. She hides the body amongst a patch of dense undergrowth, zipped up in a charcoal-lined, camouflaged body bag. The lining should conceal the odour for a while. She checks for any witnesses and strolls away through the Irish section, reading the epitaphs as she goes. Seems it's full of immigrants who died after fleeing the famine in the 1840's. She can't imagine dying, doesn't like to think about it. Killing others is one thing, that's just a discipline, an operation to be performed efficiently and cleanly. Start equating it with loss of life and you may as well give up. The best doctors keep their emotions in a hermetically sealed unit. The best killers too. It's well-paid, self-employment. Gun for hire. Just like the old west with smartphones, Glocks and multi calibre sniper rifles. She wonders if she has time for a decent meal. Cold beer and paella would go down well. She has a couple of hours. The Segovian Palace on Saint Nicholas Street gets four stars on her smartphone so she plumps for that. She reads more *Da Vinci Code* while she eats, but gives up and starts *Papillion* instead. Henri Charrière in sweltering French Guiana, making multiple escape attempts from Devil's Island prison. He's not long been arrested and beaten up a few other prisoners when she presses buttons and flips to *Pride and Prejudice* and a smouldering Mr Darcy making attempts to appear the bad guy for Miss Lizzie. She grew up with the world of Austen. Took her a while to realise not all the Darcy's turn out to be gentlemen in disguise. She flicks back to Da Vinci. The albino's still leaving vital blood trails all over his murder scenes. Back to *Papillion* and Henri's in solitary, going mad and eating bugs to survive. That's the problem with carrying a library in your pocket, it's like literary channel hopping. She gives up and starts to think ahead. The beer's good, the paella a little on the salty side. She takes up her phone and pushes buttons.

*

Brecht and Brigitta Nobel are out walking in De Hoge Veluwe National Park, 22km from their home in Barneveld. They are a gentle couple, happily retired. Brecht is a lay reader who preaches in his local church, Brigitta helps out with the homeless. They are busy, don't take much time to walk together like this, so they are making the most of it. It's said couples grow to resemble each other as they get older and it could certainly be said of these two. The same grey hair, peaceful smiles, twinkling eyes. The same slight stoop too. They have even been known to finish each other's sentences. The sort of couple you might watch from a distance, and wonder if you could ever end up like that, long-time married to someone in that same, devoted, faithful way. As Marc Cohn once sang,
'When the years have done irreparable harm, I can see us walking slowly arm in arm.
Just like the couple on the corner do, cause girl I will always be in love with you…'
Brecht's phone rings. He shrugs apologetically and takes it out. Answers in his native Dutch.
'Ja. Ja. Hallo.'
He listens, switches to English.
'Yes. This is Brecht. Pardon? Suzie who? No, I haven't.'
He stops walking, listens for a while Looks suddenly concerned. Brigitta stops and looks concerned too.
'I don't normally discuss these matters. How do you know about all this?'
He listens again. He listens for a while.
'Wait, wait a minute.'
He lowers the phone, looks at his wife.
'It's about the snake,' he says. 'A stranger from England wants to meet me.'
Brigitta shakes her head, it's brief and abrupt but effective.
'I'm sorry Miss Kruger. We can't discuss this. It's a private matter.'
He listens again. Lowers the phone.
'She says she's travelling here now. On her way to see us. She says it's a matter of great urgency. Our lives may be in danger.'

Brigitta's face loses its colour, she swallows hard.
'Brecht we don't want any trouble. You know the best way is to deny everything about the snake.'
He thinks. Lifts the phone again.
'I will meet you alone. But only once and not at my home.'
He looks around at the vast expanse of arid land, this strip of desert and scrubland. There is not a soul around.
'Do you know of De Hoge Veluwe National Park? It's about 80k from Amsterdam. Between Barneveld and Arnhem. I will meet you there. Say fifty paces from the main entrance, I'll be on the sand.' He glances around. 'Near an island of palms. We shouldn't be disturbed. When?'
He listens. Brigitta continues to shake her head furiously but it's too late. The meeting has been arranged. Brecht slowly hangs up.
'No. No. No,' she says. 'You know it is not good. The snake should not be discussed with strangers.'
He smiles. 'It will be all right. She says she wants to help us. Keep us out of danger.'
'If she wants to do that then she should stay away. Why disturb the water if the weather is calm?'
He takes her hand and they walk again.
'When is she coming?'

Fifty six

Blyton hasn't moved for a good three minutes. Blue is worried he's had some kind of seizure, perhaps the stress is too much for him.
'You okay mate?' she says, taking a few steps across the shop towards him.
He nods, but barely moves apart from this. He stands staring at a row of old copies of Enid Blyton books.
'I want you to promise me something,' he says eventually. 'If I give you this piece of snake you will do everything in your power to keep it from those who wish to misuse it. I know you want it as a bargaining chip, but you're no fool Max and there are ways to bluff. Will you give me your word?'

This is a dangerous moment for Max. He can't promise too much, he daren't. Not after his previous failures. He moves closer to Blyton.
'I'll do everything I can,' he says.
In a sense Blyton is asking for the impossible and Max can't give it, but they both say what they can.
Blyton nods and shuffles back to his room at the rear of the shop. Max follows, Blue thumbs through a few books. Blyton leans over his bed and pulls two narrow, shaped boards from the gap between the bed and the wall. He hands them to Max.
'Slot these round the chimney on the range, it'll lift. I can't do it but you can. I put it there a long time ago when I was a fitter man.'
Max positions the boards around the tiny pipe, manipulates them so they are snug against the metal. Then he tugs hard. At first the chimney won't budge, then there is a piercing screech as the pipe wrenches free and swings to one side. Blyton points at the wall. There is a discoloured brick jutting out a little. Blyton pulls on an old, grease-stained oven glove and prizes it free from the wall. Max stoops to look in the gap.
'Nothing,' he says, 'it's empty.'
Blyton chuckles. 'No it's not. You're looking in the wrong place,' he says.
Max looks in the gap again. Then he crouches and peers up the chimney. Nothing. Blyton taps his shoulder. He waves the brick, shows Max the end of it. It's hollow and there is charred rag protruding from it. Blyton eases the cloth out. Lets it fall open in his hand. There it is. The last piece of the Nehushtan serpent.
'I said I'd never let it out of my sight,' he says sadly. 'But I can't come with you.'
He pushes his hand towards Max.
Max hesitates then takes it, wraps it again and slips it inside his jacket.
'Thanks Blyton.'
'You guard it with your life,' the old man says.
'It's all I've got,' says Max.
He shoves the pipe back and locks it in place with the wooden hoists, then he hands them back to Blyton.
He shakes the old guy's hand, grips it a second longer than he would normally. Blyton holds out his hand to Blue but she brushes it aside and gives him a hug.
'My lucky day,' he mutters and she laughs.

'We'll see ya soon, Blyton,' she says.
Max pauses at the door, looks back. 'Just one thing,' he says, 'if a woman in black comes calling, with cold grey eyes, ear studs and vipers on her teeth, don't open the door. Just hit her with as many of those old books as you can lift.'

*

Anya's not coming back. Suzie Kruger has worked that out. Her phone is dead and she hasn't made any attempts to contact. Either she's run for the hills, in which case one day Kruger will catch up with her, walk into a bar and blow her away. Or she's been arrested, in which case Kruger doesn't want to be anywhere near her. There is a third option. But she didn't seem like the suicidal type. Shame. She had potential. Kruger dismisses the thought and calls Don Cortez.
'I'm one step away from completing the snake. How do you want to play this?'

*

Blue groans, and postpones shoving gum in her mouth.
'You're kidding me, not another flight?'
'We could go by bike but it might take us a while.'
'We only just got off one plane.'
'Welcome to the world of international adventuring.'
'You're assuming I'll pay again I suppose.'
Max sighs. 'I have some money. I could go alone.'
She laughs. 'Yea right, and how long will that last? You need me. You so need me Mr Maguire. I'm not only the sweet talking, goodlooking one, I'm the goose with the golden eggs, mate.'
'You also have the phone. Call up Carlyle for me would you. The number should still be on there.'
She rolls her eyes, pops the gum and chews as she searches for the number. She dials and hands the phone to Max.
'Max!' Carlyle sounds like he's all smiles and champagne over there in Madrid.
'You're in a good mood,' Max mutters, sounding the opposite.
'Oh you know, business is good.'
'How's the investigation going?'
A pause from Carlyle, Max can almost hear him thinking. 'Investigation?'

Max decides to help him out.

'Into some strange goings on in your basement. And the small matter of Anders Alvarez's death?'

That sobers him up. 'Max, I told you, I have someone looking into that. But it's complex. Especially trying to do it quietly. I can't afford bad publicity.'

'Well let me give you a clue. Suzie Kruger. Ask that doorman of yours about her, the big one who seemed pretty cosy with her.'

'Max, what do you want? Did you just call to bring me down? And what do you mean about my basement? How come you guys just took off like that?'

'We didn't take off. Someone dumped us in Segovia. Yea, no kidding. Well look, we need to come and see you. I need a favour. We'll be there in about six hours.'

They hail a taxi back to the station. Then a train back to Paddington. The Heathrow Express to the airport and a plane back to Madrid. Blue's doing her best to stay upbeat but the travelling's taking the punch out of her. She leans on Max's shoulder and asks sleepily, 'How are you going to track down Kruger?'

'That's the favour I want from Jack Carlyle.'

'Does he know her?'

'Doubt it. But his phone could be useful.'

She sits up, crinkles her nose at him. He smiles, says nothing.

Fifty seven

Jack Carlyle is waiting for them. As soon as Max and Blue approach the front desk the receptionist buzzes him. He comes out, all smiles and arms open, as if they are long lost family. Prodigals returned. He's in another insanely expensive suit, the large gold cross hanging over the silk tie. A single minder hovers in the background. He looks as relaxed as a Sunday afternoon by the pool, but Max is not convinced.

'I used your office phone to call Brecht Nobel and Kurt Danby. The numbers should still be on your system. Can I try finding them?'

'Well, hello to you to, Maguire. Nice to see you again. Cup of tea, cold beer?'

'Carlyle, I'm sorry, I ain't got time to waste. The pace is hotting up. I need to contact the last couple of seers again.'
'What about your list?'
Max shakes his head. 'Went walkabout,' he says. 'But I have to find the last couple of seers.'
Carlyle frowns, places a gentle finger to his lips.
'Easy on the 'seers' word in public,' he says quietly, then smiles again.
He takes them to another office, thankfully not the one where Andre Alvarez got murdered. He buzzes a secretary who appears with a printed list. He thumbs down it and hands it to Max.
'There,' he says, jabbing a finger at a couple of numbers. 'Try those.'
Max dials. Blue pops some more gum and takes up Jack's offer of iced tea. The same secretary, braids, smart and slim, non-smiling and efficient, appears with iced tea for them both. Max doesn't touch his.
Kurt Danby isn't answering. His phone is off. Or the battery's dead. And if the battery's dead then Danby may well be too. He dials the other number. The answering service cuts in again and he's about to hang up when he hears the soft Dutch reply break in.
'Ja? Brecht. Hallo?' The answer now is in no way breezy. It's curt, apprehensive.
'Brecht Nobel? This is Max Maguire. Please just listen.' Max starts to explain the situation to him. Brecht cuts in.
'Mr Maguire, I already have one meeting arranged concerning the snake. I do not wish to have another.'
'Who with?'
A pause on the other end. Max decides to help him out.
'Mr Nobel if it is someone called Suzie Kruger, don't trust her. Don't…'
'I have to. I have agreed.'
'She is highly dangerous.'
'She gave me her word. We have one meeting and one meeting only. And then I am done with this. To be honest, where the snake is concerned I don't trust you or her. I am sorry but that is the way it is.'
'Can I come to that meeting?'
Silence.
'Why should I let you? You may be the dangerous one.'
'You're right I may. I can prove nothing over the phone. Is it today?'
'No tomorrow.'

'Is it near you?'
Silence.
'Don't let her into your home Mr Nobel.'
'The meeting is not at my home.'
'Is it in a public place?'
'Yes but a deserted one. Very quiet. I don't want people knowing about the snake.'
'Where Mr Nobel? I need to know for your own safety. You're in Amsterdam, yes?'
'Yes, well, no. Near there.' He is starting to panic. 'I have to go.'
He hangs up. Max dials again but this time the answering service cuts in and there is no live interruption from Brecht Nobel.
'D'you have a map of the area round Amsterdam?' he asks Carlyle.
'Can do better than that, Max,' he says, and he swivels a laptop on the desk. 'We have the world wide web.'
Max punches keys and types in Holland. He studies the maps as they appear, zooms in.
'Ever been to Amsterdam, Jack?' he asks, suddenly on first name terms, but then he is after something.
'I've been all over,' says Carlyle.
'Where would you go for a secret meeting near Amsterdam?'
Carlyle takes the laptop, brings up Google earth and zooms in. Yellow sand rises out towards them as the pixels come into focus.
'There.'
He turns the laptop.
'Wow!' Blue's eyes show wide. 'Where's that?'
'De Hoge Veluwe National Park. A strip of desert land. Plenty of room there for a secret liaison.'
'Is it near Amsterdam?'
Carlyle punches keys and searches for a few minutes. He smiles.
'There you go. Brecht and Brigitta Nobel, Barneveld. About 20k from the park. I'd say it's a sure bet.'
Max looks at Carlyle. 'Thanks Jack,' he says. You may have just saved Aretha's life.'
Carlyle shrugs. 'All part of the service.'
Max and Blue head for the door.
'Off again so soon?'

'We have to get to Amsterdam. We have to find Kruger. Or we'll lose the element of surprise.'
'She thinks this is the last piece of snake but she's wrong,' Blue stops.
'Wait a minute,' she slaps her forehead. 'I should have thought of this before. They don't have all the pieces. Mr Carlyle, you still have your part of the snake right?'
'Ah,' he winces and shakes his head. 'I was going to tell you about that. It's gone missing.'
Blue says, 'What?'
Max sighs. 'No surprise there then,' he says. 'You're lucky to still be alive, Jack. Your sort are a dying breed. You're a member of a unique club. The Nehushtan Seer who got robbed and lived to tell the tale. Watch your back though. When did it go missing?'
'I checked it this morning. It was gone then.'
'How?'
'A safe. Broken open. Window forced. Should have listened more closely to you, Max. I'm sorry.'
'No point crying over spilt milk,' says Max, 'we never put our money on that one anyway. We stick to our plan. Come on.'

Fifty eight

Max and Blue fly into Amsterdam that evening. Blue's cash is getting low but they have enough for a night at The Sheraton airport hotel and a hire car for the next day.
They pay for a double room and Blue takes the bed. Max is happy with that, he isn't in the mood to sleep much. Whatever happens tomorrow he is likely to see Aretha again. He pulls the photo from his pocket. Thankfully it wasn't stolen when he and Blue lost everything else of importance. Probably the closest he's ever been to love. He's been *in* love a few times and there've been a fistful of crushes. But love is another matter. Love is the kind of thing that makes you reassess the future. Affects what you do for a living and where you might end up making some kind of life. When he met her she was in trouble. On some assignment for *Cosmopolitan*. Took too many risks for an interview, ended up in the wrong kind of club at the wrong kind of night. Too many drunks and not enough good people

around. Max was drowning his troubles. Nothing serious, just a few whiskeys to bolster him after a hard day losing treasure to a gang of amateur criminals. When he heard the commotion coming from a back room the first thing he did was look for assistance, but no one else was batting an eyelid. So he went in alone. The room was chock with bodies and sweat. Six guys in leathers, fists like chunks of granite, hate tattooed all over them. And in the centre this small, sassy girl, fighting her corner but losing ground. Clothes the worse for wear, make up smudged across her beautiful face. Eyes having to move fast to keep track of too many thugs. The easiest thing to do was hurt a couple of them. Take the focus off the girl. So Max, not usually a man for weaponry, took a chair and broke it across the shoulders of the nearest two guys. Then he grabbed a dislodged chair leg and cuffed them both round the ears. Two short sharp swings each. One back one forward. The big guys went down and the others started to take notice. Four against one is never great odds, but Max was fast and hadn't drunk as much as the others. As they came for him he leapt sideways up onto the nearby window ledge. And when two of them leapt after him he dodged and they found their heads smashing through glass. He took advantage of the extra height up there and kicked out at a huge, bearded head. Probably broke the guys nose, there was suddenly blood. And that left just the one guy, the biggest, smelliest, and still unharmed. Max caught sight of the girl slipping out as the sledgehammer fists came at him.
'Oh great,' he thought. 'She's safe and I get the payback.'
But she wasn't gone long, and was soon back with a couple of full pint glasses. She smacked them across the back of the big guys head and did the proverbial hand-dusting routine as he dropped like a sack of cement. The others were starting to come round and Max was not up for much more of the fisticuffs, so he grabbed her arm and they left before the air could clear. He finally found out her name as they recovered by the river, limping side by side in the cool night air.
'Thanks,' she said, 'that was getting nasty. I'm Aretha by the way.'
'What? Named after...' he stopped as he saw her face. 'Bet you never been asked that before,' he said and she laughed.
'I'm Marvin,' he said and she gave him a look.
'You're kidding? Not named after...'
She stopped when he laughed. 'No I'm not Marvin at all. I'm Max.'

They shook hands in that odd English way, but it was a distraction from the awkward introductions. Then she grabbed his arm and they walked for a long time. For two years in fact. Aretha globetrotting for her magazines. Max doing the same for his ancient relics. They kept it relaxed. Took time together when they were in the same country, whichever country that turned out to be. Eventually it came to that question. The 'where are we going' question. And somewhere in the background there was the sound of a deathknell. And that was that. They left each other. Promised to meet up again one day. Max just never expected that it would be on a strip of desert in Holland, over a few pieces of old snake. When they knew each other she'd mentioned the serpent once or twice, but as far as Max was concerned it was a done deal. Lost for all time. He looks at the photo again. He'd told himself this was for Ben Brookes, but the truth is, if he'd not once loved her himself he wouldn't be here now. Whatever happens to the snake happens. It's Aretha that matters.

*

There's a slight breeze disturbing the wild grass and kicking up gentle swathes of sand.
Max and Blue get there in good time. They grab an early breakfast on the way and arrive around 8.30am. They find the main entrance, park up and take a walk. There are a few dog walkers around. One or two parents entertaining early rising kids. A couple of photographers snapping the quiet vistas. Apart from that no sign of Kruger or anything sinister. Yet. They return to the hire car and chew on chocolate fruit bread.
'So – you gonna tell me about her?' she says, flicking her eyebrows up knowingly as she speaks. 'I saw you last night, I woke up and caught you looking wistfully at her little picture there. You guys got history, right?'
He nods. Tells her something of the story, a little about their first meeting and the two years after that. Blue listens, purses her lips. Looks a little contrite. He's not seen her like this before.
'Sorry about… ya know, taking the mick a bit. Lady Kiss Kiss and all that.'
He shrugs it off. 'It's no big deal. We had something, we moved on.'
'But this is why you're here isn't it? You're not really after the snake.'

He says nothing. There is nothing he can say really. She knows what she sees and anything else he might say would just be like trying to blow smoke.

'So,' she says brightly, after an awkward silence, 'what's the plan?'

'Yea, good question. We wait for Aretha to appear. We hang back till then. As soon as she arrives we can offer the deal.'

'D'you think Kruger will bite on it?'

'I think she'll pretend she does. Whether she'll actually let us go without a fight… I doubt that. She's a killing machine. Her instinct is to clean up. Do the job and eradicate any remaining traces. That's you and I.'

'So?'

'So I bought this.'

He reaches inside his jacket, pulls out a compact snub nose revolver. A Colt 38 special.

'It's not a Glock but it'll do her some damage. If it comes to that.'

He feels the weight in his hands. 'I hate guns,' he says, 'but with someone like Kruger I daren't go in unarmed.'

'Got one for me?' says Blue with a grin.

'No way. You'd probably shoot *me*!'

She laughs. 'I ain't scared.'

'Not now maybe, not here chewing on fruit bread. But when you're out there and you see the lack of soul in her eyes and she's spitting poison at everyone, you should be scared then. You should be totally focussed, ready for anything, assuming nothing. Do that and we might just make it through.'

*

De Hoge Veluwe National Park is 55 km of desert, heath and woodland. A slice of the Sahara crashlanded in the middle of the Netherlands. Every so often wild grass bursts like sunlight from the dunes and black skeletal tree limbs jut out from the sand, dead giant's fingers clawing at life. Turn up at the right time and the deer and wild boar will be roaming. The locals maintain the place for ecological reasons, and it's a handy site for a family day out and some cinematic footage. Useful too for an isolated rendezvous. Pick the right place at the right time and you won't be disturbed. Brecht arrives a few minutes early. Drives up and leaves his car parked discreetly behind a clump of trees. He walks the fifty paces or so, past the wooden

watchtower into the open sand. He's obvious there, but that's the point. He wants to be seen and to have the meeting done quickly, so he can return to his life and Brigitta back at home. He doesn't have long to wait. She's on time. A slender, dark figure steps out of the trees. Perhaps she was here before him, waiting, watching. Seeing what he is like. She is not what he expected. Not at all. Smaller, yet more sinister. Something evil about her very walk. She is certainly making no attempts to appear benign with her black clothes and fixed expression. He suddenly wishes he had listened to the other guy, the Englishman with his warnings on the phone.
Kruger steps up. Goes directly to him. No introductions. No niceties or handshakes. She looks the old man full in the face.
'Now listen to me very carefully,' she says. 'I am not operating alone and we know where you live. You have one hour to return home, get your piece of the snake and bring it back to me here. If you don't do that I will kill your wife. And I never talk lightly about killing. I stick to my word. Do you understand?'
He stares, his jaw drops open. He can't believe strangers can treat each other this way. Her tone is a world away from that friendly voice on the phone.
'I...'
'You heard what I said. You have one hour. It starts now.'
She doesn't look at her watch, or anything melodramatic like that, and she doesn't wait for his agreement. She merely turns and walks away, back to her spot in the trees. He steadies himself, takes a moment to muster strength for his walk back to the car. Then he goes, his heart in his mouth and his head swimming. He is full of terror now. And one hour is very short for his trip home and back. He wonders what his father would have done. A very different man to Brecht. Aart Nobel was a tough man, a member of the Dutch resistance during world war two. Actively involved in harbouring allied troops and assisting their escape after the failed assault on the bridges over the Rhine in 1944. After the war he went into the building trade and took three of his sons with him. Brecht was the last of four boys and very much the gentleman of the family. He went into medical research and the snake came to him via his mother. Handed down from the maternal ancestors. His father and brothers may well have turned up with a shotgun today. But he is not his father and brothers. He drives home, says nothing to Brigitta - what would be the point - and retrieves the

snake from the wall safe. This takes him twenty nine minutes, which by rights should give him just enough time. As long as the traffic is not against him.

Fifty nine

Max and Blue saw it all. They left the car a while back and took up places in the woodland on the edge of the sand. From there they could see Brecht amble across his fifty paces, counting as he went. They saw Kruger emerge and glide across the arid ground. They couldn't hear the exchange but saw the outcome. Brecht Noble looked as if he'd been given his death sentence. Blue was all for taking Kruger there and then but Max knew he needed to stick to the plan. Wait for Aretha to appear. If they took on Kruger now and lost they might never have the chance to bargain for her. The time ticks by. Kruger has disappeared into the trees and doesn't come out again. They hear the car pull away. They wait. They hear it return. Max steels himself. This could be it. They hear a second car pull up. Then a footfall and a snapping twig behind them. Max realises too late.
'On your feet losers.'
He knows before he looks. It's Kruger. No doubt with her Glock. He turns.
'Hello Suzie,' he says.
'Shut up, Maguire.'
Blue studies the other woman.
They hear a car door slam. Kruger looks beyond them to the open ground. Brecht is making his laborious way across the sand. He looks ten years older. He has a bundle in his hand. Kruger waves the gun towards the snatch of desert.
'Out there,' she says and Max and Blue walk ahead of her, hands raised in true hostage style.
Brecht sees them and stops momentarily.
'What's going on?' he calls.
'Nothing,' says Kruger, 'keep walking.'
The old man takes up again. They meet in just about the same spot where they met before. Brecht holds out the bundle.
'Wait,' says Kruger, looking over his shoulder.

They follow her gaze. A distant figure in white appears in the trees and comes towards them across the arid ground. He walks with a cane and every so often it jams in the soft ground and he struggles to pull it free. It's hard going, his age and health seem to be getting in the way. Behind him a minder walks with him, slowing whenever he does.
Blue stares, narrows her eyes, flinches. She cannot believe what she's seeing.
'You!' she says.
Max stares too.
'Cortez? You're behind this?' he says.
The old guy with the cane limps towards them. Walking on the sand is almost too hard for him, and he seems more frail than when she last saw him at the casino.
'I took this guy's money,' says Blue. 'I played him in The Siesta, in the casino there. Man, he's cool. Cool as ice. But I won. Didn't I?'
Cortez stares at her, doesn't flinch or show any surprise. He opens his mouth and replies gently, forms his words carefully.
'Actually, no.'
Blue's face falls. 'No way! I beat ya! Fair and square.' She thinks. Snaps her fingers. 'A flush. A diamond flush. I had ya.'
He allows himself a small smile. Shakes his head. 'If you recall, I folded. You never saw my cards. I let you win.'
'No way!'
'I had a full house,' he frowns for a moment. 'Fives and eights I believe.'
Blue looks from Cortez to Max, her mouth opening and closing. Eventually she finds the words. 'He's bluffing. Max I beat him. Honest. I did.'
'I won't argue with you Miss Odyssey,' says the old man, 'I don't have the energy. You decide what you want to believe.'
'Why would you let me win? Why? Why would you do that? Why? Why?'
'Because the wise people with the power know when not to exercise it.'
She thinks, creases up her face.
'Are you saying... it was charity? You wanted to help me?'
He shrugs. 'You decide, we have other things to sort out here.'
'I still don't believe you.'
She glances at the minder coming up on Cortez's shoulder. She recognises him too. He was in the casino at the game.

'D'you know this guy then?' she asks, indicating Cortez and looking at Max.
'Yea. Don Cortez. Business man and all round gangster. Knows what he wants and gets it. I take it you stole the diary, and the list, and our money.'
'Like you say – I get what I want.'
'And now you want the snake? Is this what it's all about?'
He coughs on cue, and it takes a few seconds for him to stop. The minder passes him a water bottle. He sips. They wait.
'That wasn't intended as any kind of demonstration, but as you can see I am not a well man, Mr Maguire. I need everything this snake can give me.' He turns to Kruger. 'You have the last piece?'
She beckons to Brecht, holds out her hand to him. Brecht Nobel has been hovering on the edge, if there had been a wall he'd be pressed up against it. He wants to be anywhere other than out here with these people right now. Kruger snaps her fingers and waves her outstretched hand to beckon him closer.
'Nobel – the snake.'
The humble Dutchman inches forward, pulls a bundle from his pocket. He's terrified, in no mood to argue. Hands it to Kruger. The moment he has done it he starts backing away.
'Go,' says Max to him.
'No! Wait!' Kruger raises her gun, takes aim. But Cortez lifts his cane and cracks it across her hand.
'No more killing,' he says. 'This isn't what we came here for today.'
Brecht turns and hurries away, into the trees and towards his car. He doesn't look back.
Kruger turns on Cortez, hate in her eyes. She lifts her gun again and levels it at him for a second, then lowers it and lets it hang from her arm. Max figures she's in pain from the blow, but she'll never show that. Cortez nods to the minder who speaks quietly into his phone.
'Piece it together,' Cortez says to Kruger.
She lays a torn piece of canvas on the sand. They wait.
'What are you doing here anyway, Maguire?' Cortez asks.
'You'll see,' says Blue.
'You may not be so confident soon,' Cortez says to her. 'I don't only win at poker you know.'

He glances back at his minder. The guy nods. There is a movement from the trees behind him. Two figures emerge and make their way across the sand.

Max squints into the distance.

'Aretha,' he says, under his breath.

It's her. At last. And she's walking with another familiar figure. Blue screws up her eyes again to get a better view.

'Is it her?' she asks.

Max's vision is no better than hers but he'll bet anything on it.

'Why did you kidnap her?' he asks Cortez as they watch the figures approach. The girl is stumbling, the man with her has to steady her every so often.

'I once had a tutor. An old monk who went by the name of Father Tom. Loved telling us stories. One day I came across him idling in a hammock, I think he may have had a little too much Bourbon. He called me over, regaled me with tales of his adventures, some of them may even have been true. One of them was about an ancient snake with healing powers. He talked of it then suddenly clammed up. Which made me wonder. I never forgot it. That's why I hired Miss Kruger to do some 'research' for me. To see if it was true. She was extremely keen – she'd already been this close to getting a piece on Table Mountain in South Africa. I believe you and a friend deprived her of it Mr Maguire.'

Max shrugs. Says nothing. Cortez continues.

'She'd heard about the seers, and discovered that Miss Kiss was something of an expert on the snake. So we 'enlisted' her help. Miss Kruger arranged a liaison, mentioned the serpent. Miss Kiss couldn't resist. That's when we took her. You see, collecting the pieces together wasn't enough. I need to know how to extract the power.'

'But there is no power,' says Blue, but Cortez ignores this.

'And Sophie MacManus? You kidnapped her too?'

'Yes. Unfortunately Miss Kiss had not brought her journal along when we abducted her. We needed more information. Mrs MacManus was a way into the chain. Charles MacManus was very helpful once we had his wife.'

'And you killed her?'

'Yes. An unfortunate piece of collateral damage. Unavoidable. She ran out of usefulness. And Miss Kruger thought killing her might frighten you two away.'

Max shakes his head. 'So much killing,' he says, spitting the words out. 'And we're not done with that yet,' says Kruger, spitting her words back. She unwraps a bigger bundle. Reveals the collection of snake fragments. Starts piecing them together on the canvas. Max looks up. The two figures are still approaching them. It is Aretha. She's much closer now. Along with someone else he recognises.

Sixty

'I knew you had inside help,' Max says.
Blue looks up. 'Sheez, stone me!' she yells.
'Carlyle,' says Max, 'the inside man, I should have known. It was staring me in the face. That's why Kruger could move freely around The Siesta. She didn't just know the doorman, she was in league with the owner. And that's why the hostages were being held in the basement there. And why you did nothing about Alvarez's death. You knew it would happen. In fact, you led us to that office so Kruger could blow him away.'
It's all making sense now in Max's head. 'That's how Kruger found out we were in Madrid so quickly and was able to come looking for us at Ander's apartment. She was already in town and Carlyle kept passing on the information.'
'Hello Max,' Jack Carlyle says as he helps Aretha take the final steps. Max ignores him. Looks at Aretha instead. She's looking thinner, and paler, and there are plenty of marks on her face and clothes.
'You okay Aretha?'
She gives him a weak smile. Nods. 'I knew you'd come,' she says.
'We should have guessed you know,' says Blue, 'Carlyle, you found Brecht and Brigitta's address so easily – yet how could you know his wife's name? Unless you'd seen the list. Unless you'd stolen the list. You already knew the meeting was here didn't you? Kruger had told you.'
'Actually it was Cortez,' says Carlyle. 'Kruger tells me nothing. She's a law unto herself.'
Suzie leers at him, the vipers on her teeth showing. Max can almost hear the hissing.
'Your piece of snake wasn't stolen, was it Carlyle?' he says. 'You just handed it over. I don't get it. Why did you sell out? Not for money surely.

Power? Was it pressure, threat of violence? You didn't have any loved ones they could threaten. I doubt if anyone has much love for you.'
'Touché Maguire. You know, I'm no stranger to this kind of thing. A man doesn't build up a business like The Siesta without making a few unorthodox connections. Me and Cortez go back a long way.'
'You mean – he called in a favour?'
'Something like that. He scratched my back and I well... the rest is a cliché.'
'People are dead because of that cliché,' says Max.
'It happens.'
'You...' Max snarls and makes a move on Carlyle but Cortez speaks.
'Look, there's been enough killing. Let's just get the snake reformed and finish this.'
Kruger places the last piece of snake on the canvas. The other half of the head. She adjusts one or two of the fragments. The serpent lies there, about a foot in length, wings flared on its back, that blade of fire exuding from its slit of a mouth. 'There it is,' she says. 'The finished article. Not seen since the days of... Wait a minute.'
Kruger stares. Narrows her eyes.
'What is it?' asks Cortez.
'It can't be.'
'What?'
'There's a piece missing. The head's not finished. Look.'
Cortez shoves her out of the way, he pushes hard for a sick man. Sends her staggering.
'I thought you said you collected all the pieces.'
She straightens herself, tidies her clothes.
'I did,' she hisses. 'Eleven seers eleven fragments. This was the last one. But it's not enough. The face. There's an eye missing.'
The top of the serpent's head was clearly not there. There was a jagged break in the metal where the last piece had sheared off.
'Maybe one of the pieces got broken,' says Carlyle.
'Shut up. Course it didn't. They're made of bronze, they don't break easily.'
The sound of a throat clearing. And a laugh. Considering the nature of the present company the laugh is perhaps ill-advised.

Cortez, Carlyle and Kruger turn slowly to look at Max and Blue. Blue is smiling her big smile. Another mistake. Max is calm, quiet. Stone-faced. 'That's why we're here,' he says.
Blue starts to nod vigorously but Max grips her wrist and stops her. Throws her an abrupt warning glance. They must play this thing carefully. Nobody's won yet.
'There is another piece,' Max says.
'Where? How?' snaps Kruger. 'There were only eleven seers.'
Max shakes his head. 'We thought that too. But it was Blue, she spotted that Aretha's diary specifically mentions that there are twelve.'
'So who's the twelfth seer?' ask Cortez.
'Doesn't matter. What matters is - we have that last piece.'
'Give it,' says Kruger.
'We will. But only in exchange for Aretha.'
'Oh sweet,' says Kruger, 'he's come for his girlfriend.'
'You can't have her,' says Cortez. 'I need her for the snake.'
'What do you mean?'
'She's the only one who can make it work.'
'The snake doesn't work,' says Blue. 'It's just a relic. There is no power.'
Cortez turns his eyes on Blue, his gaze burning into her. Somehow she's struck him deep within.
'It has to work,' he says. 'You'd better pray it works. Or she dies.'
'This is about you, isn't it Cortez?' says Max. 'You're sick.'
'You bet he's sick,' mutters Blue, it's under her breath but everyone can hear.
'No I mean, you're dying aren't you?'
Cortez turns his eyes on Max. Nods slowly.
'My last chance,' he says. 'It's the snake or a bullet in the brain.'
Max softens her voice. 'The snake can't do anything for you.'
'Not like this no. But when the last piece is in place, and Miss Kiss works the magic…'
'There is no magic!' yells Blue and Kruger turns on her.
'One more word from you and I swear I'll blow your freakin' head off,' says Kruger and she takes a step and trains her Glock on Blue's skull.
Blue backs up, hands in the air. 'Okay, okay, but don't say I didn't warn ya.'

'I said shut up,' says Kruger. 'I've killed a dozen people for this snake. One more won't bother me.'
Cortez turns to the minder. The bodyguard hands him a small, blue, leatherbound book. The journal. Cortez hands this to Aretha.
'Here,' he says, 'you might need this.'
She turns it in her hands. Opens it and lets the pages flick past. She smiles.
'You said you could make the snake work,' Cortez says, a slight threat to his voice.
She nods. 'I did yes. But I can't...'
'Can't?'
'Not without the final piece,' says Max quickly and Aretha looks straight at him.
'Where is it?' says Kruger.
Max looks at Blue.
'We'll only tell you if you let Aretha go.'
'No,' says Cortez.
'Then – no deal.'
'I can't. I need her for the power of the snake.'
'But without the final piece you don't have the complete snake.'
'I won't give you the girl.'
'Then we won't give you the snake.'
Cortez runs a hand over his chin. His fingers shake a little. He coughs again.
'Then we have a stalemate,' he says.
'No we don't,' says Kruger, 'hand it over or I kill the redhead.'
She grabs Blue by the neck and holds her against her, her arm clamped around her throat, she pushes her gun against her temple. Blue stares at Max, wide-eyed.
Max pulls his gun, trains it on Cortez. 'You said it was the snake or a bullet in the brain,' he says. 'Choose.'
Silence. The wind pushes sand about. Somewhere a dog barks. Time slows right down.
'There is another possibility.' It's Carlyle.
'What?' says Cortez, his eyes burning into Max.
'Get the girl to tell you what to do. If she gives you the secret then you don't need her.'
Max looks from Carlyle to Kruger to Cortez. Cortez nods.

'That may work,' he says.
'No!' spits Kruger. 'We can't let them walk away.'
'Shut up,' says Cortez and clearly Kruger does not like it. He turns to Aretha. 'Can you do it?'
Max turns his gaze on her, wills her to agree. She blinks a few times.
'Okay,' she says slowly.
'Let her go,' Cortez tells Kruger, but the woman in black doesn't move.
'When we're sure,' she says.
'What do we do then?' asks Carlyle, turning to Aretha.
Max pulls a black book from inside his jacket. Hands it to Aretha.
'You'll certainly need this,' he says.
She looks at the spine and nods. She puts her journal on the ground and lets the black book fall open in her hands, then she shuffles through a few wafer-thin pages. She clears her throat and reads, 'Then the Lord sent venomous snakes among them; they bit the people and many Israelites died. The people came to Moses and said, "We did wrong when we spoke against the LORD and against you. Pray that the Lord will take the snakes away from us." So Moses prayed for the people. The Lord said to Moses, "Make a snake and put it up on a pole; anyone who is bitten can look at it and live." So Moses made a bronze snake and put it up on a pole. Then when anyone was bitten by a snake and looked at the bronze serpent, they lived.'
Kruger sighs and scowls. 'Yea, we know all that.'
Aretha ignores her, flips forward in the black book.
She reads again, 'Hezekiah broke into pieces the bronze snake Moses had made, for up to that time the Israelites had been worshipping it.' She looks up. 'You need to look to the snake, but not pray to it. You need to pray beyond it. To the God who makes snakes. The God who healed the Israelites in the desert. Look at the snake but put your faith in God.'
'That's it?' says Kruger. 'Isn't there some magic words or something?'
'It's not magic,' says Aretha, 'it's faith.'
'We've been conned,' says Kruger. 'Let me kill them.'
Cortez's face is creased in confusion. He looks suddenly old and bewildered. The snake has unmasked him. He is just a dying man looking for a way out.
'Let her go,' he says.

But Kruger backs away. 'No way,' she hisses, 'enough of this mumbo jumbo.'
'LET HER GO!' Cortez summons his energy to bark the order.
He staggers a little.
Kruger sneers at him.
'Okay,' she says and she pushes Blue away.
Then she fires the gun and Blue drops into the sand. Kruger turns and heads for the trees.
Max pulls the revolver from his jacket, aims at her, fires. She drops and rolls and clambers up again. Runs on, weaving now. He fires again and misses. A third time and she flinches. Maybe he got her that time. She disappears into the trees. Max falls beside Blue. There is blood pumping from her chest.
'Call an ambulance,' he yells, but no one moves.
'Where's the piece of snake?' asks Cortez, his voice as measured as ever.
'What?'
'The snake. If you wan to live give it to me.'
'She's dying!'
'Where is the piece?'
Carlyle pulls a gun from his jacket. Another revolver. He aims it at Aretha now.
'Surely you don't want two dead women on your conscience, Maguire,' he says.
Max looks at the three men. Cortez, Carlyle and the minder. Not a shred of compassion between them. He holds out his hand and points to Aretha.
'It's in the New Testament.'
'What?'
'The Bible,' he says, 'the black book. Turn to the back.'
Aretha does so, the cover drops open revealing a hollow in the last third of the book. Wedged inside is the top of the snake's head.
'I told you you'd need it,' he says.
Carlyle reaches over and takes the piece of snake. He kneels and places it into the bronze jigsaw. He waits. Nothing happens. Cortez drops on his knees beside him. He touches the head, runs his fingers over the shape, then along the body. Wind kicks up sand and spatters it across the relic. Cortez rubs the body of the snake, moves his hands harder, faster as he claws at the bronze, his lips moving silently. The bronze pieces begin to

break apart. There is a rumble in the sky. He pauses, looks to the heavens. But it's just distant thunder. Nothing more.

Max kneels, searches Blue's pockets and pulls out her phone. He throws it to Aretha.

'Can you call an ambulance? It's 112.'

He scoops Blue into his arms. There is blood everywhere. And no response from her. He pulls off his jacket, pads it up and presses it against the wound. He feels movement beside him. Aretha drops into the sand next to him, the phone to her ear.

'Will she make it?' she asks.

Max shrugs. A hand smashes the phone from Aretha's face.

'No!' It's Carlyle with his gun. 'No ambulances. Not here. Not till we've gone.'

'But...'

'Make the damn snake work, just make it work.'

Cortez is kneeling with bits of old bronze in his hands, he's clutching at them, trying to wring life from the things.

'It's not like that...' Aretha says quietly.

She stands up, walks to Cortez and drops beside him. She starts to say something, but not to Cortez. The old man begins to calm down, lets the pieces of bronze snake drop from his fingers. Aretha keeps talking, reciting an ancient prayer.

'I waited patiently for my God. He turned to me and heard my cry. He lifted me up out of the depths of despair. Reached down and pulled me out of the sinking sands. He gave me a firm place to stand, put a song of hope in my heart. Blessed is the one who trust in God and does not turn to other things. Blessed is the one who hopes in the Lord.' She keeps reciting it, holding the old man's shoulders. Carlyle watches and shakes his head.

'Pointless,' he sneers, but he says nothing more as Max's fist shoots up and smashes his head back. He reels and staggers and can do nothing else before another blow knocks him onto his back. Max nurses his fist and winces. Carlyle's jaw is like iron. He's lucky not to have broken any bones in his hand. He's still shaking his fingers when Carlyle's feet kick his legs from under him. He drops onto his back, winded, and the other man is up and kicking him in the side. Doing his best to break ribs. Max rolls over in an attempt to get away. He grabs a fistful of sand and flings it as Carlyle

comes at him again. The grit hits the other man's face and he recoils. It gives Max time to get up and steady himself for the next round. Carlyle staggers away from him, spits sand, claws at his eyes. They square up to each other but Max has the advantage now. Carlyle is blinking profusely, his vision still impaired from the sand. Max moves in for the kill. Then he hears the gunshot. They both spin to look. Cortez is dead on the ground, blood seeping from his head and pooling around the pieces of snake. Aretha is kneeling beside him, her hand to her mouth, staring in disbelief.
'What the... what happened?'
She shakes her head. 'I was praying, closed my eyes for a while. Then I heard the shot.'
There is a gun lying near Cortez's twisted hand.
'What a mess,' says Jack Carlyle.
And that's when the sirens wail.

Sixty one

There are cops everywhere, coming through the trees, making their way from the car park. And an ambulance too. Brecht Nobel hovers among them talking and pointing towards the others. Carlyle's already up and running. The bodyguard too. In different directions. The cops give chase. Max scoops up Blue and runs for the ambulance. Aretha follows more slowly. Only Cortez is left there, lying in his own blood, staring wide-eyed at the Nehushtan snake.

Blue disappears in the ambulance and Max falls into a car beside Aretha. They pull away and follow. The cop wants to talk but Aretha's exhausted and Max is reluctant. He's still not sure how the land is lying here. He left his gun back there in the sand. This is a complex story to have to tell. They drive to the hospital in Arnhem and leave Blue in a mess of cables and drips about to undergo emergency surgery. Max gets his jacket back. Max and Aretha sit in the waiting area. It's the oddest reunion.
'I heard you,' she says softly, 'I heard your voice.'
'When? You mean in the hotel? In the basement at The Siesta?'
She looks at him. Smiles. It's the first time they've made contact without being under duress. She takes his hand.

'I don't know,' she says. 'I don't know where I was. I was always blindfolded when they moved me. It was in this plain room with no windows or paint on the walls. I heard you outside, thought I was dreaming at first. Couldn't believe it. I prayed you'd come. But to actually hear you out there. How did you know about me?'

'Ben,' he says.

'Ben? My Ben? Ben Brookes? Ben-my-boyfriend Brookes?' she has raised her voice a little in shock. Other people start to look.

'You know, you should get checked over yourself,' he says. 'You've been through your own trauma.'

She waves a hand, a kind of 'all in good time' gesture.

'How did Ben find you?'

'By accident. Actually I found him. He was being mugged. I rescued him.'

She laughs. 'Good old Max. Always the hero.' But he shakes his head.

'Believe it or not I've given that up. When he asked me to find you I refused. For quite a while.'

'Thanks very much.'

'If it's any consolation I didn't know who his girlfriend was, it was only when I saw your picture that I knew I had no choice. You and that stupid snake.' He leans towards her. 'Tell me something. Ben found a picture of Kruger in your room. How come?'

She shakes her head. 'Suzie Kruger's not the only one who does her research. When she contacted me I put out feelers. I guessed something wasn't right. I knew I might be heading for trouble. One of my contacts sent me the picture. I should have backed out right then.'

Max shrugs. 'I doubt they'd have let you,' he mutters. 'Was that why you left the journal behind? In case it was some kind of trap?'

She nods. They sit in silence for a while.

'So, what you been up to then?' she asks suddenly, brightening a little.

'Teaching. Biblical studies.'

She laughs again. 'Unbelievable,' she says.

'Hey, no one forgets a good teacher. I want to be that good teacher.'

'What – and not be out there saving the world?'

He looks down at his boots. 'It's complicated,' he says, 'it got to me. Screwed me up. I'm not what I was. Doing things like this get to me now.'

'And the girl,' she nods towards the hospital interior. 'Who is she? She's a bit young Max.'

He shakes his head. Smiles a little. 'She's a poker player. She's my golden goose. We met on a train.'
'Nothing more?'
He shakes his head again. 'Still getting over you,' he says.
And she laughs for a third time. He frowns. Thinks. Stands up.
'You know I reckon I've got to go. This isn't over yet. Keep an eye on Blue will you? Do you have a mobile? Can I call you?'
She goes to the desk, staggers a little as she walks.
'You should see a doctor,' he says.
Another 'all in good time' wave. She borrows a pen from the receptionist, stumbles back and takes his hand. Scribbles numbers on the back.
'Call me on that. Give me a couple of days. Okay?'
He nods. She kisses his cheek. An unremarkable, comfortable gesture. She's done it a thousand times before. He goes, keeping a low profile as he exits the hospital.

*

He gets a bus back to the National Park. Jumps off a little way before reaching it so he can approach at his own speed. The place is cordoned off. Cops come and go, walkie-talkie voices blare in the background. He finds a deserted strip of cordon tape and ducks under it. Makes his way cautiously through the trees, hugging each trunk for a few seconds like he's playing a wide game. Eventually the killing ground is in sight. Blood red blotches on the yellow sand. Forensics are finishing up. Bagging bits of snake. There are a couple of other clear packets tagged and lying on the ground. He may just be lucky. As he watches the two guys leave the evidence bags and wander back to the cars he takes his chance. Sneaks under a second barrier of tape and runs for the open ground. He sees his gun immediately, the snub nose revolver, bagged and tagged. He grabs the packet and pockets it. The bits of snake are each in separate clear bags. He fishes around, the wings, the tail, various bits of body... he glances up, the guys are still preoccupied but won't be for long. There it is. He finds the top half of the head. Pockets that. He glances up again, forensics are still at the cars, getting a box to transport the evidence. He turns and heads back to the trees. Makes it just in time, crouches to see the guys wandering back. They scoop up bags without counting them. Probably don't expect two of them to have walked whilst their backs are turned. He waits for them to return to the cars then makes a convoluted trip through the trees back towards the road. Then he spots it. The occasional spatter of red. A thin line through the heart of the woodland. No telling whether it's really Suzie Kruger's but who else did he shoot at today? He gives up his trek back to the road and takes up the trail through the trees.

*

If it is Kruger he only winged her, the trail remains constant, and the splashes are not substantial. But they are regular enough to have left a ragged course. He follows it for a good half hour. When you're leaking blood it makes it fairly impossible to take a taxi or catch a bus without drawing attention or leaving a conclusive fingerprint. So she's on foot, and the trail goes on. He stops abruptly. There's a figure up ahead. About twenty paces. Crouching, nursing its arm. He can only see the back but who else would be in these woods licking their wounds? There must have been some noise because the head turns towards him. It's her. She listens, eyes flicking from side to side. Licks her lips momentarily. The Glock comes out, she swings around. She's fast. Leaps five paces towards him. And she smiles that wicked smile.
'Got ya Maguire.'
The gun's in her hand and her arms are extended, pushing the Glock towards him. Blood drips down her sleeve and from her wrist but she doesn't seem that bothered by it.
'Thought you'd find me whimpering in a corner eh? Begging to die? No such luck. Takes more than a graze on the arm to make me curl up and snuff it. Come on, come closer.'
She beckons with her hand. He steps out from his cover behind the tree.
'Turns out to be my lucky day after all,' she says. 'Just when I thought I was gonna have to let you walk free again. Now here you are.'
'I thought you didn't do long speeches Kruger,' Max says.
She tilts her head a little, like a pet dog, not quite understanding.
'What do you mean?'
'Just shoot me if you're gonna.'
'You mean like I did with your little fast-talking friend.'
His face hardens, he balls his fists, makes a move towards her.
She laughs, steps back. She knows she has to fire soon, but she's starting to enjoy this.

'Oh Maguire. You let your emotions get in the way. That's the difference between us, I see the job for what it is. You care too much.' She gives a short, throaty laugh. 'Is that why you've given up? Is that why you've ended up teaching Sunday school kids? Those who can - do. Those who can't – teach, Maguire. That's the difference between you and me.'
'That and a whole load of other things,' says Max.
'Like?'
'You wouldn't understand. Or you wouldn't care. You're just a machine Kruger. *Woman* is too strong a word for you.'
That hurt. Resurrected memories of schoolyard jibes. Suzie Kruger the disconnected girl who feels nothing. The freak. The mad machine. She squeezes the Glock.
'Shut up,' she says and Max knows he's in dangerous territory.
He throws up his hands. Backs away a step.
'Okay okay.'
'Too late for apologies,' she sneers. 'Your time's up.'
That's what she intended to say, but he's dropped and rolled and slewed his body behind a tree before she can finish. The gun goes off but the bullet is inches away from him. He keeps moving, on his feet now, powering towards her, his head down and aiming for her stomach. Before she can get him in her sights he's on her, like a battering ram, his skull shoving the breath out of her and smashing her backwards onto the ground. The gun goes off again. Another wild bullet smacks into a tree somewhere. She lashes with her other hand, makes a fist and catches his eye. He rolls off her, grabs a thick, dead branch and swings it at her gun hand. The Glock goes off again and bursts from her fingers. He hurls the branch and piles in, she's unarmed now. They roll around on the forest floor, throwing punches and smacking into trees. Her knee finds his groin and he recoils suddenly. Pulls away and lets go of her. She's up, her face battered and bloody, but she's free of him. Backing away and looking for the Glock. She stops and grabs something. She has it, the gun, but as she lifts it and aims there's mud all over the barrel. She curses and grabs it. Starts smearing the stuff off. Then she lifts it again and takes another aim. He's gone. She swings around, there is the sound of receding footsteps kicking through branches, she spots the figure bowling through bushes and undergrowth, she lifts the gun and fires. The figure crashes on.

Sixty two

Hours later and he's back at the hospital. Max checks for cops as he makes his way through the entrance and across the foyer. There are none around and no one he recognises from earlier. Aretha has disappeared, hopefully getting some medical help herself. He goes to the reception desk. Asks if he can see Beluga Odyssey. The receptionist checks her records.
'I'm afraid not Mr...'
'Maguire. Why not? I just want to see her for a few minutes.'
The receptionist frowns, looks him up and down.
'Are you a relative?' she asks.
He considers lying. 'Not really, but a good friend. We've been through a lot.'
'You were with her when she was injured?'
He nods.
'Mr Maguire. The police may want to talk to you. They're keen to find out as much as possible about the incident.'
'Look, I just want to see my friend. That's all.'
'Well you can't.'
'Please!' he glances down the corridor, considers making an attempt to go down there.
'I'm sorry there's nothing I can do.'
'Nothing? Just two minutes.'
'She's dead Mr Maguire. Miss Odyssey died this morning. I'm sorry.'
Max stares. His world shifts a little, falls out of kilter. He grips the desk.
'She can't be. We got her here on time. I padded the wound. They were fixing her up.'
'I'm sorry.'
He backs away. Wants to run somewhere to find her.
'The doctors did everything they could. She's gone.'
He stares at the receptionist. All that life. All that humour. How could it be gone? How could she be gone? He never even said goodbye. What were his last words to her? He doesn't know. Can't remember. It was all such a mess. Aretha, Kruger, the snake. No plan for this. Before he knows it he's back outside in the rain, wandering away from the hospital. Just keeps walking. This wasn't supposed to happen this time. Maybe he was so

focussed on getting Aretha safe he forgot to keep an eye on Blue. Too many people to watch out for. He walks. Gets wet. Bumps shoulders with a few people but doesn't apologise. Can't even see them. It grows dark and cold. He barely notices. His mind races on. He never finished telling her about Moses and the snake. He'd never be able to tell her now.

*

He finds himself at a road bridge over the river. In front of a memorial plaque. 17th September 1944, de Slag om Arnhem. The John Frost Bridge, named for the colonel that led the airborne troops who defended the bridge in the battle of Arnhem in 1944. A disastrous attempt to shorten the war, but a story of incredible heroism. Five Victoria Crosses. A small pocket of men laying down their lives. Nine days of holding out against the odds. A story still told. People dying for a cause. *Men will be proud to say they fought at Arnhem.*
So many lives lost, so many other nameless forgotten people down the years. Has to mean something, has to have a purpose. And the living who know them have to remember and move on. Have to. That's hard. Hard, hard, hard. Too hard. Did Blue have a family? Bound to have had. He will have to leave that to the police. They know how to sort that kind of thing. A shocking phone call. Or a knock on the door by someone from the Australian police. He recalls something he said when she got off the train with him at Exeter. 'I want you to be okay, and if you're with me, you may not be.' He had no idea what he was saying when he said it. 'Live every day like it's your last,' Ray Charles once said, 'cause one day you'll be right.' Blue did that. In the short time he knew her, she did that. Lived for the day. Lived to the full. Probably had no conception that this day would be her last, but no one could accuse her of wasting it.
He stares across the bridge. Something about the memorial here drags his spirits out of the depths. Life and death. The way of things. He has to keep going. Has to see where tomorrow leads him. Back to his normal life no doubt. But then what?

*

He thumps on the door. It opens eventually. Blyton is there, looking just like he always does.
'For a bookshop you don't open much,' Max mutters.
Blyton laughs and it sets him off coughing.

'I forget to unlock and change the sign,' he says when he's calmed down. 'you've reminded me to do it today though.'
He looks past max. 'On your own?'
Max nods. 'I bought you something,' he says.
Blyton turns and shuffles back inside, Max follows him. They go back to Blyton's room at the back. The old guy sits, Max stays standing, he pulls a leather pouch from inside his jacket.
'I promised – here it is.'
Max undoes the draw strings on the pouch and tips it up. There's a clatter and the piece of bronze snake falls out.
Blyton smiles.
'You did it? It was all okay?'
'Well… yes… and no. the Dutch police have the rest of the snake but I doubt they'll want to piece it together and stick it on a pole. Probably end up in storage somewhere as evidence.'
Blyton picks up the snake and turns it in his fingers.
'I washed the blood off,' Max says, then regrets it.
'There was blood on it? Whose blood?'
'A gangster called Cortez, the guy who started all this. He wanted the snake cause he was dying.'
'Didn't save his life then?'
'No it took it really.'
'And your girl? You found her? Got her safe?'
'Aretha? Yes. She's fine.'
'Mission accomplished then. Cup of tea?'
'Why not.'
Max stares at the range as Blyton fills his kettle.
'You want me to put it back behind the chimney,' he says, 'you know – your bit of the snake?'
Blyton reaches for the pieces of wood and hands them over. Max does the job and conceals the serpent again.
'You never know,' says Blyton, 'one day someone may come looking for it again.'
As he says this the doorbell rattles. Blyton's eyes widen.
'A customer!' he says.
Max peers into the shop. A figure in a black coat passes by, disappears between the shelves. He tenses up, puts a finger to his lips. She couldn't

have could she? Worked out that Blyton was the twelfth seer? Come to finish the job. Or perhaps worse, perhaps Max led her to him. He eases into the shop, treading as lightly as he can. He can hear her moving around, but can't work out which part of the shop she is in. He slips between the shelves, walks down to the far end. Slides round the bookcase, crouches low and peers around the wood. Not there. The next ally is empty too. He steps into it. Listens again. She's beyond the next case of books. He feels for the revolver inside his jacket. Glances back towards Blyton's room. There is no sign of him. Hopefully he's staying put.
'Max.'
No he's not, he's right there, standing at the far end. 'What's going on?' Blyton calls. 'You all right?'
A footstep behind, Max swings round, his hand inside his jacket poised to pull the gun.
For a second he sees Suzie Kruger. Right there. The black hair, cold eyes, stud ear rings.
'Max!' It's Blyton again, calling form the far end of the bookshop.
Max looks back briefly then turns again. And his vision clears.
It's a young woman, but it's not Suzie Kruger. Not her at all. Too tall. The hair's all wrong. The face too long. She looks at him, a little startled. He forces a laugh.
'Sorry, ' he says, holding up empty hands, 'I'm just a little jumpy. Been under stress lately.'
He backs away and leaves her to her browsing, hoping that he hasn't just frightened off the first customer Blyton's had in weeks. He wanders back to the old man's room. The old guy pats his arm.
'You need a break, son,' he says. 'This has taken the steam out of you.'
Max nods. 'I know, I know.' He massages his temples. 'I think I'm gonna go, Blyton. Get some space.'
'You going back home?'
'Yea, I got things to do, a class to teach.'
'Good idea. Thanks for bringing the snake back. Come back when you're feeling better. Let's not make this farewell eh?'
Max walks to the door. The bell rattles as he pulls it open.
As he steps through it Blyton squeezes his arm, asks him one last question.
'That woman you mentioned – the one with the cold grey eyes and the vipers on her teeth, what happened to her? She never came calling.'

Max glances beyond him into the shop. The tall woman is stacking books in her arms, gathering up a pile for buying.

'That's an unfinished story, Blyton,' he says, 'I'm not done with that one yet. I'll let you know when I am.'

The End

The Valley of Eight

An extract from the next Max Maguire adventure.

One

July 1943. Choking smoke rises from the camouflaged wreck as Flight Sergeant Jack Ramone pulls himself clear, his legs smouldering. He beats at them with his hands, but he's okay. He's covered in sand and oil but that's not the problem really. The problem is he's stuck out in the Sahara miles from anywhere, with his only form of transport buckled and skewed across the sand in front of him. The Kittyhawk is a write off. He can probably salvage his water bottle and a few bits of food, and the documents of course. He must save those. But then what? If he takes the confidential folder and dies with it in the wilderness anyone might get their hands on it. If he leaves it here an enemy plane might spot the wreck and come to investigate. His radio died half an hour back so he can't call for help. That's out. He glances up towards the sun, shields his eyes from the blaze. Nowhere to shelter. In this heat he won't last long. Rescue is unlikely. He could try and fix the radio. He ventures back into the plane, bats smoke out of his eyes and reaches inside the shattered cockpit for his supplies. The first thing his hand rest on is the leather folder. What to do?

*

Suzie Kruger stands in the Valley of Eight and wonders. Her short black hair ripples in the breeze as she faces Iran. She runs her finger over the scar on her side. Max Maguire. He's responsible for this. And for the indent in the flesh on her arm. Max freaking-action-man-nightmare-on-legs-refuses–to-die Maguire. His face is branded on her mind and for a hero he's not even that goodlooking. The right kind of rugged components just not in the right order. She fingers the scar on her arm. That's the thing with Maguire, she takes his marks with her wherever she goes. That man has it coming. She won't make any mistakes this time. Payback. She walks to the nearest anchor stone. Eleven feet of solid rock, the eye at the top sheered clean off. She runs her fingers along the symbols of Nimrod etched into the surface.

Not far away other drogue stones jut from the ground and mark the way towards Arzep, the Village of Eight. She drops to her haunches, crouching there in the shadow of the Doomsday Mountain. A good place to die. A good place to come to digging for treasure and end up buried in the hole you dug.

*

Max is losing the will to live. This region of the desert is merciless. No wells, no rivers, no agriculture, no one bothering to try and live here. If it were spring there might be a flash flood to liven things up and refresh Max's water bottle. But spring is long gone. And his water bottle is dangerously light. He narrows his grey eyes, shields them and stares into the distance, his long-range vision is not good. Especially in this heat. Things start to get hazy after a fistful of feet. Could get his eyes lazered but can't stand the thought of people messing with his eyeballs. He pulls a wad of papers from his pocket. The map, the newspaper cutting, the letter. He reads aloud, the sound of his own voice startling him for a moment. It has more gravel to it than he expected.

'Dear Mr Maguire. I heard you find things and I figured you might help me. My grandfather went missing in action during the second world war…'

He knows what's coming, he's read the note too many times. A missing plane, rumours of a finding by Bedouin traders in the Western Sahara. Stories of lost treasure secreted on an abandoned aircraft. And the belief that the pilot was Jack Ramone. Grandfather to Laura Ramone. He folds the letter, studies the map and the cutting then swallows.

His throat is clogging up, feels like a hand is closing around his gullet. What's he doing out here? He swore to give this up. Promised himself to play it safe now, too many ghosts. With a past like Max's you never knew when it all might blow up in your face. Total crack up.

He lifts the water bottle to his lips. Has to tip it way back before any liquid rushes out. A few drops scatter across his face, he scoops them quickly in his fist as they race down towards the scar on his chin. Stupid to come out here alone. His pride might just get him killed. And then he'll be the next guy that they come looking for out in the wilderness. He sinks to his knees. And catches sight of something. Rags rippling in the distance. An old parachute maybe, Max can't quite make it out. He hauls himself up, squints, does his best to focus. No good. He'll have to get closer. He picks up his feet and starts to run, his boots kicking up the sand as he goes. Stretches of the desert pass by. He stops, stands over it. It's not a parachute. It's a bundle of things. He grabs the ancient water bottle, shakes it, nothing. It's long dry of course. There's a compass too. And an empty mess tin. A knife and a gun. Oh, and the skeleton of course. The bleached bones of Jack Ramone, discarded inside the torn tatters of his uniform. Max falls to his knees. He can see himself here. Lying beside Jack and discovered in another fifty years. Bleached bones and ragged clothes. And another waterless bottle. Two bodies missing in action. He lifts Jack's canteen again, shakes it one more time, hoping for a miracle. Nope. He shakes it again. There's still no liquid in it. But there is something inside. Probably the dried up corpse of a scorpion or a gecko. He unscrews the lid, sand falling from his fingers as he does it. Tips it up, flicks it a few times. Something khaki tumbles out. Not a dead lizard though. A piece of cloth, a torn scrap of uniform. He lifts it up, there is something scrawled on it. Either Jack had bad handwriting or he wrote it when his strength was gone. He twists the cloth this way and that till he can make sense of it. He reads it. Sighs. Got to stay alive now. Got to find that plane.

To be continued...

Made in the USA
Charleston, SC
30 October 2012